I0761024

JJ BLACKLOCKE

THE BEREFT

THE TRADEPOINT SAGA BOOK THREE

www.aethonbooks.com

THE BEREFT

www.aethonbooks.com

Print and eBook formatting, and cover design by Steve Beaulieu. Artwork provided by Tom Edwards Design.

Published by Aethon Books LLC.

ALSO IN THE SERIES

REFUGE

AFTERSHOCK

THE BEREFT

[1]

1023 OF 2000 ORBITS REMAINING: 47YELLOW

Wyve, Director of Tradepoint, entered the Clinic, still struggling to come fully awake. Figg was already there, waiting for him, flanked by two security guards.

"Where is the Vennan?" he demanded. "What is their condition?"

There was exasperation in Figg's tone as she replied, "The clinicians haven't let me see her yet, although they keep assuring me that her injuries aren't dangerously severe."

"Her? A female?" It was more than Figg had known when she first roused him from his bed, a short while ago. "Do we know who?"

Sixteen hours into her shift, Figg looked worn and worried. "I fear it may be Gredin te Balamont. She came to the office a short while ago, anxious to speak to me. I'll share the details of that discussion, as soon as you like. When we were through, she expressed a wish to return to the Vennan enclave. I offered to summon a transport pod but she declined, saying she preferred to walk. She left, and I went back to my reports. I was still working on them when I received notification that someone had requested station security, and that a pod had been dispatched. There were no details available as to who had placed the request or what the difficulty might be. I told them to update me as soon as they could. When Security called back, they said a Vennan had been injured and was being taken to the Clinic, unconscious. At that point, I sent for you and came straight here, but the pod had already arrived and turned the patient over to the dariiseri on duty. I suppose I could have insisted on entering the treatment room but I knew you'd be here shortly and I didn't want to impede the clinicians' efforts."

"So you don't know for a certainty that it is Gredin te Balamont?"

"No, but it seems likely. The Vennans are rarely active during my shift, and she *had* been in our office, earlier."

"Are these the security guards who brought her in?"

"Yes. I asked them to wait, in case you wanted to question them directly."

He could always trust Figg to sort fact from speculation, and to present him with first-hand accounts whenever possible. "Thank you," he said, and turned to the guards. "Do you have the call that was received?" he asked.

One of them nodded and keyed his wristcom. From it, faint but clear, a voice spoke in Tradetalk: *Prett security. Hurry. Need Prett security.*

That was followed immediately by the communications computer's reply: *Prett security call. Stay this place, you. Prett security reach you soon.*

"Was the Vennan unconscious when you reached her?"

"No, Director. She was lying on the floor by the communication panel, and she raised her head to speak to us as we arrived."

"What did she say?"

"She said, 'I am lost. Can you help me?' Then she lost consciousness. We loaded her onto the pod and brought her here. And… sir? When she spoke to us, she spoke in Prettian."

That certainly increased the likelihood that the patient in the Clinic was Gredin te Balamont. "Do you have any guess as to why she lost consciousness?"

The two guards exchanged glances. "Yes, Director. She was bleeding, mostly from her arm but also from her head, and there were streaks of blood on the floor panels. It looked as if she had crawled quite some way along the corridor to reach the communication panel."

Heavy-hearted, Wyve said, "Please record a full account and add it to the Night Report. And dispatch a Collection Team to the location where you found her. Have them take a full set of samples. Append a copy of the pertinent surveillance footage to your–"

"Director? Assistant Director?"

It was a new voice, and Wyve turned to see a Third Level dariiseri at the inner doorway, neat and professional in her green smock and flowing pants.

"Identify," Wyve requested.

"Binn. I was summoned because of my familiarity with Vennans, such as it is."

"Account," Wyve directed.

The dariiseri nodded and said, "The Vennan female Gredin te Balamont is awake now. When she first arrived, I applied a topical antibiotic and coagulant to several small cuts. She is currently experiencing vertigo, possibly from blood loss, possibly from several blows to the head, but is refusing all further treatment. She requests an immediate return to her enclave to consult with her native healers. When I informed her of your presence, she requested to see both you and the Assistant Director."

"Conclusion?"

"This was assault, not accidental injury. I suggest visual documentation and a Collection Team, for the individual as well as the site. I would appreciate it if you would conduct an interview and make an advisement regarding her request to be returned to her people for further treatment."

"Your opinion?"

"Given our lack of knowledge about her race's physiology, and the fact that her injuries do not appear life-threatening at this time, I am inclined to cooperate with the request. But the Clinic would like to reexamine her, tomorrow, and to intervene further at that time if the Vennan healers prove ineffective or insufficient."

"We will see her now," Wyve announced, somewhat reassured.

With a nod, the dariiseri turned and started back down the inner hallway. They passed one doorway, then a second, and stopped at the third.

"She is here," Binn said. "I would prefer to stay while you speak with her, in case her condition worsens. If you grant permission for her to return to her enclave, we can bring transport on which she can be transferred. Until her vertigo abates, she should not attempt to traverse the halls without assistance."

"By all means," Wyve said. "Come in with us, and we will look to you for guidance once a decision has been reached about where she will pass the remainder of the night."

Binn opened the door but stood aside for Wyve to enter first.

As he stepped forward to do so, he heard a sharp *click*, and something struck the toe of his boot. Looking down, he saw that it was a stone, perhaps an inch long, shaped like a fat triangle with rounded points. Its outer edges were nearly transparent, but the interior was a peculiar shade of muddy green.

"Stop them!" a voice called sharply from within the room. "They're getting away!"

The cry came from Gredin, lying on a treatment bed on her side, curled in on herself.

Wyve looked about, but there was no *them*, only the solitary stone. Bending, he picked it up and carried it with him into the room.

"Who is getting away?" Figg asked, following after him. When there was no answer, she asked again, more strongly, "Gredin? *Who* is getting away?"

"The Beng!" came the reply, and Gredin lifted her head to look at Figg for a searing instant before collapsing with a moan onto the pillowy support of the bed's surface.

Wyve felt Figg's fingers settle on his arm and clamp down, hard. The same sense of shock was running through him, and he faltered to a stop, stunned by what they had both just seen: Gredin's face, pale and bruised… beneath a mop of short, untidy curls.

Turning his back to the bed, Wyve faced Binn and mouthed, in a horrified whisper, "What has become of her hair?!"

Binn shook her head and replied, just as quietly, "This is how she came to us."

Figg tugged at his arm, urging him along with her as she approached the bed. "Gredin? Don't try to raise your head. Just answer our questions if you can. All right?"

"Yes." Gredin's normally vibrant voice was thready and thin. Wyve bent low to hear her.

"You name the Beng," Figg continued. "Are they the ones who did this to you?"

"Yes."

"Is that who you meant, just now, when you said they were getting away?"

"My stone."

"Pardon?"

Gredin slipped one bare arm out from beneath the thermwrap cover, and Wyve saw the beautiful curves of the golden hlette that hugged her bicep, and the gleam of the coagulation gel that covered several angry red gashes in the skin just above and below it. Shallow cuts had been treated on her forehead, as well.

Splaying her fingers, Gredin rasped, "Give me my stone."

Wyve realized that he still held the triangular pebble in his hand, forgotten in his astonishment over seeing Gredin. Stepping forward, he pressed it into her palm. "Here it is."

Her fingers closed over it, encompassing one of his fingers, as well. After a moment, she whispered, "The Beng have run away. You cannot catch them now."

Wyve knew that the Beng were, indeed, scheduled to leave within the next few hours. Had they actually physically attacked Gredin? If so, such an incident was unprecedented on Tradepoint. There was an occasional scuffle between hot-tempered traders, and there had been the unfortunate accident where Gredin herself trod upon a Hesch's foot by accident and broke a bone within it, but those were rarities, and carried a heavy penalty. They were nothing like the damage he was seeing here, deliberate and vindictive. "Figg—" he began.

"I'm calling," she said, and retreated to the corridor, lifting her wristcom to her lips.

Binn stepped up to take her place beside him, gazing down at the wounded Vennan.

"Please…" The whisper came from Gredin.

"What?"

"Please… I don't want to feel this way. Take me back to our enclave."

"Very soon. We have three brief matters to conclude here, and then we will take you." He looked to Binn. "If you could summon a Collection Team…?"

"Certainly, Director. They will be here in a matter of minutes."

"Very well." With a sigh, he turned back to Gredin. "Clinicians are coming to gather necessary samples from you, and to make images for our records. None of it should cause you any pain, and it will not be a long process. Once they finish, I will take you to the Vennan enclave, with a security escort. But you should not be left alone, tonight. Can someone within the enclave watch over you? If not, we will bring you back here to the Clinic after the healing."

His words seemed to confuse her. "Once I am Healed, I will sleep. Ingarra can sit with me, if you are concerned, but I would rather that she stay with Beda."

"Let us wait and decide when we get there," Wyve said. "For now, can you explain what happened tonight between you and the Beng?"

A cautious nod. "I went to talk to Figg. When I left…" She shifted slightly, under the thermwrap. "… I was lost in thought. I didn't pay proper attention. I stepped on something – on someone – and fell. I struck my head. Beng were all around me, shouting that I had injured one of them, and that I must get up and help him, since I was big and they were small…" A sigh. "Their voices jumbled together in my head. When I couldn't stand, they began to push and drag me. They took me into an antechamber, and bio-mist came down." Her breathing quickened. "They tried to open my jacket. They wanted my necklace, the flamestone – to make up for the Judgment, they said. But I wasn't wearing it. Burlon wouldn't let me. So they tried to take my hlette and hlao instead. But they wouldn't come off." She was panting now. "The Beng left but one stayed behind, searching my pockets. I wasn't going to let him take my pouch of stones, so I… I scratched his face. I'm sorry, Wyve, but he was trying to—"

"Chee, chee, chee," Wyve crooned. "Be at peace. You defended yourself and your belongings. There is no need for apologies."

"I must have hurt him because he ran away. I was alone."

"In the antechamber."

"Yes. The mist had stopped." Her breathing quickened again. "I left my jacket there! If the guards find it…"

"If the jacket is found, we will most certainly return it to you."

That seemed to calm her. "I don't have enough clothes," she murmured. "I can't afford to lose any." Then she squirmed, beneath the thermwrap, and said sharply, "My clothes!"

"Are safe in our care," Binn volunteered.

Gredin closed her eyes tightly. "I feel so wretched. When can I…?"

Figg strode back into the room, her expression grim. "The Beng have indeed departed, and they left a last-minute revision of instructions regarding the cargo they off-loaded. It is keyed to your access only, Director. We attempted to contact their ship but they declined to respond."

"Hardly surprising, under the circumstances," Wyve said, anger simmering. Were the Beng so self-deluded as to think they could simply slide out of port and return in a hundred days' time to find that this had all blown over? Hardly. Evidence would be gathered. Charges would be filed. Gredin and the other Vennan survivors would receive compensation for this outrage.

The door opened again, this time admitting the Collection Team.

Wyve turned to them. "This Vennan was subjected to physical attack by a group of Beng. Do your collecting carefully and thoroughly, for there will be a legal proceeding in this matter, and the magnitude of the Judgment will be founded in part on the work you do here."

"Yes, Director," the head of the Team said, looking suitably impressed.

"Gredin," Figg said quietly, "Binn will stay with you while the Collection Team does their work. Then Wyve will take you back to your enclave."

"I…"

Wyve and Figg waited patiently.

"I would rather you both stayed, as well," Gredin said.

"Then that is what we will do," Wyve replied, and sat down with Figg on the far side of the room, out of the way of Binn and the Team.

He understood, in detailed theory, the procedures that the Collection Team would carry out, but he had never before watched them in action. Contamination prevention barriers in place, they moved harmoniously as a unit, easing Gredin onto her back and positioning her, limbs splayed. Next, they sealed the sides of the thermwrap, and closed its top seams snugly on either side of her neck. Then they activated the collection field.

Gredin cried out, but she sounded more startled than distressed.

"Done in three… two… one," Wyve assured her, and the field cut out, allowing the thermwrap to resume its former shape above and beneath her. "Now, close your eyes and allow them to place the mouthpiece between your lips. Bite down on it and breathe through your mouth. It will supply enough air for five minutes, but you will only need it for one, possibly less."

He watched protectively as their shielded hands slipped the hood over her head, secured it in place, and again briefly activated the collection field. Afterward, meticulously, they released the hood and removed it, folding it in upon itself and bagging it. Then they slipped the mouthpiece from between Gredin's lips and bagged it separately.

"Nearly done," Wyve assured her.

The Collection Team unfastened the sides of the thermwrap and asked Gredin to extend both of her hands.

She turned toward Wyve, looking distressed. "My stones!"

Figg walked to the bedside. "Gredin? Would it be permissible for me to hold them for you, right here next to you, for the short time it will take for the Collection Team to deal with your hands? I will not leave your sight."

With obvious reluctance, Gredin passed a small pouch into Figg's possession.

True to her word, Figg stepped out of the path of the Collection Team but made certain to stay close to the bedside, with the pouch visible.

The Team worked swiftly, two on either side of the bed. Of each pair, one held the small bags as the other passed the tip of a sonic tool beneath the curve of each of Gredin's fingernails. With that accomplished, one held little vials as the other immersed each of Gredin's fingertips in a clear liquid and then capped the vial.

Wyve noted with bleak interest that the liquid in several of the vials instantly took on a rusty orange hue – the color of Beng blood. He hadn't doubted Gredin's account. But the visual confirmation intensified the knot in the pit of his stomach.

"All done," Wyve told her, as the vials and bags were taken away. "In a minute or two, we'll be ready to take you to the enclave."

Figg pressed the little pouch of stones back into Gredin's hands.

"I need my clothes," Gredin said.

"The Collection Team will need to keep your clothing, for now. Binn will find something else for you to wear back to the enclave, won't you, Binn?"

"Of course. I'll bring a patient covering, right away. Collection Team, wait until I return before you remove the thermwrap."

"Certainly," one of them said to the dariiseri.

Binn left, and they all stood around awkwardly, waiting for her return.

In an effort to fill the time productively, Wyve approached the bed and said to Gredin, "So, do you think the Beng did this to your hair out of frustration when they were balked in their attempts to take your necklace and your hlette and hlao?"

"My hair?" she repeated, sounding nonplussed. One slender hand slid out from beneath the thermwrap and reached up to explore her head. As her fingers met the ragged assortment of short curls, her mouth dropped open and her gaze flew from Wyve to Figg and back again. "My braids. They cut off my braids!"

Wyve's heart sank. "You didn't know? I am so sorry. I assumed… " He hung his head. "Forgive me."

A tremulous sigh escaped her. "They could have done worse to me. They had a knife. I remember now, one of them said, 'Not go home with nothing!' And then my head struck the floor, over and over. I didn't realize what he was doing." Again, her fingers skimmed her head. "I must look very… odd."

"Not odd," Figg said. "Just different. And your hair will grow again, will it not?"

"Eventually. But I will look like a small child to my people. Only young children have short, curly hair. Their Guides braid their hair as soon as it is long enough. And children's hair becomes straighter and straighter as it grows in length. This will look… very strange to everyone." Her fingers clenched in the curls. "And to think I asked Ingarra to help me look older… "

"Let go." Wyve touched the back of her hand gently. "You will hurt yourself."

After a moment, she withdrew her hand. "Figg?"

"Right here."

"After I return to the enclave, will you explain our talk to Wyve?"

"Of course. Forget about that for tonight. Tomorrow will be soon enough for us to talk again about what to do."

Wyve glanced down at his wrist to see how much of the night remained… and froze. "Gredin, did the Beng take your communication band?"

Binn said, "Director, we removed it when she was brought in."

"So, Gredin, you were wearing it at the time of the attack?"

"Yes."

"Then why didn't you use it to send for help?"

She looked at him blankly, as if he were speaking in Chibi.

"I told you, when I gave it to you, that you could press the colored oval to summon Prett security, if you were ever in need."

She stared at him for another moment, and then said, "I forgot."

"Gredin!"

"Believe me, I wish I had remembered. It would have been much,

much easier than crawling to the corridor intersection." An exhausted attempt at a smile. "Forgive me, please. My head has not been working well, tonight. Figg will tell you. I was already muddled, even before I encountered the Beng. And then… Well, my thoughts have all been in a tumble. Please don't be angry with me."

"Angry with…? No. I am not. Truly, I am not. I am just so very regretful that this has befallen you. You must rest and recover. We will not expect to hold a morning meeting with you for at least the next two days."

The door opened and Binn came in. She carried a white garment over her arm, and she was followed by a clinic worker pushing a slender rolling bed. "Gredin, you will feel chilled when we remove the thermwrap, but we will have you warm again as soon as you are settled on this transfer cot. Are you ready?"

"What do I need to do?"

"Almost nothing. Lie still while the Collection Team removes the thermwrap. Then I will help you pass your hands and arms through the sleeves of this robe, and we will lift you, as gently as we can. Once you are on the cot, we have a heated blanket to cover you from chin to toes. It contains its own power source and will keep you warm all the way to your enclave. Will there be someone there to help you from the transfer cot to your bed?"

"Yes. We will manage well, once I am there. My thanks for your kindness, Binn. I understand all the better why Keegan feels so safe in your care."

Wyve retreated with Figg, making way for the Collection Team. Again, the Team moved with crisp synchrony, smoothly removing the thermwrap and folding it in upon itself, then bundling it into a collection bag. Binn stepped forward to cover Gredin with the robe, but not before Wyve caught a sickening glimpse of an enormous bruise discoloring Gredin's leg, just below the hip. Unbidden, his mind offered up an image of the stout boots the Beng habitually wore, and his temper surged again.

The clinician maneuvered the cot close and transferred Gredin onto it, then spread a fresh thermwrap over her, tucking it around her. As she did so, the Collection Team gathered up the liner on which Gredin had lain, folding it in and over, in and over, until it fit into the bag allotted for it.

Figg touched Wyve's arm. "I can accompany Gredin to the Vennan enclave, if you wish to go and examine the document the Beng transmitted, since it is keyed for your access only."

It wasn't what he wanted to do, but it made sense. "Thank you. I will see you at the office, once Gredin is settled." He cast Figg a rueful glance. "You can enlighten me, then, as to what drew her to our door so late in the first place, since I gather it was no trivial matter."

"Indeed, I will update you on the matter later," Figg confirmed. "For now, however, I will make the final arrangements with Binn for Gredin's release."

"And I will go to the office," Wyve said.

He wanted to take proper leave of Gredin, but her eyes were closed. Hoping she had found a moment's peace, he nodded silently to the Collection Team and to Binn, then left the Clinic, intent on finding out what *else* those malicious Beng had gotten up to before they departed.

[2]

1022 OF 2000 ORBITS REMAINING: 48BLUE

Beda was encouraging seedlings.

Actually, he was having a night-thought. Part of him even knew it was a night-thought. But the rest of his mind was utterly engaged in the loamy scent of the soil, the glow of the luminth, the brave, fragile stems that had broken through from the darkness below and now stood, heads bowed by the weight of their very first two leaves.

=Beda?=

Sometimes, it was enough just to observe and encourage them, making sure enough water reached the thread-like roots. Other times, if a clump of soil clung too tenaciously to those initial leaves, he might ease it off, freeing the fledgling plant from that extra, unfair burden of weight. Soon, the stalks would strengthen and the leaves would spread, able to fend for themselves. But on occasion, in the earliest going, a bit of gentle assistance could make all the difference…

=Beda!=

The row of seedlings faded from his mind's eye, their delicate green darkening into the shadows of night. He became aware of his body, of Ingarra's warmth beside him, of the heavy appetite for sleep that yet lingered within him, far from satisfied. And something else, something outside of himself, reaching in, asking for connection…

=Who…?= he queried, not yet awake enough to Focus clearly.

=Keegan te Fliss. Your pardon for waking you, but there is need. Gredin has been harmed. She requires a Healing.=

The shock of that news jolted him fully awake. =Where is she?=

=Here in the enclave, in her bed. The Prett just brought her from their Clinic. They have done their best to treat her injuries but she needs far more. She needs an Intercession.=

=I am coming. Should I bring Ingarra?=

=Yes. Please. I think Gredin needs you both.=

And so it was, soon thereafter, that he and Ingarra made their way to the little hallway outside of the suite of rooms Gredin and Keegan shared, and announced their arrival.

The door opened instantly and Keegan te Fliss welcomed them in.

The entire suite was aglow with luminth light, and the inner doors to both Keegan's sleeping chamber and Gredin's stood open. "She was set upon by the Beng," Keegan explained before he brought them into Gredin's presence. "They knocked her down and kicked her, then tried to steal her necklace and her hlette and her hlao. Thanks to a caution from Burlon, she wasn't wearing the necklace, but the Beng didn't understand the nature of the hlette and hlao. They thought they could pull those from her arm and forehead. When that didn't work, they used a knife. When that, too, failed…" He looked at them, clearly distressed. "…they cut off her braids."

"What? Why?!"

"Who can know? Out of spite, perhaps?" He shook his head. "She wanted you to know, before you saw her. She seems more concerned about that than about her injuries."

Ingarra, as staunch as ever, said, "No matter. We will see to all of it. Go back to bed and find what sleep you can, Keegan. Thank you for summoning us. We will care for her from here."

"If you need anything, don't hesitate to summon me," he said, and left them.

Beda took his Chosen's hand, and they went in together.

Even forewarned as they were, the sight of Gredin's shorn hair and the unkempt mop of curls made Beda's breath catch in his throat. It was a poignant reminder of her early childhood, when her adventurous spirit propelled her from room to room at a pace her little legs could scarcely manage. It was unsettling to see such curls now adorning the head of their mature, lanky nifflin.

Beda sank to his knees beside Gredin's bedmat. "How are you feeling?" he asked, and reached beneath the coverlet for her wrist, anxious to Assess her.

Shivering, she said, "Dizzy. Cold. But I need to talk with you both before I sleep, so do not Heal me quite yet."

"Nonsense," Ingarra protested. "Whatever it is, tell us when you wake, after you have been restored."

"It cannot wait."

"But the Beng–"

"It has nothing to do with the Beng. It is far more important than that." She groaned. "Beda, please, can you help me a little before you restore me completely?"

He stared down at her. "What are you asking?"

She breathed through parted lips, her distress apparent. "Can you Intercede for me, but only briefly? Can you help me to feel enough better for me to tell you what I must, and then complete the Intercession? The safety of the community may rely upon it."

No one had ever asked such a thing of him. It ran counter to his gyfte and to his training. But this was Gredin, and it was clear that her request was no frivolous thing. "I can try," he said, dubiously.

"Your willing effort is all I ask." Gredin looked past him. "Ingarra, will you help him? After the Intercession begins, can you interrupt him?"

"Nifflin, you are asking me to tamper with a gyfte not my own."

"Yes."

"This is important enough to justify such a risk?"

"Yes."

Ingarra nodded. "Very well. If Beda is willing, I will add my efforts to his."

Beda smiled at his Chosen. "Simply lift my hand from Gredin's wrist. It should take no more than that. But first I will Assess her."

Quieting his mind, he prepared himself. Gredin's vessel was one he knew well. All her childhood bumps and bruises had been his to soothe. He had even aided her here on Tradepoint, after she suffered punctures from an alien's claws. Whatever harm the Beng had dealt her, he would soon know.

He placed one hand on her brow and wrapped the other around her wrist, drinking in the sense of her as she relaxed beneath his touch. He took careful account of her physical injuries: an array of bruises and cuts on her head, more cuts on her upper arm, and an angry welling of blood beneath the skin on her upper leg, radiating pain and a sullen heat. Lesser complaints emanated from her forehead, her shoulder, her knee, her wrist. And, beneath it all, the dizziness she complained of shifted and seethed like an angry tide.

But even more worrisome was the state of her hlinga, for it guttered like a candleflame in a breeze when it should be strong and unwavering.

Nodding, he disengaged. "Nothing that can't be handled," he assured her, and looked to Ingarra. "There are many small things to be attended to, which should help. Once I've begun, count to fifty, then lift my hands from her. With the Power's blessing, that should be enough for a start." He grimaced, for it was a strange thing to say. You didn't simply 'start' a Healing. You carried it through to its conclusion. But that was not Gredin's request, and there was little he would deny her. They would try to do this her way, in stages, although he was resolved not to leave her, tonight, until she had been Healed of all her injuries. "I'll begin now," he told Gredin.

"Yes," she whispered. "Please."

Again, he positioned one hand at her brow, then grasped her wrist, seeking the faint, wild flutter that lived there. It should have been a strong, steady rhythm; soon, it would be again.

He closed his eyes, Focusing on the beat against his fingertips, then working his way deeper…

With a jolt, he came back to himself. "What?" he demanded, disoriented.

Ingarra held both his hands between her own and was chafing them gently. "You said to count slowly to fifty and then to take your hands away."

"But… but… that wasn't possibly fifty," he protested.

"It was, actually."

He felt scattered, as if part of his awareness was still within Gredin, while the rest of him was out here, trying to deal with light and sound and–

"Beda?"

Looking down at Gredin, he saw that her eyes were open.

Her face looked less pale and pinched than it had when he first came in, but she made no attempt to lift her head from the bedmat, only smiled up at him. "The pain in my head has eased. Thank you. Can you and Ingarra listen now, while I tell you what I must? Then you can finish, and we all can sleep."

"Of course. We are listening."

Her smile was wan. "Ingarra, this involves what I learned from Miri tonight. It is serious and affects many, many people here in the community." She took a breath and said more strongly, "For now, the enclave contains three kinds of people – those like Keegan who have not yet found their Chosen, those like you and Beda who have your Chosen with you here on Tradepoint, and people like Miri and me who lost our Chosens in Venna's destruction and are now alone." Gredin's gaze moved to Beda. "When you Assessed me, could you feel it?"

Beda said, "I felt many things."

"Could you feel how far from true Balance my hlinga has strayed?"

"Yes," he answered, sobered by the memory.

"And when your own hlinga strays from Balance, how do you correct it?"

Automatically, his hand sought Ingarra's. "I seek out my Chosen."

"Indeed. And what recourse is there for Keegan, who has no Chosen?"

"He sees to his own needs, as we were all taught to do in our youth."

"Precisely. And what should I do?"

He suddenly perceived the difficulty. "Robbed of your Chosen, I suppose you must once again see to your own needs, as you did before Dreff came into your life."

"No. Unfortunately, you are wrong. That door is closed to me now."

He had never heard anyone say such a thing. But he realized, on a moment's reflection, that he had never known anyone whose Chosen had returned to the Source… until now. "Your touch brings your body no pleasure?"

She shook her head. "It is not painful, but there is no satisfaction to it. No excitement. No way to coax my body to a completion."

Alarm filled him. "But without a completion–"

Gredin nodded. "Without a completion, my hlinga drifts farther and farther from Balance." She frowned. "At first, I thought it was because I was grieving. But Miri spoke to me tonight of her House member, Ulm te Kendar. Ulm's Chosen returned to the Source long and long ago. In the time following that sad event, Ulm became this third thing, neither Unchosen nor Chosen. Her hlinga strayed farther and farther from Balance, and she eventually lost all ability to exercise her gyftes. And I am not referring just to her major gyfte. Before long, she could not Send, could not Fetch, could not Convert her own waste, could do nothing that required a connection with the Power. And yet she lived on, miserable in the knowledge that she had become a burden to her House members, and that she had lost all touch with the Power."

"How terrible," Ingarra whispered.

"Since she was the only member of House Kendar to have suffered such a fate, it was no huge burden for her kinsmen to continue to care for her, out of love and pity. And her life ended when Venna was destroyed, returning her to peace at the Source. But Ulm's fate is now my own, and Miri's, and Hayla's, and that of every other survivor whose Chosen has now been lost. Hundreds of us. One in three, Keegan has said. Can you imagine what that burden would do to the community?"

Beda bowed his head, shaken by the picture of life to come. "We will need to be strong."

"But we are *not* strong, right now. When Miri told me, I feared we would not be able to cope with such a wide-spread difficulty in our current state… and so I went and talked to Figg, the Assistant Director of Tradepoint. She has a calm, methodical mind. I thought perhaps, since she was Prett, and used to solving problems, she might think of something that would help. And, if not, she needed to know that I would not be able to lead our community for much longer."

"Oh, Gredin," Ingarra said. "My poor nifflin. You know that you will always be able to rely on us to care for you."

"But I don't want to lose my gyftes. I don't want to be a burden. I have lost enough. I don't want to lose anything more. And so I took the tale of this calamity to Figg, hoping she might think of a solution." Gredin reached out to Ingarra and gripped her hand. "And she did."

Beda exchanged a look with Ingarra, trying to reconcile the meaning of Gredin's words with the near-frantic aura rising from her.

"The Assistant Director suggested a solution?" Ingarra asked uncertainly.

"Yes."

"Is that not good news?"

"Possibly. She came up with a plan. Something that *might* help. But our people won't like it. And we aren't certain it will help. The only way to know is for someone – for me – to try it."

"You are in no fit shape to try anything, at the moment," Ingarra said.

"But I will be, as soon as Beda has Healed me. Ingarra, I have to be. I can't bear not knowing. And I cannot discuss this with anyone beyond the three of us and Figg until I find out. Not even Miri."

"The Assistant Director is not Vennan. How can she know what you need?"

"She has studied many races. She listened closely to what I told her. She asked questions. There is a certain sense to what she recommends. But it isn't anything we have ever…"

Beda took Gredin's hand from Ingarra. "Enough. Name this thing. You have been circling around it, exhausting yourself and postponing the Intercession that you need. Be direct. What does Figg of the Prett bid you to do?"

Gredin closed her eyes. “She says that those who have lost their Chosen should mate with one another.”

For Gredin’s sake, Beda swallowed his first three responses. She was in need of calm counsel, not startled exclamations. At last, after consideration, he said, “She believes that a man who is not your Chosen could restore your hlinga?”

A nod. “And his own. She sees it as a way for us to help one another.”

“Vennans have never done such a thing.”

“Vennans have never needed to, until now.”

He sighed. “You are right to think that our people will not welcome such a suggestion.”

“I don’t intend to mention it to any others unless I know it will help.”

Beda squeezed her hand. “You would actually attempt this?”

“Either I try or I condemn a third of our people to the loss of their gyftes.”

“And if it doesn’t work?”

“Then I will have tried, at least, and I will try to think of something else, before it is too late.”

“And if it does help?”

“Then we are saved from a terrible fate!”

“For the moment,” he said, reluctant to distress her but wanting to be certain she had considered the matter thoroughly. “Hlinga is not an object you can grasp and place upon a shelf, yours forever. It is like hunger and thirst. You satisfy it… for a time. But then it will rise again. Balance is ever-changing. You must continue to nurture it.”

Beneath her child-like curls, Gredin’s face looked suddenly burdened with maturity. “Yes, you are right. This is not a solution for a single night. And that frightens me. Who can I approach? Who can I trust? How can I possibly mate with a stranger? And if I find someone, and this actually helps, what should I do when the need arises again, as it will? This will not be a Choosing. Those are the work of the Power. This would only be a mating, a thing I do because I *must* do it if I am to retain my gyftes.” Her fingers trembled in his grasp. “I know of no one to ask. It must be a man who has lost his Chosen, and it must be someone we can trust, because if this fails to help… Oh, Beda, if I do this thing, and it fails to help, then no one else must ever know of it. Can you and Ingarra think about the men you know, here on Tradepoint? Perhaps someone within your gyfte? Perhaps an acquaintance? Think of those who have lost their Chosen. Think of those I could rely on. Is there one among them who would most keenly mourn the waning of their gyfte, and might therefore be willing to take this chance. I can think of no one, and yet this must happen – yet tonight, if possible."

"Yet tonight? You cannot be serious."

"I am entirely serious. Time has become our enemy. Each day that passes takes its toll on the hlinga of everyone who has lost their Chosen, making it that much harder for us to regain our Balance." She bit her lip, then said, "Heal me, Beda. And afterward, while I sleep, find someone I can trust, and have him come here to me."

This was their nifflin. All her days, she had walked a different path, drawn by something they could neither see nor understand. But Beda knew she loved them, just as he and Ingarra loved her. He believed her when she said that the Power had come to her in her night-thoughts, here on Tradepoint. He was proud of how she had conducted her duties as First Speaker, and profoundly grateful that First Speaker's hlette had broken free of Tetralanna and come to Gredin instead.

He would do the things she asked. First, with joy in his gyfte, he would Heal her. And then, despite his apprehension, he would confer with Ingarra, and they would select someone they thought well of, someone gentle, someone trustworthy, someone whose Chosen was now gone, as Dreff was gone. They would disturb that person's night and explain this strange turn of events. Somehow, they would convince this man to undertake an action that might become a source of shame and regret… or that might, if the Power willed it so, turn out to be the source of salvation their community so desperately needed.

"Rely upon us," he said to Gredin, "and close your eyes. It is time for you to be Healed."

[3]

1018 OF 2000 ORBITS REMAINING: 3BLUE

In Khest te Bentain's opinion, the metal nests provided by the Prett were peculiar places to sleep. Narrow, tall, and deep, with no opening except for the lack of a front wall, and stacked upon each other in blocks that were six high and twenty wide, they were a bit like the colonies that kamesta dug for themselves in hillsides. He had come upon kamesta warrens, a few times, when he went walking outside of the House walls: a grassy slope punctuated with neat rows of small tunnels.

Each wall of Prett nests formed a slope, as well, with the second row set a bit farther back than the first, and the third row set a bit farther back than the second, and so on. Staggering them in that way created a small platform at the entrance to each nest – a platform that was actually the front-most portion of the roof of the nest below. It served as a handy place for individuals to Send, to gain access to their nest.

Khest's assigned nest was on the top row at the far left end, and he enjoyed knowing that no one lived above him. It made his quarters seem a little less confining. But he was wary about pacing when, as often happened now, he couldn't sleep. Tonight, when he had once again awoken far too early, with most of the night still stretching before him, he had worried that his footsteps would disturb Pipla and Jarn, in the nest below.

And so, instead of pacing, he had formed the habit of sitting, cross-legged, at the entrance to his nest, gazing out into the enclave that House Bentain shared with House Calidane. The combining of Bentain with Calidane was an uneasy arrangement, based as it was upon the number of survivors in each House rather than on any traditional triad association, and it consisted of six blocks of nests. Four blocks were Bentain. The remaining two were Calidane. The extra nests that weren't needed as sleeping quarters were used for storage, or simply sat empty.

From his vantage point, Khest could look down on the open area near the entrance door. People had taken to calling it 'the courtyard,' although it really wasn't one. Perhaps some of them drew comfort from using familiar words to name pieces of this strange shelter at Tradepoint. He did not. It only made him long for home...

Below, something moved in the darkness.

Peering, he realized that the double doors of the enclave had separated at the middle and were sliding open. They made no sound but they did reveal the faint glow of a luminth that had been dimmed nearly to extinction.

So, someone else was up and about in the middle of the night. If it was a House member, should he go down and see whether they required his gyfte?

He was still sitting, undecided, when a contact whispered against his private mind. =Khest te Bentain?=

=Here,= he replied, and saw the luminth below jerk, as if its owner had not expected such a prompt response.

=It is Beda te Balamont. There is need. Can you come?=

He knew Beda, of course. They shared a minor gyfte for Healing. It troubled him to think that someone within the community had suffered an injury that required more than one minor Healer. Or was it because the other Healers were also faltering in their gyfte, as he was?

=Of course,= he replied. =A moment, while I dress.= Hastily, he Fetched a teslan and pulled it on, stepped into the comfortable ankle boots he had taken to wearing in deference to the chilly metal flooring, tucked his pack of oils under his arm, and Sent himself down to where Beda waited.

Or tried to. To his displeasure, he arrived some distance away from where Beda stood, and the impact of the landing forced him to take a staggering step to steady himself.

=Can you come out into the corridor, so that we don't wake anyone?= Beda asked.

Silently, Khest did as he requested.

In the past few days, with the establishment of the expanded enclaves, the Prett had disconnected the bio-mist in the antechambers so that community members could venture anywhere within the Vennan area without having to undergo that protective cleansing. Currently, only the new door installed at the point where their area connected with the new public corridor was equipped with a functioning bio-mist antechamber. As a result, Beda was able to take him without delay along the inner hallway and into the main enclave's reception hall, where their meals were served.

Khest had never before seen that room empty. Although Beda had increased the light from his luminth, it didn't penetrate far into the vast chamber. Khest had the strange sensation that he was walking forward into an endless void, with only the next few panels of flooring visible before them as they walked. And a quick glance over his shoulder showed him a darkness broken only by a faint hint of luminous green that he assumed was the number display above the entry door.

"Where are we going?" he inquired uneasily, finally daring to speak aloud. "No one sleeps in this enclave anymore."

"No *Houses* sleep here," Beda corrected, "but four members of our community do."

"Truly? Who?"

"Chenna and Burlon te Laith are residing here for the duration of their dydanin, and there are also private quarters for the historian, Keegan te Fliss, and for First Speaker, Gredin te Balamont."

"And one of them requires a Healing?"

"Not precisely."

Khest felt irritation flare within him, no doubt fueled by the broken nights he had recently endured. Stopping, he said, "I thought we were coming to help someone in need."

"We are," Beda assured him, coming back to stand with him. "In fact, there are two people in need. I am taking you to the private quarters of Gredin te Balamont. She was set upon, earlier tonight, by a group of Beng."

"Beng?"

"An alien race that trades here. You might remember them from the reception. They were short and wore green clothing. Tonight, they dragged Gredin into a bio-mist antechamber and attacked her, hoping to steal all that she had of value, her flamestone necklace, First Speaker's hlette, and her hlao. Fortunately, on Burlon's advice, she wasn't wearing the necklace, and they were unable to remove the hlette from her arm or the hlao from her head, although they injured her in their attempt to do so. But they were angry at being thwarted, and so they kicked her, as well, and cut off her braids."

Khest listened, horrified. Although he had resisted Burlon's offer to take him on a tour of the Traders' Market, it had been due more to a lack of enthusiasm for exerting himself in such a venture, not because he thought he might be in actual danger of attack from the individuals who came to Tradepoint. And now some other race had threatened First Speaker and done actual damage to her… "Your pardon," he said. "I did not understand. Of course I will do whatever I can to Heal her. Are you seeing to the other one?"

"What do you mean?"

"You said two people are in need. First Speaker is one of them. Who is the other?"

"That," Beda said, "will take a little explaining. Come sit and we'll talk."

"Sit? Talk? Shouldn't we be hurrying to reach them?"

"That is part of what I need to explain," Beda said, and motioned for the two of them to walk on.

Have patience, Khest told himself, following. What Beda said didn't make sense, but very little had made sense to him since he'd learned of the loss of their world and the death of Silandra and the others of his House. Everyone was acting oddly, himself included. But Beda te Balamont was a kindly man. Something had driven him from his bed and caused him to come to House Bentain's enclave in search of Khest. Better to cooperate and find out what it was.

The luminth soon revealed the departure dais. Beda lowered himself onto the second of its steps and gestured for Khest to do the same, then set the luminth between them. Lit from below, Beda's face looked odd, like that of a stranger. "How are you faring, Khest?"

It was not a question he expected to be asked. "In what sense?"

"Your hlinga. Your gyftes. How are you faring, in this time of sadness and loss?"

Khest shrugged. "Better than some. Less well than others, I suppose."

Beda shook his head. "If you will trust me, I need a more specific answer. Some in the community are having difficulty exercising their gyftes. I need to know if that is true of you."

"Are you worried I won't be able to Heal First Speaker?"

"I will answer that question in a moment." Beda reached out and touched his arm lightly. "Would you permit me to Assess you first? I assure you, there is a purpose to my request."

"My thanks, but no."

In the luminth glow, Beda's expression softened. "If you are like the last individual I Assessed, you may well be out of Balance, in which case an Assessment would steady you and improve your condition. There is no shame in it."

"You assume that your Balance is better than mine?"

"I am quite certain of it. If I am wrong, no harm is done. And if I am right, I will tell you why I was so certain. May I?"

Khest nodded, embarrassed by his own stubborn resistance. Stiffly, he shifted his position and reclined, until he was lying on the broad, hard step. Beda's hands were deft, settling at his brow and wrist…

A sudden flow of warmth eased muscles Khest had not realized were clenched. He relaxed into the Assessment and felt the dark shadow of the past days become more bearable.

He took a deep, shuddering breath as Beda's hands lifted away.

"Better?"

"Better," Khest admitted, sitting up again. "So, what do you make of me? Are you worried that I won't be able to Heal First Speaker?"

"No, for I have already Healed her."

Khest stared at him. "Then why did you seek me out? Why are you taking me to her quarters, if not to Heal her injuries?" he demanded.

"Because your hlinga is in disarray."

"That is true of us all," Khest protested.

"Yes. But a specific malaise is harming many individuals in our community, a difficulty beyond the mourning and fear that has struck us all. It preys upon a particular set of individuals – those who have lost their Chosens – and the harm it does goes far beyond sadness and grief. As you may have begun to realize, it strikes at your very ability to Focus and Control your gyftes."

"But everyone–"

"No. Not everyone. Not to this degree. And, left untreated, it will intensify until the exercise of your gyftes is utterly beyond you."

Mindless panic rose up within him. He wanted to force Beda to stop uttering such frightening words. He wanted to be in his bed, asleep, not sitting in this dim reception hall, listening to someone describe the very dread that had begun to stalk his days. "How can you possibly know?"

"I wish I could tell you that the Power informed Gredin of this danger, and that it imparted the cure to her, as well. But that is not so. The knowledge comes to us from a member of the community whose House harbored such a one, back home – a kinswoman whose Chosen returned to the Source, long and long ago, and who gradually experienced these same losses and limitations. Are you aware of anyone in House Bentain who has suffered such a fate?"

"No. Never."

"I suspect they were few. Very few. But the problem did exist, and this is how it presented itself – a waning of hlinga, a disruption of Focus and Control, and finally a failure of Balance so complete that even the simplest uses of the Power became impossible." Beda sighed.

"And now, instead of that situation being rare, nearly a third of our community members have suffered the loss of a Chosen and are beginning to feel the impact."

"Why are you telling me these things?" Khest asked. "We are of different Houses. My major gyfte is Touch, while yours is Growing. Silandra, my Chosen, has returned to the Source, while you are still united with Ingarra. Why, then, have you singled me out tonight?"

"Because Gredin is in desperate need, as are you. I cannot help either of you, but there is a chance that you can help each other."

"Help? How?"

"By joining with her."

"You are recruiting allies for her? Surely you know that Naria te Bentain, who leads my House, does not support Gredin."

Beda smiled ruefully. "That is not the sort of joining I mean."

It was an odd thing to say. If he wasn't referring to publicly supporting Gredin te Balamont in the on-going disagreements within the community, then what could he possibly…?

Oh.

But…

"You cannot mean what you seem to be saying," Khest objected.

"Ah, but I do," Beda replied, his voice so quiet and calm that it left Khest no shelter of disbelief behind which to hide.

And so he met Beda's gaze squarely, speaking past the emotions that clogged his throat and distorted his voice. "Then you waste your time. I have lost my Chosen. There will be no more mating for me in this life."

"If that is your final word on the matter, I am saddened for you twice over," Beda said, "for your decision dooms you to lose your gyftes, as surely as you have lost your Chosen. Indeed, I suspect you already feel Control over your gyfte beginning to elude you. And that will only become worse, until all of your gyftes, large and small, fall away from you, never to be recovered." He shook his head. "I see that you find my words cruel. But would you truly prefer the gentle comfort of a lie that lulls you long enough for your gyftes to drift beyond your reach?"

Khest wanted to rise and stride away, or to shout down the other man's words, but a glance at his own hands stopped him. Yesterday, one of his House members had come to him, seeking relief from a brutal headache. Khest had placed his hands carefully upon the man's head, his neck, his shoulders… and nothing but a dull jangle of misery had reached him, with no clear sense of how to alleviate the problem. Concerned, he had summoned Likal, and she had banished the man's headache within moments.

At the time, Khest had blamed his own failure on fatigue, and hunger, and sorrow… but had not Likal been just as tired and hungry and sad as he?

Well, no, not quite, for Likal still had Reller, her Chosen.

Beside him, Beda continued to speak, looking out into the darkness of the room. "Tonight, Gredin heard of this for the first time, and was deeply affrighted by the tale. She sought counsel with Tradepoint's Assistant Director, who listened, and questioned, and came to the conclusion that a loss of Balance from no longer being able to mate with a Chosen was at fault. The Assistant Director said to her, 'Since so many of you are affected, why won't the afflicted attempt to help one another…?'"

"By mating," Khest finished for him, forcing his lips to form the shocking words.

Beda nodded. "Gredin's Balance is eroding by the day, yet she has been charged by the Power with protecting and leading our people, and so she believes an answer to this problem must exist. But she refuses to talk to the community about the Assistant Director's suggestion until she has discovered whether the solution will work. She is determined to attempt this thing, in secret… but for that she needs someone who can be trusted to say nothing, and who also stands to benefit if the effort succeeds. Because she knew of no such individual, she confided her difficulty to me, since I was her Guide. And I, in turn, have come to you."

"But why? Why me, out of so many others?"

Beda suddenly looked sad. "Because we are both minor Healers, you and I… and because I knew your Chosen, Silandra. She was a fine

Grower, with a particular skill in the raising of berries, which was an interest we shared. She and I would meet, on occasion, to exchange cultivars or confer on some detail of berry care that was too particular to be of interest to any but the two of us. Frequently, she spoke of you, always with great love and praise, not only for the skill of your gyftes but also for your steadiness and kindness. The community cannot afford to lose your skills, if that loss can be prevented, and Silandra's words make me believe that I can trust you to deal gently and honorably with Gredin, whether this desperate venture succeeds or not."

Khest bowed his head into his hands. "But to do such a thing..."

"Who does it harm? To our great sorrow, Dreff and Silandra are both gone beyond recall. Will it benefit you or your House for you to lose Control of your gyftes? This is not a selfish act that I ask you to consider. It is an act for the benefit of the community. We have few Healers, and not many more individuals with gyfte of Touch. If you attempt this and it succeeds, you can continue to be a source of strength and well-being for those around you. But if you decline this chance and descend past the use of any of your gyftes, you will need to be cared for by your kinsmen for the rest of your days."

"I notice that you do not mention the other possibility."

"That being...?"

"That Gredin and I attempt this thing and find it does nothing to restore our Balance. In that case, the worst of your predictions comes to pass, and we bring shame down upon ourselves and our respective Houses by acting against the ways of our people."

"Shame? I disagree. Neither the Power nor the Houses themselves have ever spoken on this matter. From childhood, we are taught precisely what is expected of us in the days before we find our Chosens, and it then becomes our heart's delight to devote ourselves to each other once we *do* find our Chosen. But I am aware of no teaching or prohibition concerning the sad fate of someone whose Chosen has returned to the Source. Is it different in House Bentain? Were you taught some rule of behavior which is unknown to me?"

In all honesty, Khest had to say, "No."

"What I *have* been taught, all my life, is my sacred duty to serve my gyftes to the utmost of my ability. Through study, through practice, through Tutoring and Mentorship, I have devoted my days to becoming the best Grower and Healer I could be. Is it so unreasonable, then, lacking other instruction, to assume that our highest duty is still to serve our gyftes? And if something threatens to wrest our gyftes from us, against our will, should we not do everything we can to prevent that from happening, so long as our efforts harm no one?"

Khest dredged a faint, wry smile from deep within himself. "Are you certain that gyfte of Speech is not among your talents? You paint a persuasive picture, especially when nothing but loss and darkness appears to await me if I decline your plan." Gingerly, he rose from the step. "Very well. At the very least, I will meet Gredin te Balamont and discover how she feels about the matter."

"You will find that she feels much as you do – wary of taking this step but determined to do so, considering the alternative. Filled with hope that it will help stem the tide of loss, but aware that it may not. And determined that all awareness of this night's activities be known to no one but the three of us, should it fail. She counts upon your discretion."

"As I will count upon hers. And yours."

Beda nodded and gestured at the deserted reception hall. "You may depend upon me. I brought you here in the dark of night, unobserved. And this room is a place where any member of our community may spend time without exciting comment. None but the three of us know that you are here, let alone why. My Chosen is aware of Gredin's need and knows that I thought of someone who might agree to help and be helped, but even she does not know your name or House. Be assured, you have much to gain and little to lose."

If Khest thought about it much longer, his courage would fail him. "Take me to her."

Beda stood. "In truth, we are nearly there."

They walked past the edge of the departure dais, then on through an archway Khest had not noticed before. It led to a hallway that offered five doors, all on the right side of the corridor.

Gesturing, Beda murmured, "That door at the end leads to the room where Burlon and Chenna te Laith are spending their dydanin."

At the sound of Burlon's familiar name, Khest dropped back a step, disconcerted.

Beda didn't appear to notice. "These middle three doors were storage rooms, but they are empty now," he said. "The musicians kept their instruments there, as did some of the Makers who had more fragile equipment, before the enclaves were enlarged and the nests were built. The one closest to us was changed inside, once it was no longer needed for storage. The Prett removed the wall panel inside that separated the storage area from the final suite of rooms, to make additional space for the historian and his equipment." Beda pointed to the final door on their right, only a few steps away . "Gredin is in there."

When Beda opened the door, Khest could see a small, dimly lit room equipped with a metal table and five stools. The far wall was punctuated by three doors. Beda gestured, this time to his left. "Keegan te Fliss resides there."

"I thought you said the door to his room was out there."

"Since his room has been enlarged, it now has two doors – this one and the one we saw."

Khest looked around uneasily. "And if he comes out and encounters me here?"

"He will not. Keegan knows a little of what is happening. After the Beng attacked Gredin, she was taken to the Prett Clinic. When they had done all they could for her, they brought her here and placed her in Keegan's care. He summoned me to Assess Gredin and perform an Intercession. When Ingarra and I arrived, we told Keegan to return to his bed. For the time being, he has agreed to come and go from his room by the door in the corridor, so as not to disturb Gredin." Beda pointed to the middle door. "That is the Cleansing chamber. And there," he said, gesturing to his right, "is Gredin's room. The door will open when you approach it. A good night to you, Khest te Bentain. Summon me at need." And he stepped back toward the entrance door.

"You're leaving now?" Khest asked.

"Unless you have further need of me."

"You aren't going to wait and… introduce us?"

"You and Gredin can manage that for yourselves. It is as good a place to begin as any." Beda's smile was sympathetic. "Remember what you hope to gain, and what you stand to lose. Treat one another gently. This has been a trying time for you both."

And he left.

Khest resisted the temptation to follow him.

Continuing to stand in the common room seemed unwise. If, despite Beda's assurances, Keegan te Fliss emerged from his sleep chamber, there would be no hope of evading his notice. And the Cleansing chamber served no better purpose. No. Unless he intended to go directly back to his own nest in House Bentain's enclave and forget this entire encounter with Beda, the only sensible choice was to enter Gredin's room.

He walked toward her door.

The panels opened, revealing a chamber sunk in near darkness.

Entering, he let the door slide closed behind him, then waited while his eyes adjusted. It gave his body time to calm itself. His breathing gradually slowed, and he began to make out details in the dimness.

The luminth itself, placed on the floor, emitted only a dull glow.

Gredin's covered form was motionless on a sleepmat.

Shelves along the far wall held what looked like a few piles of folded clothing and… something else, roughly the size and shape of someone's head. It even appeared to have distorted features, although that must be the darkness playing tricks on his vision.

And then, in a sudden jolt of memory, he realized what the object was, and the unexpectedness of it provoked a bubble of nervous laughter that formed in his chest and escaped from his lips in a soft huff of sound.

"What?" asked the figure on the bed. "Who is there?"

Khest froze. "I'm sorry. I didn't mean to wake you."

"I was awake. Who are you?"

"Khest. Khest te Bentain."

"Should I remember you?"

"No. We do not know one another."

"Then what are you doing here?"

He couldn't say *I have come to mate with you.* "Beda brought me," he said instead.

"Ah. You know Beda?"

"Yes. We are both minor Healers."

"I see." Silence. Then she said, "You may turn the luminth up, if you like. I… I've been having some difficulty with it, today, or I would do it myself."

He found her confession reassuring. "I, too, have had difficulty with my luminth. Shall we leave that one as it is, rather than risk too great a glare?"

"Yes, that might be for the best." Bedclothes rustled, and the figure on the bed sat higher. "May we talk, before we...? For the moment, may we simply sit and talk?"

"Of course," he agreed, because that was the polite reply. But his thoughts were whirling. What could Beda have been thinking? What was *Gredin* thinking? She could not possibly be serious, and yet she was First Speaker. Falsehood had no place in her gyfte. The spoken word was the instrument of a Speaker's gyfte, just as physical contact was his.

"Come and sit," she invited, and he caught a glimpse of her pale arm gesturing toward the end of her bedmat.

"Very well." He sat down and set his small pack of oils on the floor at the foot of the mat. "Is there something you wish to know?"

"Yes. Why did you laugh, after you came in?" she asked, sounding more alert.

"I didn't."

"You did. Under your breath. I heard you. You went…" And she replicated the little huff of air that had escaped him.

Embarrassed, he said, "Oh. I didn't think you heard that. I laughed from astonishment, when I realized what I was seeing on your shelf."

"And what did you see?"

"I believe it is a container of amarantha wine. Where did you come by such a thing?"

"The jug shaped like a creature's head? From the Hesch. It was their gift to us, at the reception. You are familiar with amarantha wine?" Gredin asked.

"Burlon once described it to me."

"Oh! You know Burlon?"

"We grew up together in House Bentain. Despite the difference in our basic natures – or perhaps because of it – we became fond kinsmen. Once, when he returned from a mission to Tradepoint, he described just such a peculiar-looking jug, and he told me a wild tale about it. But I had never actually seen one, and so the sight of it here startled me into a laugh."

"And will you mention seeing it here, when next you speak with Burlon?"

It sounded like a casual question.

It was not.

"No. Nothing about this night will figure in my conversations with Burlon. Or anyone else."

"Even if you and I do nothing but talk?"

"Even if you and I do nothing but talk."

A sigh. "I should find that reassuring," she said. "But soon it will be too late for us, if we do nothing but talk."

Her words seemed to reverberate in the quiet room, echoing in his head.

"Doing something may not help, either," he said, and his own words shocked him, for they revealed how far forward his thoughts had already traveled.

"That is a truth," Gredin said, and sank into silence.

But it might, his own mind supplied. *And if it does…*

If so, they could retain their Balance, and thereby retain their gyftes and their sense of the Power's approval. It would give them the strength to persevere in this strange new life, despite the massive losses of world and kin and Chosen.

But he was still wary. "Who knows?" he heard himself ask.

"Who knows… what?"

"Who knows that I am here?" he asked, wanting to be assured that her answer would be the same as Beda's. "Who knows why you wanted me to come?"

"Only Beda and Ingarra. I confided in them and asked them if they could think of anyone who might help me. They said they would think on it... and apparently they selected you."

"Ah. And Beda tells me he has not even spoken my name to Ingarra. But I am still uncertain why he came to me."

"He must feel we can trust you. I was shocked when this notion was first suggested to me. In all honesty, I am shocked by it still. But I am horrified by what is happening to me. I must ask others to heat my food, if it becomes too cool. My temper is uncertain, and it is becoming more and more difficult for me to Speak with calm authority when I need to. It is like being at the Ocean Holding and casting my nets into the sea, only to find, when I draw them back, that they are emptier with each new attempt. And the days are passing."

He recognized her fears all too keenly. His losses differed from hers because his gyfte differed from hers, but it was only a matter of time before they would both lose everything. "So then," he asked, torn between dread and a reluctant hope, "what do you want?"

"I want not to diminish."

"No, I mean what do you want of me?"

"Nothing you do not want for yourself. You are Beda's choice, not mine."

Khest's newly growing confidence faltered. "There is some other you would rather approach?"

"No. There is no one. And I dared not decide blindly. Can you imagine what Tetralanna and the other House volunteers would say if they knew you were here, having this talk with me? I have no wish for our tale to sprout legs and go walking about, unless…"

"Unless what?"

"Unless we succeed. If we *do* manage a return to Balance, then…"

He found himself imagining the uproar such a confession would cause within the enclave. He did not want to drown in the torrent of idle gossip that would ensue, or to become the focus of the outright censure it would draw from Naria, the Head of House Bentain.

"No," he said, the word bursting from his lips.

Gredin looked at him, her eyes widening in alarm. “You must be more specific. ‘No,’ you do not wish to explore this matter with me? If so, you can leave and I will trouble you no further, except to entreat you to silence.”

Feeling a stab of panic, he shook his head. “I wish to stay.”

“Then you must explain your ‘no,’ for it perplexes me.”

“Your pardon. I only meant…” He tried to find an explanation that would not offend. “I live a quiet life. I do not wish my name associated with matters that are… controversial.”

“Ah, I see,” she said. “You wish to reap the benefits, if benefits there be, but you would prefer me to stand alone, not naming you when I explain what we have done and why we have done it and what benefit it can bring to others.”

“Yes. No. I mean…”

“You mean ‘yes,’” she said, her tone cool.

He sighed. “I mean that I wish there were a way for us both to retain our privacy.”

“There is,” she said, still in that detached tone that told him clearly that he had wounded her. “In fact, there are two ways.”

“And they are…?”

“The first is for us not to try. The second is for us to try and fail. In either eventuality, there will be no need for anyone beyond Beda to know you ever came here to me. And so I ask again, quite seriously, do you wish to leave?”

It would be so simple to say yes. There were scores of others she could approach. It was only due to Beda that he had been singled out. He could distance himself from this mad scheme, secure in the knowledge that Gredin would find someone else willing to aid her.

But that would leave him fading, less capable each morning than he had been on the previous day. Was he truly so craven that he would prefer a safe but inevitable decline?

Well, perhaps not inevitable. If Gredin and another explored the matter, and their efforts bore fruit, there would be time enough then for him to seek a partner for this wild endeavor.

Or would there? What if Gredin had trouble finding someone reckless enough to make the attempt? During that delay, might he himself not drift so far from Balance that no return was possible?

And, if so, would it not be a fitting punishment for his lack of bravery?

He would not be so foolish as to allow his misgivings to dictate his choices. "I will stay," he said, feeling as if each word were a heavy stone forced from his mouth.

"Even if it brings you to the attention of others?"

"Even then. I will stay."

"How do I know you will not change your mind?"

That made his smile, however ruefully. "You do not know me yet. You will find that I am not changeable. Cautious, yes. Slow to reach a conclusion. But, once I have done so, not changeable. All who know me well would describe me so."

Gredin sighed. "Who are you?"

"I told you. I am Khest te Bentain."

"Yes. That much I know. But you have told me very little beyond a few bare facts. Your name. Your House. Your minor gyfte for Healing. I know that Beda approached you, and so I believe that you must be kind and trustworthy. And you have told me, just now, that you are not changeable. But beyond that… who are you?"

He shook his head, at a loss. "No one of importance."

"You have no other gyftes of note, beyond your gyfte of Healing?"

"My major gyfte is Touch."

"Oh! Of course. I kept thinking that I had heard your name somewhere before. You are on Keegan's list."

"Keegan's list?"

"Keegan te Fliss, the historian. He is making lists of people's major gyftes. Your name was among them. And your minor gyfte is notable, as well. There are only as many Healers remaining as there are fingers upon my hands. Therefore, although your gyfte for Healing is minor, it is far from unimportant."

"No gyfte is unimportant, I suppose," Khest conceded. "All gyftes are granted to us by the Power. But it would be foolish to pretend that the dimension of a gyfte makes no difference. If you have stubbed your toe, if your head aches from a change in the weather, if you have nicked your finger while working in the kitchens, feel free to apply to me for aid. But if you have broken a bone or suffered a serious blow to the head, do not waste precious time by seeking me out. Go directly to Cayman and entreat her to Assess you for Salderon's care."

"You belittle your gyfte."

"I am honest about it. I wish it were greater. I have studied diligently to make the most of it, and I will continue to do so, if Salderon is willing to act as my Mentor. But there is good reason why I am not a ranked Healer." He shrugged. "My gyfte of Touch is far greater. And, together, my gyftes have brought ease to many. I try to be content with that." He shifted where he sat. "Indeed, if you and I together cannot improve our situation, I may soon have to be content with a great deal less." He shifted uneasily. "And I admit that there is something else that troubles me. What if what you and I attempt displeases the Power?"

"Then I suppose," she said dryly, "the Power will let us know."

That shook him. "Your night-thoughts… You truly believe the Power spoke to you?"

She did not reply for a long moment, then said, "My Chosen spoke to me – my Chosen who is dead. It was Dreff's voice that I heard in my mind. But his voice was telling me things he could not have known. So yes, I believe it was the Power that spoke to me."

"And you believe it would do so again, if our actions displeased it?"

She laughed, but it was not a happy sound. "The Power has stated that it will not Speak to me again... and I sincerely hope that proves to be so."

She sounded sad and weary, worn down by the same losses that dragged at him. "And you, Gredin te Balamont," he said softly. "Who are you?"

"I am First Speaker. The community's Voice."

"And when day is done and your duties are set aside? Who are you then?"

"An instrument of the Power, weary and drained, waiting for the new day to arrive and fill me with fresh purpose."

"I am less than that," he said. "What grace and wisdom I possess dwells in my hands. With a simple contact, they learn more about a person than all the talk in the world could teach me. When I lose that skill… Well, that is a day I do not wish to live to see." Slowly, he flexed his fingers. "What say you, Gredin te Balamont? Shall we attempt to change our fate?"

"Yes," she said firmly, then added, in just as firm a tone, "Khest, I am afraid."

"As am I. At least we are honest with one another." He folded his hands in his lap. "You are First Speaker. I ask you to use your words to state precisely what we intend to undertake. If we are to act, there must be no misunderstanding between us."

Gredin considered. "Very well." She took several slow breaths. "I have lost Dreff, my Chosen. You have lost your Chosen, as well. What was her name?"

"Silandra," he managed to say, although his throat tried to close around the syllables.

Gredin nodded. "I have lost Dreff. You have lost Silandra. You and I are among the many who have lost their Chosen. Already, in the days since our Chosens returned to the Source, our hlinga has begun to ebb, taking our Balance and our gyftes with it. But I am First Speaker, and you have the gyfte of Touch and are one of our ten remaining Healers. For our own sakes, and for the sake of the remaining community of Vennans, we cannot surrender passively to these losses. Therefore, you and I will attempt to act upon the advice of Figg of the Prett, Assistant Director of Tradepoint. Her counsel was that two who were Bereft – or as the Prett define it, *garamog* – might be able to regain their Balance and retain their gyftes by…" She hesitated, then cleared her throat and continued, in the same resolute voice. "…by joining in a physical mating. That is what we are going to attempt. But we approach this action out of desperate necessity. I am not Silandra. You are not Dreff. Our Chosens have returned to the Source and are lost to us forever. We do not seek to recreate the bond we had with them, for that cannot be done. The pairing of Chosens is crafted by the Power. What you and I undertake will be a physical joining only, done so in the hope that we may continue to serve the Power. If our joining does nothing to improve our hlinga, we will not undertake such an action again." A sigh. "There. Does that suffice?"

"Yes," Khest said, reassured.

"I am glad… and yet, for all my words, I do not know where to find the courage to attempt what I have just described."

Khest found her admission rather endearing. Smiling, he said, "Actually, you have a source of courage in this very room."

"I don't know what you mean."

"That jug on the shelf holds the courage we both fear we may lack."

"It is only wine."

"Only wine?" Khest repeated, amused. "Have you sampled it?"

"I have opened the jug and sniffed it. It has a pleasant aroma."

"It has far more useful properties than that, according to Burlon's tale."

"He has said nothing about it to me."

Khest smiled, unsurprised. It was very like Burlon to be secretive. Traders *seemed* like a friendly and outgoing lot, but they kept matters confidential when it suited their purposes.

In general, Khest considered himself to be more of a listener than a talker. The nature of his gyfte encouraged him to Focus inward, alert to information that could not be conveyed through words. But he knew, as Gredin did not, that Burlon's story had a direct bearing on their predicament, and so he spun that memory into words for her.

"Shortly after Burlon became the head of Bentain's Tradeteam, we chanced to share a meal. He was clearly brimming with some tale to tell that he did not wish to share with the others at table. So, afterward, we walked together in the House gardens, and he described his first official meeting with the Hesch since being placed in charge. At the meeting, the Hesch insisted on honoring his good fortune with a toast and brought out the most unsightly stone jug Burlon had ever seen."

Gredin nodded in recognition. "Like the one over there on the shelf."

"Just so. As Burlon told it, they pulled the strange, stone-creature's tongue out to open the jug and poured a generous cup of liquid for each person at the meeting table. When Burlon inquired as to the drink's nature, they told him it was a wine made from amarantha berries. He took a sip, expecting it to be as mild and innocuous as it smelled. Instead, he said it felt as if something cold and prickly was dancing upon his tongue. But when he swallowed, the liquid burned inside his throat and chest, growing hotter with each sip. Still, Burlon is nothing if not bold, and so he drank down the rest of the measure he'd been served. And when they poured for everyone again, he let them refill his cup. And then they all drank for a third time, before settling down to business. He said that the amarantha wine made the Hesch almost friendly, and he was able to easily talk with them about the proposed Trade. But then he realized that the wine was having quite a different effect on him, and so he excused himself and hurried back to the privacy of the enclave."

"It made him sick?" Gredin asked, sounding alarmed.

"No. But he needed the privacy of his room, nonetheless. And he stayed there, shut away by himself, until the next morning."

"Why?"

"Burlon's words were these: 'It made my ilian tingle. I pleasured myself to a half-dozen completions before it finally let me sleep.' We laughed about it, the two of us. But now Beda has brought me here, and this jug sits upon your shelf, and it makes me wonder whether perhaps it might help us both. Do you have a cup?"

"What?"

"A cup. Do you have one? Unless you would rather drink directly from the jug…?"

"I have a cup here on the floor next to my bedmat," she said. "I suspect it has… yes, water in it. Beda must have left it by the bedside after his Intercession, for when I woke."

"Drink it and then I will pour the wine… unless you have changed your mind, after all."

"No. But, in truth, I have no desire for you to touch me," Gredin said. He could hear no anger in her tone, just a weary honesty.

"Nor do I desire you," he replied, equally honest. "But those attitudes will not serve us, if you are right about what ails us, and so I suggest we begin by sharing a glass of amarantha wine while we discuss the matter further."

Brave words. In an attempt to live up to them, he made his way to the shelf and picked up the stone jug, which proved heavy for its size. "Have you finished the water?"

"Yes," Gredin replied, and Khest heard a faint sound that might have been the empty cup settling onto the metal floorplate. "Do you have the jug?"

"I do," he assured her. "But I didn't expect it to weigh so much!"

"I know." He heard a faint thread of amusement in her tone. "The Hesch warned me, when he brought it forward at the reception, and I *still* nearly dropped it on his foot. Can you imagine? I would forever have been known as the Vennan who breaks the feet of Hesch."

"Where do you want it?"

A rustling sound. Then, "Bring it here and put it in the middle of the bed. I will sit at the head and you can sit at the foot. With the jug between us, I will feel quite safe."

That took him aback. "You feel unsafe with me?"

"I feel unsafe with what we propose to do. But with the jug between us, no action we undertake will be impulsive."

"True," he said. "Can you hold the luminth up? I can barely make out where I'm going, and I don't want to drop this."

Gredin obliged.

Khest walked carefully across the floor, his gaze cast on his feet as he made his way cautiously to the foam bedmat. When he reached the edge of it, he lifted his gaze to Gredin, and almost *did* drop the jug, astonished by the sight of the luminth light filtering up through the short, curly floss of her hair.

... so they kicked her and cut off her braids. That was what Beda had said. But Khest hadn't truly pictured it. He had vaguely registered that her hair would look different, perhaps with a braid or two severed.

But he had not expected her hair to be so short, nor had he anticipated seeing the way it coiled into soft, loose ringlets, as if she were still a youngling.

Gredin te Balamont was First Speaker. Daily, he watched her address the community, her expression somber, her hair elaborately braided, with First Speaker's hlette gleaming upon her arm. She had looked poised. Serene. Untouchable.

Now she sat on her bedmat, the coverlet pooling around her waist, the luminth's glow revealing the symmetry of her bare breasts and, even in bed, the intricate beauty of First Speaker's hlette clinging to her upper arm. It was the oddest blend: the vulnerability of her pose, the impact of being so near to an object of Power, the disarming incongruity of her curls…

"What's wrong?" she asked. Then, before he could answer, she raised one hand to her head and said, "Oh. My hair. Did Beda explain?"

"Yes."

She smiled. "It will offer a change in topic for the idle gossip in the enclave."

"What will you tell people?"

"The truth, of course. I can't hide it, and I'm going to look like this for quite some time, so there's little point in avoiding an explanation." She lifted her chin. "It's only hair. It will grow back."

She said the words firmly, but he saw the way her fingertips traced over the curls, as if she could scarcely believe they were her own.

A sudden surge of sympathy made it difficult for him to swallow.

To divert her attention and his own, he set the jug on the coverlet, stepped out of his ankle boots, and sat down on the far end of the foam bedmat, facing her. "So, you say you have not sampled this wine. Nor have I. Shall we give it a proper try?" He grasped the tongue of the ugly stone carving and gave it a tug – to no avail.

"Not like that. I will show you." Smiling, Gredin leaned forward, her breasts shifting as she reached to grasp the jug.

The impossibility of what Beda had brought him here to do troubled Khest afresh. This woman was a stranger to him. She was not even of his House. And she seemed no more eager than he for this strange encounter. Why had he not flatly rejected Beda's plan at the outset? Why had he come to this chamber? Why did he not leave it now, before he and Gredin could be distressed and embarrassed further?

Because I cannot bear to be parted from my gyfte.

That answer rose in him with such urgency that he stayed silent, watching as Gredin grasped the jug, twisted its stone tongue, removed the ugly stopper, and picked up the cup.

"Can you lift the jug and pour?" she asked.

It would be rude to refuse. Khest lifted the jug and tilted it so that a stream of liquid flowed, filling the cup nearly to the rim.

When jug and cup and stopper were all safely at rest on the floor beside the sleepmat, Gredin said, "You should be cautious when you take the first sip. If Burlon was speaking truthfully, it may cause a most peculiar sensation."

"Oh, so *I* am to take the first sip?" Khest asked. "You think me so brave? Very well. We shall educate ourselves in this matter by degrees." He accepted the cup and lifted it. As it neared, he inhaled, and smiled at the wine's pleasing scent. Encouraged, he put his mouth to the rim and, resolved, took in a generous measure of the liquid.

He had heard Burlon's tale. He had listened to Gredin's caution. Despite both, he sat up straighter as the wine bathed the surface of his tongue in a ripple of intense sensation. It felt almost as if he held some living creature in his mouth, something that scurried this way and that on tiny, clawed feet.

It took an effort of will to swallow. When he did, a surging warmth rose from deep within him, radiating out to the tips of his fingers and toes before it receded.

Belatedly realizing that he still held the cup an inch from his mouth, he lowered it, careful not to spill the liquid that remained.

"Well?" Gredin said, and he saw that she was watching him closely.

"Remarkable," he replied.

"It smells like the gardens."

Khest lifted the cup again and sniffed. "Wilder than that. It reminds me of green things running rampant, like the meadows at the Bentain Holding."

Gredin put out her hand. "I may as well keep up with you." Taking the cup from him, she drank. As she swallowed, her cheeks grew red and her eyes shimmered with moisture.

"Does it make you feel warm?" Khest asked, unsure if their reactions would be identical.

"Yes. Did it prickle on your tongue?"

He nodded. "And yet it was pleasant, when I swallowed. And the taste is mild. It reminds me a bit of… something. I'm not sure what."

She passed the cup back to him. "Perhaps you need to try it again."

"Perhaps I do," he agreed, and took another mouthful.

This time, he was braced for the tingle it caused on his tongue, and he let the wine wash around inside his mouth for a few moments before he swallowed. A reflexive shiver shook him as heat blasted through him again and retreated.

"Well? Did you place the taste?"

"No," he admitted. "But it is enjoyable." And he handed the cup to her again.

"You say that Burlon drank three glasses?" she asked as she accepted it.

"So he claimed."

"Then we had best get on with it," she said, and this time took several long swallows of the wine, while Khest watched apprehensively.

Her immediate reaction was a brief spate of coughing, as tears escaped to bead on her lashes. But then she smiled.

"Something amuses you?" Khest asked.

"It amuses me not to be timid," she said. "I feel as if I have been tiptoeing around for days, cringing and creeping, waiting for the next disaster to strike. This, at least, is action of a sort." She held out the cup. "But you will need to pour more. I have finished what there was. You are falling behind."

And so he lifted the jug, filled the cup to just below the rim, and put the jug down again, noting that it felt no lighter than before. "Then I shall not be timid, either," he stated. Taking the cup from her, he raised it to his lips and emptied the entire cup in five determined swallows.

That was, it would seem, a mistake. It left him feeling as if the very air around him were smoldering as he drew a breath and let it out again.

Gredin, he saw, was struggling to refill the cup.

Khest helped her, then held up a hand. "Do not drink all of that at once," he cautioned, his voice little more than a croak. "The sensation afterwards is quite unpleasant."

"Unpleasant in what way?" she asked, the cup already rising toward her mouth. "What are you feeling?"

"I am far too hot," he said, "as if there were a brazier blazing beneath this bedmat."

"You are wearing too many clothes," she said dismissively, and slowly upended the cup.

By the time she had emptied it, she was gasping for breath, her cheeks scarlet, her eyes streaming with tears. But she met his gaze with brazen courage. "Your turn again."

Khest held up a cautious palm. "Perhaps we had better wait and see what effect the first two cups have on us."

"It has not yet been two," she objected. "We shared the first, so each of us has actually only had a cup and a half. Burlon drank three; he would not be impressed with our efforts."

For some reason, that struck him as funny. "Well," he said, reaching for the jug, "we would not wish to fail to impress Burlon."

"Certainly not," Gredin concurred, then pressed her palms to her cheeks. "Hot," she said. "Quite, quite hot. And what of you? Has the sensation passed? Are you feeling cooler?"

"No," he admitted.

"A pity there are no windows to open," she said.

Again, he found himself amused by her words. "From what Burlon has told me, windows on Tradepoint would not be wise."

"Well, I am not wise. I am too warm," she said. "And I wish this wine would hurry and do whatever it is going to do to us. I cannot waste the entire night here with you."

And that, somehow, was the funniest statement of all. He could not hide a grin. "Ah, but it is not a waste for me. I have been given this chance to make the personal acquaintance of Gredin te Balamont, First Speaker and appointed Voice. When I retired for the night, I had no such expectation."

"And I am such delightful company," she said, her tone scathing.

"You are someone new. For those of us with gyfte of Touch, every new person with whom we interact is an exciting event."

"Exciting? You may be assured, Khest, there is nothing exciting about me."

"You are mistaken. No two people are alike. I mean, yes, many things *about* them are alike. Two arms, two legs, a face with eyes and a nose and a mouth. But even then, no two faces are quite the same. No two bodies are quite the same."

Gredin scowled, offering no reply.

With a smile, Khest said, "Here. Hold the cup while I fill it again. Now drink, and so shall I. And then I am going to massage your feet."

"My feet?" Gredin echoed, her tone scornful.

"Did Dreff never rub your feet?"

"Feet are for walking upon."

He pushed the cup toward her. "Hush. Drink."

For a moment, he thought she might refuse. But she raised the cup and took several long swallows. "There," she said hoarsely. "Half. Drink the rest, and then we will each have finished two cups."

Khest took it from her. "You seem to put great store in Burlon's tale of three cups."

She shrugged, wiping at her streaming eyes. "Thus far, I have felt hot, and my eyes have watered, but no great wave of excitement has overcome me. I am counting upon three cups to kindle extraordinary longings – extraordinary enough, at least, to make this plan seem more pleasant than terrifying."

"Indeed," he said, and drank off the liquid that remained in the cup.

This time, the heat was a little frightening, as if his blood were attempting to boil within him. It stole his breath away. Setting the cup on the floor beside the bedmat, he grasped the jug and set it there, as well.

Now nothing separated him from Gredin but the coverlet.

"It is time that I brought your poor feet some relief."

"My feet are fine."

"So you say. But I do not believe you. Stop your arguing."

"Refill the cup first."

"Very well. As you please." He poured more amarantha wine into the cup and passed it to Gredin. He hoped that employing his gyfte would ground him, in the face of this unsettling encounter. Doing so would allow him to know Gredin better, once he was able to feel her living flesh beneath his hands…

Her living flesh.

As Silandra's flesh was no longer living.

Despair welled up within him, turning the moment dark and bitter. He should not have come here. He wanted no part of this strange scheme. He was weary to his bones. If he returned to his own bed, he could close his eyes and sink into the temporary oblivion of sleep…

But, when he woke, he would be that much farther from proper Balance.

"What should I do?"

It was so exactly the question reverberating in his mind that it took him a moment to realize the words had been spoken aloud by Gredin. And hearing her question confirmed for him what *he* should do – he should trust in his gyfte. Had he not resolved to do so, just a few moments ago? These shifting thoughts, this changeability of mind, these doubts, they were all offshoots of how depleted his hlinga had become. He resolved to stop thinking; he would simply cling to his gyfte for as long as he was able, by any means offered to him.

"Lie down on your front, with your feet toward me," he instructed Gredin.

"If I lie down on my front, I won't be able to drink from the cup," she objected.

"Then drink first," he said, nettled by her quibbling.

Drink she did, the entire cup, long swallow after long swallow. Then she cried out breathlessly and leaned over to press both hands to the jug. "I'll pour for you," she said huskily, but he saw the way her hands shook as she tried to lift the heavy jug. "Or no, I'm won't," she said, and instead pushed it toward him. It made a disagreeable scraping noise as it slid on the metal floorplate. "There," she said. "You do it. If I attempt to pour you more, I will spill it."

He grasped the jug, unsettled by the fierce color of her cheeks. "Lie down," he counseled.

"Drink."

"I will. But you need to lie down."

She pushed restlessly at the coverlet, thrusting it aside, and collapsed onto the mat on her front. Then she reared up, twisting to look back over her shoulder at him. "Drink," she insisted. "Then we will each have had Burlon's measure."

"There is no guarantee it will have the same effect on us," Khest protested, but he filled the cup and set the jug aside, turning it so that its bulge-eyed gaze was directed at the wall.

"The wine is having *some* sort of effect," Gredin maintained. "I feel…" She shrugged helplessly and said, "Hot. Odd. Different. I feel different, as if there is something my body urgently needs to do, but I have no notion what it might be."

"Lie down," he counseled again.

"Drink."

He gave her an exasperated look. "If I drink, will you lie down?"

"Yes. But you must drink it all."

"And if I do, you will hush and let me get on with this?"

She nodded.

"Very well." He lifted the cup, reflecting that Burlon had much to answer for.

A swallow.

Still, he doubted Burlon would care, ensconced as he was with his new-found Chosen.

A swallow.

Burlon and Chenna would be intent entirely on one another, secure in their devotion.

A swallow.

Were they entwined at this moment, fueled by passion, with no need of amarantha wine?

Khest let the rest of the liquid pour down his throat in a steady flow, tilting the cup until it surrendered the final drops.

As he did, something ignited deep within him, sending fingers of flame up from his middle to sear his throat and fill his head. He couldn't see, could scarcely breathe. The cup slipped from his grasp, and he heard the sound of pottery breaking. He felt a pang of shame and regret for its destruction, but the furnace inside him demanded his full attention. He was too hot, far too hot. If this sense of burning did not recede soon, he would need an Assessor.

The thought of having to explain his plight was so embarrassing that it intensified both the inner heat and his resolve. He would talk to no one about tonight's mad encounter – except perhaps to admonish Beda for involving him in the first place.

The heat faded just enough for him to take an easier breath, although he felt as if he were melting, his edges less distinct than they should be.

Focus. He needed to Focus.

"Let us begin," he said, and his voice was that of a stranger in his own ears, hoarse and wavering. But he took several slow, calming breaths, and his vision cleared. He saw that Gredin had finally followed his direction: she was stretched out on the mat, face down, her feet nearest him. He resettled himself at the end of the mat, brushing aside a shard of broken pottery. Then he removed a bottle of oil from his pack, uncapped it, and poured a measure onto his palms.

Gredin had oddly delicate feet for such a tall woman. Slowly, gently, he spread the oil, exploring from the slender circumference of her ankles to the tips of her toes. Then he turned his palms up and slid his hands beneath, to lubricate the tops of her feet.

"You are putting me to sleep," Gredin said, but her tone was not one of complaint.

"Hush," he said, disgruntled at having to reach for words again. "Close your eyes. No more talking. You will only sleep if your body requires it."

When she subsided, he closed his eyes, the better to Focus.

It was a dance, of sorts, the interplay between his hands and the fragile structures beneath the skin of her feet. He courted her trust, proving that he would do her no harm. Everywhere he stroked, tension lay in wait, over-sensitizing her so that she twitched and winced and recoiled as he broached each new area.

It was slow work, with layer upon layer of repetition built into its patterns. You could not reason with the body through words. The body knew what it knew, felt what it felt, needed what it needed. Truth and experience was in his Touch, and the deft strokes, repeated over and over, resulted in deeper and deeper layers of trust.

In time, her feet became utterly pliable and her breathing told him that, although she had not fallen asleep, she had abandoned all of her conscious concerns. She was a little animal beneath his hands, warm and trusting, tension banished, worry forsworn. Her feet were hot, as his hands were hot. His knowing fingertips and clever thumbs worked her flesh like bread dough, kneading and pulling, kneading and pulling, first the left foot, then the right, then both together, one slender foot in each hand. There was a pleasing symmetry to that, a rhythm that comforted him as much as it seemed to comfort her. And in time, when his fingers promised him that he had brought her peace, he grew determined to bring her more than that. It only took a slightly different rhythm, a subtly firmer pressure, a minimal change of angle to find the little spot at the curve of her arch, revealed now that she was completely unstrung, where a different and more instinctual hunger could be fed. It was largely a question of patience, like a very small question whispered, then whispered again, and then again, until the quality of her breathing began to alter, and a new blush of warmth awoke beneath his hands, faint at first, steadily building into a glow, the spot small but distinct, arresting his attention, begging to be stroked, and so he stroked–

She recoiled sharply, her foot slipping through his grasp as she abruptly rolled over and sat up, her eyes wild in a red-cheeked countenance, her breath coming in gasps.

It was not Silandra who faced him.

Khest felt his own breath lodge in his throat at the shock of that realization. He had become lost in the task, submerged in his gyfte. By arousing Gredin, he had aroused himself, and he had somehow come adrift in time and circumstance.

"What *was* that?" Gredin whispered, her gaze searching his with desperate intensity.

Khest didn't know how to answer, or explain, or apologize.

Gredin was still breathing in gasps, and the dark centers of her eyes were immense. "Did that happen on purpose?" she demanded, still whispering. "I mean, did you *make* that happen?" Another snatched breath as she leaned even closer. "Can you make it happen *again*?"

The world turned upside down as Khest realized what she was truly asking. "Yes," he said in simple honesty.

"Will you?"

"Yes, if you wish, but–"

"But what? *Will* you?"

"Yes, of course," he heard himself say. "But… that was just your foot."

"What do you mean?"

He risked a very small smile. "There are a great many other places on your body that will make you feel even better. You know this. Surely you know this?"

"Mating," she said, and blushed.

"Well, yes, of course, but…" He tried to collect his wits. "Give me your hand."

"Which one?" she asked, looking disappointed.

"Either. It doesn't matter."

She extended her right hand.

"Sit back. Close your eyes. Relax." Capturing her hand, he turned it palm upward. Then, when he had taken a moment to gather himself, he slid his upturned hand under hers, with his thumb above it, and ran the pad of his thumb over her palm, tracing patterns in glancing moments of contact.

She trembled.

When he had found the places that were most sensitive for her, he simplified the pattern, moving from one to another of them, over and over.

Without warning, her fingers closed convulsively around his thumb, trapping it, and her eyes flew upon, brimming with an anguished question she could not seem to voice.

He waited.

Seeming on the verge of tears, she released him and pulled her hand away.

Still, he waited.

"How do you know to do that?" she asked, her voice a mere thread of sound.

He could not bear to give her the truest answer: *Because these are some of the things that most pleased Silandra.* And so he told her the broader truth. "Touch is my gyfte. Bodies speak to me, and I listen."

She made a little sound midway between a laugh and a cry. "But you keep stopping!"

He stared at her. "Because you keep pulling away."

She inhaled deeply. "And if I do not pull away?"

"Then I will not stop until you tell me to."

"Until I…? Why would I tell you to stop?"

He smiled. "Because, when a body achieves a completion, there is a short time thereafter when it can no longer bear such touches. It wants only to calm itself and recover."

Gredin gripped both his hands, her gaze pleading, her tone urgent. "Khest. Please. Make me need to tell you to stop."

[4]

1010 OF 2000 ORBITS REMAINING: 11YELLOW

What is Gredin up to?

Miri sat at one of House Kendar's tables for morning meal, which was *not* where she wanted to be. For more than a dozen days now, it had been her responsibility and privilege to eat morning meal with Gredin, Burlon, Sill, and Keegan in the privacy of the tiny suite of rooms that Gredin and Keegan shared. Early this morning, however, while Miri had been working in the kitchens with the other Tenders to prepare the first meal of the day, Gredin's voice had intruded on her private mind, proclaiming that their usual meeting was postponed.

And then the sense of Gredin's mind had gone, leaving behind the direction: *Do me the kindness of attending morning meal in the reception hall with the community. I will join you there and explain.*

So here Miri sat, picking at a bowl of food she couldn't even properly taste. At least she had managed to convince Keegan te Fliss to join her. Burlon sat at one of the House Laith tables with Chenna. Sill was with her Chosen, Marin, at House Torr's tables.

And there was, as yet, no sign of Gredin.

"This is my fault," Miri murmured.

Keegan turned to her, eyebrows lifted. "Fault?"

"That Gredin isn't here."

His smile was kind. “I doubt that. She has many commitments to fulfill.”

“You think I’m being silly, but it *is* my fault. I went to her, yesterday evening, and told her… a thing. A troubling thing. And now she isn’t here, and I am to blame. I should not have gone to her at the end of the day, when she and I were both tired and easily distressed. I should have waited, or not spoken at all. But I felt that I *couldn’t* wait. It was too dangerous a situation for that, if I was right.”

“Dangerous? What was it?”

Did she dare to tell him? Not sharing her condition, could he possibly understand? She had no wish to be the object of his pity if he believed her, or to face his empty reassurances if he did not. Either would be intolerable. She liked and admired Keegan te Fliss. They had participated as equals in the small group that assembled every morning with Gredin. How could she bear it, now, if he looked at her as if she…

There was some sort of tumult at the back of the hall. Beside her, Keegan rose from the bench, peering over the heads of the seated diners. A moment later, his fingers gripped Miri’s shoulder and squeezed. “It’s Gredin.”

“Peace,” a voice said – Gredin’s voice, rich and strong. “Peace! Sit down, everyone. Be at ease. I will explain when I reach the dais, where you can all easily see and hear me.”

The other voices dimmed. Keegan sank back onto the bench, his face still turned away, tracking Gredin’s progress toward the front of the large hall.

Miri felt her anxiety ebb. She had lain awake for most of the night, feeling guilty over alarming Gredin, worrying about the fate that awaited her and all of the others who had lost their Chosens. Rising to prepare morning meal had been a grim relief, since at least it gave her hands something to do, although she had restricted herself to the most menial of kitchen tasks, no longer trusting her skills. But now Gredin was here, and everything would be…

A collective gasp rose from the community as Gredin mounted the steps, placing herself clearly in view.

"Her hair!" Plithik te Kendar exclaimed from her seat near Miri, as other cries and questions continued to erupt.

On the top step, Gredin raised her arms. The overhead lights struck flashes of gold from her hlao and from First Speaker's hlette, as well as awakening vivid colors in her flamestone pendant. "Hush and listen," she said.

The community fell silent.

"There are matters of great importance that I need to share with you," Gredin said. "But before I begin, look around at your kinsmen. Are any absent from your table? I wish to speak to all of you, and it is particularly urgent that I be heard by all who have lost their Chosen. If you think anyone might still be abed, or may simply have wandered apart, please say so now and I will wait while they are brought." She scanned the room. "No? You are certain? Everyone is here?" Again, her gaze traversed the group. "Very well. And please feel free to continue your morning meal while you listen."

Standing there on the step, Gredin was such a peculiar sight that Miri couldn't tear her gaze away. Yesterday, Gredin had looked much as Miri felt: pale and slack and sad. Now, one short night later, her posture was proud, her voice compelling as she began her explanation to the group. But her hair…!

"Last night, as I returned from a conference with the Assistant Director of Tradepoint, I was attacked in the public corridor by a group of Beng traders."

A cry of horror rose from the community.

Gredin raised a hand, and the noise subsided.

"I took no harm that an Intercession could not set right but, as you see, the attackers also cut off my braids. It was an act of malice and mean-spirited frustration. The incident has been made known to the Director, and the Beng tradeteam has departed from Tradepoint. Have no fear; the Director wishes me to assure everyone that you are safe, both within our enclave and in the public areas." She let the silence gather for a long moment, then said, "However, there is another danger – one that threatens not just me but *many* of us, and it cannot be as easily managed as my attackers were. I only became aware of this danger last night. In fact, it is why I was abroad in the public corridors so late, to ask the Assistant Director for her thoughts on the matter."

She's talking about Ulm, Miri realized with a shock. *That's the danger she means.* The realization made her feel sick: Gredin had left the enclave because of their talk and had been attacked. It *was* her fault!

"Falling victim to the Beng was a small price to pay for that conversation," Gredin said. "The fear and pain of the attack, the loss of my braids, are of little consequence to me because the Assistant Director did indeed suggest a solution to this danger we face. But the danger and its solution apply solely to those who have lost their Chosen, those who the Assistant Director refers to as the *garamog*, a Prettian word which translates in our language to 'those who are Bereft of that which they held most dear.' Those of us who have lost our Chosen have, indeed, become the Bereft. Therefore, I ask those of you whose Chosen have returned to the Source to come with me now, into the side room that was formerly the sleeping quarters for House Balamont. There, we will discuss this danger and how best to protect ourselves. You are welcome to bring whatever remains of your morning meal with you."

Raggedly, hesitantly, people began to rise.

"As to the remainder of the community," Gredin said, her voice ringing through the chamber, "I ask those of you who are Unchosen or who still have your Chosen with you to respect our privacy by remaining here in the reception hall to finish your morning meal. We will return to you as quickly as we can, at which time I will explain this danger to the rest of you." Then Gredin descended the steps and started toward the side room she had indicated.

Abandoning her food, Miri rose from the bench. When Keegan began to rise with her, she said, "No. You are Unchosen. You need to stay here."

"But I am the historian!"

"Nevertheless, you are not one of the Bereft. Your place is here. Afterwards, with Gredin's permission, I will speak to you fully about what was said and what transpired."

She left him sitting there, alone and forlorn. When she passed House Torr's tables, she saw that Sill had remained seated, although her expression was conflicted. Miri offered her a nod and as reassuring a smile as she could manage as she continued to walk with the flood of solitary individuals making their way across the reception hall.

As she merged with them, she felt an odd upwelling of emotion – not pride, certainly, but a sort of abashed relief at seeing that she was far from alone in her condition, and that many of the others looked as disheveled and distressed as she felt. She thought she glimpsed Hayla in the crowd but couldn't be certain. Some of the people around her were exchanging furtive glances and occasional watery smiles. Others looked angry, trudging along as if they resented the effort Gredin had asked of them. Chief among those was Tetralanna te Balamont, accompanied by a cluster of women whose expressions were equally grim.

When Miri reached the room in question, she found that it was of a good size, although small in comparison to the reception hall they had just left. There were no benches or tables, just an empty expanse. Grumbling, people lowered themselves to the floor. Most, Miri noticed, had made no attempt to bring the last of their morning meal with them. Perhaps she should have the kitchen Tenders serve midday meal a bit on the early side, today…

"My thanks to you all for coming here at my request," Gredin said as she closed the door after the last of the stragglers. She went to stand at the front of the room, and the look she bestowed on them was as gentle as it was sad. "Many of you may have noticed, over these past days, that some of our kinsmen are feeling better than they were when we first learned of Venna's destruction. They cry less often. They are able to Focus on their tasks. They have more vitality. They converse with others, instead of retreating to their beds. Their appetites have improved. They find it easier to sleep. Some of them have even begun to laugh again, or at least to smile."

There was a silent stirring in the group.

"I noticed these things and wondered to myself whether they had loved their kinsmen less dearly than the rest of us did. Was that why they could escape the worst of their grief so quickly?"

A wordless murmur of agreement broke the stillness.

"I particularly wondered because I, unlike them, was sinking deeper every day into my sorrow. It took less and less activity to weary me. I became impatient, or angry, or even tearful over the slightest mishap. Worse, I began to find it more difficult to exercise my gyftes properly."

Someone to Miri's left gasped, and someone behind her began to weep.

"You may recall a recent day when I began to address the community, and those at the back of the room could not hear me. I had to Focus my efforts anew and start again. Little things – simple things – began to evade me. I had difficulty adjusting my luminth. I made mistakes when warming my food and had to be careful not to burn my tongue. If I wanted an object from across the room, it was easier and more reliable for me to rise and retrieve it than to attempt to Fetch it from where I sat."

By now, isolated exclamations from the others had become a steady hum of recognition and reaction.

"And it was not only me," Gredin conceded. "I heard reports of individuals having difficulty Sending safely down from the new nests the Prett provided for us. Reports of Needleworkers pricking their fingers so often with their needles that they required the attention of a minor Healer. Reports of kitchen Tenders suffering burns, or finding it difficult to properly prepare or season the meals they created. At one extreme, more arguments were taking place. At the other extreme, more people were reluctant to leave their enclave, or their nest, or even their bedmat."

The room seemed to throb, as if it could not contain so many unhappy emotions.

"And then a friend came to me, last night. Deeply distressed, they told me of one of their kinsmen, back home, who had lost their Chosen. It happened long and long ago, and yet the Bereft kinsman still lived on within the House. Over time, however, the same lapses I have just described befell this person – changeable temper, difficulty sleeping, trouble Focusing. According to my friend, that kinsman eventually lost all ability to exercise a gyfte, however small or basic that gyfte might be. They could not Send. They could not Fetch. They could not reach the private mind of another. They could not Freshen their clothing. They could not Cleanse themselves with a touch. They could not even Convert their own waste. They had to be attended at all times by another member of their House, as if they were the newest of younglings."

For Miri, it was strange to sit in the midst of the group and listen to the facts of Ulm's life set forth like a sad tale someone had invented. Of those present here, only she knew for certain that all of it was true.

"You may wonder why my friend came to tell me this thing," Gredin said, her voice patient but inexorable. "They told me because they had just realized that they were descending along their kinsman's path toward helplessness, and that it was happening for the same reason – because they had lost their Chosen. Indeed, they realized that each of us who has lost our Chosen has begun that fearful journey, a journey toward a place of dependence and incapacity, with all our gyftes stripped from our grasp, a place where we will have to rely evermore on others within the community to care for us and keep us safe."

Several people began to moan, and more to weep.

"I was afraid, for myself and for all who were like me," Gredin said, her words vibrant in Miri's ears. "But that is no longer true. I have found a way for us to escape that fate, and I will share that way with you."

Dumbstruck, Miri stared at Gredin. Their talk, last night, had ended in dread and despair. Now Gredin spoke with confidence of a way to avoid Ulm's fate. How was that possible?

Every gaze in the room was fixed on Gredin.

"As I told the community a short time ago, I went last night to talk to Figg, the Assistant Director of Tradepoint. She is a Prett, and the Prett are a methodical people, much given to the solving of problems. I hoped, if I told her of our plight, that she might see some solution that had not occurred to us. And she did."

"Then tell us!" a man shouted from the back of the room. "What must we do?"

"What must we do? Something we have never done before, in all the history of Venna. These are new times, with new troubles to be overcome. At home, the loss of a Chosen was so rare that most Houses held no kinsman who had suffered such a blow. But now – well, look about you. See how many of us have been brought low, all at the same time. Left to our fate, we would become an intolerable burden on the other survivors, and a misery to ourselves. And so we must take bold steps to elude that bleak future, for our own sake, for the sake of the Unchosen and the Chosen in the reception hall, and for the sake of Vennans yet unborn who would have to participate in our care." She eyed them, and Miri felt the challenge in her gaze. "Are you ready to hear? Are you ready to know what the Power calls upon you to do? Be assured, it is something of which you are all capable, something you have done countless times before… but never in these circumstances. When I explained our terrible predicament to Figg, she responded by saying that we should help each other. I didn't understand. I told her that those of us in the community, within each House, always help one another. But I had mistaken her meaning. Figg stated her belief that we might restore our hlinga and retain Control of our gyftes if those of us in this room, those of us who have lost our Chosen, those of us who are now Bereft, are willing to mate with one another."

Miri gaped, unable to credit that she had heard Gredin properly. The room was suddenly alive with whispers and low-voiced rumbles reverberating with shock and anger.

Gredin let them react amongst themselves for a short time, then spoke again, her tone firm. "You have all been graced by being part of a Chosen pair. You know the solace and strength that mating with your Chosen always brought to you. Deprived of it now, your hlinga recedes farther and farther, preventing you from maintaining a proper Balance. And where else are we to turn?" She held up a single finger. "If we do nothing – as we have done since learning of Venna's loss – we begin to lose Control of our gyftes, and that condition will worsen until we have no abilities left to us. We need to mate, but our Chosen has returned to the Source." Gredin raised a second finger. "We cannot interfere with an existing Chosen couple by taking our need to them." A third finger.

"And we cannot interfere with the Unchosen. Burlon and Chenna te Laith are in their dydanin right now, proving to us that the Power still moves among us, revealing new Choosings." Her gaze raked the room. "Who does that leave? It leaves *us*. It becomes our responsibility to help ourselves by helping each other. Who do we harm? No one, for our Chosen has been taken from us, never to return. And who do we help? We help everyone. We renew our hlinga and restore our own Balance. We do the same for the Bereft individual with whom we mate. We prevent ourselves from becoming a massive burden on the rest of the community. And we perpetuate our connection to the Power, maintaining mastery over the gyftes that have been given to us."

"Empty promises!"

Miri turned her head toward the sudden shout and saw Tetralanna rising to her feet at the back of the room, her cheeks starkly crimson in a face white with emotion.

"She talked to this Prett," Tetralanna accused, her voice shrill, "someone who is not even of our race, and let herself be lured away from the proper teachings of our people." She pointed at Gredin. "Look at her wrist, all of you. She wears a piece of Prett *griimoni* to allow them to summon her whenever it suits them. She has become their creature, and they are filling her head with bizarre notions. Every day, she dispatches one of our own people to them, and they do things to him that make him ill. Nevertheless, she forces him to return to them the next day, and the next, and the next. And now *this* abomination!"

"Tetralanna, calm yourself and listen," Gredin urged. "I am saying all of this for the well-being of everyone in this room. Can you honestly claim that your own Control of your gyftes is what it was when we first arrived on Tradepoint? Or even what it was five days ago?"

"I am mourning the loss of my world, and my House, and my Chosen!" Tetralanna retorted, and Miri winced at the raw pain conveyed by the words, underwritten as they were by the former First Speaker's gyfte.

"As are we all!" Gredin replied, her anguish equally apparent. "But while you have been clutching your sorrow around you like a shawl, I have been searching for ways to keep our situation from becoming even worse. And I have found one."

Tetralanna's voice dropped to a sneer. "So the Prett claim. But what do they know of us, of our needs, of our ways?"

Gredin cocked her head, her eyes widening. "Is that what you think? That I have brought you some suggestion of the Assistant Director's on the mere hope that it might help? No. I care too much for this community to do such a reckless thing."

"Then what?"

"I listened to her plan. I put it to the test. And it works."

Tetralanna's eyes narrowed. "Are you saying…? Do you mean that you actually…? Gredin te Balamont, are you standing before us and admitting that you have mated with someone other than your Chosen?"

"Yes. And I am much the better for it."

"No! Stop! I will listen to no more of this. *None* of us should." Her gaze was wild as it swept the room. "Rise to your feet, all of you. Do not pay attention to this wrong-headed girl who has so swiftly forsaken her Chosen's memory. I am leaving, and I call upon every true and honorable Vennan to leave with me!"

Miri watched in horror as first a few, then a dozen, and finally a hundred or more people struggled to their feet, threading their way through the seated crowd to follow Tetralanna to the door and out into the reception hall beyond, where the rest of the community sat waiting.

As the door closed behind the last of them, Gredin spoke in the daunted silence to the many who remained. "Do not think ill of those who left. They are frightened. And, although we are frightened, too, we are just a little braver than they are, or perhaps our Balance has deserted us a little less thoroughly. But believe me when I say that your bravery will quickly be rewarded. You will feel your hlinga revive and strengthen. And as all of us here begin to recover and thrive, we will become living proof that we have selected the proper path, and those who just left will reconsider." She sighed. "The day has scarcely begun, and already I have asked you to absorb a great deal of troubling news. At its briefest, all of us who lost our Chosen are in danger, but I have found a path to safety. We will weather this together and become strong and steady in our gyftes once again." The set of her shoulders eased. "I would tell you just a few things more, and then I will gladly answer any questions you may have."

Sensing the tension in the room slacken, Miri offered Gredin an encouraging smile.

"What I am describing," Gredin said to the group, "has nothing to do with our Chosen. The Power selects the one individual in all the world who is perfect for us, and reveals that relationship in its own time, to the joy of both members of the couple. To have lost that one perfect person is a tragedy that can never be put right. We will each cherish the memory of our Chosen for the rest of our days, and we will never cease to mourn their loss. Through all that we discuss today, and all the actions that follow, remember this one thing – no one can replace your Chosen, and no one will attempt to do so. That relationship is like no other we will ever know again."

Miri saw tears, heard weeping, but it was not the wild keening that had so often overtaken members of the community in the past days. There was now, at least, a tempering of hope.

"But we live in our vessels. Our bodies have needs. They must have water to drink, food to eat, air to breathe. And, to nourish our hlinga and retain our Balance, we must mate. It was different before we found our Chosen. We could satisfy our body's longings ourselves. But mating with our Chosen changed our bodies, tuned them to a different pitch. To be deprived of mating now starves our hlinga as surely as refusing to eat would starve our bodies. And the Balance through which we exercise and Control our gyftes depends upon the state of our hlinga. We can do without it, for a time. We can hold our breath, for a time. We can walk and talk and work despite being thirsty, for a time. But the need does not go away. It redoubles. And the vessel begins to weaken, then to falter, and finally to fail. Is there anyone here who has not yet felt the weakening of their Control over their gyftes?"

No one replied.

"I assure you, it has been the same for me," Gredin told them. "This morning, for the first time since learning that Dreff had returned to the Source, I feel stronger instead of weaker, steadier instead of less certain. That is what I want for all of you, as well. Ask me your questions and I will answer. Understand, please, that I only learned of this danger yesterday evening, so there has been little time to make plans and take action, but I have done what I can, and I will continue to do more. Now, who has a question for me?"

"Were you injured in last night's attack?" a woman called, and Miri recognized Hayla's voice. "Are you all right?"

Gredin looked startled, then shyly gratified. "Thank you for your concern. Yes, I was injured, and yes, I have been Healed. I am quite well now, except for –" She raised a hand to touch her curls. "– this."

A different woman's voice from somewhere behind Miri asked, "You truly mated with someone, last night?"

It was a bold question, and Gredin's voice was equally bold as she answered. "Yes, I did, with someone else who has lost his Chosen. And we are both much the better for it, this morning, which is why I am here, telling all of this to you."

"Who was it?" a man asked.

"No," came Gredin's firm reply. "That is information the two of us share, but no one else has a right to ask. Think on it. Will you want the community – or even those of your House – to ask such things of you? And even if you don't mind, perhaps your partner will feel differently. Some Houses are practical and will likely be sympathetic to our necessity. Other Houses cling rigidly to tradition and may react with hostility, as you just saw proven by Tetralanna te Balamont. This is a new problem that demands a new solution. No one can help us but ourselves, and yet we are all in a damaged and vulnerable state. We each feel the loss of our Chosen keenly, and so it is no happy impulse that brings us to mate with another. Our House cannot help us. Healers cannot help us. The Unchosen and those who still have a Chosen cannot help us. But we can help each other. We can *Heal* each other. Look around at the other faces in this room. These fellow sufferers are your allies. And it is not strictly a question of looking to the Bereft kinsmen within your House. All of us here in this room, regardless of House, are part of the same group. In isolation, each of us can do nothing to save ourselves. But together, two by two, we can escape a frightening fate and regain the glory of our gyftes. It is a mutual salvation, a gift we can bestow upon one another."

Shyness swept over Miri as she looked at the others seated around her and saw them looking back at her, every gaze seeming to brim with apprehension and hope.

"Another question?" Gredin invited.

Miri gathered her courage. "Most here are unfamiliar to me. How can we find one another to attempt this thing, once we leave this room and return to our Houses?"

Gredin nodded. "A sensible question, and one we are working to resolve quickly. This morning, before I came to the reception hall for morning meal, I met with the Director and Assistant Director of Tradepoint and told them of our need. Is there anyone here whose House has not yet been moved into the new quarters provided by the Prett? No? Then you all know what those quarters are like. 'Nests,' as we have taken to calling them. Well, this very morning, the Prett are preparing a new enclave for the exclusive use of those of us in this room. The nests there will only be two stacks high – ones that open directly out onto the floor of the enclave, and an upper level that can be reached by means of a single flight of steps. For some of us, Sending down from the upper levels has become a dangerous thing to attempt, so this will be safer for all of us. You will each continue to sleep with your House, in the nest already provided to you. The new nests being prepared are intended only as a place for the Bereft to go when we need to mate. There will be a foam mat in each nest, and a drape to cover the entrance. When the drape is pulled to the side, that is an indication that the nest within is available for any pair of Bereft who have need of it. When they enter, they will release the drape, and anyone else coming into the enclave will know that the nest is occupied."

Miri sighed, and saw Gredin notice. She gestured at Miri again.

"That all sounds very helpful," Miri said, "but how do we… find someone willing?"

Gredin smiled. "We are setting aside a place just within the entrance to the enclave that will hold a scattering of tables and stools. You are all encouraged to spend time there. If you have small tasks to accomplish, feel free to bring those tasks along and work on them there. Failing that, it will at least be a private place where those of us who share this challenge can chat and get to know one another. If the community were not so short of supplies, I would have liked to provide food and drink, but that will have to wait. But anyone there should feel free to approach another, and retire with them to an available nest. It is why each of you will have come there, so try not to feel ill at ease. And it will become easier, once you have proven to yourself that doing so improves your hlinga and that of your partner." Her expression brightened. "Yes, your 'partner.' That is an apt term. Think of this as a dance you cannot perform alone, a dance which will enrich you both." Her hand swept out in an expansive gesture that included them all. "This dance will enable us to live our proper lives, and the others in this room are your potential partners. Only we can take part in this particular dance. And we *must* take part in it, if we are not to wither and fail."

"But we are not talking about a mere dance," someone protested.

"True," Gredin replied. "We are talking about an alliance of survival, to save us from dependency. We are talking about a partnership where neither participant needs to feel beholden. We come together out of mutual need, for our mutual benefit." Again, she gestured at the group. "These, seated around you, are your alliance partners. We are fighting to overcome a common affliction, determined to regain our Balance and retain our gyftes. We will help one another in every way we can – not just by mating to strengthen our hlinga, but by befriending one another and lending support in every way possible. When we encounter one another in the new enclave that the Prett are creating for us, we will smile and greet one another, applauding one another's courage. When sadness for all that we have lost overwhelms us, we will seek one another out, to remind ourselves that some things *can* be regained."

"Seek one another out?" asked a man sitting near where Gredin stood. "How? I have seen no faces here that I recognize. How am I to know whether someone I encounter has lost their Chosen?"

Gredin gazed down at him, her expression pensive. Then a new smile transformed her. "Like this," she said, and raised her hands to one of the free strands of her hlao. Her fingers moved deftly, then dropped away, revealing a simple knot near the end of the strand. "I tie this knot in remembrance of Dreff, to proclaim myself as one of the Bereft. Anyone who looks closely at me can see this knot, and will know me for what I am – a person who has lost their beloved Chosen, and who stands ready to take whatever steps I must to keep my hlinga replete and maintain my Balance so that I may continue to serve the Power." She looked to them in inquiry. "What do you think? Will this suit our need?"

All around the room, hands were rising to hlaos, and knots were being tied. It made Miri's skin prickle to see the speed with which Gredin's gesture was adopted. She tied a knot at the end of one strand of her own hlao, and the gesture felt right and proper. Miri could feel her panic and uncertainty recede. If Gredin's words were true – no, *since* Gredin's words were true –there was a path to lead them out of the darkness that had threatened to swallow them and sever them from their abilities. There was a path… and she would take it. She sensed that same resolve forming all about her, rising from the other afflicted strangers.

Her fellow Bereft.

Her alliance partners.

[5]

1000 OF 2000 ORBITS REMAINING: 12BLUE

Burlon stared as the doors to the former House Balamont enclave opened and a stream of people exited, led by a stone-faced Tetralanna te Balamont. Seeming oblivious to the stir they were creating, they marched to a corner of the reception hall, ignoring the seated diners, and formed a tight huddle with Tetralanna at its center.

"Scrapes and gouges, what's happening now?" he exclaimed, and waved a hasty hand of apology at the outraged faces that turned in his direction. "I ask your pardon," he said to his new Laith kinsmen, "but I fear something untoward has occurred."

"What could it be?" Chenna inquired, wide-eyed. Her slender hand came to rest on his forearm, gripping tightly. "Are we in danger, as well?"

Burlon stared at her heart-shaped face. They had only recently left their cozy bed, and the heightened pink of her cheeks and bright violet of her eyes made him think of the Bentain hills in a spring sunrise, when giessen flowers carpeted the ground in waves of purple under a pink-and-gold sky.

It was a vision he would never see again.

"I don't know," he admitted. "But with Tetralanna involved, it's trouble of some sort."

"I hope Gredin comes out soon to explain."

"As do I. People are getting restless." He turned his head, half-rising from the bench in an effort to better view Tetralanna's group. Was it his imagination or had they huddled even closer to each other? All he could see were the backs of those standing at the circle's outermost edge.

"Finish your breakfast," he urged. "We have to wait, so we might as well eat while we do." So saying, he applied himself with grim resolve to the remainder of his porridge, and was rewarded by the sight of Chenna doing the same, her expression less troubled.

After a delay that left Burlon's nerves taut, the doors finally opened again and Gredin stepped out, followed by the remaining folk who had lost their Chosen. Even at a distance, it seemed to Burlon that there was a new air about them. Dispirited individuals had risen from morning meal in response to Gredin's words. Now, heads were higher. Shoulders were straighter. Expressions were sober but appeared less despairing.

Whatever Gredin had said to them behind closed doors seemed to have awakened a renewed sense of determination.

Why, then, had Tetralanna and the others left early, their outrage clear for all to see?

To his surprise, Gredin walked calmly through the tables, seeming not to hear the many questions aimed at her. She returned to the dais, sparing no glance at all for the group surrounding Tetralanna.

Reaching the top step, Gredin said, "My thanks to you all for heeding my request to wait," she said, her gyfte making her words impossible to ignore. "I spoke at length to those who, like myself, have lost their Chosen. But 'lost' is an odd word, usually applied to an object misplaced or thoughtlessly left behind. For anyone whose Chosen has now returned to the Source, that word more properly describes our emotions, for we *feel* lost without them. But we did not lose them through any action of our own.

"A short while ago, I spoke of the word the Prett use to describe our situation, *garamog*. It means 'shorn of' and, it seems to me, affords a much more accurate description. Those from our private meeting agree. We are Bereft, each of us shorn of our Chosen through no fault or will of our own. So, going forward, we prefer that you refer to us as the Bereft."

Burlon cast a look around. Everyone appeared to be intent on Gredin.

"I informed all of you that the Bereft face a danger, a significant one, and one that is uniquely ours. I have explained it to those who now bear this title, and I have informed them of what must be done to eliminate that danger from our lives. Now I will explain it to you."

Burlon felt his breathing quicken, much as it did when he encountered an unexpectedly tricky Trading situation. He waited for Gredin to continue.

"Perhaps you have noticed erratic behavior in those members of your House who are Bereft. While you are managing to cope, and even move forward, they are still mired in tears and despair. Have you not seen them try to exercise their gyftes, and fail? Or, worse, injure themselves in the attempt? And when you tried to help and comfort them, were they not irritable and short-tempered, instead of being grateful?"

Burlon saw heads nod, while others gave their seatmates a swift, telling look.

"No doubt you made excuses for them, thinking that their grief was still to blame. But it was not just grief. Or fatigue. Or arrogance. Or self-pity."

Gredin paused, and Burlon felt as if the entire room held its collective breath. Even Tetralanna's group seemed frozen in place.

"It was their hlinga."

But that made no sense. Was Gredin implying that the Bereft, as she called them, couldn't sufficiently pleasure themselves because they were still mired in grief?

"Those of you in the community who are blessed by the Power to have your Chosen at your side renew your hlinga each time the two of you mate and experience a completion. Unchosens pleasure themselves to completions, as well, in order to restore their hlinga and maintain their Balance, as we were all taught to do from childhood by our Guides." Gredin's gaze made a slow sweep of the room. "The Bereft no longer have those options. When one's Chosen has returned to the Source, and attempts at self-pleasuring no longer bring any benefit."

A concerned murmur filled the room.

No benefit? Then how…

Gredin nodded, setting her curls in motion. "You begin to comprehend the danger I spoke of, the danger the Bereft now face. With the door to self-pleasuring closed to us, and with our Chosens returned to the Source, the only outcome I could see for us was the gradual loss of our hlinga and, consequently, our ability to exercise our gyftes. A day would come when all of our gyftes, even the simplest and most basic, would be beyond our reach. On that terrible day, the Bereft would be as the smallest younglings, able to do nothing gyfte-driven, dependent on our Houses for care, forever unable to Fetch our meals, or Cleanse ourselves, or Convert our waste."

Burlon's gut felt as if he had swallowed rocks instead of porridge for his morning meal.

"Do not doubt my words. This has happened to others in the past, however rare the instances. And it has happened just as I describe."

Had Gredin known someone within Balamont who suffered this way? If so, why hadn't she spoken of it sooner? Burlon grimaced. There would be much to discuss at their meeting, once it convened.

"Fortunately, with help from our hosts, the Prett, a solution has been found to save the hundreds of us who are Bereft from becoming an intolerable burden on the remainder of the community. But the solution is both simple and difficult. Those who are Bereft must find a partner who is also Bereft, and mate with them."

A wind of whispers and shocked exclamations swept the room, then died away as Gredin gestured for silence.

"I reacted in much the same way when this solution was first proposed to me. It is a new idea to us. We had no need of it on Venna, for very few individuals ever returned to the Source." She smiled sadly. "But that life is lost to us. Our situation here on Tradepoint requires new ways, if we are to prosper. For the Bereft, there are but two choices: mate… or dwindle to nothing. And before you judge or condemn or retreat behind the thick and comforting wall of tradition, ask yourself which choice you would make, and think deeply and honestly upon the consequences."

Burlon scanned the faces of those around him. Chenna was pale and teary-eyed, but he sensed no outrage from her. That didn't seem as true for the Laith folks nearest him. Most wore pinched expressions of shock and disapproval, although a few just seemed stunned. He couldn't see Palla te Laith, but he had no doubt that the stiff-necked man who opposed Gredin was enraged and indignant, wherever he was seated.

As for Gredin's question, Burlon was profoundly glad *he* didn't have to make such a choice. He took Chenna's hand, seeking the comfort of her skin against his.

"I know which choice *I* would make," Gredin continued. "Which choice I *did* make."

"Who is the man who shares your shame, Gredin te Balamont?!"

Tetralanna.

Gredin shifted to face her. "Shame? Do you not mean courage?"

"Courage?" Tetralanna sneered. "It took no courage for you to disgrace our House. You are already well-versed in doing so."

Gredin lifted her head, her stance serene. "Hear me," she ordered, her voice resonant with Power. "Hear me and heed my words. There is no shame here, only an urgent need to improve our situation and renew our hlinga. What the Bereft decide to do, and with whom, is no one's business but their own. They require no one's permission. No Head of House on Venna ever spoke against the choice they must now make in order to recover their Balance. Do not belittle their courage for deciding to take such a step. Refusing to act to improve their condition would condemn them to a life without the touch of the Power, a kind of living death."

"So you claim," Tetralanna responded, but Burlon noted that her voice sounded weak and thin in comparison to Gredin's.

"So I state," Gredin said with solemn emphasis, and turned back to the larger mass of the seated community. "We are one people. Here in this room are all of the Vennans who still exist. I cherish each of you. I am grateful that you have survived. I look forward to the day when we find New Venna and resettle there. When that glorious time comes, I want each of you to be ready for it, in Balance, able to fully exercise your gyftes. To do less would dishonor the Power."

Burlon braced himself for a hostile response from Tetralanna, but she remained silent, as did the rest of the community.

"The Bereft are entitled to privacy as they press forward in their efforts to restore their hlinga. To that end, the Tradepoint Director has ordered the construction of an additional enclave, solely for the Bereft's use. He says it will be ready by the end of this day, a place for them to meet and become acquainted, since many of us who are Bereft are strangers to one another." Gredin lifted an entreating hand. "If you are Unchosen, or have your Chosen at your side, be grateful and be kind. Show your understanding. The Bereft are in great need of it. And now, if you have finished your meal, I encourage you to proceed with your day. I will address you again at midday meal if there are any new developments to report. A good morning to you all."

Burlon watched her descend the steps. Doing his best to tune out the clamor of voices, the clink of dishware, even the touch of Chenna's hand in his, he Focused and reached out with his private mind. =Gredin?=

=Yes?=

=We need to meet.=

=Of course. Please gather the others. I do not wish to tarry here in the reception hall.=

=I understand. We will join you.=

Releasing the connection, Burlon became fully aware of his surroundings again. People were beginning to leave, and kitchen Tenders were clearing the tables. Burlon gave Chenna's hand a gentle squeeze before releasing her. "The circle of five must meet. Will you be content without me for a time? Given all that has been said, this meeting may take longer than usual."

Chenna smiled and gave him a swift kiss. "I am never content without you, but I will be fine. I promised to help Hayla with the nest curtains, this morning. Go about your business and do not fret."

Burlon gave her a kiss in return, one that left her cheeks glowing.

"I will find you when I am finished," he promised. "For now, I must seek out the rest of the circle."

It didn't take as long as he had feared, despite the milling crowd. He did have to dodge a few individuals intent on speaking with him, and he walked the long way around the departure dais in order to avoid a grim-jawed Palla te Laith, but soon he was seated at the little table with the rest of the circle, listening to Gredin recount her meeting with the Bereft.

"…and then Tetralanna and her followers stood up and walked out. Those remaining were shaken but grew steadier as they listened to what I had to say. By the time I finished answering their questions, they looked hopeful," she concluded.

Burlon abandoned his stool and began to pace in agitation. "Bloody blisters, Gredin! You're fortunate the entire lot of them didn't leave! Have you lost your mind?"

He winced, suddenly aware how harsh his words sounded. Of late, Gredin had been less than comfortable around him, and he had been working to mend their relationship, softening his words and actions to avoid upsetting her. Had his outburst just undone all his progress?

To his relief, she responded calmly. "Tetralanna's resistance, along with those who followed her, was to be expected. My resolve is not swayed. Please, come and sit. I will share my thoughts with all of you and answer your questions. There is much I need to clarify."

Relieved, Burlon reclaimed his seat. "Your pardon, Gredin. Please continue. What did you discuss with those who remained?"

"Mostly matters of practicality and reassurance. I stressed that they were entitled to privacy, and I explained the special enclave that the Prett are constructing."

"Do you really think that several hundred people can keep their activities secret?"

Gredin shook her head. "Not secret. Private. Within their individual Houses, the Bereft are already known. It's not who they *are* but what they *do* that will remain private. The community has no need to know the identity of the partner with whom any Bereft mates."

"I think of them as alliance partners," Miri said shyly. "Gredin reminded us that we are not seeking a new Chosen, for we could never replace what the Power has already given to us. That was a comfort to us all, I think. None of us will ever forget our Chosen. Instead, we are helping each other return to Balance by coming together in temporary alliances. Finding an alliance partner is a different thing altogether from finding your Chosen."

Burlon shifted restlessly on his stool. "It may seem different to you, Miri, but I doubt the rest of the community will be so easily persuaded." He turned to Gredin. "You do understand that, don't you? You've boldly proclaimed that people will take such a partner to a nest and…"

Gredin raised an eyebrow. "…and mate with them. That is precisely what I am saying. It is what I have *done*, and will need to do again and again, if I am to recover my hlinga and maintain it."

The blunt words were shocking. Burlon growled, causing Miri to flinch. He heard Sill catch her breath, and even Keegan's fingers grew still on his *crabe*.

Gredin sat calmly. "I am Bereft, as are many, many others in our community. Would you condemn us to a life without access to our gyftes, cut off from the Power?"

"I would rather be dead," Miri blurted into the silence.

"Miri!" Sill said, sounding aghast.

"Well, I would," Miri insisted. "If you had ever seen my kinswoman, Ulm, you would understand why death is preferable to that… that husk of a life." She mustered a wan smile. "Gredin was very brave to put Figg's suggestion to the test. And it worked as Figg predicted. Surely you can see how much better Gredin looks. She has recovered some of her hlinga." Miri's lips firmed. "I intend to follow her example, as soon as I can locate someone willing to mate with me."

Keegan looked thoughtful.

Sill looked sober.

Burlon felt beleaguered. How was he to convince the House volunteers opposed to Gredin that she was a steady, reliable leader when she kept making such contentious proclamations? And it would be even harder now, with her looking like a child, with her hair in unruly curls.

"I understand how all of you who are not Bereft must be feeling.

Sill, your Chosen is safe, having accompanied you to Tradepoint. Keegan, you have yet to find your Chosen, so your body has not become attuned to another's touch. And Burlon." Her gaze sought his, blue and earnest. "You are still in your dydanin with Chenna. How incomprehensible the idea of mating with anyone other than your Chosen must seem to you!"

She was right. He could barely take his leave of Chenna in the mornings, despite the duties that required his attention. Her mind, her body, her very self was perfection. When he tried to imagine finding his completion in some stranger's body, his mind recoiled.

Gredin touched his arm lightly. "What I did was not an easy thing. Far from it. But my alliance partner and I are both much the better for it."

"Who mated with you?" Burlon asked. He was deeply unsettled, but logic, his instinctive Trader's logic, understood her actions. However strange, however unlikely, she had found the path to a mutually successful… Trade.

"Another Bereft, of course."

"But who in House Balamont consented to do this thing? Certainly not one who was part of Tetralanna's little group, the ones who walked out?"

Details would help him understand. Information was what allowed him, along with the rest of the circle, to make good decisions.

"Before I answer," Gredin said, "consider the matter of the Bereft carefully. How can we best accommodate their ongoing needs? How much privacy are they entitled to? How do we identify and aid those who are reluctant to proceed? How might we help if someone has difficulty securing a partner?" Gredin lifted her hands. "And that is only the beginning of the questions we must try to sort out. I shared these questions and others with Wyve and Figg, during this morning's meeting with them."

"You went back out into the public corridors alone, after what occurred last night?" Burlon demanded.

"Not alone. The security guard accompanied me. But I would have felt quite safe if I *had* walked alone to our meeting, and nothing untoward occurred," Gredin answered calmly. "Wyve and Figg were reassured to see me so soon after my Healing, and we had a productive discussion. They are both pleased to hear that the mating I experienced was successful, and that my hlinga has improved – Figg particularly so, as it was her idea. Although I arrived somewhat earlier than normal, Figg had already informed Wyve about the Bereft and their problems. They are quite relieved, I think, that we found a solution so quickly. As you heard, Wyve has authorized construction of an additional enclave exclusively for the Bereft to use."

Burlon frowned. "Why is the need for privacy so great? A new enclave means more space, and more space means higher costs. If people are determined to do this, can't they simply use their own chambers?"

"No!" Miri said, her tone vehement. "Would you be at ease, Burlon, walking into your House's enclave with a stranger at your side, and entering your chambers with them under everyone's gaze? I certainly would not. An enclave that only those who are Bereft will enter sounds… comforting."

"That's all very well," Burlon said evenly, "but it places an additional burden on the community to pay for it."

"A lighter burden than hundreds of our people cut off from their gyftes," Gredin retorted.

"Well then, what is Wyve charging us for the additional space?"

"I didn't ask. We need this thing, whatever its cost."

"Gredin!" Burlon leaned forward, his temper spiking. "You can't keep making independent decisions that involve the community's finances. You have asked us to advise you and to give you the benefit of our experience. Why bother meeting if communication is all one-way, and all of the decisions are already made?"

"There was a need for haste. I was doing what was needed to keep us safe."

He sighed. "You could have waited. You learned of this problem late yesterday evening, and immediately ran off to see Figg. It gave the Beng an opportunity to attack you – a subject we should discuss in detail. And you committed yourself to decisions on behalf of the entire community that caught me… that caught us all unprepared, this morning."

Despite her childlike appearance, Gredin didn't cry or look abashed by his words. She simply nodded. "My apologies. You are right, Burlon. I made hasty decisions, perhaps because my Balance was significantly eroded, and those led to even more decisions, all without consultation with the group." The ghost of a smile played on her lips. "But I am glad I took the chance of mating with another, for it has resulted in a significant improvement in my hlinga, which in turn is helping me make better decisions than I recently would have." She made a little gesture. "I doubt I could have discussed this subject with any equanimity, if I had not first restored some degree of my Balance. But I should have tried. We are a circle of advisors. I will strive not to forget that, in the future."

"Our thanks," he said tersely. He wanted to say more. Truthfully, he wanted to give her a tongue-lashing for relaxing her guard around the Beng, but now did not seem to be the time, when she was finally behaving sensibly.

Gredin cocked her head. "In my own defense, I did try to contact you when I first learned what the Bereft are facing, but I couldn't reach your private mind. Where were you?"

I was passed out, drunk, on the Rodornon ship. He cleared his throat. "The Rodorno arrived in port, last night. Their crew invited me aboard."

"Aboard…? You entered their ship?"

"Didn't I just say so?" he asked irritably, anxious to repress the flood of guilty memories created by his actions. He had abandoned his Chosen during their dydanin, and he had drunk himself insensible. The Rodornon ritual had eased the emotional burdens he carried, but he still felt foolish and vulnerable for speaking so frankly to Artett Abna-gul and her crew.

On the other hand, if he was honest with himself, he had known that such an experience was nearly inevitable, given the empathetic nature of the Rodorno and their fondness for *kippi*.

"Was it safe to do so?" Gredin asked.

"As safe as sitting in this chamber," Burlon said briskly, wanting to leave the topic of the Rodorno before more details of his visit could slip out. "They are good friends to us. But let us return to our discussion of the Bereft. You were about to tell me the name of your alliance partner – our new ally in House Balamont, and one we sorely need there."

"You are mistaken. I wasn't about to do any such thing. It is no one else's business who my alliance partner was, last night."

Burlon opened his mouth… and closed it.

Sill and Keegan looked uncomfortable, avoiding his gaze. Miri smiled defiantly.

All right then, he would try a different approach.

"If any of the Bereft refuse to find an alliance partner, won't we need to know? At worst, their House will need to make plans for the future care of such folk."

"I intend for everyone to participate," Gredin stated. "We can't afford to lose any more gyftes, and life would become unbearable for that individual."

"So we will need names."

"Individual names, yes, but not pairings," Gredin said.

Burlon gave a grudging shrug.

"Wyve claims that the enclave for the Bereft's private use will have special *griimoni* to open the enclave doors," Gredin continued. "After midday meal, I will ask all of the Bereft to assemble, to register the pattern of their palm and to speak their name and House into a device Wyve has provided. Figg also suggested that the groups be allowed to step inside the enclave and view its layout, so that it will be familiar to them before they go there to mate with an alliance partner for the first time. That way, if everyone knows where to come, and how to get in, and what it looks like inside, their first real visit will be less intimidating. Once they have registered, they will only need to place their palm on the *griimoni,* and the door will record their identity and open."

"I would like to see that new space," Keegan said, "so I can describe it for my histories."

Gredin's lips tightened. "I believe admittance to the new enclave should be solely for the Bereft."

Burlon considered reminding Gredin that she was once again making decisions without seeking advice from the circle.

But then she added, "What do the rest of you think about Keegan's request?"

"I see no harm in it," Sill said slowly. "Keegan would only visit the area before it is in use."

"Does that satisfy your requirements for privacy?" Burlon asked the others.

Miri and Gredin shared a look, and Miri said, "Or I could simply share a mind picture of it with him afterward, and answer any questions he might have."

Burlon sighed. Apparently Gredin wasn't alone in her belief that privacy needed to be a key component of any arrangement made for the Bereft.

"That would be acceptable," Keegan said earnestly. "I have no wish to intrude, Miri, truly I don't." He gave her a lop-sided smile. "Curiosity has always been a failing of mine, according to my House."

Miri looked a bit flustered. "Your pardon, Keegan. I spoke badly. Your desire to see the new enclave is understandable. You're a historian, after all. It's just…" Miri folded and unfolded her hands, where they rested atop the table.

If she were a Trader, she would have to erase such a tell-tale sign of her inner agitation, Burlon thought. "Why does the idea of others who are not Bereft visiting the new enclave upset you so, Miri?"

"I don't know," she cried. "It just does! I truly do trust Keegan. I trust all of you. But it comforts me to think that no one but another Bereft will ever go there. I feel so unsettled that anything offering comfort and safety seems doubly precious." Miri sighed. "Gredin, please thank the Director for giving us more space, and for the new door *griimoni* so that we can enter the Bereft enclave without having to state our name aloud, in the future. It will be hard enough to find the courage to go there at all, without having to worry that I might be overheard by someone out in the corridor." She shuddered. "I don't want to be the subject of idle gossip, especially regarding a matter as personal as this!"

Gredin gave the kitchen Tender a smile. "Be assured, Miri, I will thank him. Wyve and Figg seem certain the device will meet our needs, giving the Bereft as much privacy as possible, showing us who has made use of the enclave without indicating who they mated with."

Burlon was fairly sure the Prett *griimoni* would function exactly as Gredin described. The Prett were clever with their machines. But… "How will that information be relayed to us, so we know who is participating?"

Gredin brightened. "Figg says the names will appear on Keegan's *crabe* daily, with the individuals listed by House. I had no idea *griimoni* could perform such tasks."

Keegan looked up. "What if someone doesn't participate?" he asked. "I'm concerned about Tetralanna and those who followed her out of the Bereft meeting."

"The entire Bereft community will encourage them to change their minds. When they see others improve, it should increase their confidence in what we are urging them to do. And I will ask the House volunteers to monitor their Bereft members and inform me if someone is having difficulties."

"Your pardon, but… the volunteer for House Balamont is Tetralanna."

"A truth. And a difficulty. Soon, however, an individual whose hlinga is still failing will become fairly obvious. Keegan can provide us with a daily update."

It was a fair plan, Burlon thought. Any sane person, seeing their kinsmen and fellow community members on the mend, would want the same for themselves.

"I do have some questions, although they have little to do with privacy," Sill said. "Will alliance partners remain… fixed?"

"Always the same two together, you mean?"

"Yes."

Gredin shrugged. "I suppose that will depend on the two individuals. Perhaps, for some. But there need be no formal requirement. An alliance partner is not a Chosen. Some people may find it easier to have several different alliance partners. Or many."

"And if children result from these matings?"

Burlon's mouth went dry. "*Can* children result from such a mating?"

Gredin looked troubled. "Keegan, do your histories hold any such information?"

Keegan shook his head. "Becoming Bereft is nearly unprecedented, so I would hardly expect such a thing to be mentioned in any of the histories I read."

A gloomy silence fell.

"Sill's questions are good ones," Gredin said slowly, "and we have no ready answers. Babies may result... or they may not. In the past, our people have not borne children often, despite having Chosens. Alliance partners may have even less of a chance."

Burlon crossed his arms. "But what if they do? Would you make the Bereft who are involved select a single House to claim, as you did with myself and Chenna?"

He didn't understand precisely why the idea of children resulting from an alliance mating unsettled him so, or why he was pushing Gredin on this issue. It had to be painful for her to contemplate, since she had lost her Chosen on the heels of her dydanin and, therefore, had seemed to lose any chance of a child... until now.

Gredin shook her head. "An alliance partner is altogether different from a Chosen, I believe. A Chosen is selected by the Power. We who are Bereft will be making our own selections." Her blue gaze was steady on his. "We do not intend to make a life with our alliance partner, in the way that you and Chenna will do."

"But if a child results...?"

Miri slapped the table. "Then let the child belong to the mother's House! Whether she has taken one alliance partner to her bed or many, she is the one carrying the child. She knows which House *she* belongs to."

Burlon stared at the kitchen Tender, a woman he had personally recruited from House Kendar because of her reputation for calmness, and felt abashed by her flushed face and glittering eyes. "Again, I ask your pardon for upsetting you, Miri. I only want us to be ready for any consequences that may result from the actions of the Bereft. I don't want to leave such decisions in the hands of people like Tetralanna."

Miri took a deep breath. "I should be the one offering apologies, Burlon." She gave him a shaky smile. "My outburst is a clear sign that my hlinga is in great need of repair. I only hope my courage does not fail me when the new enclave is finished and I have the opportunity to seek a mating with another in need."

"Don't be so hard on yourself, Miri," Gredin said. "It took three servings of the Hesch's amarantha wine before *I* could proceed, last night."

Burlon blinked. "You drank three cups of amarantha wine?"

"Yes. It is all that gave me the courage to follow through on Figg's suggestion. We'll be needing much more of it now," Gredin said. "I doubt I could have achieved a completion without it, and other Bereft may find that it bolsters their courage, as well."

Burlon grimaced, his spirits sinking. "I really shouldn't approach the Hesch again for several days, at the soonest, so use what you have wisely. In fact, if Nitikikani's temper doesn't cool, I may not be able to make a deal with them before they leave port."

Gredin looked alarmed. "But…"

"Trading is a chancy thing," he said forcefully. "Trading partners like the Wilra are not always in port when you wish them to be. And conditions, or prices, or attitudes can change without warning, as we've experienced with the Hesch and the Beng."

An odd expression crossed Gredin's face. Despair? Embarrassment? Worry? Sympathy? It seemed similar to all, yet not completely one thing or another.

"Burlon, Wyve gave me news regarding the Beng at our meeting, this morning, and asked me to pass it on to you."

Apprehension tightened his insides. "What about the Beng?"

"They left Tradepoint after attacking me."

"So you said. They were due to leave. And it won't save them from a massive Judgment when they return." He was grimly certain of that.

The little toe-stubbers were finally going to get what they deserved. Maybe he would demand Beng grain in compensation. Starting with *piprill.* At little or no cost, of course. He would have to discuss it with the other Traders and come to a decision about how much to request and for how long. If the Power blessed them, the penalty might even last until they found New Venna…

"Burlon!"

Reluctantly, he set aside his thoughts of retribution on the Beng. "Your pardon, Gredin." He gave her a smile that was *g'ril*, as the Shodekekeen would say, all teeth and no humor, and shrugged. "I'm sorry the Judgment will be delayed. But the Beng will return eventually. I was just thinking that perhaps we would ask for Beng grain as part of the compensation for your injuries. In the meantime, we have the grain I bought from them to tide us over."

"No. We don't. The Beng left port and cancelled their contract with us."

"What?!"

"And that's not even the worst of it. Wyve says that, according to the *chronorb* records, the Beng had just finished off-loading their cargo to the Prett warehouses, both the grain to satisfy contracts made while they were in port and sacks that were as yet unsold, when they attacked me. Figg thought it might explain why some of the Beng were out in the corridors when I passed by." She waved her hand, impatiently. "That hardly matters, though. The attack isn't our most pressing problem, although I have lodged a formal complaint with the Director."

Burlon braced himself for whatever news she was about to impart.

"Unfortunately, the Beng left word with Wyve that they were accepting the alternate terms of the previous Judgement. They won't be returning to Tradepoint for six sectora. And they instructed Wyve that under no circumstance was the Prett Director to sell any of their grain to the Vennans. To others, yes. But not to us."

Burlon felt as if all the air had been sucked from the room. There was a pounding in his ears, and his hands were sweating. *What now? How are we to recover from this? What food can I find to fill the gaping hole in our kitchen stores that the loss of the Beng grain has now created?*

He wanted… no, he needed Chenna. Her touch, her very presence would comfort and sustain him while he waited for the shock of Gredin's news to pass.

But that succor would have to wait. Tonight, he would seek solace in Chenna's arms, and let their mutual passion hold his worries at bay until morning. Right now, however, he was a Trader. And a member of the circle. He would not abandon his duties, leaving the others to wrestle with such weighty problems.

Gredin was watching him, one hand clasping the flamestone pendant at her neck.

He considered remarking that his caution against wearing the eye-catching stone outside of the Vennan enclave had proven to be wise advice. Otherwise, that necklace would now be in the hands of the Power-forsaken Beng – gone, as their food was gone.

But, looking at her child-curls and vulnerable expression, he refrained. It seemed that the flamestone, given to her by her Chosen, brought her a kind of comfort. And comfort was another commodity currently in short supply. He said only, "Take care with that necklace, Gredin. I would not want you to lose your Chosen's gift."

"I will," she responded, with a trace of defiance. "I will hide it beneath my clothing when I venture out. But make no mistake, I *will* wear it, now that the Beng are gone. It... steadies me."

Who could blame her? But it made him uneasy, all the same. Suddenly, Tradepoint seemed unpredictable. The Beng had carried their spite to a violent and unprecedented level. And the Hesch had withdrawn into arrogance and impenetrable anger.

Burlon wanted to bury his head in his hands. He wanted to indulge in a glass of potent *kippi* and let the mournful chant of *dok-watorn* ease the unwelcome burdens that had just descended with such crushing weight onto his shoulders.

But that would not help the community.

"Let's discuss our options," he said instead, and straightened his back, rallying to assess their predicaments anew.

[6]

0881 OF 2000 ORBITS REMAINING: 40GREEN

"They'll be coming for us soon," Chenna murmured.

Burlon groaned, then groaned again as Chenna trailed her fingertips across his chest. They were sprawled on the bedmat, waiting for their breathing to ease in the aftermath of a completion that had just overwhelmed them both.

"I will miss this room," Burlon admitted, smiling up at the ceiling. It was the final day of their dydanin, and he had spent all of it with Chenna, except for the morning meeting with Gredin and the others.

"Yes, but we will have our new nest with the others of House Laith," Chenna soothed. "I went and examined it, yesterday, with Ulin and Payt. Their nest is on the same level." She smiled. "The foam mat provided by the Prett for Chosens is broader than this one."

"That may not be happy news," Burlon teased. "I want you close beside me."

"Oh, you will find me within arm's reach." She stifled a yawn. "We are on the topmost level, and the panel that hangs across our entry pleases me greatly."

"Because it will hide us from curious eyes?"

She laughed. "No. Because it is fashioned from pieces of fabric in every shade of green you can imagine."

"Fabric pleases you?" he asked, still teasing.

She leaned her forehead against him. "Green pleases me," she said, and shivered within his embrace. "I miss the Holding." Her voice shrank to a whisper. "I miss my poor bees."

He tightened his arm around her. "Do not be sad. When we finally reach New Venna, you and I will live at a Holding. And I intend to demand a second dydanin for us, one where we will be alone together for the days as well as the nights. The Power has promised Gredin that New Venna awaits us. We need only be brave for a time, until we can find it."

"You sound so certain. But where was the Power when Gredin was attacked by the Beng? Where was it when Venna was destroyed?"

"Oh, beloved, you are asking the wrong man. I am a Traveler and a Trader. I know little of the Power, beyond the glory of the River, which has always been enough for me. I have no grand answers to offer you, only my love and devotion." He sat up, then, braced on one arm, leaned over her to kiss a tear from her cheek. "There is nothing I would not do to make you happy again. Just give me time." He peered down at her in adoration, then grinned.

"What is funny?" she asked, frowning up at him.

"A tiny crumb of d'limten is clinging to your face, daring to mar your beauty." Thanks to Miri's kindness, they had eaten their evening meal in bed, feeding one another bites of food in alternation with kisses. "I see I must perfect my skills at feeding you." Leaning down, he touched the tip of his tongue to the spot…

…and encountered nothing but the smoothness of Chenna's skin.

Startled, he drew back and looked again.

The tiny brown speck was still there.

Shifting to sit more upright, Burlon brushed his fingertip over the spot.

The little speck remained.

A glimmer of astonished excitement awoke, deep inside him. Touching a fingertip lightly to her chin, he Freshened her.

The speck remained unchanged.

Thrilled, he bent and kissed her. "You will draw the attention of every eye, this evening."

She clasped her hands around the back of his neck. "We both will."

"Well, yes, but..." Gently disengaging her hands, he drew back slightly and said, "View yourself through my eyes." He gazed upon her face, letting her sense his adoration and excitement. Then he narrowed the Focus of his attention and asked, "What do you see there?"

Chenna's hand flew to her cheek, her fingertip hovering just below the tell-tale mark. "Is that... a glim?"

"I believe it is. If so, we should see several more, by morning."

It was exactly the encouragement they needed to coax them from their bed and into their clothes. Soon thereafter, as tradition dictated, he became aware of attempted contacts with his private mind, first a few, then more, and more, and more, until Burlon opened the chamber door and swept Chenna out into the midst of the waiting crowd.

He had expected the crush of people they found in the narrow corridor, but he was unprepared for the size of the crowd that had gathered in the reception hall itself to celebrate with them. It was expected that House Laith would turn out in numbers, and Burlon had felt confident that Gredin and the rest of the morning group would be there, but it was quickly apparent that the entire community had come – if not precisely to wish them well, then at least to take part in the celebration.

And celebration it was. Burlon marveled, wondering at the effort it must have taken to keep him ignorant of the plans being laid. Musicians were playing, and tables were being cleared in the wake of evening meal to provide a space for dancing. Ingarra came up to Chenna and placed a band of artfully wrought fabric flowers on her head.

Accepting it, Chenna darted a look of inquiry at Burlon. He nodded. Good news was meant to be shared. Chenna murmured in Ingarra's ear, and the older woman peered closely at her, then embraced her.

When she released Chenna, Ingarra turned to Burlon, her face alight with pleasure. "May I tell Gredin?"

"You may tell Gredin, and Gredin may tell everyone," Burlon replied. It would have been more traditional to approach House Laith first, but he had no wish to lend an aura of authenticity to Palla te Laith's pretensions. The man was only his House's volunteer, *not* its Head of House.

Moments later, Gredin's voice reached everyone in the enclave. "Chenna and Burlon have emerged from their dydanin, and Chenna is going to have a child. May the Power grace them as they increase the numbers of House Laith and this entire community!"

After that, the atmosphere within the community achieved a true glow of gaiety for the first time since the news of Venna's destruction. Clinging to his Chosen's hand, Burlon found himself congratulated again and again. Even Tetralanna te Balamont unbent enough to smile upon them.

Gredin came up, soon thereafter, and Burlon felt his happiness waver at the shocking sight of her short-cropped hair. Each time he encountered her, it struck him anew, reigniting his fury at the Beng… and his own sense of guilt. If Gredin had been able to reach him after hearing Miri's frightening tale about Ulm, he would have accompanied her to and from her conference with Figg. He would have insisted they make use of the security guard Wyve had provided, coming and going. The guard's presence would have prevented the Beng attack from occurring. But he had been with the Rodorno aboard their ship, out of range of Gredin's attempts to reach his private mind. And even if he had been closer, within the Rodornon enclave, he would have been unrousable, afloat on a reckless sea of *kippi*-induced night-thoughts. By the time he had finally awakened in the midst of the Rodornon crew, his head cradled on the warm lap of Artett Abna-gul, it was too late; the attack on Gredin had already occurred, and the Beng had made their craven escape from Tradepoint…

"Smile," Gredin prompted. "This is a joyful night, and your new House has many eyes."

He nodded and gave Chenna an apologetic squeeze. "With a Chosen such as mine, a smile should be my permanent expression."

"Indeed," Gredin concurred, and Burlon felt another stab of guilt. Here he stood, proclaiming the joy that his Chosen brought him, while Gredin would forever be a solitary member of the Bereft.

But it was not now so hideous a fate as it would have been without Figg's wild suggestion.

Alliance partners. The very notion had shaken the enclave to its core, but the alternative – a third of their community rendered helpless and gyfteless – was far worse.

"How goes use of the new enclave?" he was forced to ask Gredin, having spent his day in Chenna's arms, oblivious to all other events.

"Well enough. Keegan says some Houses are proving slower than others to participate."

Burlon had the impression she was being intentionally vague, distancing him from the issue. A dividing line seemed to be forming within the community, with the Bereft huddled together on one side of it and the remainder of the community left behind on the other, wishing them well but powerless to aid them. Perhaps that was unavoidable. Perhaps it was not even such a bad thing. It was hard not to pity the Bereft, and hard not to show that he did. For pride's sake, the Bereft might need a sense of solidarity with one another, along with the setting of an intentional boundary past which the rest of the community could not intrude.

The new enclave was just such an intentional restriction. Upon its rapid completion by the Prett, the Bereft had assembled two days ago in a long line, advancing one by one to place their palm against the lock and solemnly speak their name and House. They had done so under Burlon's watchful eye, since he was far more comfortable with Prett *griimoni* than most Vennans.

All of the Bereft had been required to come and register themselves, even Tetralanna and the others who had walked out of Gredin's initial explanation of their condition.

"Very well," Tetralanna had snarled, removing her palm from the pad after stating her name and House. "Register me, if you insist. I have lost my Chosen. I do not deny it. But you cannot make me enter here." And she had refused to do so, although she had taken a cursory glance through the open doorway, and given a dismissive sniff before stalking back to the Balamont enclave…

"Burlon!" Gredin said, and the gyfte-laced snap of sound pulled him from his reverie.

"Yes," he acknowledged, chagrined. "Your pardon. You said…?"

"I *said* that you should dance with your Chosen."

Dancing! His gyfte came suddenly alert. "If it can be arranged discreetly, might I…?"

"Might you what?"

"Invite the F'lala to join us?"

She looked amused. "Are you so determined to outrage your new House?"

He shrugged. "I am newly appointed First Traveler, and Chenna is going to bear a child. I am likely in as much favor with my new House as I am ever apt to be. And the F'lala are a mild-mannered race whose appearance is unthreatening. I could ask Ellis to attend them."

"And if Palla te Laith and Tetralanna take exception to their presence here?"

"Then Palla te Laith and Tetralanna can retire to their respective enclaves."

The corners of Gredin's mouth twitched. "You are a mischievous man," she accused. "Very well. So long as there are no more than ten of them, and they are attended at all times, you may invite them to come. After all, this celebration is in honor of you and your Chosen."

"Well, I promise that the F'lala will not attempt to join in the dancing," Burlon said, and grinned. "Seriously, I will have Ellis seat them over there, against the wall, where they can see the dancing and listen to the music without drawing undue attention to themselves."

Gredin smiled. "My thanks for your reassurance. Still," she teased, her smile widening, "I can imagine how a dancing F'lala might look, with its cloud of hair floating two steps behind where its feet are treading..."

And so it was, a short time later, that a silent octet of F'lala settled onto benches near the arrival dais, wide-eyed and admiring, while Burlon partnered Chenna in the community dance, his spirits soaring at the sight of three new glim already visible on her cheeks.

[7]

0808 OF 2000 ORBITS REMAINING: 13BLUE

Keegan tucked his *crabe* securely under his arm and trudged off, intent on completing the task he had been dreading since giving his report at the morning's circle of five meeting.

As a youngling, growing up in House Fliss, he had been naively unaware of the oddity of his gyfte. His Guides, Ilthet and Jaisel, from House Fliss's orchard holding, had been patient with the endless questions that tumbled off his lips from the moment he could clearly speak. Everything about his small world was fascinating to him, and almost all of his sentences began with "Who" or "Why" or "How." *Who carved the frieze along the top of the walls in my room, and why did they decide to depict placrim blossoms? How long did it take them to complete it? What tools did they use? Was it done freehand, or did the maker use a pattern?* He had never run out of questions, just the opportunity to ask them.

As he grew, and his world expanded to include a group of Tutors, his questions only increased. He had long supposed it was just as well there had been no easy match to his gyfte within the House, so that the Head of House was forced to select a variety of House members whose gyftes complemented elements of his own.

No doubt he would have driven a single Tutor mad with all his questions.

Still, it had often plagued him that there was no one else within the House with his gyfte. Few of his kinsmen had shown patience when subjected to his unending curiosity, and even his Guides had been grateful to escape back to their lives among the fruit trees at the Holding when he grew older, or so it seemed to him.

So he had learned to fade into the background, allowing others around him to talk. He listened carefully to conversations, in order to keep the intrusion of his questions to a minimum.

In truth, he became almost too successful in that practice, as evidenced by the reactions others exhibited when he asked them to clarify a detail or provide additional information, as if they had forgotten he was there. And when they did acknowledge his presence, it seemed to him that their comments always carried an air of disapproval or censure.

"Keegan, you startled me!"

"Why do you creep about so silently, listening to others?"

"What are you writing in that journal of yours, Keegan?"

Always, he had smiled to show he took no offense, and he had clung to the belief that, now that his hlao had unfurled, he would find his Chosen at the dances. A Chosen would love him *and* his gyfte, however strange and useless others considered it to be.

But his life, to date, had proceeded along other, mostly solitary, paths.

He well remembered the sorrow and shame that had risen like a rogue wave to swamp him when the Head of House explained tersely that the House had no one to Mentor him, and no reason to expect that his gyfte would generate any significant future profits. As was his custom, he had smiled and thanked the Head for her honesty, before leaving with her final words echoing in his thoughts. *"Please yourself however you like with your future studies and the exercise of your gyfte, as long as it does not place too heavy a touch on the House's financial reserves."*

He had worked hard to swallow his hurt and disappointment,

telling himself that his future still held the brightness of a Chosen, uniquely suited to him, who would spread the gentle balm of loving acceptance over his pain, so that it would be as nothing. Eager and determined, he had attended the House dances. But, over time, it was his hope, not the pain, that had worn away to nearly nothing.

At the last House dance he attended, shortly before the journey to Tradepoint for the Trisectoriana, he had tried not to let the jests of his kinfolk spoil the evening. *"Still no Chosen, Keegan? Perhaps you have slipped the Power's mind! Why, just yesterday, Egilene was remarking that you must have extraordinary patience, more than any man he knows, for it has been long and long since you started attending the dances – longer than anyone except the Oldest!" And everyone had laughed.*

When Venna was destroyed, returning every member of House Fliss except himself back to the Source, he had mourned, not least because he believed that his House's destruction had forever denied him a Chosen. But then the strange miracle of Burlon and Chenna – members from two separate Houses – discovering their Choosing had occurred at the reception, and hope had been reborn within him. *Patience*, he told himself. *Have patience. There is yet time and opportunity for the Power to find the perfect match for you.*

And patience was a skill he had, by now, honed to near perfection.

Perhaps that did make him the best choice from the circle of five to seek out Tetralanna and discover why no one from House Balamont had yet entered the enclave of the Bereft.

The former First Speaker made no effort to hide her contempt for Gredin and Burlon, and readily opposed any stance they took, so there had been little sense in sending them. Sill's time was taken up with an ever-increasing load of petitioners. As members of the Bereft began to experience an improvement in their hlinga, they were anxious for Sill or Vik to Harvest their precious memories before they could blur. And no one wanted to take Miri away from her beloved kitchen, now that her Balance had improved.

Which left him. And the *crabe*.

His Prett *griimoni* collected information and reported it in neat columns, but it was his responsibility to interpret those results for the other members of the circle, each morning. And that, too, made him the likely candidate to verify the oddity of House Balamont's information as reported to his *crabe*.

Entering House Balamont's new quarters, he was pleased to see that a number of softening touches had been added by its residents. Metal benches padded with newly sewn cushions had been arranged to create conversation and workspaces, decorated here and there with small, plump pillows in soft shades of blue and green. People were socializing, some seated, some strolling together. And the colorful curtains in the doorways caught his eye. From the nests that were occupied, a soft glow from luminth shone through the airy hangings, making a pleasing design of light and color reminiscent of the stained-glass windows that had existed in House Fliss...

"What are you gaping at, Historian?"

Keegan turned around, stung by the familiar, sharp-tongued voice.

Tetralanna te Balamont stood watching him, her arms crossed, her lips pursed in a tight line of displeasure.

"Good day, Tetralanna," he said. "I was admiring the decorative touches your House has added to its new quarters. They make it much more home-like and welcoming."

"Everyone is doing their best under trying circumstances, but nothing will ever make these ridiculous metal boxes seem like home." Her blue eyes were like chips of ice. "What brings you here, uninvited, Keegan te Fliss? Surely you did not come solely to admire the handiwork of our Makers."

Pleasantries, it seemed, were unwelcome. "Might we find a place to talk, Tetralanna? There are several questions I must ask you, in your role as House Balamont's volunteer."

"*Volunteer*," she sneered. "I am not some pathetic individual anxious to fill my empty days. I am the new Head of House Balamont." She glared at him, oozing arrogance. "You would do well to make note of that, Historian, if you have not already done so."

Keegan repressed a shiver at the animosity in her voice.

"Ask your questions," she continued, "and then leave my House."

Keegan slipped the *crabe* free. "May we please sit, Tetralanna? It is easier for me to make notations while sitting."

Tetralanna gave the *crabe* a wary look, as if she expected it to snap at her.

"If we must," she said curtly, and led the way to a vacant bench. "I see that you, like Gredin, have become a creature of the Prett."

"They were kind enough to provide me with a way to record information needed by our community, once my paper supplies were exhausted," he said, gently refuting her implication. "There is no need to be worried or afraid. The *crabe* will not harm you."

"I fear nothing," she snapped.

Keegan's hands grew damp as he observed how seriously Tetralanna's Balance had eroded. With a sigh, he touched a finger to the screen, triggering it to awaken.

Its voice said, in Vennan, "Welcome, Keegan te Fliss. Please enter a selection."

Tetralanna recoiled violently. "It speaks! And it recognizes you!"

"Only because the Director set up to do so. A moment, please." Tapping on the familiar choices, he worked his way to the section of the report on the Bereft that had raised alarm in the group at the morning meeting. Rotating the *crabe* so that Tetralanna could see the lighted screen, he pointed at the area in question. "Do you see this section here? It contains information concerning House Balamont."

Tetralanna gave the screen a dismissive glance. "I hardly need a Prettian device to inform me about the members of my own House."

"I am glad to hear that," Keegan said, "for I received information – which is displayed here – stating that none of House Balamont's Bereft have yet entered the new enclave prepared for their use. You see?" He enlarged the screen display and extended it toward Tetralanna, but she recoiled with a shriek and threw her hands up as if to ward him off, knocking the mechanical tablet from his grasp. The device landed with a loud clatter on the metal floor.

The low hum of conversation in the gathering area ceased at once. Heads popped out of nest entrances. People stared.

Keegan scrabbled for the *crabe*.

Tetralanna laughed harshly. “If we are fortunate, your clumsiness has killed it, Historian, releasing you from its influence.”

To his profound relief, the *crabe* appeared intact, without even a scratch on its smooth surface. Cautiously, aware that his hands still wanted to shake, he tapped the screen to power it off, then set the precious *griimoni* next to him on the bench. “I am sorry the noise disturbed your House members, Tetralanna.”

“You should, instead, apologize for disturbing me with your foolish questions.”

“Foolish?”

Tetralanna leaned forward. “Yes, foolish,” she hissed. “Foolish to think I would allow anyone under my charge in House Balamont to bring shame upon themselves, or upon the House, or upon our proud history by following Gredin’s dark path.” She straightened. “We are the keepers of cherished traditions. That is why you find no Balamont names listed on your talking device. I have instructed the House in proper behavior, and have scolded into silence those reckless enough to question me. There are no Balamont names now, and there will be no Balamont names in the future.”

“You think it right to prevent your House Members from recovering their hlinga?”

“I think it right for the Head of House to set an example and lead the way. I will do everything I can to prevent those of my House from taking such a step.”

“But… you can’t be serious. You are condemning them, and yourself, to a living death!”

Tetralanna shrugged. “If so, it is the Power’s will, and we will have the comfort of knowing we made the honorable choice.”

He was horrified, and knew that it must show on his face.

“Don’t you see, Historian? You have fallen into that foolish girl’s trap, believing whatever tale she tells you, to your detriment. Besides, *you* have lost no Chosen, and therefore have no right to question my decision in this matter. Go back and inform Gredin that she has no say in House Balamont’s affairs.”

“Gredin is still a member of House Balamont. She is concerned for all of you. She wants no one to be separated from their gyfte.”

“I care nothing for Gredin’s concern.”

“You should,” Keegan said, anger beginning to build in his chest. “She only wants what is best for the members of our community.”

“She embraces new words and new ways far too easily. And she will say anything to entice the weak-minded to her side. She is set on destroying the very foundations of our way of life. We came here as a delegation of Houses, and a delegation of Houses we shall remain.”

Tetralanna was wrong – dangerously, tragically wrong. And yet, confronted by the force of her words, clothed in her gyfte, Keegan found it hard to defy her assertions. She might be out of Balance but her gyfte had not yet deserted her, although she seemed to have lost all scruples about how she put it to use.

“I am sorry for you and the members of your House, Tetralanna te Balamont.”

Anger tightened her face. “We neither want nor need your pity, Historian. And we do not want you here.”

“What *do* you want? Surely you wish to preserve your House.”

“You seek to understand me? To know what I want?”

“Yes. Please. I need to understand.”

But Tetralanna sagged and held out her hands in appeal. “Help me,” she said, her voice gone suddenly thin.

Concerned, he offered his hands to steady her, and turned his head to see who else might be close enough to aid them.

But Tetralanna’s hands closed on his, her grip firm. “Hear me, Keegan te Fliss,” she said, and her voice was no longer thin, but rich with her gyfte. “Hear me and attend. You will leave us in peace. I forbid you to address me or any other member of House Balamont who has lost their Chosen. You will not ask us your prying questions. You will not urge us to defile the memories of our Chosens by seeking to mate with another.” Tetralanna’s voice had somehow become his entire world, echoing inside his head. “And you will not seek Gredin out and speak of what has passed between us. Remember my words and obey them.” With that, she flung his hands away, swaying slightly.

“What…?” Keegan croaked, feeling somewhat unsteady himself.

Tetralanna’s smile was cold. “You are Silenced, Historian. And do not approach this House again, for none here will speak with you. Now go. Do not trouble yourself on our behalf in the future. And take that nasty thing with you. Its presence sullies the very air of my House.”

His mind reeling, Keegan picked up the *crabe*, hugged it to his chest, and staggered out of the Balamont enclave.

[8]

0788 OF 2000 ORBITS REMAINING: 33GREEN

"So, here we are again," Burlon said.

Wyve looked up from his work. "Indeed. Come in. Sit."

Reluctantly, Burlon obeyed. Eleven days had passed since his last visit to Wyve's office, and he had an unhappy feeling that he knew what the topic of this meeting was going to be. But he would let Wyve make the first move. If he had been summoned to the Director's office to discuss something *other* than geddel crystals, Burlon certainly wasn't going to introduce that topic voluntarily.

Wyve continued to twiddle with the hologram on his desk. "The new enclave is proving satisfactory?"

"Yes. Gredin seems particularly pleased with whatever you did to program the entrance lock. It has performed flawlessly, which is a relief to her, since she is anxious not to discourage anyone who attempts to gain entry. We aren't much used to *griimoni,* so some folk were apprehensive."

"And the data from it has downloaded properly to Keegan te Fliss's crabe?"

Burlon shrugged. "It seems so. I haven't heard anything to the contrary."

"Good. So, is it your sense that matters are settling down, somewhat? Your people have weathered the first impact of your world's loss and are finding a new pattern to their days here?"

"Some more than others, but that's to be expected."

"But, generally speaking, the larger quarters have helped, and matters are calmer?"

"Yes." He made a face. "Food is still a concern, of course, thanks to the Beng."

Wyve frowned. "I have just been reading Binn's latest report from the Clinic about Keegan te Fliss's testing. It begins to look as if no Prettian food is going to be compatible with Vennan digestive systems. I am truly sorry for that. It would have been a quick, simple solution if we had been able to augment your supplies. What is the current state of your kitchen stores?"

Burlon chewed on his lower lip. "Haven't you discussed that with Gredin?"

"Well, yes, but…"

Burlon let the unfinished sentence hang in the air.

Wyve sighed. "…but a second opinion can be helpful."

"And?"

"And I want to be sure that you are personally aware of where things stand."

"Why? I'm a Trader, and a Traveler. Why should I keep myself up to date on how the kitchen is stocked?"

Wyve looked amused. "Because knowledge of what your community needs makes you a better trader and a wiser traveler. And because I know you to be a curious man who prefers his own direct knowledge to the voiced opinions of others."

Burlon could find no ready reply to that.

"Moreover," said Wyve, "you are a leader. It is your nature. You are poor at following, and worse yet at following blindly. So I ask you again, what is the current state of your kitchen stores?"

Burlon sighed. "Bland and bleak. Not yet desperate, but… bland and bleak. I was counting on that Beng grain to win us time in which to explore new avenues of Trade. I wish the Mamora and the Thalken had not left so soon."

"You are regretting your decision to keep Venna's destruction a secret?"

Burlon waved a hand in annoyance. "It isn't a fact we can hide forever. I never pretended that it was. But it seemed best to be cautious about when that news was allowed to spread. I feared that some of our trading partners here would take advantage of the situation."

"And now?"

"Now, I am wondering whether we should have been frank about it, immediately. If we had been, the Mamora and the Thalken would have returned to their home worlds knowing that we were actively seeking edible tradegoods. Now, we'll have to wait through another cycle and a half of their travels before we can hope for any such items from them. And even then, we'll have to be cautious. Keegan's experiences at the Clinic have shown that truly new items will have to be tested before we dare to buy any quantity." Burlon inhaled and made himself don a brighter expression. "But I have told the Rodorno, in confidence, and they'll help, if they can. There's nothing edible in their current cargo but they've assured me they'll bring a broad sampling of items on their next trip. And there would have been no benefit in telling the Beng. It would only have amused them or raised their prices even higher." He slapped the surface of the bench with his open hand. "Gashes, Wyve, what's the point of all your security guards and monitors? None of it kept Gredin safe!"

The accusation stretched between them, quivering on the air like a rope held taut.

It was Burlon who yielded first. "Forget I said that. I'm just frustrated, with no Beng here to take it out on. Figg offered a transport pod, that night. Gredin turned it down. And it's not as if anything like the Beng attack had ever happened before."

"Still," Wyve said, "we are deeply regretful that the attack occurred, and deeply grateful that the harm she took was no worse. I have reminded her, as well, that the bracelet she accepted from us gives her the power to summon security, should the need ever arise again." He shook his head. "That said, I think we may have seen the last of the Beng here on Tradepoint."

"Really?" Burlon asked, making no attempt to hide his skepticism. "I think they'll bank on the fact that six sectora is a long time, and people's memories are short."

"*My* memory is not short, where this matter is concerned, and I have collected images and evidence that I will use against them, if they are so foolish as to return."

"In six sectora? Will you still be the Director here in six sectora?" he asked, and saw the question take Wyve aback.

"Well, if not me, then Figg." Wyve leaned forward in his chair. "How does Gredin seem to you? She has seemed quite energetic at our morning meetings, of late, but those come early in the day. Does she still seem well when you encounter her later, in the enclave? This odd matter that she and Figg discussed, this loss of… of…"

"Hlinga," Burlon provided. "Yes, she seems much better, though there is yet room for improvement. A fair number of the other Bereft seem steadier, as well, although it is early to call what they are doing a success."

Success or not, there was apparently a great deal of mating going on. But there was no need to say so to Wyve.

Still, it struck a different thought, something he *did* intend to share with Wyve. "You may recall that I wasn't at the reception, on the night of the Trisectoriana…"

"Indeed. We were told that you had found your chosen and entered your *dydanin*."

"Yes. Chenna is my Chosen. Two days ago, our dydanin came to its end… and soon Chenna will give birth to our child."

"Burlon! That is wonderful news. I am astonished and delighted. My best wishes to you and to her." His forehead furrowed. "You say that she will give birth to your child 'soon.' How soon do you mean?"

Burlon stopped to figure. "Chenna's first glim appeared two days ago, and so the child will be born on the hundred-and eighty-ninth day of our time on Tradepoint, if we have not departed for New Venna by then."

Wyve blinked. "I don't understand. How can you be so precise?"

"Easily. Two days ago was our twenty-third day on Tradepoint.

And the child will come forth one hundred and sixty-six days after the appearance of Chenna's first glim. It is simple addition."

Wyve looked skeptical. "It was simple addition on your home world."

"What do you mean?"

"You say 'a day,' as if that is a measured item upon which we can all agree. But a F'lalan day is much shorter than a Prett day, and I have no precise knowledge of how long a day would be on the Shodekekeen homeworld, or the Polpethtiran. You are confident that your chosen's body will accomplish the growth of your child in one hundred and sixty-six Vennan days, and that may very well be so. But how does a Vennan day compare to the length of a day here on Tradepoint?"

Burlon felt as if the hard metal floor beneath his feet had suddenly become soft and unstable, like the ground on the edge of a bog. "They have always seemed much the same, to me. Gredin comes to speak with you and Figg quite early in the morning, and yet I have not found her nodding off like a F'lala over her evening meal."

"A good point. But 'much the same' is not 'precisely the same.' If there is even a small difference between our respective day-spans, that difference will multiply itself over the hundred and sixty-six days of your baby's development, making it a near certainty that this child will not arrive precisely when you think it will."

Burlon scowled. It was a worrisome thought. He had never given much thought to babies and their births, but it had been reassuring to think that he could name the very day on which the child and Chenna would separate. It that was untrue on Tradepoint, what else that he had not anticipated might differ?

"Also, if you will be patient with me," Wyve requested, "what is a *glim*? I have never heard anyone speak that word before."

"Oh! Your pardon. A glim is simply a mark, a small fleck of color on the skin. When a Vennan woman is creating a child, little glim appear on her cheeks and nose. They are the earliest sign that a child has begun."

"And do these *glim* disappear, once the child is born?"

"Of course. Otherwise, you would see them on the faces of a great many of the women in the community."

Wyve looked suddenly stricken. "So you are telling me that a great many of the women in your current community here…"

Burlon realized where Wyve's words were headed. "Yes," he affirmed somberly. "They had children, back on Venna. Some were infants, others were younglings, and many were adults with children of their own. All gone, now. All returned to the Source."

Wyve shook his head slowly, then brightened. "The entire community must be thrilled to hear that your chosen is going to have a child."

"Thrilled… and yet saddened. As her body swells, it will make them recall when they had that same experience, and our child will be a sharp reminder of their loss."

"And yet it is a very hopeful sign," Wyve insisted. "The first step toward increasing the number of your survivors."

"Yes. All will see it so. But, for many, it will be a sweetness laced with salt."

"Indeed, I can see why that will be true. But let me assure you that this is news of unalloyed happiness to me, as it will be to Figg. We will do all that we can to help."

Burlon wondered if he had misheard. "Help?" he echoed, smiling. "I assure you, Wyve, the deed has been accomplished. No 'help' is required."

But Wyve did not return his smile. "Nothing must go wrong with this pregnancy. If there are foods or medicines that Chenna requires while the baby is developing, we will do all within our power to procure them for her."

"Medicines? Have you not understood what is happening, Wyve? Chenna is not ill. She is creating our child."

"Yes. And that will be the work of over a hundred days, by your own admission. We would gladly examine her at the Clinic, to assure that everything is–"

"No. There is no need. Babies are not a cause for worry. They are a cause for joy."

Wyve studied his hands, then met Burlon's gaze. "May it be so, my friend. May mother and child both pass unscathed through this time of development. But surely you – or the older women in your community, at least – must realize that it is not always so."

"But it *is* always so. What concerns you, Wyve? What is it that you fear?"

Wyve eyed him with an air of suspicion. "You are telling me that every Vennan pregnancy ends with the birth of a healthy child to a healthy mother?"

"Of course. Why would it not be so?"

"And what if a child is born who is not healthy, or whose body is malformed? Do you end its life?"

Burlon stiffened, horrified. "What are these notions that plague you, Wyve? Is this something that befalls the Prett? I tell you clearly that it is not so for Vennans. Often, a Chosen couple must wait long and long before they are graced with a child, but once a glim appears, the result is exactly as you just put it – the birth of a healthy child to a healthy mother. How could anything less be the Power's design?"

Wyve was making visible efforts to calm himself. "I hope with all my heart that it will be so for Chenna and the child. Truly. But your lives have undergone a massive upheaval and a terrible shock. The food you eat is different. The water you drink is different. The air you breathe is different. You no longer walk freely under the Vennan sun. Chenna may be lacking a sufficiency of certain vitamins or minerals. There may be trace elements that her body requires in order to form this baby properly. For all of these reasons and more, I am anxious on Chenna's behalf, and on behalf of the child-to-be. Surely it will do no harm to have her come to the Clinic so that Binn can examine her, at intervals, and–"

"No. It would distress Chenna to no purpose. She is well. She is surrounded by the women of our House and our community, many of whom have borne children of their own. She is within easy call of our Healers, should any problem arise. But it won't."

"Burlon, I only–"

He held up his hand. "Enough, Wyve. I have shared my good news with you. You have congratulated me. We need say nothing more on the topic. Let us turn our attention, instead, to your reason for summoning me, shall we? What prompted you to inquire about our kitchen stores?"

Wyve tapped on the surface of his desk, and Burlon saw the display there alter. "I have been looking at your trading balance, now that the remaining Houses have pooled their accounts. And I have also examined the listed contents of your warehouses."

It wasn't the reply Burlon had expected. "To what end?" he asked.

"With an eye toward ensuring your self-sufficiency, if you are required to journey elsewhere before New Venna is located." He sighed. "The search hasn't yet even begun, as I understand it."

"Correct," Burlon said, the word unpleasant on his tongue. "What has happened, Wyve? Why this sudden summons?"

With a slow shake of his ponderous head, Wyve replied, "Because I had a call this morning from Pord, our Melding Mediator. He reports that certain… factions within the Vokastra are growing increasingly vocal. He suggests – not demands, but strongly suggests – that you take utmost care not to miss your upcoming delivery date regarding the geddel crystals."

Burlon found himself feeling an unexpected empathy for the Vokastra and their worry over whether this shipment of geddel crystals would be punctually delivered. Had his own fear and anger not risen in his throat when he learned that the Beng had reneged on the grain purchase he had fought so hard to obtain? Could he blame the Vokastra for their anxiety? True, he didn't altogether understand what purpose the crystals served for the Prett, but it did not appear to be a frivolous one. Nothing so elemental as food, of course, but important to them, nonetheless.

Wyve released a huff of air. "Understand, Burlon, I want you safe. I want *every* Vennan safe. If Gredin has good cause for restricting you from traveling the river, that restriction is something you should honor, not least because your chosen is now with child. But if, perhaps, Gredin is being overly cautious…" He shook his head sharply. "I want you to understand that missing a delivery would most likely result in reprisals from my government. I make no demand. But it is important that you understand my limitations. I cannot thwart their decisions, Burlon. Therefore, I want you to act prudently. But you cannot act prudently without all of the facts. I called you here today to provide you with these new facts. That is all. You hear what I am telling you?"

"I do," Burlon acknowledged. He knew something else, as well, something Wyve had forborne to point out: earlier in the day, the countback monitor displaying how many orbits remained to the Vennans had changed from green to yellow. The sight had sickened him, and it would only get worse. "You are a friend to the Vennans," he said to Wyve. "We do not doubt it. But the Vokastra rules your people. Balancing between those two realities as you do is a chancy thing." He managed a smile. "I appreciate your honesty. I will give the matter serious thought."

"I ask no more than that."

Burlon rose, and so did Wyve.

"A good day to you, Director. And if you should suddenly find that you cannot reach me, over these next few days, I trust you will not distress yourself."

Wyve gave him a long look, heavy with comprehension, then said, "Be safe, Burlon. And know that I wish you well."

[9]

0779 OF 2000 ORBITS REMAINING: 42ORANGE

"I need to talk to Gredin."

Gredin turned at the sound of the unexpected voice, and saw Keegan in the outer room, his face turned away from her, apparently addressing the wall.

"Certainly," she told him. "Come in. We'll talk."

But he stayed where he was, visible through her open doorway.

"Come in," she invited again. "Are you all right?"

"I need to talk to Gredin," he said, then shuddered. "I *can't* talk to Gredin."

"Of course you can. I'm not busy. Come and sit down. Or I'll come out there, if you'd rather."

"No."

"Why not?"

"It's taken me most of the day to get this close. I can't be in the same room with her."

That sounded like nonsense, but Keegan never spouted nonsense.

"Can you tell me why?"

"I've written things down on my *crabe*. I'm setting my *crabe* on the table here. I'm going to my room now."

"And you want me to come out and read it?"

Keegan made no reply. He simply set the *crabe* on the table and retreated to his room.

Her curiosity awakened, Gredin went out and sat down at the table, drawing the *crabe* toward her. Unused to handling it, she lifted it gingerly and tilted it until the words on the screen became visible. Keegan had typed:

Tetralanna has Silenced me from speaking to any Bereft of House Balamont –

which, of course, includes you. And she forbade me to approach you. She has

informed the Bereft of Balamont that they are not to use the new enclave. She has likely used her gyfte to Speak this order, as well, since not a single Balamont Bereft has entered the new enclave since it opened, including you. Is she preventing you from going there?

Gredin put down the *crabe*, her hands shaking with anger. "No," she announced aloud, facing the open door to Keegan's room, "Tetralanna is not preventing me. I have met elsewhere with my alliance partner, not at the new enclave. But it is intolerable for Tetralanna to set herself between other members of the House and their chance at redemption!" She stalked to Keegan's doorway, and grimaced as he backed away into the far corner of his expanded room. "You are not approaching me," she pointed out. "I am approaching you. And this ridiculous Silencing and Compulsion of hers should fade by tomorrow morning. I am very sorry you've been subjected to it. Tetralanna takes entirely too much upon herself. If she dares such a trespass again, I will have harsh words with her. But no small part of the reason she does these things is her lack of Balance. If she would only mate and improve her hlinga, she would see for herself how unacceptable her actions have become. We circle, around and around – her lack of Balance makes her refuse to take an alliance partner, and so her hlinga fades further, and so her actions become even more objectionable." Gredin ran her fingers through her curls in frustration, then dropped her hands to her sides. "Enough. I am going to change my clothes and go to the Balamont enclave. I will converse directly with any Bereft that I find there. Again, my apologies for what she has put you through. I will see you – and speak with you without her interference – in the morning."

Striding back to her own bedchamber, she looked with disapproval at her clothing choices. For an errand such as this one, where she would be exerting her authority in direct opposition to Tetralanna's, the casual traveling clothes she preferred to wear would not suffice, but she would feel pretentious if she donned the scarlet Shodekekeen gown to visit her own House's enclave. And it saddened her to think of wearing Trethen's lavender gown, now stripped of its geddel crystals in order to placate the Vokastra…

Which left the teal and bronze garment that Ingarra had made for her, which she had worn on the night of the Beng's attack. Prett Security had recovered the jacket from the bio-mist chamber where she had abandoned it after her assault. They even found the button the Beng had torn off and returned both items to her so that Ingarra could mend them. The fabric no longer showed any sign of damage or blood, but a disagreeable chill crept over Gredin as she stepped into the outfit for the first time since that night.

After a moment's hesitation, she decided not to don the jacket. Better to wear First Speaker's hlette in plain sight. Then, to counteract the dark memories the outfit engendered, she fastened her flamestone pendant around her neck, and felt the tension ease from her body as the stone settled against her skin. The Beng were gone. She was safe, here within the Vennan enclave. Indeed, she was safe on all of Tradepoint. The Beng had taken nothing from her but her braids, and the braids would grow back, eventually. Her hlao, her hlette, her pendant, and her stones were all safe, in defiance of the Beng's wishes. The Beng were gone, and she remained.

Secure in that knowledge, she left her room, crossed the reception hall, passed through the deactivated Enclave 1 antechamber, entered the interior corridor, turned to her right, and walked past Enclave 3 to the entrance to Enclave 5, which had become the exclusive residence of House Balamont.

The hour was late and the outer doors had been closed for the night, but a touch of Gredin's palm was enough to trigger the door panels to open and admit her. Inside, the enclave was still thoroughly lit. The harsh overhead lights, however, had been replaced by dozens of robustly stoked luminth. By their glow, she surveyed the stacks of nests that rose up before her.

Many of the nests were twice the normal width, their entrances off-center, indicating that a Chosen couple resided there. Tonight, she had no need to call on kinsmen who still possessed their Chosens, although she hoped to look in on Ingarra and Beda when her current task was done.

She knew that an effort had been made to move as many of the Bereft as possible down to ground-level quarters, so she approached the first single doorway in sight and, when she reached its concealing panel of cloth, said softly, "May I talk with you? It is Gredin."

She heard movement inside, but no one came to admit her.

"A calm night to you," she said. "Perhaps we can talk tomorrow." Then she moved on to the next panel and tried again. "May I talk with you? It is Gredin."

Again, no reply.

It was not until she approached the fifth entryway that someone responded, retracting the cloth panel a few scant inches. The woman's face was unfamiliar, her eyes red from weeping, and the dark circles beneath them attested to a string of broken nights. "What do you have to say?" the woman demanded, making no move to allow her inside.

"I am Gredin."

"I know who you are. Why are you here?"

"To try to help you."

"Can you return my Chosen to me?"

"Your Chosen, like my own, has returned to the Source. They cannot return."

"Then go away and leave me in peace."

"But you are not at peace. What is your name?"

"Tharnin."

"Tell me, Tharnin, what is your gyfte?"

"Ask Keegan te Fliss. He knows. Be on your way now. I need my bed."

"You need to restore your hlinga."

Tharnin answered by letting the cloth fall back into place, shutting Gredin out.

"A calm night to you, Tharnin," Gredin said to the barrier, and walked toward the next doorway. Before she could reach it, however, a group of people – a dozen or more – stepped around the far end of the block of nests and came toward her. None of their faces were familiar to her, but it was clear that she was their goal. Tightly bunched, they came closer, and it wasn't until they were only a few steps away that she realized they were not slackening their pace. Instead, pivoting, they insinuated themselves between her and the line of nests, forcing her to back up hastily to avoid being trodden upon.

Gathering her wits and her Focus, she said sharply, "Stop there."

The force of her words made them stumble to a halt, but they shifted restlessly. A man near the front of the group pointed at her. "You need to leave. No one asked you here. No one wants you here."

Indignation heated her response. "This is my House. I am Gredin te Balamont."

"I know who you are," he sneered. "I also know where you sleep at night – and it isn't here among us. You act as if you belong to this House only when it suits your purposes. The rest of the time, you are far too busy claiming titles for yourself and ordering people about. Well, we have no appetite for that, here. You are young and head-strong, and we have no need of you. Be on your way."

"The only title I bear claimed *me*," she said, gesturing to First Speaker's hlette. "And the reason for my presence here tonight is to offer encouragement and assistance to my fellow Bereft. I have only just learned that no one from my House has yet availed themselves of an alliance partner, and it saddens me beyond bearing to think that my kinsmen will falter and fail, while the Bereft of other Houses regain their hlinga and reassert mastery over their gyftes."

"Our Bereft are our own affair," the man said.

It seemed to Gredin that a man who spoke with such authority was not likely one of the Bereft. That made him a more formidable opponent, but it also gave her hope that she would be able to reason with him, if he was in Balance. "Might I ask your name, kinsman?"

"Marakett."

The name seemed familiar. Had Keegan said something about this man? If so, what?

And then the recollection came to her, words that Keegan had confided on the morning that House Balamont's volunteer was to be named: "*...Last night, the position was being contested by Marakett, Crovek, and Ibbin. Now Crovek has stepped aside, but a choice is still being made between Marakett and Ibbin...*" Instead, the position had gone to Tetralanna.

"Well then, Marakett," Gredin said, "am I correct in assuming that yours will be the first name on the list of individuals who volunteer to be paired with a Bereft, to undertake their personal care for the remainder of your time and theirs in this life? You will need to keep that person with you always, for they will be unable to Send or Fetch or contact your public mind. You will need to Freshen them, and care for their clothing, and monitor the temperature of their food, and Convert their waste, and do your best to solace them when they are overwhelmed by the grief that results from their inability to exercise their gyfte. You do understand that this is where your decision leads, yes? And that you are making that decision not only for yourself but on behalf of all of the Chosens and Unchosens within the House? There are two of you for every one Bereft, so you will have someone with whom to share this responsibility, but it will occupy much of your time and theirs for–"

Marakett backed up a step, looking appalled, and the people with him began to mutter uneasily.

"Has Tetralanna left you unaware of all of this?" Gredin asked, relentless. "Or are you aware, but intending to turn your back on a third of your kinsmen, leaving them to their fate? Of course, that will not be easy to do, living in such close quarters and sharing table with them at meals. And it is a great sadness, because their only error was to come to Tradepoint without their Chosen." Gredin spread her hands and reached out to him. "Would it not be better for everyone, Bereft and

Balanced alike, to encourage each House member whose Chosen has returned to the Source to at least try taking an alliance partner? It is the only path that can replenish their hlinga and restore their Balance, returning the mastery of their gyfte. How can that be anything but the Power's will?"

She became aware that a scattering of people had emerged from the ground-floor nests and were standing in silence, listening to her. Carefully, she kept her gaze trained on Marakett, but she pitched her voice to reach the listeners, as well.

"Three days ago, every Bereft registered their palm print, along with their name and House, at the new enclave dedicated to their use. Any who wish to try an alliance partner, or who simply wish to converse with other Bereft who have already done so, have the ability to admit themselves to that enclave at any time, simply by pressing their hand to the panel. And they can leave it whenever they wish. But I speak from direct experience, as well. My Focus and Control were draining from me, and my ability to exercises my gyftes, both large and small, was becoming unreliable. I felt cold, much of the time, and I was easily moved to anger or tears. That has all changed for the better since I took an alliance partner. But Tetralanna refuses to do so, which means that you are listening to a woman who is falling farther and farther from Balance. Please take care when listening to her advice and be thoughtful about how you proceed. All here in this enclave are members of my House, as well as being part of our larger community of survivors, and my true hope is for us all to be safe, well, and secure in our gyftes. Happiness is too much to hope for, so soon after the losses we have suffered. But I would at least wish that we be handed no reason for our current sorrow to increase, as will doubtless happen if any of us lose access to our gyftes."

Many had now come out to listen, and some were weeping softly. To release them gently without affrighting them, she said, "If you will excuse me, Marakett, I am going deeper into the enclave now, to visit with my Guides for a short time before I retire for the evening. My thanks for listening to my words, as I have listened to yours. A calm night to you all." And she skirted his group, walking toward the back wall where Ingarra and Beda had their new nest.

They let her pass, although several of them watched her sharply. Her other listeners, the phantom Bereft who had appeared in their doorways while she spoke, had all withdrawn, but Gredin was comforted to know her message had been received by many of those who most needed to hear it. She hoped they would discuss her words amongst themselves, and that a few might find the courage to try and improve their situation with an alliance partner. That might well be all they needed – a few. If those few had a positive experience, they would share the news with the others, and…

"Where? Where is she?!"

The words cut sharply through the air. Gredin looked back over her shoulder just in time to see Tetralanna come boiling around the corner of the front line of nests, every angle of her body bespeaking outrage.

"You!" she shouted, pointing at Gredin as she approached. "I want you out of here *now*!"

Gredin stood firm. Ignoring Tetralanna's demand, she responded in a much quieter voice, one that nonetheless could be clearly heard throughout the enclave. Pointing her own finger at Tetralanna, Gredin said, "You were wrong to Silence the historian, Keegan te Fliss. He is only working to protect the interests of House Balamont's Bereft. If you take such an unfair action again, I will–"

"Will what?" Tetralanna interrupted, stopping before she came within Gredin's reach. "Silence *me*, in your turn?"

Gredin shook her head. "Tetralanna, why are we at odds on this matter? Can you not see that the Bereft of this House are suffering? Can you not feel the truth of that decline within yourself? Are you truly content to allow your gyftes to slip from your grasp forever? And even if you are, can you not understand that the other Bereft have a right to make that decision for themselves?"

"Stop filling our ears with your nonsense. Leave us. You no longer have a place here."

"Now it is you who speaks nonsense. Of course I have a place here. This is the House of my birth. I am Gredin te Balamont. Where I am currently lodged does not change that. Our kinsmen who are already Chosen or Bereft will always be of Balamont, as well. The only members whose House might change are the Unchosen among us, since they might find their Chosen elsewhere and decide to align with their new Chosen's House."

"More of your wild talk," Tetralanna protested. "Without your encouragement, Burlon and Chenna would never have done such an aberrant thing!"

"And yet, as the direct result of that 'aberrant thing,' the Power is now blessing them with a child." Gredin waved her hand. "But that is another matter altogether. The important thing, tonight, is for the Bereft of Balamont to be encouraged to avail themselves of the new enclave, where they can find an alliance partner to help them. Time is passing, and time matters. The longer they wait, the more their hlinga will have ebbed and the farther from Balance they will become. If they go to the enclave and try, and decide afterwards that it was a mistake, they need only abstain and they will soon lose whatever small benefit they gained and be back where they began. But if they go to the enclave and try, and find afterwards that their condition has improved, moving them closer to the Power and better able to exercise their gyfte, how can that possibly be a bad outcome?"

Tetralanna's glare was poisonous. "I am sickened that you would stand there and use my hlette to strengthen you while you utter such twisted notions. Return it to me now! Or, if you will not, then at least have the decency to go away and leave us our privacy."

By now, Marakett and his group had gathered at Tetralanna's back, and several of them added their voices to Tetralanna's, demanding Gredin's departure.

She considered insisting on her visit to Beda and Ingarra but decided, instead, that more could be gained through a graceful exit. "The hlette is not yours," Gredin said. "It belongs to no individual. For the time being, however, it has elected to reside with me. I will leave this enclave now so that everyone may settle themselves for the night, but I will be back, and I will see you all when I address you tomorrow at midday meal. In the meantime, I encourage all of you – and especially the Bereft – to think upon my words. Right now, the choice is still our own. Soon, however, time will make those decisions for us in ways that we may deeply regret. If you feel conflicted as to which path is right and good, select the path that brings you closer to the Power and your gyfte."

She took a last look around. Although many of the faces appeared as closed against her as Tetralanna's, she believed that a few showed signs of deep and conflicted thought.

"A calm night to you all," she said, and the crowd parted in silence, allowing her a clear path to the enclave doors.

[10]

0765 OF 2000 ORBITS REMAINING: 6BLUE

It was no longer night, but not quite morning.

"Go back to sleep," Burlon murmured. He pressed a kiss to the lobe of Chenna's ear and felt her quiver in reaction. That, in turn, sent a wave of arousal through his own body, a sensation so sweet that he nearly climbed back beneath the coverlet to join with her again.

But no. The day would be beginning soon. Already, Gredin would be sitting down to her daily conference with Wyve and Figg. And that meant that he needed to get started, if he was going to be on his way before she returned to the enclave.

Chenna's hand rose to cup his jaw. "When will you be back?" she murmured.

"Soon. Not tomorrow, but the day after. Today, I will Travel to Sprygale. Tomorrow will be spent in formal delivery of the *timte* gifts, and settlement of the geddel crystal payment. Sprygalians are a strange lot – you cannot hurry through a Trade with them without giving offense, and it is essential for our community that they remain willing to continue the geddel crystal exchanges. Then, the next morning, I will return."

She sat up. "Here. Lean down. Let me tie your hlao." When she had done so, she sank down again and murmured, "I am afraid for you."

"Don't be silly. Everything will be fine. I have First Traveler's hlette."

She whispered something in reply, but the coverlet muffled her words.

He bent and, this time, kissed her temple. "I will return in two days' time to count your glim," he promised, and left her there.

It wasn't until he Sent himself down to floor level of Enclave 6, which House Laith shared with Indirin and Torr, that his mind unscrambled Chenna's half-heard words. *I have First Traveler's hlette*, he had said, to reassure her.

And her whispered answer, all but lost in the bedding, had been: *So did Cirin.*

Slivers and scrapes.

He hated the fact that she was worried. But the best cure was for him to make a speedy trip and return to her safely. And he still had two errands to carry out before he could depart.

His first destination was directly across the corridor, where House Balamont resided in Enclave 5. Not that he intended to enter. To do so would be tempting trouble. He had absolutely no wish to start this day in a confrontation with Tetralanna. Instead, stopping short of the Balamont antechamber, he closed his eyes in concentration and reached out with his public mind.

=Ingarra? Ingarra te Balamont?=

No response.

Focusing, he tried again. =Ingarra?=

Contact flared to life. =Yes. Here. What is wrong?=

=Nothing is wrong,= he soothed apologetically. =It is Burlon. I am sorry to wake you, but I have come for the quilt and coat.=

=In the middle of the night?=

=Early morning is nearly upon us. I regret disturbing your rest, but…=

He received the clear sense of a sigh. =I will bring them out,= Ingarra said.

=I am grateful.=

=You should be,= she grumbled, but there was no great heat in her words.

Before long, the Balamont doors slid open, and Ingarra emerged, her hands empty.

Burlon eyed her with alarm. "Please don't tell me that they aren't ready!"

She gave him a patient smile. "Come with me," she said, and walked up the hallway to the entry to Enclave 1.

It wasn't a place he wanted to go. Not yet. If Gredin should return early from her meeting with Wyve and Figg, on this of all days, he didn't want to be drawn into an energy-wasting argument with her. He had only planned to enter Enclave 1 at the last moment, when he could simply step up onto the departure dais and leave.

Of course, at need, he could depart from anywhere. But Travelers were trained to develop rituals that helped them Focus as they launched themselves onto the River. At home, the Travelers of House Bentain had all departed from the center of an elaborate mosaic set into the floor of a special chamber. Here on Tradepoint, the departure dais served the same purpose. And its bio-mist offered an additional protection, since he encountered other races here and had no wish to spread any contagion he or they might have encountered.

But it was increasingly clear that Enclave 1 played an integral part in Ingarra's plans. They went inside, and Burlon removed two small luminth from his pocket. Handing one to Ingarra, he powered the other, and followed as she headed straight for the departure dais. Had she left the quilt and coat there, ready for departure? He hoped not. It would be disastrous if anything harmful befell those Trading items at this late date… But no, as he approached the dais, Burlon could see that it was clear of all objects, as was right and proper. So where, then, was Ingarra taking him?

She veered to the right, and Burlon's breathing quickened nervously as he realized that she was leading him straight to the hallway that led to the chamber that Gredin and Keegan shared, as well as Keegan's former room, which had been the site of his own dydanin with Chenna.

And indeed, to his astonishment, it proved to be the dydanin room to which Ingarra was leading him. "It wasn't in use," she explained as she opened the door and reached inside to turn on the bright overhead lights. "Come and see how everything turned out."

With a sigh of relief, Burlon slipped in after her and closed the door behind himself, then turned… and froze where he stood, faced with a stunning display of color and workmanship.

The *timte* quilt was spread over the room's sleepmat, dwarfing the foam pad. At its heart, it depicted a massive sun, its center made up of concentric circles in varying hues of red, gold, orange and yellow that seemed to vibrate with intensity. From the outermost edges of that sun, sinuous tongues of flame wavered in molten curves, dancing out in all directions against a background sky that varied through a dozen different shades of purple and dark blue. And over it all, in matched shades of threaded stitchery, hundreds of tiny designs covered the fabric, inviting the eye to examine the quilt more closely.

"Help me turn it over," Ingarra said.

Burlon had been so taken with the front that he had neglected to give a thought to the quilt's back. Curious now, he assisted Ingarra in flipping the quilt over and smoothing it out to its full dimensions again.

The reverse side was a startling contrast to the front. Instead of a single, massive sun, and a series of circles and curves, the back of the quilt was a study in crisp, diagonal lines depicting dozens of shimmering fabric 'jewels,' set off by a soft-napped black latticework that contained tiny, unexpected flecks of vivid color.

Burlon wasn't sure how long he stared at the quilt before he could finally force his gaze from it and turn his attention to what Ingarra referred to as 'the moon coat.'

The back of the coat depicted a scene: a full moon shining down on a tumbling waterfall, seen through the delicate branches of a flowering tree. The background fabric was a rich, deep purple. The moon was silver-white. The lavender of the tumbling waterfall was interwoven with silver 'reflections' from the moon, and the multitude of tiny blossoms bore petals of pink, lavender, purple, and white, rising from leaves in shades of soft grey-green from moss to mint.

The front of the coat bore a crescent moon, high on the left breast. The rest of the front, along with the sleeves, bore occasional sprays of blossoms and leaves, and the hem of the coat and the top edges of the two commodious pockets were embroidered with blossoms, as well.

The coat had a tall collar. And draped around that collar was a long scarf in shades of lavender, white and pink, with a few bold dashes of purple woven through it.

"I asked Nunellin te Vell to weave the scarf," Ingarra said. "She is a wonder at the loom. I had her make it quite long so that, on bitter days, the girl will be able to wear it over her head with plenty left over to keep her throat warm." She shifted slightly. "Will they do, Burlon? Are they enough?"

He turned to her, stunned by the doubt he heard in her tone, and took both her hands in his. "They are beyond anything I could have hoped for," he told her fervently. "You have surpassed my every expectation. I am deeply in your debt, as is the entire community. Indeed, you are setting my mind alight with ideas for future projects… but we will discuss that on another day. For now, please know that I am deeply delighted by what you have created. Return to your bedmat, which Beda has no doubt kept warm for you, confident that you have done a wonderful thing."

"Silly man," she said, blushing with pleasure. "Travel well and return to us safely. We will keep a friendly eye on Chenna until you are back to do so for yourself." With that, she crossed her palms, bowed her head briefly, and left him there.

Immediately, Burlon set himself the task of folding the quilt and, separately, the coat. Then, Focusing, he Fetched two large carrysacks from the shelf where such things were stored in House Bentain's warehouse. No doubt Naria te Bentain would be quick to tell him that he no longer had a right to do so; she disapproved openly of Gredin's views on 'community.' But no one else was Traveling anywhere, so the sacks wouldn't be needed. He had not yet learned where House Laith stored such things, and he had no time for petty arguments between the Houses. His trip to Sprygale was for the benefit of all.

The sturdy carrysacks materialized at his feet, and he bundled the quilt into the green one and the coat and scarf into the blue one, nodding approvingly when the items fit neatly into the space available. It was part of a Trader's gyfte to have a keen sense of volume and space, and he knew all of the Bentain carrysacks well from long use. Folding the quilt and coat had been enough to give him an accurate notion of the size of sack they each required.

Only one more task stood between him and his departure. Securing the fastenings on the loaded carrysacks, he left them, turned off the lights, and tiptoed out to where the corridor met the reception hall. Gazing out into what had been a vast darkness when he and Ingarra first arrived, he now saw lights showing from the kitchen area.

Good. Miri was up.

It took no real effort at all to Send himself across the reception hall to the glow of the kitchen doorway. Entering, he said, "Good day to you, Miri."

Two short days ago, he would have worried that his sudden arrival would upset her. But Miri, true to her word, had bravely been among the very first to avail herself of an alliance partner, and the improvement was already perceptible.

She set down her cup at the sound of his voice in the otherwise-empty kitchen, and turned with a ready smile to face him. "And a good day to you, Burlon. What has you up so early?"

This was the tricky part. He didn't want to compromise Miri or trouble her conscience, and so he simply said, "I have an odd morning ahead of me, one that will keep me away from this morning's circle of five. I am here to see what I might be able to glean to eat now, instead. Perhaps a few *chingee* wafers that I can tuck in my pocket?"

Miri made a wry face. "It is your misfortune that you've come so early. Nothing fresh has been baked yet. But we can see what is left from last night. And, as you say, there are the *chingee* wafers. I've set those safely away until the Polpethtira return with enough for us to serve everyone, but no one has a better right to them than you." She opened a series of deep drawers, glancing into each. "With no morning or afternoon snack, people bring bigger appetites to evening meal," she said in apology, "and those of us whose hlinga is improving find that we come to table more eagerly, as well. But there are always at least a few things left over, for we would never want to find ourselves unable to fill the last few plates."

With deft moves, she assembled a small meal for him: three slender d'limten breadtwists, a bowl of what looked like pureed vegetables, thinned with water to a soup-like consistency and a pair of *chingee* wafers.

"Here," she said, glancing down at the bowl until the soup in it began to steam. "These should tide you over until midday meal."

Wishing there were more, Burlon forced a smile and thanked her. She was right that what she had just presented to him was sufficient food for a quiet morning on Tradepoint. It was his own fault that he hadn't been honest with her about how much more demanding than usual his tasks would be.

Sticking stubbornly to his original plan, he drank the soup, relishing the flavor of the kuma leaves with which it was spiced, and ate the breadtwists, then tucked one *chingee* wafer in his pocket and bit a corner off of the other. "Give my best to the others at the meeting," he said.

"I will," she promised. "If you share midday meal with Keegan, I'm sure he will tell you all that you missed."

Burlon smiled and nodded but he said nothing, knowing that another two days would pass before he had a chance to catch up on the latest decisions. He contented himself with saying, "Thank you for the meal. I will see you later." And then, with a nod of farewell to Miri, he Sent himself back to the dydanin room, where his carrysacks awaited.

Arriving there, he took a short while to calm himself and finish chewing the little mouthful of *chingee*. Then, with the soup warming his insides, he picked up the carrysacks, one in each hand, and walked through the darkness to the steps of the departure dais. There was still only a small glow of light from the kitchens, so the other kitchen

Tenders had not yet arrived to begin the preparation of morning meal for the community.

First Traveler's hlette pulsed and warmed around his upper arm as he stepped onto the dais, as if it sensed the journey ahead and was eager for it. The dome shifted into place. The bio-mist descended. Burlon devoted one last thought of rueful longing to Chenna, torn to think that he must leave someone so precious to him behind in order to exercise his gyftes. But then the hlette pulsed again, and he turned his attention fully to the joy of the present moment as he inhaled, Focused, and launched himself upon the River, bound at last for Sprygale.

[11]

0761 OF 2000 ORBITS REMAINING: 10PURPLE

She was late.

Miri took a firmer hold on the shallow-rimmed plate in her hands and hoped that her food offering, along with a sincere apology, would be enough to smooth any irritation the others felt about her tardiness. She hurried into the now-familiar room… and stopped short, as three faces turned to her.

Three faces, not four. It felt odd not having Burlon at the table, his level gaze friendly, even though she had known ahead of time that he would be absent from today's meeting. However, to her relief, she was able to calmly smile, rather than feel flustered at being the center of everyone's attention. *The benefits of an alliance partner.*

"Your pardon for my late arrival." Miri placed the pretty plate with its offering in the middle of the metal table, then took her usual stool. "I couldn't resist waiting for these to finish baking. Please, try them and tell me how they taste to you."

As they did so, Miri looked around the small table, eager for the others' responses. She was relieved to see that Sill and Keegan did not seem unduly disturbed by her tardiness. They both offered her a ready smile before turning their attention to the food she had brought.

Gredin, however, looked out of sorts. A frown pleated her forehead, and her lips were tightly compressed. Miri felt a frisson of apprehension. Gredin was her friend and fellow Bereft, but perhaps she shouldn't have let her delight in being so easily able to exercise her gyfte this morning cause her to tarry in the kitchens.

Full bowls of porridge and cups of water sat before each of them, untouched. Gredin, along with the others, had patiently waited to begin the morning meal so that they could all eat together, as was their custom. No wonder Gredin looked displeased. She was likely hungry, as well as annoyed by the delay.

"What are these?" Keegan asked, selecting a small, golden square from the dish.

"Baked benroot brushed with spiced oil."

Keegan popped the small square into his mouth and chewed. "Delicious, Miri. And so crisp!"

Sill nodded. "I agree. Normally, I don't care for benroot, but these have quite a nice texture and they're full of flavor."

"I thought we had finished off our supply of benroot," Gredin said. She chewed the vegetable carefully, her eyes narrowed in concentration. Miri suddenly recalled how refined Gredin's sense of taste had proven to be, that first day on Tradepoint when the dinner offering had been various filled, savory pastries being tested for the reception. How long ago that seemed. They had all been different people then.

"We did," Miri confirmed. "This is newly harvested benroot from the Prett Growing area. There wasn't enough of this first offering to make a meal of it for everyone, although there will be plenty in another day or two, according to Beda. So I experimented. The other kitchen Tenders and I want to be ready when the harvest is brought to us. These just came out of the ovens, which is why I was late in arriving. I wanted all of you to be the first to taste them."

"How will you serve them?" Gredin asked.

Miri smiled. Oh, she had missed this feeling of satisfaction and confidence that resulted from the exercise of her gyfte. "We plan to give everyone a small plate of them, instead of a d'limten roll, to accompany midday meal. It should make a welcome change." She smiled as she saw Keegan and Sill reach eagerly for a second square.

"I'm so pleased you like them. It's too bad Burlon is not here to try them."

Irritation returned to Gredin's face at the mention of Burlon's name. Miri watched as Gredin eased a hand into the pocket of her travel pants, and heard the familiar faint *clicks* as the stones in Gredin's pouch slipped past each other beneath her restless fingers.

"Even during his dydanin, Burlon was never this late," Sill commented. "Would you like me to contact his private mind and ask what is keeping him?"

"Please," Gredin said.

Miri blinked. Had Burlon expected her to tell the others he would not be attending this morning's meeting? She quickly cast her mind back to the early hour in the kitchen when he had appeared, and their short conversation.

"Wait," Miri said, again becoming the reluctant center of attention. "I spoke with Burlon earlier, before the community awoke, and he said he would be absent from our meeting today."

"Why did he tell you and not me?" Gredin asked, now looking thoroughly annoyed.

Miri flushed. "Likely because you were already at your meeting with the Director. All I know for certain is that he approached me in the kitchens and asked for something to eat. He said he had an odd morning ahead of him. I just assumed he had an early Trade meeting and would miss morning meal, so I gave him the best of what I had on hand. It wasn't much."

Sill sighed and shook her head. "He is not responding to my mind touch, Gredin."

"I can contact Chenna, if you wish," Keegan offered. "She should have knowledge of his whereabouts."

Gredin did not respond. Head down, she seemed oblivious to their words as she withdrew the pouch from her pocket.

As Miri watched closely, Gredin loosened the drawstrings of the little pouch and slowly stirred the stones inside it with her forefinger. Then Gredin nodded, as if answering a question, and poured them into her hand. Head bowed, she studied them intently as she shifted them to and fro between her cupped hands.

A taut silence filled the room. Gredin seemed mesmerized by what she held, as if the faint chinking caused by the shifting stones were some language only she could understand.

Miri caught a glimpse of flashing colors as Gredin suddenly spilled the stones across the surface of the table, toward the spot Burlon normally occupied. The abrupt movement caused Miri to flinch, but she made no move to interfere with the tumbling stones.

Keegan watched, open-mouthed and wide-eyed.

Sill was a pool of stillness. Was she using her gyfte of Memory, Miri wondered, to capture this strange behavior on Gredin's part?

The polished stones clattered loudly against the metal surface of the table as they rolled, miraculously avoiding bowls and cups and spoons, then came to rest. But one careened off the table and landed in front of the door to the reception hall.

Gredin slumped on her stool, her hands braced against the tabletop, making no move to regather the stones.

"What…?" Miri started to ask, concerned for Gredin, who was pale, her breathing rapid in the silence. Rising, Miri picked up the cup of water at Gredin's place and held it to her friend's lips. "Drink," she urged, and waited as Gredin released her white-knuckled grip on the table edge to raise first one, then both shaky hands to the cup.

Caught between concern and relief, Miri monitored Gredin carefully as she took quick gulps of the water.

Silently, Keegan got up from his stool and retrieved the stone that had fallen to the floor.

Not fallen, Miri amended, the tumble of bright stones clear in her mind. *Flown.* That stone had seemed to have a life of its own, barely touching the table before flying off on its own trajectory.

Keegan picked up the stone that lay in front of the door to the corridor and placed it gently on the surface of the table in front of Gredin. With the edge of one hand, he carefully swept the spray of other stones into a neat pile in front of Gredin, then nudged the errant stone closer to the pile.

The sight of them seemed to rouse Gredin. With steadier hands, she set the cup aside and pointed at the stone Keegan had retrieved.

"Burlon has gone to Sprygale," she announced, in a thin, dispirited voice.

Had the stone spoken to her? Miri wondered. If so, it was in a voice only Gredin could hear. The stone itself seemed innocuous, although it was pretty, containing multiple shades of red and pink, with inclusions resembling leaves and fern-like trees. Miri had never seen its like before. If she indulged her imagination, it made her think of some wild place at sunset.

"Sprygale?" Keegan asked. "What makes you think such a thing, Gredin?"

Miri noted that color was returning to Gredin's face, although she took another long sip of water before responding to Keegan's query. When Gredin set the cup down again, Miri refilled it, then cooled the water, with a flick of her newly returned Balance.

"The stone told me. But if you need confirmation, I will contact Ingarra."

Sill looked puzzled. "Why would Ingarra know anything of Burlon's plans?"

"Because," Gredin said, "if Burlon has gone to Sprygale, he would not leave without the *timte* quilt and coat." She took a deep breath. "A moment, please, while I contact her, and then I will open my mind to all of you so that you may share our mind-speech."

It didn't take long.

=Ingarra?=

=Niflin! Fair morning.= Ingarra's cheerful response was astonishingly prompt.

=And to you. Tell me, please, did Burlon te Laith approach you, this morning?=

=Yes, quite early. So early, in fact, that I nearly didn't answer his mind touch.=

=What did he want?=

=The *timte* coat and quilt. Did I tell you Nunellin made a beautiful scarf to wear with the coat? They look stunning together. Burlon was quite pleased.=

Miri could taste the happy pride in Ingarra's response through the link Gredin shared with the three of them.

=It seems Burlon made an early start for Sprygale.=

=Early enough that I was thankful to return to my bed next to Beda and sleep a bit longer, afterward. The new bed cushion is so comfortable, it is hard to leave it.=

=My thanks, Ingarra. A good day to you.=

=And to you, nifflin.=

The loving warmth of the contact faded as Gredin terminated the mind touch.

"Are you now persuaded that Burlon has Travelled the River to Sprygale?" Gredin asked softly, and reached yet again for her cup of water.

"Yes, of course. But I don't understand why he would defy you and leave without permission," Keegan said, clearly troubled by the turn of events.

"Nor do I," Sill said. "I will have strong words for him when he returns. Burlon wears First Traveler's hlette and Travels a familiar path on the River, so he will likely come to no harm... and yet I worry," she confessed.

So do we all, Miri thought, stricken. *Why didn't I give him better food for his morning meal? Will that offering be enough to sustain him on the River?*

Sill broke the quiet that had followed her confession, jolting Miri from her anxious thoughts. "Gredin, would you enlighten me about your stones?" Sill reached out with a single fingertip and touched the 'Sprygale' stone. "How do you know what messages the stones intend to impart?"

"They are mine," Gredin said simply. "Most of them have been with me since I was a child. I find comfort when I hold them – doubly so, now that Venna is no more. Sometimes, their shapes or colors remind me of people, or of places. And sometimes they tell me things. Not literally, of course, but I experience a kind of... of...

knowing. Today, that stone told me that Burlon had gone to Sprygale."

Sill regarded Gredin thoughtfully. "A channel for your intuition, perhaps." She turned to Keegan. "Have you ever heard of such a gyfte?"

"No. But there are many tales I have not heard. Fliss was only one House of many, and I did not often leave it."

Miri could see that Gredin considered the subject of her stones an uncomfortable one. Perhaps she felt they were a private matter. Or perhaps she simply didn't want to deal with the criticism or ridicule that public knowledge of her stones might create within the community.

Well, I can provide a diversion of sorts. "Gredin, shall we move on to today's agenda, now that Burlon's whereabouts have been confirmed? I am sure there are important topics for us to discuss."

With gentle hands, Gredin herded the stones into the little pouch and secured the drawstrings before slipping the pouch back into her pocket. All of her movements with the stones, Miri realized, had the look of actions taken countless times in the past.

Gredin looked soberly around the table. "You're right, Miri. To begin, there is a new development with Tetralanna and House Balamont of which I need to make you all aware."

"And we should eat," Miri said, mock-sternly. "No one can feel their best or make good decisions with empty insides." She reheated the bowls of porridge and cooled the cups of water, taking pleasure in tasks that had been beyond her only a few short days ago, and reveling in how easily the Power answered her call.

She waited until the others began to eat before sampling her own bowl, finding the porridge satisfyingly thick, if simple. Today, the kitchen staff had flavored it with a bit of finely ground astinelle, and hunger provided a stimulus of its own.

It didn't take long for everyone to empty their bowls. The remaining squares of benroot quickly disappeared, as well.

"Yesterday," Gredin began, "we learned from Keegan that no one from House Balamont had yet taken an alliance partner. I directed him to seek out Tetralanna and discuss the matter with her, to be certain the *crabe* had given us accurate information."

Miri remembered how badly she'd felt for the historian, and her guilty relief that Gredin had not asked her to undertake the task. The thought of meeting with Tetralanna made her shudder. The former First Speaker had become nearly impossible to deal with, responding more rudely at each new encounter. Miri had to admit she was more than a bit afraid of the woman and her sharp tongue. Whyever had the members of House Balamont selected such a person to hear their concerns and represent them?

"Keegan's discussion with her was short and unpleasant. Tetralanna confirmed that she had made it very clear to the Bereft of House Balamont that they were not, under any circumstances, to seek out an alliance partner."

Miri was shocked. "Why?"

"She declared they would rather preserve their honor than take such a step."

"But they will become unredeemable if they continue to refuse!"

"So Keegan warned her, as I have warned her. But she refused to hear his words of concern. Or mine."

Miri bit her lip, troubled. "The more her Balance wanes, the less capable she will be of making wise decisions."

Gredin nodded. "It is already happening, to judge by her actions and words. Indeed, it has likely been the case for far longer than I am comfortable acknowledging. This time, however, when Keegan tried to reason with her for the sake of her kinsmen, she grew irate, and then insulting. Finally, when he persisted, she Silenced him to prevent him from reporting the matter to me, and ordered him out of House Balamont."

"Silenced him?" Sill asked sharply. "But Tetralanna is well aware that it is only a temporary measure."

"It was effective enough at the time," Keegan said dryly, and trained his bleak gaze directly on Gredin. "I didn't truly appreciate what a terrible experience you endured, that first morning here, when Tetralanna Silenced you. I felt badly for you because it seemed cruel, under the circumstances, and because I didn't care for Tetralanna's cold arrogance. But when she did the same thing to me, it made me feel as if Tetralanna had burrowed beneath my skin, claiming mastery over my mind and body." Keegan shuddered. "I can hardly express how happy I was to wake, this morning, and find her hold on me gone."

"Which is exactly my point," Sill insisted. "Tetralanna affected your life for a day, and tarnished her reputation further by doing so. What did she think she was accomplishing?"

"Propping up her pride, I would guess," Miri said tartly. "Tetralanna is the one who started this 'Head of House' nonsense. No doubt she hoped to prevent anyone within House Balamont from overhearing your discussion with her, Keegan – especially the Bereft."

"You are more right than you know, Miri," Gredin said softly, looking sad and weary. "I visited my House last evening and discovered much amiss there, and with Tetralanna most of all."

Gredin, with her short curls, looked to Miri like a forlorn child. But Gredin wasn't a child. She was the leader of their community, as well as being a friend and fellow Bereft. Miri had come to admire Gredin's strength of character, and her willingness to seek new paths for the community to walk, in their quest to survive and prosper. It was hardly surprising, Miri supposed, that Gredin had gone to House Balamont, her own House, in an effort to set things right with her kinsmen.

"I managed to speak to a few individuals before Tetralanna intervened. She is quite out of Balance." Gredin's eyes glittered with unshed tears. "Indeed, she has spoken so harshly against me that many no longer consider me a part of House Balamont."

Miri felt anger on Gredin's behalf. "That's nonsense. Tetralanna has no right to say such a thing."

Keegan spoke up, his tone grim. "Tetralanna does as she pleases. And because of her gyfte, others follow. You are the only one, Gredin, who can remedy that situation."

"I believe Keegan is right, Gredin," Sill said. "Tetralanna is working hard to undermine your authority. Her pride will not let her yield a position she sees as being rightfully hers."

Their words, while true, sounded harsh. Miri touched Gredin's arm. "I believe the Power came to you because you, out of all within the community, are intended to lead us. I have confidence that you will find a way to manage Tetralanna and the others of your House."

"Oh, I understand what I must do, even if I do not yet see how." Gredin straightened her shoulders. "Unless there is other urgent news, I suggest we end today's meeting now. I need time before midday meal to think on Burlon's absence and what I should say about it to the community."

"It will stir the other Travelers like a strong wind in the trees," Keegan warned. "They will want to begin the search for New Venna, once they learn of Burlon's departure."

Gredin nodded. "I know. And I must talk to Ellis and ask her to make the other Traders aware, as well. One of them will need to take up Burlon's duties in our maartza until he returns."

Burlon has Traveled the River to Sprygale.

Burlon is no longer on Tradepoint.

"Oh," Miri exclaimed, as the implications of Gredin's words set her thoughts awhirl. "I just realized… I wanted to reopen the food stall at the maartza today. I intended to ask Burlon to accompany me there, once his morning tasks were completed." She gave Gredin a rueful smile. "I've been sitting here, listening but not really thinking. When you talk with Ellis, would you ask her if there is another Trader willing to escort me to the Traders' Market? I'm sorry. I wish I could speak Tradetalk. Then I wouldn't be such a bother."

"I can take you," Gredin offered. "And you're not a bother. The walk will do me good, and I've been wanting to see the food stall."

Which was how, a short time later, Miri found herself clad in her travel clothes, with a food basket on her arm, walking at Gredin's side toward the Traders' Market.

"My thanks for accompanying me," Miri said, noticing that Gredin, too, had changed her clothing after their meeting, donning an outfit similar to Miri's own. With her short curls and plain clothing, Gredin looked very different from the regal woman who had escorted Miri and

Ingarra and Hayla to the Traders' Market, just days ago. "I hope you're not nervous."

"Why would I be nervous?"

"Those bird people were angry with you for being at the Market. What if we meet some of them again?"

"The Hesch?" Gredin shrugged and kept walking. "They may sound sharp-tempered but they wouldn't actually harm me, the way the Beng did. And you've heard Burlon's reports. The Hesch refuse to engage with us at all, at the moment, so there's no need to worry. We are quite safe."

Gredin sounded utterly calm and certain, but Miri noticed that she maintained a vigilance as they walked. And the flamestone necklace was hidden beneath her shirt and jacket, as was First Speaker's hlette. Gredin had even bound her hlao around her brow in a smooth band of gold, and insisted that Miri do the same, without the knot that identified them as Bereft. Aside from Gredin's hair, she could have been any Vennan Trader.

Miri resolved to hold her tongue until they reached the Vennan maartza. Gredin had already experienced a number of upsets between yesterday and today. A peaceful walk was likely what she needed most.

But Gredin said, "I hope Burlon is safe, as well. Desh! Nothing has gone as I intended."

"Don't be so hard on yourself, Gredin. You've done what you thought best."

Gredin laughed harshly. "My best? Many in the community who would not agree. Even the Power must be disappointed in me, by now. I've let Tetralanna do as she pleases, out of deference to her declining Balance. And what has been the result? Conflict and angry words that have raised a thick wall between the two of us."

Miri shook her head. "That woman treats everyone in her path much the same, Gredin. Look at what she did to Keegan, who has been unfailingly polite and kind."

Gredin grimaced. "Tetralanna is my kinswoman. She and I share a gyfte. Of all here, I should be able to reason with her. If the Bereft of my own House reject my entreaties–"

"Plenty in the community *have* listened, including myself, and I am much the better for it. Thanks to you, and to time spent with my alliance partner, my Balance is nearly restored, and his even more so."

Gredin was silent for a dozen or more steps along the metal corridor.

"You are finding the… process bearable, then?"

"Yes. Awkward, of course. Embarrassing even, at times," Miri responded, soberly. "But the two of us vowed to laugh about the difficulties we encounter, and to persist, rather than weeping or recoiling. Thus far, that promise has stood us in good stead." She forbore mentioning how much willpower it required from her, each time, to follow through on the sessions with her alliance partner inside the Bereft enclave. She hoped, in time, that it would become easier, and that repetition would wear away the guilt she felt each time she mated with someone other than Zanther. But it was not yet the case…

"I am glad for you."

Miri shook her dark thoughts aside. "And I am glad you had the courage to find a solution for the Bereft," she said, and meant it. "I was terrified of becoming unredeemable. And now, instead of that horror, I am able to exercise my gyfte again!" Miri felt like dancing at the happy realization, and would have, if she hadn't been in a public corridor. "The benroot dish you tasted this morning was the first new offering I've created in days. I'd nearly forgotten how pleasurable it was to do such a thing."

"It was very good." She gave Miri a sidelong glance. "Is it unkind of me to admit I'm pleased that Burlon's arrogant actions deprived him of tasting today's treat?"

Miri wondered how to respond. "Burlon is… was… the head of Bentain's Tradeteam. He was a coordinator for the Trisectoriana. And now he wears First Traveler's hlette. He's used to being in charge. I'm sure, once he returns, he'll offer both an apology and an explanation."

"That hardly helps me now! When the Travelers learn he is gone, how am I to stop them if they decide to leave, as well? I fear they will go, putting themselves at risk, despite me telling them to wait."

And that would further undermine Gredin's role as leader of the community. Miri began to appreciate the larger implications of Burlon's actions, occurring as they did at a time when Tetralanna was publicly contradicting Gredin and denigrating her leadership abilities. In his own way, Burlon had done the same by departing, against Gredin's express wishes. Small wonder Gredin was upset.

An idea presented itself.

"Gredin? Is there any reason the community has to know that Burlon left without your permission?"

Gredin gave her a quick glance and shook her head. "Too many people in the community already know he's gone – not just we four remaining circle members, but Chenna, Ingarra, and whatever folk Ingarra may have told, beginning with Beda. If I try to claim that Burlon is still here on Tradepoint, Tetralanna will demand that I produce him. And when I can't, she will *use that* failure against me, further influencing those who support her views."

"No, you misunderstand me," Miri said. "Of course you must tell the community that Burlon has gone. But must you tell them that he left against your wishes?"

"But that's precisely what he did!"

"Only we four of the circle know that for a fact. Keegan and Sill will hold their tongues. None of us ever share what we discuss in the meetings." Miri gave Gredin a rueful smile. "Most of the time, it's too depressing to repeat to anyone, anyway."

Gredin gave her a cross look. "So, I am to say that I have sent Burlon te Laith to Sprygale with my best wishes for a successful trip and a safe return?"

"You're being testy," Miri admonished. "Tell everyone Burlon is gone. Simply omit the fact that he made that decision on his own."

Gredin's brow knit, then smoothed. "You are suggesting I imply that, for Burlon alone, I lifted the sanction against Traveling the River?" Gredin's lips quirked. "Miri te Kendar, you are a devious woman. I thank you."

Smiling, Miri let a more comfortable silence descend between them, content to let Gredin think in peace for the remainder of their walk to the Vennan maartza.

But Tradepoint, it seemed, had different plans. At the sound of someone behind them, Miri glanced over her shoulder and saw a pair of the bird creatures advancing swiftly. "Hesch," she murmured to Gredin with apprehension, and directed her gaze ahead again, but her shoulders hunched protectively in spite of her best intentions.

"We are quite safe," Gredin replied softly. "Maintain your pace."

The Tradepoint corridors were broad, with ample room for the two Hesch to pass them. Instead, Miri heard the odd clicking of their footsteps grow louder as they neared and then settled in right behind them.

Gredin walked no faster or slower than before, and Miri stepped in careful rhythm with her, although her nerves grew ever more taut as she imagined the tall, gaunt creatures peering down at her, close enough to reach out and grasp one of her braids.

Then the pair of Hesch quickened their steps and veered to the left, passing the Vennan women. One of them said something that Miri didn't understand, and she saw that Gredin's expression remained unchanged, as if she, too, failed to comprehend.

The bright, bead-like eyes of the nearer Hesch seemed to be trained on Miri, the black orbs glistening in the harsh overhead lights.

She neither smiled nor frowned, but the basket's weight on her arm suddenly seemed intolerable. What would she do, if the Hesch threatened them?

Then the other Hesch spoke, and uttered a harsh laugh. Its companion clacked its bill, and the two lengthened their strides, proceeding down the corridor and around the first corner they reached.

Miri let out a shaky breath. "Are they gone?" she dared to whisper.

"Most likely."

"Will they come back?"

"I doubt it. As I told you, the Hesch make a show of intimidating others, but I don't judge them to be a true threat. Besides, the Market is just ahead. Calm yourself, Miri. All is well."

"What did they say?"

Gredin grinned. "Just that we looked harmless – which I take to mean that they didn't recognize me."

They reached the tall Traders' Market doors without further incident, and Miri beamed with relief as they walked the familiar aisle to the Vennan maartza. One of the two Traders manning it came forward to greet them with a wide grin. "Good day, Miri. Good day, Gredin te Balamont. I am Devik te Shelahn." He indicated the other Trader. "And this is Tirwin te Darius. We are pleased to see you. Customers have been sparse today."

Miri scanned the underpopulated halls of the Market. "Burlon had the right of it, as usual. He warned us that there were few in port currently, but I was eager to reopen my little food stall, so I insisted on coming," she said, ignoring the narrow-eyed glance Gredin gave her at her easy use of Burlon's name.

"Would you like some help in setting up?" Devik asked.

"My thanks, but no. That won't be necessary."

"What have you brought to sell today?"

"Fourteen d'limten rolls, six with herbs, eight with bits of dried placrim. Thirty-seven packets of crackers, sprinkled with horvin seeds. A large crock of broth with dumplings. The dumplings are filled with minced vegetables. And two loaves of d'limten bread to slice. Each slice will be spread with softened rista cheese."

"My mouth is watering. Too bad we Traders agreed not to buy our own merchandise," Devik said, his green eyes twinkling.

Miri entered the small tent the Prett had provided, and set her basket on the metal table at the back. She motioned for Gredin to come inside as well and, once she had, Miri swung the retractable arm of the counter into place along the front of the tent. Now she and Gredin were neatly barricaded behind its width, with Devik lounging on the opposite side.

Miri Fetched a gaily striped cloth from the basket and covered the counter, smiling as the surface immediately looked more inviting. While the Prett had been kind enough to provide the tent and the well-made table and counter, everything had looked far too drab.

The tent color hovered between gray and white, while the table and counter were made of the same metal that abounded everywhere on Tradepoint. To Miri, it all cried out for color and softness, so she had brought the prettiest things she had in the kitchens to help her display the food. To her eye, food looked more inviting that way, and it helped disguise the meagerness of the morning's offering.

Which reminded her…

"Devik, I have spent the past few days thinking about ways to use the food stall's popularity to sell items in our maartza. And then I remembered how much Burlon enjoyed the food items the Polpethtira shared with him, during their Trade negotiation, and I thought perhaps we could do that here at the food stall." Miri took a deep breath to quiet the nervous excitement building within her. "Would you consider giving me two jars of the relish? If so, I will use them as a sample."

"Only two jars?" Devik looked dubious. "That amount of relish won't go far."

"I brought a number of tiny spoons with me. Customers would be able to try a taste of relish to see if it was to their liking. The more adventurous could spread it on their food purchase. I think it would be particularly good with the slice of bread and cheese."

"And if they want more relish than a spoonful?"

Miri gestured broadly to the maartza. "I will tell them there is plenty available for purchase within."

Devik's expression grew thoughtful.

"And, once inside the maartza, a customer might well find other items to buy," Miri added earnestly.

Devik nodded. "True enough. It's a good idea, Miri, worth the risk of two jars of relish to see if it will work as you describe." He grinned. "Are you sure you don't have a small gyfte of Trading hidden beneath your gyfte for kitchen Tending?"

Miri smiled back. "I'm no Trader, Devik. And I can't speak a word of Tradetalk, which is why Gredin is here to assist me."

"Perhaps, then, it is time for you to learn the language – enough Tradetalk, at least, to understand the compliments that come your way."

Devik's words held more than a hint of teasing, and Miri smiled, but she continued to think about them as she prepared the food items for sale. Finally, with the last tray ready, she surveyed the table.

"Here," Gredin said from behind her, making her jump.

When Miri turned around, she saw that Gredin held a jar of relish in each hand.

"Your pardon, Miri. I did not intend to startle you."

"No need for apologies. I was deep in thought, and you were so quiet that I forgot you were there." Miri accepted the jars and turned back to the table, shifting a platter with a little flick of Power in order to make room for them. Picking up a bright orange tray neatly layered with thin slices of bread and cheese, she turned and carried it to the counter, then repeated the trip between table and counter with a plate adorned with streaks of sunset colors upon which she had arranged six of the d'limten rolls, three of each type.

"The ones with dried placrim are on the right side of the plate. The ones with herbs on the right," Miri said, pleased to see that Gredin was paying close attention.

Next, Miri placed the deep-blue basket of seeded crackers in the center of the counter, letting the rich color anchor the display.

"Where will you put the soup?" Gredin asked. "There isn't enough room for that big crock."

Miri set three yellow cups of broth, each with a single dumpling, next to the blue basket. "I'll replace these as we sell them. As long as there is a cup on the counter, we still have more to sell. We haven't tried selling anything in cups before. They'll have to consume the broth here, and hand the empty cup back to us. Everything until now has been something folks could eat out of hand as they strolled the Market."

"Clever," Gredin said. "It all looks very inviting, Miri. The colors will draw people in, just as the Shodekekeen do with their fabrics."

Miri set an open jar of relish and a short pottery jar containing a number of small spoons on the other side of the basket from the broth cups. "Don't worry, I'm not relying solely on the colors to draw customers in." Miri flicked a hand from plate to platter; almost immediately, the aroma of freshly baked bread began to fill the air. Another flick, and the enticing smell of soup also made its presence known. "Now, we wait."

Miri imagined a widening ripple of enticing aromas wafting out from the small tent, stirring noses everywhere. Sure enough, before long, a pair of F'lala hurried into view, heading straight for the tent, their white hair waving madly behind them due to their haste.

And, behind them, a trio of large-eyed, large-eared Rodorno.

From the corner of her eye, she saw a Prett security guard slip into place just to the side of the tent's opening.

Miri turned her head and smiled in satisfaction. "Brace yourself," she said to Gredin. "We are about to become quite busy."

[12]

0744 OF 2000 ORBITS REMAINING: 27PURPLE

When Gredin was finally alone in her room, shut away from the bustle of the Traders' Market and Miri's irrepressible high spirits, she paced the floor, filled with frustration.

The Hesch were still clinging to their resentment of everyone in the Vennan enclave, and it was entirely her fault. She could only be grateful that her shorn hair and the way her jacket had hidden the flamestone necklace had prevented them from identifying her individually, or she and Miri might have had a much harder time of it in the public corridor.

Meanwhile, Burlon was gone to Sprygale, after she had specifically forbidden him to go. She would gratefully adopt Miri's suggestion that she allow people to think he had done so with her permission. But she knew – and he knew – that it wasn't true. She had surrendered the geddel crystals from Trethen's dress for nothing. Nothing! He had launched himself upon the River this morning in flat defiance of her decision...

Something nagged at her mind, half-remembered – something about that day when she had thrust Trethen's gown into Burlon's hands, and then had been forced to hide her tears while she dealt with

Rig te Indirin. How long ago had that been? More than a day or two. In fact, it had been quite some time ago.

Her pacing slowed as she thought through recent events, counting backward from the current moment… and was appalled.

A dozen days. She had parted with Trethen's dress a dozen days ago. And in all that time, despite the changes that had swept through the community, she hadn't once seriously considered lifting the edict that bound the Travelers to Tradepoint.

Stranger still, Burlon had not renewed his request. Why?

Her feet stopped.

Burlon hadn't bothered to renew his request because he'd given up any hope of persuading her. Instead, he had settled back to wait for Ingarra to finish the coat and quilt. Which Ingarra had done. And Burlon had gone.

Gredin sighed. She should have remembered that patience was a common Trader's virtue, along with self-confidence. As House Balamont's Traders had long ago explained to her, there was no room to dither when you made a Trade. If the moment was right and the terms were advantageous, you had to act.

Well, Burlon had acted.

What if it was still too soon? How could she ever make that up to Chenna, if Burlon failed to return? The glim on her cheeks were multiplying, and the child inside of her was growing. It would be an unparalleled tragedy if Chenna now became one of the Bereft.

But, of anyone in the community, surely Burlon was the likeliest to be in Balance. His dydanin had ended just a few nights ago. His hlinga should be strong.

Well, Cirin's had been strong, as well. His last act, before departing to find out whether Venna still existed had been to mate with Hayla. And now Hayla was forever alone, one of the Bereft, because Gredin had failed to convince Cirin of what she knew.

Gredin began to pace again. Why had the Power selected *her* to hear its message? She hadn't prevented Tetralanna from dividing the community. She hadn't been able to keep herself safe from the Beng. She couldn't even make a decision and stick to it. She…

The stone jug caught her attention, its bulging eyes seeming to catch her in a disapproving gaze.

"I hope you enjoy sitting alone on that shelf," she said to it, "for you are the first and last jug of your kind that we will ever possess, if the Hesch have their way."

She grimaced at the absurdity of talking to the ugly stone object, then fell back a step as the truth of her words struck her fully. So long as Nitikikani and his people refused to Trade with the Vennans, this solitary jug of amarantha wine was all that they had to help the Bereft. Some, like Miri, seemed to have no need of it. But the others, the ones who were having difficulty…

How much liquid did the jug contain? It was large, yes, and heavy, but much of its weight must come from the stone itself, and she had no idea how large the hollow cavity within it might be. Five days ago, she and Khest had each filled a cup three times. Surely, at that rate, the wine that remained would not last for long, and would not serve many.

Five days ago.

For five days, revitalized, she had resumed her normal activities, and memories of her time spent with Khest had drifted to the back of her mind. But now she was talking to jugs. She was bouncing from one half-made decision to another. She was fretting to no good purpose, letting anxiety swirl through her without forming any clear plan of action.

She looked across the room to her bedmat, where the embroidered pillow sat atop her coverlet. Doing her best to calm herself, she looked intently at the pillow and Fetched it.

Instead of arriving in her hands, it toppled off the edge of the foam mat and fell to the floor.

She was out of Balance. Smug in her recovery, she had taken her condition for granted, not noticing as her hlinga slowly ebbed away.

Dejected, Gredin walked to her bedmat and sat down on it, scooping the pillow into her arms and hugging it to herself for comfort.

Contact Khest, she told herself.

But she shrank from the thought.

Contact him. He will be as badly in need as you are.

Then why hadn't he contacted her? Why did she have to be the one to make the offer?

But that wasn't fair. The first time, at Beda's bidding, Khest had come to her. And since then… well, since then, she had made no effort to contact him, nor had he reached out to her. Perhaps he was regretting their first encounter. Perhaps his House had discovered what he'd done and was making matters difficult for him. Or perhaps he had been availing himself of the new enclave and had moved on to other alliance partners.

It was a frightening thought. She knew no one else to approach. And she felt ill at ease about going to the new enclave. Others had anonymity, if they wished it. She did not. Everyone in the community knew her on sight, now that the Beng had taken her braids. A number of the House volunteers had taken a stand against her. Would their kinsmen feel the same way? It would be a sad and upsetting thing, if she went to the new enclave and no one there would agree to mate with her.

Then contact Khest.

And there it was again – her thoughts had carried her in a neat circle. Was she going to surrender to that? Was she already so badly out of Balance that she could only watch helplessly as her mind staggered from worry to worry?

No. That was pathetic. She would not let it be so.

Hugging the pillow even more tightly, she composed herself as best she could and reached out in search of his private mind. =Khest te Bentain?=

=Gredin.= His response came at once, solid and clear.

Unsure what to say, she took refuge in the truth. =My Balance is not what it was when we parted. I thought your situation might be the same.=

=Are you free? Would you like me to come to your quarters?=

She was both relieved and alarmed. Midday meal had ended, a short time past, but the day's activities were going on, all through the enclaves. Keegan was off at the Clinic but he might return soon, depending on how the day's testing went. What if he sat down to work at the table in the outer room that she shared with him, and the time came for Khest to leave? In a true emergency, she supposed he could Send himself elsewhere, but Burlon's early cautions against the community doing so were still in effect.

An alternative occurred to her. =I am indeed free,= she confirmed. =But today, instead of coming to the door of my quarters, you will find another door in that short corridor, all the way to the end on your right. It is where Burlon and Chenna te Laith passed their dydanin, but it is not being used now. Could you meet me there? Would that be agreeable to you?=

=Certainly. I will arrive shortly.=

=My thanks,= she said, and let the contact lapse.

Having failed to ask him where he was, she had no precise idea of how long it would take him to arrive. Putting down the pillow, she left her bedchamber, walked through the room where she and her advisors gathered in the mornings, and went down the short corridor to let herself in through the last remaining door on the right.

The room was disconcertingly bare. The foam pad provided by the Prett was there, but Burlon and Chenna had taken their bedding and other belongings with them to their new nest. Embarrassed to have invited Khest to such an unwelcoming place, Gredin hurried back down the hallway, gathered up her own luminth, bedmat, and coverlet, and carried them back. *You could have just Fetched them*, she chided herself, but then she remembered her failure to Fetch her pillow, just a short time earlier. It was dawning on her, with unpleasant clarity, that she had become dangerously complacent as soon as her Balance returned.

She knew better, of course. But she hadn't wanted to face the new reality.

Her hasty dash had quickened her breathing and left her uncomfortably warm. Chagrined, she spread the bedding, hoping that the mundane task would quiet her. But the uncertainty of when Khest would arrive, coupled with the certainty of why he was coming, kept her feeling agitated. And indeed, she had only just finished smoothing the coverlet when she heard a light tap at the door and turned to find Khest entering.

He looked dauntingly well, offering her a warm smile as he closed the door behind himself. "A good day to you, Gredin." Then his gaze sharpened, and his smile faded. "You look as if your day has already been a challenging one."

"It has," she conceded. "But you look rested. Indeed, you look as if your Balance has lasted well."

He shook his head. "It did not. But someone came to me who had experienced a difficult first attempt, and I was able to help her. You have been with no one since we parted?"

"No."

"Then small wonder you are feeling less than well. We of the Bereft have barely begun our recovery. In time, I suspect we will learn to sense the early signs when our Balance begins to waver. But first we must restore our hlinga completely." He sat down on the mat and gestured for Gredin to join him. When she hesitated, he asked, "Did you light the luminth yourself?"

"Yes."

"Good. That was beyond you, before. I am pleased to know that we both benefited from our time together. But you look uneasy. Have I become frightening, since I saw you last?"

"No, but you have become real. What we propose to do here has become real. The last time, it was the middle of the night."

"The last time, we had both partaken of amarantha wine. I managed without it, on my second mating, and so I trust that I can do so again. But you would benefit from a cup or two. Shall I Fetch it?"

"No."

"No?"

She shook her head wearily. "I am quite certain you're right… but it wouldn't be fair to the others. I have only the one jug, and no immediate prospect of obtaining more. There isn't enough to share with all of those who might need it, and so we will leave the jug stoppered until there is enough for all."

"What a very foolish notion," Khest said.

"What?"

"I said that you are being foolish."

"I am striving to be fair!" Gredin protested.

But Khest shook his head. "It might be 'fair,' but it isn't sensible. And there is no need to look so angry about it. Sit down here. I will rub your shoulders while I explain." He patted the coverlet. "Come along. Sit down."

She could tell him to leave. If she did, she had no doubt that he would go. But there was a small, uncomfortable, suspicion wriggling within her that what he said might be right, that perhaps she *was* being foolish. Surely it would do no harm, at least, to listen. And if she was going to listen, she might just as well let him chase the knots from her shoulders while he talked.

With a sigh, she sat.

Khest chuckled. "I did not offer to rub your jacket. My gyfte would find no sustenance in that, and you would experience little benefit. Take it off."

With another sigh, she did so, and found herself wondering if what Khest had just said about his gyfte might apply to Keegan, as well, when he spoke about the difference between writing with his reed pen on paper as opposed to poking at letters on the *crabe* the Prett had provided.

"And your tunic," Khest prompted.

She complied.

A few moments later, a warm, spicy scent filled the air.

"What is that?"

"Tadema oil." His hands came to rest lightly on her shoulders, and his thumbs began to move in slow circles. "It helps my skin speak to yours."

"What will you do when it is gone?"

His hands stilled. "What?"

She regretted having put her question so bluntly, but she would not be less than honest with him. "You brought this tadema oil with you from home, yes?"

"Yes."

"What will you do when you have used it all?"

"There are other oils. There are other people with the gyfte of Touch who no doubt brought their own supply."

"And when those are gone, as well?" What unkind mischief drove her tongue? Was she trying to alarm him and drive him from the room?

His thumbs began to move again, prodding at her rigid shoulders. "Then we will Trade for oils from other worlds, I suppose. Or discover oils of our own, on New Venna."

"Good," she said. "I am glad for you, and glad for those of us who benefit from your gyfte. But the amarantha wine is a different matter altogether. Imagine, if you will, that the bottle of tadema oil you are using were the only bottle of its kind, and all of those with gyfte of Touch needed to share the contents of that one bottle, and the only other source of oil was refusing to sell or Trade with you. That is our situation with the amarantha wine. We have whatever remains in that one jug, and we cannot obtain any more. Someday, perhaps. But not now. What wine we have is not enough for every Bereft, or even for every Bereft who is finding it difficult to mate. These are my people, the ones the Power has directed me to protect. How can I justify using the wine myself and leaving them to do without?"

Instead of answering, Khest said, "You are as hard as a branch of glinn wood beneath my hands. Lie down and let me chase the worries from your bones."

With a groan, she obeyed. "Would that you could. But worrying is the task the Power has assigned to me."

"Hush now," Khest said as she settled full-length on the soft pad.

"If you were a Prett, you would say *chee, chee, chee,*" she told him.

"Why? What does that mean?"

"I suppose you could say it means 'Stop your worrying and be calm.'"

"Well then," Khest said, a smile audible in his voice, "*chee, chee, chee.*" Fingers had now joined thumbs, spreading the oil, kneading the clenched flesh beneath the skin. Soon, his palms took part, as well.

Then the heels of his hands came into play, pressing down in long, heavy strokes as if to herd the worries to where his clever fingers could dismantle them. When his efforts rose to her neck, it was if he had found a way to suspend her thoughts. She let him lift her head and turn it this way and that, to an accompaniment of crisp little popping noises. And then, at some point, he began to tell her a tale, his words pitched soft and low.

"There was a night of storms, long ago, at one of the Holdings. Rain and wind and darkness. There was a trail from the mountain meadow to the upland shelter, but it was narrow and winding, bordered sometimes by thorn bushes and sometimes by a steep ravine. The Tender of the rista flock could have Sent himself to the upland shelter with a moment's effort to spend a dry night in relative comfort, but he adjudged the night to be too harsh for the flock to remain outside, unprotected. Instead, he cast a Binding on each of the rista, telling it which of its fellows it was to follow, and he cast a final Binding on the youngest, smallest rista, instructing it to follow directly behind him. Then he powered his luminth and made his way down the steep trail, through the wind and rain, walking at a rate that the youngest, smallest rista could manage. It took them much of the night, and along the way the rain turned to sleet, and then to snow, but he brought every rista in the flock down safely from the mountain meadow, and settled them in the shelter with dry bedding, and Fetched food and water for them. And when he had done all of that, and the bodies of so many rista had made the shelter a warm and cozy place even on so bitter a night as it had become, the Tender made a sleeping nest for himself in the dry bedding, and fell into a well-earned slumber."

Gredin floated on a sea of sound, buoyed up by Khest's words, thinking about nothing but the scene he described.

"Many people within his House— people who did not share his gyfte – told him that he should have made some other choice, rather than risking himself," Khest said. "They pointed out that he could have Sent down to the shelter and simply rung the bell to call the rista home. Or he could have started them down the path and taken up a position after the last of them, to see to it that no rista lagged behind and was lost. Another person thought he should have sought a cave in the rocky slopes and sheltered with them there, in the mountain meadow. Someone said that he should have reasoned that they were sensible beasts who would see to their own salvation, while he spent the night down at the Holding, sitting by the fire with his feet up. One even claimed that he should have broken his luminth into small pieces, and bound a piece around each rista's neck, so that they could each find their own way down. Would that have been a good solution?"

"No," she murmured into the mat. "Better to keep the luminth whole, so that he could see clearly and lead the way."

Khest's fingertip traced a pattern behind her ear. "Say that again, please," he requested.

She blinked, confused, trying to remember what she had said. "Better to keep the luminth whole, so that he could… Oh."

The fingertip continued to tease. "Yes. 'Oh.' Better that he be able to see clearly and lead the way. And better that you be able to *think* clearly and lead the way. Fetch the jug, Gredin. Or shall I?" When she hesitated, he asked, "Is it stored where it was before, on the shelf?"

"Yes, but…"

The jug appeared on the floor beside the sleepmat.

"I won't need any, this time," Khest assured her, "so in truth we will only be using half as much as we did before." A moment later, an unfamiliar cup appeared beside it, glazed in blue with white speckles.

"What cup is that?" Gredin demanded. "Where did it come from?"

"I Fetched it from my room, from among my belongings. You may keep it, if you like. As you may recall, I broke your cup, the last time."

"Did you?" She had no memory of that, none at all. "Well, perhaps we won't need it. You say that you won't require any amarantha wine. Perhaps I won't, either."

"Perhaps," Khest said, but there was an undertone of doubt in his voice. "Just recall that the act alone is not enough. You require a completion. Several, if possible."

She wished that she could deny the point, but it was something every Vennan learned as they grew from childhood toward maturity. The explosive moments of a completion reinvigorated the hlinga, restoring Balance. Nothing else created the same effect or yielded the same benefit.

"Start with a cupful," Khest urged, pouring for her, "and we will judge from there."

"Judge what?"

"We will judge when you have begun to listen properly."

"What do you mean?" she demanded crossly. "I am listening."

"Yes, but your body is not." He traced a pattern behind her ear again. "How does that feel to you?"

"Fine. Pleasant."

"When you and I were last together, your reaction to such a touch on such a spot was quite different. Right now, it is as if your body stands out in the reception hall, vaguely aware of my presence here but distracted by a hundred other people approaching you with their concerns. Sit up and drink your wine, Gredin. Let us see what that wins us."

The cup was a pleasant fit in her hand, cool and smooth. She raised it and realized that she had forgotten the inviting scent of the amarantha wine, like the Balamont gardens on a summer morning. She inhaled twice, savoring it, then lifted the cup to her lips and drank, in long, thirsty swallows.

And there it was, that peculiar sense that something was skittering across her tongue on tiny, pointed feet. And then the rush of heat, blasting everything else out of its path, demanding her entire attention as it raged through her.

When it passed, she became aware that she was panting, and that her forehead was damp. She realized, too, that Khest had removed his tunic. Both of them were bare to the waist, but there was a rosy flush to her skin that was absent from his. The wine, no doubt.

"Now what?"

"Now we wait a bit and try again. In the meantime, I wanted to give you my thanks."

"For what?"

"For not naming me to the community when they demanded it. I should have spoken and risen in support of you, but…" He looked down at his hands. "I have always led a quiet life. I wish to go on doing so. Still, it was unkind of me to make you face their criticism alone."

She shook her head. "They were going to be upset, whether faced with one person or twenty. Your presence beside me would not have spared me. It would only have given them another target for their ire. What you and I did was right and necessary. In time, the community will understand that. But the Bereft deserve their privacy, insofar as we can provide it – and that includes you. I am already a target of disfavor for many within the community. One reason more for disapproving of me is of little consequence. You were there when I needed you. That is what matters."

"Bravely spoken," Khest said, "but I am still in your debt. If there is anything you need…"

A thought came to her. "You could satisfy my curiosity on a matter, if you would."

"Certainly. What do you wish to know?"

"When you first came in, you said that you were closer to Balance than I was because you had been with another Bereft since I last saw you. Can you tell me… did that take place at the new enclave?"

"Yes, it did," he said, looking so relieved by her question that Gredin wondered what he had been afraid she would ask.

"Can you give me your impressions of the enclave, and point out anything about it that you think we could improve? It was kind of the Prett to provide the enclave, but their preferences are not ours."

"Gladly. Lie down again and I will rub your back while you listen."

It seemed a fair Trade. Gredin stretched out and tried not to react as Khest's hands came to rest on either side of her back. "You say you were with someone who had a difficult first encounter?" she asked.

"Yes. Her first alliance partner is a kinsman of mine, and he was distressed on her behalf. He approached me, hoping that my gyfte of Touch might be of help, and so I agreed to try. I contacted the woman, and we arranged to meet at the new enclave during evening meal, when most people's attention would be turned elsewhere."

Gredin inhaled, lulled by the faint fragrance of the tadema oil.

"Most of the door pads were drawn aside, signaling that they were not in use. And it was clear, from how widely scattered the few lowered curtains were, that people were being considerate, selecting nests distant from others that were being used. That wouldn't be possible at a busy time, but it was a comfort to us. We selected a nest near the back of the enclave, well away from any others that were occupied, and lit the small luminth that we found inside. Do you remember the luminth that hung from the ceiling on the night of the reception?"

"The ones in little lace cradles?" She stirred beneath the comforting pressure of his hands. "Of course. They looked like stars, that night."

"Well, they are being used now in the nests of the Bereft enclave."

It struck Gredin as an excellent idea. The lace would diffuse the light from the luminth, and the patterns created would soften the austere metal walls of the nest.

"Other than that, the nests contain nothing but a foam pad and the necessary bedding. Much like this room, now that I reflect on it," Khest said, sounding mildly amused. "It does no harm. People come there for one purpose only, and then they Freshen it, and tidy the bedding, and leave. It isn't meant to be a personal space, any more than our alliance partner is meant to be our Chosen. Some may find the plainness regrettable but it seemed fine to me. No one is intended to linger there."

"Was anyone using the upper floor of rooms?"

"Yes." His fingers centered in on a particular spot, coaxing it to ease. "A few."

"I am relieved to hear it. I thought people might consider the staircases provided by the Prett to be an insult."

"No, I think most see the staircase as a good reminder of why they are there – so that they will no longer need such a thing, in future."

"I hope so. I hope, as people make use of the new enclave, that their Balance will improve, and they will view our efforts with a sympathetic eye."

"Many of us are deeply grateful, and we will do what we can to persuade the rest to come and benefit, as well."

For a time, she sank into silence, wondering if Khest's hands found the state of her body as easy to read as Keegan found the words on the screen of his *crabe*. Then she regretted the thought, because it reminded her that other people existed, people to whom she owed a deep responsibility. "That woman…" she began.

"Hush. Relax."

"No, please. I need to know. Is she better now?"

"Your pardon?"

"The woman whose first attempt at a mating was unsatisfactory. The one your kinsman asked you to approach. Were you able to help her?"

"Yes. She is much improved. Now hush."

"I only wondered whether–"

Khest lifted one hand slowly from her back, then the other. "You," he said on a note of decision, "are in need of more wine."

"Because I asked a question?"

"Precisely. I am not here to listen to your questions. I am here to listen to your body." Lifting the jug, he poured until the liquid neared the cup's rim. "Sit up and drink."

She disliked being told what to do but she could see little point in arguing with him. Feeling awkward, she knelt upright and accepted the cup.

By the time she had emptied it, each breath seared her throat, and the air felt thick and hot against her skin. "I have rumpled my trousers," she complained, and rose to slide them down her legs. When they were pooled around her ankles, she leaned over to remove them, but the sudden change in position made her head spin. Crying out, she began to topple, and instead found herself sitting in Khest's lap, one foot still tangled in her trouser leg.

"Be more careful," he admonished. "The wine is strong." Flicking her curls aside, he traced a pattern behind her ear.

She shook her head, dodging his touch. "Don't! That tickles."

He sighed. "Well, I suppose a tickle is *some* improvement, but you still have quite a distance to progress."

"To progress?"

"Before your body is ready to welcome mine."

She frowned. "I don't recall anything tickling, the last time."

"Your body was relaxed, not carrying the tensions of a busy day."

"I had just been attacked," she reminded him sharply.

"And then Assessed. And then Healed. And then you slept for a time. Beda does his work well. Your body was quite at peace, even though your mind was not."

"So you are saying, this time, that I am more difficult?" she asked, and scrambled away to sit on the bedmat again.

He made no effort to detain her. "I am saying, this time, that you are different. As am I. And that will be true every time we meet to join. Just like our hlinga, we ebb and flow." He smiled. "Do not look so displeased. It makes life interesting. Even if I used my gyfte on the same individual every day, they would be different under my hands on each occasion. Everything changes, and we are part of everything. It is why Tetralanna and her followers are so desperately unhappy. They hate the present reality, yet they fear change. They wish with all their hearts to do the one thing that is impossible."

Gredin couldn't resist asking. "And that is…?"

"To move backward in time. If they had Sill te Torr's gyfte of Memory, they would retreat within it and never come out." Reaching down, he ran a fingertip along the bare sole of Gredin's foot.

She recoiled with a shriek. "Don't tickle!"

"Are your feet usually that sensitive?" Khest asked.

"No. Never." She grimaced. "Well, now, apparently."

He shook his head. "Ticklish is not a state that will serve us." Lifting the jug, he poured again.

Gredin eyed him warily. "More, so soon?"

He held the cup out to her. "Whatever you feel after this third cup, I am quite certain that 'ticklish' will not be the word to describe it."

And so she drank.

Soon thereafter, dizziness drove her to flatten herself on the bedmat, and the heat coursing through her made the bedclothes unbearable. “I am aflame,” she confided to the ceiling.

“Then I will extinguish you,” the ceiling promised, and cool puffs of air touched her skin, first her brow, then her shoulder, then the inner bend of her elbow.

It made her shiver.

“Are you cold?”

“No.”

“Does it tickle?”

“No.”

“Would you like it to stop?”

“No.”

The ceiling chuckled, and the little breeze revisited her elbow, causing the same delicious shiver. Then the breeze moved on to her hip, her knee, her ankle.

A new shiver, different but equally delightful.

A breeze on her other ankle brought nothing but coolness. Then it returned to the first ankle, and she couldn’t suppress a little sound of pleasure and entreaty.

But the breeze moved on, as breezes always did. It drifted along the inner curve of her calf, played for a moment at her knee, then teased upward along the valley where her left thigh touched her right.

Her legs grew restless, parting to welcome the cooling breeze.

“Come inside,” she invited. “Burn with me.”

“You know what you are asking?”

He was not the breeze, nor was he the ceiling. “Yes. You are Khest. And you are welcome.”

When the two of them were finally exhausted, she slept, and woke some unknown time later to the soft rhythm of Khest’s fingers combing through her curls.

“Have we missed evening meal?” Gredin asked. “If we have, I must beg Miri not to sell everything that was left or I will perish before morning!”

Khest laughed. “There is no need to fear. We are still some distance away from evening meal. But I am pleased to hear that you are eager to eat."

Gredin found herself smiling. "Perhaps it was poor planning on my part to rouse the Bereft to better appetites just when we are most pressed to feed them well."

"A burden we will bear, and a problem we will solve," Khest said, then slid a glance her way. "We *will* solve it, won't we?"

"In time. Certainly no one will starve. But we will experience lean times for a while. There are fewer other races here at Tradepoint than usual, which limits our opportunities. And the food testing Keegan te Fliss undergoes with the Prett has yielded no encouraging results. But our Traders are all aware of the difficulty, and they will set things right as quickly as they can."

Khest nodded. "I leave such complicated matters to you and the High Council."

"No." She sat up, jolted from her languor. "Understand me clearly. There *is* no High Council, just as there are no Heads of House. There are only House volunteers who have taken titles and authorities upon themselves that are not theirs to claim."

Khest's tone was wary as he said, "Your pardon. I did not mean to distress you. But…"

"Speak your mind," she requested. "Indeed, I will take it as a kindness if you do. I have little opportunity to hear what is being said candidly in the Houses. The content of your words may not please me, but I would always rather hear the truth, and I will never blame you for being the one to tell it to me."

Still looking abashed, Khest said, "There is little I know, except that we are all long-used to thinking in terms of Heads of House and the High Council, and so those titles come naturally to people's tongues. No one in our enclave ever refers to House volunteers."

"It is a new way of thinking, so that is to be expected, I suppose. But, also, Naria does not think well of me, and she thinks quite well of herself. Judging by you and Burlon, House Bentain contains many fine people, but when I look about for support, my gaze is not apt to land there first."

"You feel strongly about this," he said, "and yet I have not heard you speak out against Naria and the others."

Gredin sighed. "The community is shaken. The Bereft are only just beginning to recover their Balance. It hardly seems the proper time to upset everyone by criticizing those who stepped forward to offer some sense of structure within the Houses."

Khest made a little noise, then fell silent.

"What?" Gredin asked. "Say what you are thinking."

"It's just… well, when a thing is said, and said often, and goes unchallenged, it soon takes on an assumption of truth in people's minds, regardless of its merits."

Hadn't Burlon and the others tried to warn her, when she raised the notion of asking each House to appoint a volunteer, that it might not be the best solution to the problem? At the time, she had dismissed their concerns, confident that she had decided upon the correct path forward. And she had persisted in that way of thinking, even when things took such an unexpected turn with Tetralanna's appointment and the claim of the volunteers to be so much more than she had ever intended. But now, having won back a measure of her Balance, she could see the merit in Khest's words. By letting matters move forward as they were, and voicing no meaningful protest against it, she gave the appearance of approval. And the longer matters continued down the wrong path, the more disruption correcting them would cause, for herself and for the community as a whole.

Some different solution was needed. But what?

Her hlinga was sufficiently strengthened for her to look back over the past days and see how erratic she had become, sometimes taking bold, solitary action, consulting no one, and other times shrinking back and refusing to take any action at all, no matter how dire the situation, for fear of offending someone… or because she could not bear to be the target of anyone's criticism and displeasure.

What sort of leadership was that?

From this moment forward, she would have to do better, and that must include making better use of her circle of five's advice. Her circle of five… which, unfortunately, was currently a circle of four.

A fine time Burlon had picked to take decisions into his own hands and leave Tradepoint.

A fine time she had picked to force him into doing so.

"Gredin? Have I angered you?"

She shook her head. "No. You have made me think, and for that I am grateful." Meeting his gaze, she said, "Truly. You have helped me in every way."

"Then I am glad. Before we part, may I offer another thought?"

She nodded.

"Until your instincts have fully returned, you might benefit from adopting a pattern."

"Like the one you trace behind my ear?" she teased, and they shared a smile.

"That, as well. But what I mean, for the present, is that you and I might agree to meet at least every second day, if not daily. Five days was too long for you. Or you are free, of course, to seek some other alliance partner–"

"No. Please. At least for now, I would much prefer it to be you. And yes, I see the sense of your suggestion." Again, she smiled. "I would not want to lead the rista astray on the hillside."

"Just so. In two days' time, then?"

"In two days' time."

Rising, Khest deftly Freshened himself and donned his clothes. "Shall I return the jug to its place on the shelf?"

"No, I feel quite capable of doing so. But several of your braids are in disarray. Shall I restore them for you?"

"It would be a kindness."

And so she unplaited three of the braids at the back of his head, and finger-combed the freed locks. The hair of those of House Bentain was subtly different from that of Balamont, its yellow tinged with a hint of palest red. Burlon's hair was like that. He would look slightly out of place in his new House of Laith. What sort of hair would his child with Chenna have?

With long-accustomed fingers, Gredin rebraided Khest's locks. She had often played at braiding Trethen's hair, and Beda's, and Ingarra's.

And, of course, Dreff's. In a way, this braiding felt as intimate as the joining of her body with Khest's. It was not a thing you did for a stranger. It was a service you offered to those who were close in your life.

Carefully, she finished the third braid and secured its end. "There. Now you are ready to carry on with your day, with my thanks."

"And with my thanks to you. It is the beauty of this solution that you found – both who take part will benefit from it."

After Khest left, Gredin moved slowly, accustoming herself to the silence around her and the renewed sense of harmony she felt. When she had Freshened herself and dressed, she Fetched the bedding back to her own room and raked her fingers quickly through her curls. But when it came time to move the jug of amarantha wine, she lifted it into her arms and cradled it there. She had little doubt that she could replace it by using her gyftes… but what if she was wrong, and it broke? No. Better to carry it back to her room and be certain of its safety.

Back in her own bedchamber, when she placed the squatty jug on its shelf, her hands lingered upon it for a moment, stroking the cool stone. What an unlikely vessel it was to hold such a valuable substance within it. Dozens, perhaps hundreds of the Bereft might benefit from its properties… and yet they were denied the chance because of her.

It was her fault.

And it was her responsibility to put it right.

This one last time, she would act alone.

Hastily, she removed the travel outfit she had just redonned. It would not do, not for what she must do next. Instead, resolved, she Freshened the one-piece teal and bronze outfit that Ingarra had sewn for her, then donned its jacket and buttoned it all the way up to her chin. There was nothing she could do about her hair, but she could explain why it looked the way it did. Indeed, she could explain a great many things. And she would.

The time had come for honest answers.

Gredin left her bedchamber, closed the door behind herself, and made her way through the reception hall and the Vennan corridor, not easing her pace until she reached the bio-mist antechamber. Entering it, she waited through the mist cycle and emerged into the public corridor, where she strode to the nearest intersection and pressed her hand against the screen.

"Where want go?" the mechanized voice inquired in Tradetalk.

And Gredin, determined, replied, "Want go Hesch enclave."

[13]

0741 OF 2000 ORBITS REMAINING: 30PURPLE

For Keegan, going to the Clinic had become a familiar walk to a familiar room where he underwent a familiar routine.

Ellis te Vell no longer consistently accompanied him, depending on what tasks she was called upon to perform as part of Venna's small group of surviving Traders. Ever since Burlon had reopened the maartza, the demands on her time had steadily increased, and Keegan had assured Ellis that there was no longer a need for her to act as his minder or interpreter.

While his vocabulary in Tradetalk was still quite limited, it was increasing, thanks to the *crabe* he carried, and he could now easily manage the words he needed for a food-tasting session with Binn. Creative pantomime on his part augmented the few language failures that did occur and, along with Binn's unfailingly close scrutiny, had long since eliminated any anxiety he felt about visits to the clinic.

Indeed, there had begun to be an air of inevitability about them: take his place on the odd-looking but comfortable bed; allow Binn to make her adjustments; begin the food tasting; and, finally, make a mental guess with himself as to how many bites he could swallow before it all came spewing up and out again. Despite having become quite adept at expelling the noisome mess neatly into the pouch Binn provided, Keegan had no wish to subject Ellis to the sight of any more failures. He was quite sure the time she normally spent warming the seat of her chair next to his bed could be spent more productively elsewhere.

Entering the clinic, Keegan briefly bowed with crossed palms to the Prettian seated behind the desk before saying, slowly and clearly, in Tradetalk, "I Keegan. I go Binn. I go six?"

The awkward rhythm, along with the scanty number of words, always reminded him of how a youngling, new to the ways of talking, would make their wishes known. Of course, no one in the Vennan community would mistake him for a young child, despite the cadence of his speech. Indeed, nothing could be farther from the truth; he had lived beneath the hand of the Power for long and long.

"Yes. Is good. You go Binn."

"I thank," Keegan said, and walked through the doorway that led to the corridor that held Room Six.

It was the same room he had used on his first visit to the medical clinic with Ellis and Gredin, and the same room the Prett at the entry desk had directed him to for the food tastings at every visit thereafter. Curious, he had asked Ellis to ask Binn whether the room was permanently assigned to her. Or was there something particular about the bare little room that she preferred over other available rooms? After a back-and-forth exchange with the Third Level *dariiseri*, Ellis had reported, with a shrug, that the healer simply liked consistency.

And apparently that had been the truth for, as usual, he could see Binn waiting for him in the open doorway to Room Six. Her large, dark eyes tracked his movements down the hallway, and Keegan wondered what information she was gathering as she watched him come ever nearer.

"Good day, Binn," Keegan said when he arrived, bowing over crossed palms.

Binn returned the courtesy, saying, "Good day, you. Glad see Keegan come. Begin now?"

"Yes," Keegan replied and, sighing, followed Binn into the room. What would today's Prettian offering taste like? He hoped for something bland; the stronger-tasting samples were always the ones that produced the strongest pains in his middle, and the ones his body rejected the soonest. That had been true of yesterday's trial, and he had still felt a bit nauseous at evening meal. He had managed a few bites of bread before giving it up as a lost cause, gratefully retiring to his bed, and telling himself that morning would find his mind and body restored to normalcy. And that had been the case, praise the Power.

Except for Binn, whom he genuinely liked, he would be glad to leave behind the strange, *griimoni*-ruled world of the Prett clinic when the food trials ended.

Keegan paused to remove his jacket and boots before first sitting, then lying back on the Prettian bed. He had learned through previous experiences that the soft, heated cushion kept him comfortable without his jacket, and that Binn would quickly provide a thick, warm blanket if he requested one.

Reclining, Keegan laid the *crabe* that was never far from him on the metal table, and waited for Binn to provide the day's food offering.

But Binn did not open the cabinet containing the metal plate. Instead, she reached for his *crabe*. Keegan watched as she swiped through a number of screens, too quickly for him to absorb more than a fleeting impression of color and strange symbols. Binn paused on a dark blue screen that held only a flashing circle – a circle, he realized upon looking at it more closely, that was a match to the symbol on the door to the Prett clinic itself. On the day that he, Gredin, and Ellis had first come here, Ellis had pointed out it out as the symbol for a healer.

Binn pressed her finger to the flashing circle. The *crabe* spoke and she answered, the exchange clearly in the Prettian language. Binn gave a grunt of satisfaction as the circle stilled, then dissolved into a long list of unfamiliar symbols. Another tap of Binn's broad finger and the screen image quickly reconfigured itself into something that looked like the roots of a strange plant.

"This," Binn said, pointing at a large orange circle, "Prett food."

A number of straight black lines radiated from the bottom half of the orange circle for a short distance before branching, with sharp angles, into at least two, three, or more, thinner black lines. On the far right of the screen, the line leading from the orange circle branched twice, but in green, not black.

Binn's finger traced the first black line on the left downward. "Keegan eat this food. No good." She continued to move her finger downward, encountering the area where the line branched. Slowly, she stroked each thinner line, repeating as she did, "No good. No good. No good. No good." She peered at Keegan. "See you? Keegan eat this. This. This. This. This." Binn's finger deftly traced each of the other black lines leaving the orange circle. "All no good. No good, Prett food."

Keegan pointed at the green line. "What this?"

"Last try. Last food. No more." Binn pointed at the circle of orange. "Mother this. All Prett food." She pointed at the black lines. "Like children. All make family. Prett food is name family." She cocked her head at him. "Keegan understand?"

"I think, yes." Keegan said slowly. "Green today food? Other food that no good food?" He thought about her description of the Prettian foods as a 'family'. Did she mean…? "Food here." He traced his finger down the first black line, following each thinner line, as well. "Children. First child, four finger. Four finger, four food, not same. Close, but not same. All no good. True?"

"Yes!" Binn's eyes were shining. "Keegan have one child to try. No more. Then we finish. Want be good. Fear not good. Child with two finger? Finger close same."

Keegan thought about what Binn was telling him, and his spirits sank. The last two untried food items were very similar, and Binn expected them to be as unsuccessful as the others he had tried.

For the first time, Keegan was glad Burlon wasn't on Tradepoint, and he sighed. His failure to tolerate any of the Prettian food offerings would be unwelcome news to the circle of five. Keegan had no idea where Burlon would find another food source so willing as the Prett to aid the Vennans.

Binn turned the *crabe* off and placed it on the table. “Binn make plan. Tell Keegan plan. Keegan say yes, maybe?”

“Binn plan is what?”

“Binn see Keegan each day. Keegan smaller. Binn not happy food no good. Binn think. Maybe Prett have more to offer. Vennan might eat thing Prett not eat. Vennan maybe call that thing food. Prett say no, not food for Prett. Understand?”

Items that the Prett didn’t eat but that the Vennans might? Keegan supposed it made a kind of sense. On Venna, the rista ate grasses and other kinds of fodder that the Vennans didn’t. But Vennans ate other kinds of greens and enjoyed them. Grasses and greens were quite similar, overall. So what Binn proposed sounded logical.

Keegan nodded. “Yes. I understand. You ask Director bring other thing to Tradepoint?”

“Maybe,” Binn said. “Need know more about Vennan. Inside Vennan. Inside Keegan. Then tell Director what bring.”

And Keegan supposed that was also logical, if disheartening. The Vokastra were unlikely to sanction such an idea without knowing their efforts were likely to be successful.

“What need do?” he asked.

“Take small piece, here, there, inside Keegan. Keegan not need, be same again soon.”

She was talking about the tissue and blood samples.

“Want help Keegan. Want help all Vennan,” Binn said. “Hurt Binn here,” she placed a broad hand in the middle of her chest, “that Keegan smaller each day.”

Fear for his vessel warred with the desire to bring Gredin and the others good news for a change. Keegan was weary of seeing their faces fall, each morning, when he announced that the previous day’s food tasting had failed yet again. He would give much to lighten the look of worry that Burlon habitually wore to the meetings despite having just left his bed with Chenna.

But no decision had yet been made by the circle regarding Wyve’s original request for samples. Discussion around the table on that first day had centered instead on the need to test the Prett food to ensure it was safe for Vennans to consume. In retrospect, Keegan could see that the food testing had been a wise decision.

And when Gredin had spoken of the Director's appeal, Burlon had instantly dismissed the idea of allowing Prett scientists to take tissue and blood samples, in order to expand their knowledge of Vennan bodies, saying it was not worth the risk, since the Vennan community included Healers. Gredin hadn't seemed as certain, given Cirin te K'lar's death, but the discussion had returned to the need for finding a volunteer willing to taste Prett food. Consequently, they had failed to make a final decision about the Director's request for samples.

Binn, who had been nothing but kind and solicitous, waited patiently for him to speak. If he refused, Keegan had no doubt she would proceed without complaint with the next food tasting, and that her bedside monitoring would be as scrupulous as it had been on each previous occasion.

There are only two foods left to taste.

"You wait. I ask," Keegan said, coming to a decision, and reached out with his private mind. =Gredin?=

There was no response.

He tried again, this time more insistently, in case she was sleeping… or mating with an alliance partner. =Gredin? Gredin te Balamont? I have need of you.=

Nothing.

Vexed and puzzled, Keegan considered what step he should take next. Gredin and Burlon were the only ones he trusted to make a decision this important. As wise as Sill and Miri were, they had as little acquaintance as he did with issues that were not Vennan.

But Burlon was on Sprygale, and Gredin was not answering his mind touch.

Meanwhile, Binn was waiting.

And there are only two foods left to taste, he reminded himself again.

"Yes," he said. "Binn take small piece. Binn use much care when take piece, yes?"

Binn nodded. "Much, much care," she repeated as if to show she had heard him. "Binn help Keegan."

"Yes. What Keegan do?"

"This," she touched his shirt, "off. This, also," she said, indicating his pants.

Keegan removed his clothes and handed them to her, grateful for the warmth of the bed against his bare skin. "What now?"

"Make flat. Keegan not move. Binn tell griimoni what do."

With trepidation fluttering his insides, Keegan felt the bed flatten until he was horizontal. The position gave him a view of nothing but the immaculate white ceiling, and he wished there was a window or a picture there, anything to slow his thoughts and distract him from what was to come. He turned his head to watch Binn, rather than stare blindly at that sea of white.

Binn moved with smooth assurance, pressing panels that opened silently beneath her touch, although he couldn't decipher the purpose of the screens they revealed. Binn's broad hand moved again, and suddenly a pale blue light encompassed the bed, and Keegan became aware of a faint vibration, as if the bed itself were humming.

"Make you, make all, much clean," Binn said.

Like a Cleansing. Keegan smiled to himself. How odd it would look and sound if Vennans hummed and produced light each time they Cleansed themselves or their surroundings. Nevertheless, it was reassuring to think the Prett and the Vennans performed similar functions, the Prett with their *griimoni,* the Vennans with the Power.

Keegan expected both the light and the vibration to cease but they continued. He made a sweeping gesture, encompassing his bed. "This blue stay?"

"Yes," Binn said. "Blue go when finish take pieces."

Keegan wished Gredin were present. With her ability to speak fluent Prettian, she could have asked the multitude of questions that hovered on his tongue. Her assistance would have enabled him to obtain many more details for the account of this experience that he would write for his histories. Perhaps, Keegan mused, he could persuade her to accompany him when he returned to the clinic tomorrow for the penultimate food tasting. By then, he could have a neat list of questions compiled for her to ask Binn.

Binn applied something cold and sticky to his chest, jolting him from his thoughts, and he instinctively flinched.

"…chee, chee, chee…" Binn murmured, then said, "Is good. Cold. Make not feel. Griimoni see Keegan, tell Binn where put." She continued, picking up another filmy disk and placing it near the first. A third followed, this time on his right side, just beneath his ribs. A fourth and a fifth were placed on his left hip and at the bend of his inner arm, respectively. "Good," Binn said.

Keegan lifted his arm to more closely examine the strange object affixed there. The material was so thin that he could see his skin through it. In the center of the disk was a circular opening not much bigger than the eye of one of Ingarra's tapestry needles.

Whatever substance the disk was made of neither pinched nor pulled uncomfortably at his skin, despite adhering tightly to it. The coldness emanating from the disks, however, was annoyingly acute, causing him first to tense, then to shiver.

Binn noticed immediately and turned to touch the control panel she operated. "Make more warm come," she said.

And it was true. Almost before she finished speaking, the surface beneath him began to radiate delicious waves of heat along the length of his body. It didn't eliminate his awareness of the cold spots on his skin, but the new level of warmth made them decidedly more bearable.

"My thanks," Keegan said, knowing Binn understood that phrase of Vennan. The same sentiment, in Tradetalk, never sounded sincere enough to him.

Binn's big hands made gentle adjustments to the position of his body, straightening his legs and moving his arms until they lay extended, palms up, close to his body. Then she placed a pillow beneath his head. "Good?" she asked.

"Good," Keegan assured her.

"No move. Time take piece," Binn said, and touched a new panel on the wall, one she had never opened before.

The panel door folded back on itself, revealing a narrow cupboard rather than another screen, and Keegan watched with interest as Binn coaxed a strange *griimoni* from its depths. A polished metal oval made of thin, curving, jointed metal rods emerged. It was roughly half his length, mounted on a long neck-like arm. Binn stretched the *griimoni*'s long neck until the bottom edge of the oval ring hovered a handspan above his chest. Then she returned to her control panel.

Lights bloomed along the circumference of the oval, and it rotated silently, halting when a corresponding oval of light lay on his skin, one that encompassed the cold disks attached there. Binn touched the control panel once again and the disks lit up, one after the other, glowing like small stars against his skin.

"No move," Binn requested again.

His curiosity at its peak, Keegan watched the *griimoni* silently descend.

Five eyes opened along the curving rods, spilling bright light as they each extruded another length of metal. Keegan squinted against the glare, trying to make out details. The new extensions seemed thinner, and the light glaring down from each open hatch began to pulse and spin.

Or was it the extensions themselves that were spinning?

It was the last coherent thought Keegan managed.

The previously silent *griimoni* made a high-pitched sound and the needle-like extensions darted downward, penetrating the openings in the disks with swift precision.

Stunned by the rapidity of the process, Keegan began to tremble. The sight of the metal extensions invading his body sickened him. A feeling of intense pressure began to build, quickly transforming into a smothering wave of pain, and he tried to cry out to Binn.

More pain followed as the *griimoni* bit him, deep inside, before withdrawing as quickly as they had attacked.

Keegan felt a wave of scorching heat sweep through him, leaving ice in its wake. He shuddered, gasping as hot agony flared in his chest, his hip, his arm – everywhere the *griimoni* had penetrated.

He heard shrill alarms, quickly joined by Binn's agitated voice.

His vision darkened.

He couldn't breathe.

The room noises grew fainter, then stopped.

The darkness expanded, swallowing his pain and his panicked thoughts, and he relaxed.

For a brief moment he felt a sense of gratitude. Then awareness vanished.

[14]

0741 OF 2000 ORBITS REMAINING: 30GREEN

The foot ached.

It was a bitter thing to have uprooted the nest and undertaken this journey, only to find that few other races were currently in port. And now, thanks to the accursed Vennans, he had to confine himself to his chair for long passages of time. But it was either that or risk showing weakness in the Market. He could only tolerate a half-day of walking and standing before the discomfort grew distracting and his temper grew dangerously short.

"Nitikikani?"

Anger flared. "I left orders not to be disturbed."

"Yes. Deep regret. But…"

He clacked his bill before he could master the impulse, and grumbled, "Whatever it is, have Ragar handle it." As if Ragar's conceit needed any more nourishment. Oh well. It would, at least, get rid of this unctuous underling.

But it didn't. "Nitikikani… It is Ragar who sent me."

Something had finally arisen that Ragar admitted he couldn't handle? That was a wonder. "What does he need?"

"He needs you to come."

"Come where, fool? You think I want to wander the ship on this foot, seeking Ragar?"

"No, of course not. Your pardon. But Ragar is not on the ship. He is in the enclave."

"I am *not* walking all the way out to the enclave again. What is Ragar's difficulty?"

"Someone is at the entrance, asking for you."

"Prett security?"

"No, Nitikikani."

"Then tell whoever is there to leave a message and go away. Or make an appointment to meet with me at the maartza, tomorrow."

"Ragar suggested those things. They were not… acceptable alternatives."

Against his will, Nitikikani felt his curiosity awakening. "Did Ragar identify this importunate visitor?"

"He said to tell you… a Vennan."

Carefully, Nitikikani lifted his foot from the cradle and lowered it to the floor, freeing himself to swing his chair around and stare directly at the young messenger. "I find that unlikely. Did Ragar have anything to add?"

"Only that it is not a trader."

Not a trader, Ragar claimed, and yet Nitikikani felt his trader's instinct stir. "Very well," he said. "Go back. Tell Ragar that I am on my way."

"Yes, sir. Shall I have him admit the visitor?"

"No."

Nitikikani took his time, rewrapping his sleeves, then claiming his stick. Let his uninvited caller pace the public corridor, waiting for him. And, by the nebulae, if it was the one he'd had Prett Security evict from the maartza… Unlikely. That one had been a trader. This one wasn't, or at least claimed not to be.

The riddle managed to distract him somewhat from the throb of discomfort that every other step cost him. He rode down from the perch and wound his way through the ship to the rigid umbilical. At its far end, he went through the double lock and emerged, at last, into the enclave, that little piece of Tradepoint allotted to them for the duration of this stay.

Ragar was there, waiting for him, but at least had the good sense not to betray nerves or impatience.

"The visitor is still in the public corridor?" Nitikikani asked.

Ragar nodded.

"Anything to add?"

Ragar's shoulders twitched. "It just stands there, saying your name. There is a security guard watching it."

"Very well. Get on with your work. I will see to it."

With a quick nod, Ragar moved on, perhaps relieved not to have to deal further with the stranger. Well, Nitikikani had no fear of strangers. Beng carried knives. Shodekekeen had claws. Vennans were tall but mild – like Mamora, but without the stink. Annoying but harmless.

His foot throbbed.

Well, mostly harmless.

With Ragar gone, Nitikikani took a moment to make the mental shift to Tradetalk, then went to the nearest comm panel and activated it. "Nitikikani," he announced. "Who you? What want?"

"Greeting, Nitikikani. Gredin te Balamont here. Want talk."

Well, *that* was not the answer he'd expected.

He could see little point in speaking with that Vennan, beyond the pleasure of berating it for troubling him at his enclave. Still, the day had been short on amusements, and he had already risen from his comfortable chair and come this far.

"You wait," he said, and keyed the comm off.

Grumbling beneath his breath, he hobbled through the rest of the enclave and entered the antechamber, beyond which lay the public corridor. While the bio-mist cycled, he took up a position near the outer door where he could lean one casual-looking shoulder against the door frame, and keep his support stick out of sight.

The mist receded.

The outer door parted and slid open.

Nitikikani eased a half-step forward, to prevent the door from closing prematurely.

And there, framed in the doorway, stood a Prett security guard, standing back a few respectful paces from the threshold, accompanied by a most peculiar figure.

The shape and height and general coloring were right for a Vennan. But Vennans wore their sleek hair in long, complicated plaits. This individual's hair was less than a center talon long, and what there was of it waved and twisted in little coils all over its head, without a discernible pattern.

No. This did not look like the young one who had stepped upon his foot and then wept and cowered through the Director's Judgment. Nor did it seem to be the bold one who had worn the scarlet clothing and accepted their gift at the Trisectoriana reception. Both of those Vennans had asked to be called 'Gredin te Balamont,' and he had reconciled himself to the contradiction by reasoning that it must be a title rather than a name, and that the Vennan in the scarlet outfit had supplanted the weeping one after the shame of the Judgment. But then he had encountered a Vennan in the public corridor who wore the fire-stone and claimed to be the one who had injured his foot. And now a fourth one stood before him, again claiming that title.

Or had he misread the entire situation?

That was not a pleasing thought… and yet the Judgment had been passed, much to his advantage, and so his understanding could not be too badly awry. He would, he decided, listen to what this new creature had to say. Perhaps its words would make matters clearer.

"Nitikikani," he said, touching his chest with his free hand. It seemed as good a way to begin as any. "You come here, ask talk me."

A small movement of the lips, and a nod. "Yes. Thank Nitikikani. Need talk."

He gestured at it. "Name you."

It looked startled. "Gredin te Balamont."

He cocked his head.

It seemed to read his skepticism. With a nod of its head, it said, "Look different. Hair gone." Then it added, "Beng push me down, cut hair, take hair, leave Tradepoint."

He knew that the Beng were gone. Their orbital countback had been deep into the orange. But he had heard no rumors of an attack by Beng on a Vennan. That was shocking. The Director must be furious. Such things simply did not happen on Tradepoint.

Until now.

Remembering the little knives the Beng were so fond of, he asked, "Hurt you, they?"

The Vennan shrugged and nodded. "Make many small cut. Make big bruise. Make threat do worse." It touched its brow. "Beng want take hlao. No could make come off." It touched its arm. "Want take hlette. Same." It touched the jacket collar, buttoned up to its chin. "Want take flamestone. Lucky I no wear, that night, or Beng have now. At end, angry, they cut braids, take."

But Nitikikani hardly heard those final words. The firestone! His heart doubled its beat. So then, this *was* the same Vennan, or at least one who held the same title. Was the firestone a badge of office? Was the Vennan wearing it now, beneath the concealment of that high collar?

He tried, without success, to calm himself. The firestone had first come to him in a ta'akdream when he was a mere fledgling, and the crisp, unfading memory of it had haunted him ever since, shaping his life, influencing his choices, inspiring him first to explore even the most remote areas of Heschanda, and then to hone his skills as a trader and undertake missions to Tradepoint, where individuals from so many worlds came to barter their goods.

Until this trip, however, his efforts had all been in vain.

As a first-fledged, he had been taught to expect such a dream, but it was rare for anyone to have their ta'ak revealed to them at such an early age. He had spent much of his free time in childhood recreating its image in paints or in clay, striving always to craft something that was more closely true to the sight he had been vouchsafed in his ta'akdream. It was shaped like a tear falling from the Ta'akgod's eye, just such a size, and width, and thickness, and weight. Its background was the black of night, the impenetrable darkness of space, the color of a Hesch's great primary feather. Against that expanse of black, colors blazed across it diagonally, like the spreading tail of some perfect comet: greens and golds, blue and reds, in delicate layers that seemed lit from within.

And when he had finally lain eyes upon it in reality, not just in his dreams, it belonged to another, to this Gredin creature. Walking the corridors of Tradepoint with a group of other Vennans, this one had displayed a flash of color at the throat that caught his eye – and then held his complete attention when he realized what he had just witnessed.

A day later, when that same Vennan appeared from nowhere and blundered into him, breaking a bone in his foot, the painful event had offered him an unlooked-for opportunity. By charging kegitt against the Vennan, and agreeing to allow the Prett clinic to confirm the damage done to his foot, he had insured that the Judgment against the Vennan would be ruinously high. In return, after giving the Vennan enclave a night to despair over what had befallen them, he had planned to offer them an exchange: cancellation of the Judgment in return for giving him the firestone. But the Director had interfered, transferring the bulk of the Judgment debt onto the Beng, thereby ruining Nitikikani's plan.

He had been heartsick ever since.

And now this Gredin Vennan was here, wanting to speak with him?

Why?

"Say," he invited. "Why come? What want say Nitikikani?"

It sighed, then squared its shoulders. "Tradetalk not good way speak. Not… smooth. I come say important thing. Nitikikani be patient. If word come out wrong, I want fix. Please."

He nodded. "You talk. I listen."

A breath. Then it said, "I come say sorry. But more. Want do more than speak word. Word be easy. Empty. Want Nitikikani understand. Want Nitikikani believe. Want Nitikikani hear sorry from inside me. Want Nitikikani think hard, say what I do make sorry not be empty. What Nitikikani want? What Nitikikani need? If I have, I give. Want Nitikikani not be angry at me. Want Hesch not be angry at Vennan. Want all be good with Hesch and Vennan. Not easy, I know. Nitikikani think, please. How we fix? How we make fix last? How we be good together, Nitikikani and me, Hesch and Vennan?"

That forced a painful laugh from him. This Vennan seemed sincere in its determination to mend the breach. But there was no way it would agree to give him the one thing that he truly desired. Once it heard his demand, it would turn and leave. And his heart would break again.

But the Vennan was watching him closely, its eyes suddenly alight. "You know a thing?"

He said nothing.

It persisted. "Nitikikani think hard, think of a thing, maybe? Yes?"

Hesch did not lie. Stiffly, knowing the futility of it, he nodded.

"You name thing to this Vennan, yes? Please? Nitikikani name this thing to Gredin te Balamont?"

He wanted, at the very least, to see his ta'ak clearly, even if this was the only time it could ever be so. Reaching out, he pointed his finger at the Vennan's throat.

It blinked, its expression one he had learned to identify as confusion, but it did not retreat. "Not understand," it said, with only a slight unsteadiness in its voice. "Show, please. Show what want."

Extending his arm, he used the tip of one talon to tap against the top button of its jacket. "Open," he said.

The Vennan's eyes widened, and it glanced up and down the public corridor, but then it returned its gaze to Nitikikani, and unfastened the button.

In silence, he tapped the second button, and then the third.

"Take jacket off?" the Vennan asked.

Nitikikani nodded.

It obeyed, unfastening the second button, and the third, then shrugging the jacket off of its shoulders, down its arms, and off.

The corridor lights set the firestone's colors ablaze, and Nitikikani felt a rush of heated longing sweep through his body. He tried to sear the moment into his memory, so that he would always have at least the sight of it to remember.

"What Nitikikani want?" the Vennan asked. "Tell. Use words."

His voice came out so thinly that it could barely shape the sounds. "Firestone."

A shocked look crossed the Vennan's face, followed immediately by something that might have been horror. It said nothing, did nothing, simply stood, scarcely seeming to breathe. But its body pulsed, every few moments, causing the light to dazzle on the firestone.

"If…" it said at last. Just that. *If.*

He waited, afraid to fracture the moment.

It tried again. "If I give Nitikikani flamestone…" Its face contorted, then smoothed. "This be fix I seek? You say words, please. You say what this do, if…"

The burden, suddenly, was on him. It frightened him to think that what he wanted might actually be possible, if only he could find the right words. Slowly, watching the Vennan's face for any sign of confusion or anger, he said, "If."

The Vennan nodded, seeming to understand that the two of them were building something here, piece by fragile piece.

Nitikikani said, "If Vennan Gredin give ta'ak–"

"*Ta'ak*? Not know this word."

He started over. "If Vennan Gredin give firestone to Nitikikani…" He took a breath. "If Nitikikani keep firestone for always…" The Vennan had to understand that he was proposing a permanent arrangement, not a loan or a temporary solution. "Then… Then Nitikikani and Vennan Gredin be good always together. Hesch and Vennan be good as long as Hesch listen to Nitikikani." There were limits to what he could promise; the Vennan needed to understand that fact, as well. "Cannot speak for Hesch Nitikikani not know. But Nitikikani, Nitikikani Tradeteam, Nitikikani ship, Nitikikani crew be good always together with Vennan Gredin, Vennan Gredin Tradeteam, Vennan Gredin ship, Vennan Gredin crew. Hesch tell truth always. You ask Director. Nitikikani promise good always. If trouble come between Vennan and Hesch, then Vennan Gredin talk Nitikikani, we solve, we make good. This what Vennan Gredin want, yes? I understand?"

"Yes." The Vennan's face was wet, its hands shaking visibly as it reached up and tried to unfasten the cord from which the firestone hung. When it had tried for a time, unsuccessfully, it approached Nitikikani, turned around, and bowed its head, exposing the slender column of its neck. “You take,” it invited.

Instead, Nitikikani grasped its shoulders carefully and turned it around to face him once again. “Soon,” he said. “You come inside. We sit. Talk. I show you a thing. Then I give you a thing. Yes?”

The Vennan looked past him to the antechamber, and he saw a shiver race through it. It said something over its shoulder in Prettian to the security guard, then raised its gaze to meet his and said, “Yes. I thank. Yes. I come inside.”

[15]
0741 OF 2000 ORBITS REMAINING: 30ORANGE

Wyve, Director of Tradepoint, tapped his desk to raise the holographic screen.

The day had been an exceptionally busy one, and he was tired as he neared the end of his shift, but Figg was due in the office shortly for the changeover report.

There had been two arrivals, this day: the Nairn and the Yaylay. The Nairn had approached the station late morning, signaling their desire to dock after offering a friendly hail. Once permission was granted, they accomplished station docking with brisk efficiency.

The Yaylay ship had exited FTL one revolution later, at what the Yaylay considered a safe distance from the station, and they had stood off without contact for an additional two revolutions before requesting docking instructions. In the twenty sectora since First Contact, the Yaylay had initially spent twelve revolutions observing Tradepoint and its surroundings for possible dangers before asking for a dock assignment, their concerns apparently appeased. The Yaylay were nothing if not cautious, and Wyve considered it a testament to the station's smooth operation that the Yaylay had gradually reduced their observation time from twelve to two revolutions during his tenure.

The delay had not been without additional benefits, since both

Docking and Security had consequently been able to perform the routine tasks associated with an arriving trade ship sequentially, rather than simultaneously, eliminating any pressure on the two departments that might have resulted if two ships had reached dock together.

And now, happily, the organized Nairn had sent their ship manifest.

Wyve tapped his desk again and the list of trade goods the Nairn would be offering filled the holographic screen. He planned to review it with Figg before turning station authority over to her, and Wyve strongly hoped the Nairn manifested contained edibles, ones the Vennans might find safe and useful.

Without warning, the border around the screen turned red and began to flash, the signal for a station emergency. Whatever the unknown situation, it was dire.

The manifest dissolved, revealing the distressed face of Murnn, a communications tech. "Director, I have been ordered to declare an emergency in the Clinic."

"Report." *Had there been another incident in the Traders' Market? Was someone else hurt?*

"The Third Level dariiseri..." Murnn looked away from the screen for a moment, and Wyve heard a muffled voice speaking, the words unintelligible, the tone one of distress.

"Director, Binn urgently requests that you contact the First Speaker for the Vennans and request her immediate presence in the Clinic."

"What precisely is the matter, Murnn?" Wyve asked firmly, but he feared he already knew. Something serious had apparently happened to Keegan te Fliss, for Binn was involved, and he had personally selected Binn to oversee the food challenges with the Vennan historian.

"Director, Binn says the Vennan is dying. A full medical team is in Room Six trying to prevent it but they are having little success in their attempts to revive him. Binn requests the presence of the leader of the Vennans in the hope she will have some essential piece of knowledge they currently lack."

Wyve took a deep breath, masking his own distress, before replying, "Very well. I will be there shortly with Gredin te Balamont. Urge Binn to spare no effort in preserving the Vennan's life."

"Of course, Director," Murnn replied.

Wyve terminated the contact almost before Murnn finished speaking, and sent an emergency signal to Gredin's wristband, drumming his broad fingers against the desk as he waited for the signal to connect, mentally rehearsing the unfortunate news he would have to share with her. He needed to impress Gredin with the extreme urgency of the situation without unduly frightening her.

But instead of hearing Gredin's voice in response to his signal, his desk displayed an unwelcome message: *Connection failure. Repeat attempt?*

Cursing under his breath, Wyve programmed his desk to continue to send the emergency signal to Gredin until contact was established. With that done, he contemplated his next action. Hopefully, Gredin would respond momentarily, but the dire situation did not allow for delay.

Hesitating for only a moment, Wyve accessed the station communication system and entered the code that allowed him to broadcast throughout the Traders' Market and the public corridors, then hurriedly searched the remaining symbols for the one denoting the Vennan enclaves. Finding it, Wyve swiftly added it to the broadcast area. The sound of his voice might stir fear among those hearing it – particularly the Vennans – but it couldn't be helped. There was no time to waste.

"Attention! Priority alert! Burlon te Laith, report to Director. Burlon te Laith, report to Director. Immediately!"

Wyve had just finished keying the message to repeat until further notice, when Figg, looking a bit ruffled, strode into the office.

"What is happening?" she asked. "Are the Hesch making more trouble for the Vennans?"

"No. The alert involves only the Vennans. The Clinic says it is imperative that we bring Gredin there immediately, but she has not answered my calls to her communication band. The situation is dire. If Gredin cannot be located, then Burlon must act in her stead. Keegan te Fliss, is experiencing a medical crisis. Binn fears he is close to death."

Figg assimilated his words, the line of her mouth grim by the time he finished. "I agree, then, that Burlon is the next best choice."

"He should have heard the alert by now. Contact should happen any–"

His desk signaled an incoming call and Wyve expelled a breath of relief. Burlon could always be counted on to understand the nuances of station life, and a Priority Alert had no doubt caught his immediate attention.

"Wyve speaking," he announced, accepting the call.

"Director? This is Ellis te Vell. I am one of the Vennan Traders."

Wyve well remembered the hapless female trader who had looked so upset on the day one of her charges, Gredin te Balamont, had accidentally broken the foot of Nitikikani of the Hesch. Fortunately, she spoke Prettian clearly enough.

"Ellis te Vell, where is Burlon?" Wyve asked, wasting no time on pleasantries. "I have urgent need of him."

There was a momentary silence. Then Ellis te Vell said, "Burlon is on Sprygale, Director."

For the geddel crystals he had pressured Burlon to acquire....

"Where is Gredin te Balamont? She is not answering our calls."

"I... I do not know, Director."

Wyve felt anger begin to build, alongside his fear. Without Gredin or Burlon, the Vennans seemed lost and ill-informed, uncertain of how to proceed. Did they have no protocols in place for such a situation?

"Listen to me carefully, Ellis te Vell. Your historian, Keegan te Fliss, is dying. I urge you to bring your best... healer to the medical clinic immediately. There is no time for delay. The situation is... not good."

"I will do my best, Director. I just wish you had been able to reach Gredin."

"As do I. Hurry, Ellis. Bring your healer."

"Yes, Director. Please, don't let Keegan evanesce. He is the last of his House... and my friend."

"We will do my best to prevent that from happening," Wyve assured her. But he couldn't help adding again, before he terminated the connection, "Make all haste, Ellis, or our efforts to save Keegan te Fliss may be in vain."

[16]

0740 OF 2000 ORBITS REMAINING: 31PURPLE

Standing beside Nitikikani as the bio-mist came down, Gredin kept her gaze fixed on his lanky form towering over her. *You are standing upright, not huddled on the floor. You entered this antechamber by your own choice. This is nothing like what you encountered with the Beng.*

But no one else knew she was here.

Nitikikani issued a civilized invitation, which you accepted. He didn't drag you in here. And remember, this time, that you are wearing Wyve's wristband. At need, you have only to press its jewel and Security will come.

But would they? The public corridor was one thing. But she was now preparing to enter the Hesch enclave. Did Prett Security have Wyve's permission to enter another race's enclave, uninvited?

Stop it. Breathe. You aren't afraid of Nitikikani. You're just upset because... because of what you have agreed to give to him.

Choking back a whimper, she raised her hand and clasped the flamestone pendant, her only surviving keepsake from Dreff, given to her in the sweet moments of their Choosing…

Fine. If it is that important to you, keep it. But be honest with yourself about the price. If you go back on your word and refuse to part with it, the Hesch will not Trade with us, and there will be no more amarantha wine. You will endanger those of the Bereft who are finding this transition most difficult. And you may be condemning yourself to becoming one of the Unredeemed, as well. Will you throw all of that away in order to hang a pretty bauble around your neck? Is that the decision of a leader?

The mist was nearly gone. Gredin forced her fingers to unclench, releasing the flamestone. When the door at the back of the antechamber slid open, she let Nitikikani lead the way, and was dismayed to see that he was still using a stick to support part of his weight as he walked.

As they emerged into the enclave, another Hesch came toward them, then stopped in obvious shock when it saw Gredin.

She nodded. “A good day,” she said in Tradetalk. “Peace.”

Nitikikani spoke in what she assumed was the Hesch language, a series of harsh sounds that made her throat ache in sympathy. Whatever he said, it appeared to reassure the other Hesch, for it returned to its work.

Looking down at her, Nitikikani said, “I take you my rooms. We talk, sit, drink. No one come there, make bother. Quiet.”

She nodded and followed, suppressing a wince when she saw the way he limped. Their progress was slow as they walked between assorted stacks of crates and containers, sometimes having to detour around large pallets of goods. Gredin soon realized, with a pang of alarm, that she was no longer quite certain which direction would take her back to the antechamber.

Don't worry about it, she admonished herself firmly. *Either all is as it seems, and Nitikikani or one of his people will escort you out when the visit is at an end, or things are not as they seem, and you already have far larger concerns than the direction of the antechamber.*

Eventually, they reached an odd-looking door. When Nitikikani opened it, Gredin saw that it was several layers thick, opening onto a small, empty room with an identical door on its other side.

Unsettled, she took a step back and said, “Is what, this?”

Nitikikani answered promptly with a single unfamiliar word.

“Not understand,” Gredin protested. “Use other word?”

Nitikikani's shoulders moved in what might have been a sigh. "Between place," he said.

"Between what?"

"Enclave here. My rooms there," he said, pointing at the far door.

"Why empty room between?"

He tried to explain. Gredin had to admit that he made a genuine effort. But, as happened sometimes when she talked to Figg and Wyve, all of the truly necessary words were unfamiliar to her, and attempts to define them only seemed to lead their efforts farther astray. Finally, with a shake of the head and what might have been a small laugh, Nitikikani said, "You want we stay here, talk? Not need go my room. Just… better there. Quiet. Sit. But stay here if want."

She could see nowhere in the enclave to sit. It was a working warehouse. And Nitikikani's posture bespoke discomfort.

Either everything is all right or nothing is.

She decided to trust.

"We go Nitikikani room," she said, and walked into the little empty space, stepping over the raised sill of the door.

Nitikikani followed her in, closed the door behind himself, touched a series of buttons on a panel, then crossed the room and did the same on the panel next to the other door. Three beeps sounded. Then he opened it and gestured for Gredin to go through.

When she did, she found herself in a long, narrow, barren corridor.

"Is good," Nitikikani assured her. "Just walk."

And so she did, although she felt less sure and more foolish with every step. Twenty, fifty, a hundred steps, and still there was no end in sight.

Surely the walk must be unpleasant for Nitikikani, using his walking stick behind her.

After nearly two hundred steps, she saw what appeared to be the end of the corridor in the distance – a blank wall without a door. But that was nonsense. He would not have brought her all this way for nothing. And so she walked on, with Nitikikani silent behind her.

Why did he want Dreff's pendant? Why did he want it so badly that he was willing to forgive his injury and promise peace between the Hesch and the Vennans, in exchange for it?

Or was she being naïve? The pendant was a tangible object; peace was not. Once she surrendered the pendant to him, would he and the rest of the Hesch simply continue their grudge, denying that the agreement she had made with Nitikikani ever took place?

No. *Hesch tell truth always*, he'd said, and her gyfte had resonated to the authenticity of his words. This was no time to start doubting him – or herself, for that matter.

Another hundred and fifty steps brought them to the end of the corridor and another heavy door.

"I open," Nitikikani said, and moved past her. Reaching the door, he pressed a button and said something, apparently in Hesch.

A brief reply.

More words from Nitikikani.

A longer reply which, to Gredin's ear, sounded agitated.

She expected a sharp reply from Nitikikani. Instead, he spoke quietly. Was he attempting to calm? To coax? To persuade? There seemed to be elements of all of those things in his tone.

Silence. Then three beeps and a click.

Nitikikani tugged on the broad handle of the door, and it swung slowly open.

"In," said Nitikikani, and stepped aside for her to enter.

"In where?" Gredin asked. "What there? Your room?"

"Between place."

"And then?"

"Ship."

Ship?

Gredin hesitated. She had heard that word often since coming to Tradepoint, but it made little sense to her, despite Burlon's descriptions. She understood Sending herself from one place to another. She understood Traveling the River to cover greater distances, and that the Travelers' gyfte enabled them to take other people and goods along with them. But if someone was doing all of that, why would they want the further burden of encasing themselves in a metal shell?

She had been touched and quietly amused when Nitikikani pledged to 'be good always together with Vennan Gredin, Vennan Gredin Tradeteam, Vennan Gredin ship, Vennan Gredin crew.' There *was* no 'Gredin ship' or 'Gredin crew,' but she had understood the intention of his words.

Now, however, she wondered if she had made a dangerous assumption.

She lifted her hand in the gesture traders used when they needed to request a clarification. Pointing down to the floor beneath her feet, then at the bare corridor that surrounded them, she asked, "Tradepoint, yes?"

"No." Nitikikani extended one long, thin arm and pointed diagonally, back the way they had come. "Tradepoint there."

More urgently, she pointed at the floor beneath their feet again and asked, "What this?"

He said a word she didn't know.

She shook her head.

He said a different word.

She shook her head.

He hesitated, then said, "Empty."

In a sickening rush, words that Tetralanna had spoken on their first day on Tradepoint rushed back into Gredin's mind: *This place is like a cloud, hanging in the sky far above the surface of the Prett home world. Burlon says there is no air to breathe, on the other side of these walls... If you made an error while Sending, you could end up outside of Tradepoint, and it would end your life.*

And all that stood between her and that emptiness was this corridor? This narrow tunnel? Compared to that, Nitikikani's ship suddenly sounded like a beacon of safety. "We go in?" she asked. "We go in now, please?"

"Yes." Nitikikani gestured for her to go first through the open door.

Anxious, she plunged ahead, stepping over the raised sill, and found herself in yet another small, bare room. Well, not altogether bare. Benches lined one wall, with what looked like a row of cupboards above them. She sat down on the far bench, watching as

Nitikikani entered and secured the outer door behind himself. When he turned to look at her, she gestured around them and asked, "Your room?"

"No. Ship between place." He did something to the inner door, and it opened. "Come. No more between place. Ship. We go my room now."

Her fears might have been groundless. Nevertheless, Gredin was relieved to step over the sill and enter Nitikikani's ship. Hesch traveled to and from Tradepoint all of the time; surely they had found a safe way to do so.

"Stay close," Nitikikani said, and headed off to their right.

His pace was slow, for which Gredin was grateful; she had no wish to get lost aboard the Hesch ship.

Their path offered little for her to see – a solid metal wall to their right, and a similar wall on their left that was punctuated by doors that were mostly closed. Of the two they passed that were open, Gredin glimpsed a room that bore a wall of blinking lights, and another where a seated Hesch met her curious look with a jerk of its head that might have been an expression of surprise. Or perhaps not. It was difficult for her to read the movements and minimal expressions of Hesch. She preferred it when they spoke, allowing her to gain a sense of the emotion beneath their words.

"Here. We go up," Nitikikani said, and stopped.

Gredin looked, confused by what she saw. There was an alcove, and within it there was a metal rope as thick as her arm that moved upward silently, ceaselessly, like a stream flowing to the sky. Then a section of the rope appeared with a small metal platform affixed that extended horizontally, filling most of the alcove. As she watched, the metal rope carried the platform upward, out of sight.

A while later, another platform appeared, and also vanished into the space above. And then another.

"Step," Nitikikani said. "Step take you up, take you my room." The Hesch gestured, tracing the shape of a tall loop in the air. "You understand?"

Unsure, she said, "Maybe no."

Nitikikani nodded. “Step come. I walk on step, stand. Step go up my room. I walk off.”

She bit her lip, trying to envision doing such a thing.

“Step come slow. Walk on step, stand. Go up. Walk off step. Yes?”

She nodded, but she supposed her nervousness was apparent.

For just an instant, Nitikikani touched her shoulder, and she understood it to be an expression of reassurance. “You watch. I go first, show Gredin Vennan. Next you go. I wait up there, help you walk off. Yes?”

“Yes,” she said quickly, before her nerve could desert her.

“Is good,” Nitikikani said, and took up a position within the alcove, looking down over the edge. “Step come now.”

The step appeared.

Nitikikani moved forward onto it, gripping the metal rope with one hand, the walking stick with the other, and was carried upward, out of her sight.

Gredin looked back over her shoulder. What if a member of the Hesch crew came along and found her standing alone? On the whole, that possibility seemed more frightening than the stately ascent she had just watched Nitikikani make.

She edged forward into the alcove and peered down, as she had seen Nitikikani do.

A step was right there, so close that it startled her. She froze, and the step continued to rise, now at the height of her knee, now her waist, now her shoulder. She watched it vanish upward, her breath coming quickly.

Be ready for the next one, she chided herself, and looked down again. Dry-mouthed, she waited and watched, waited and watched, waited and… Ah. She saw a glimmer of silver rising out of the darkness. Watching it come ever closer, she tried to judge when to step and when to reach for the rope.

Now.

She moved forward in two quick steps and gripped the metal rope.

And up she went.

After the first anxious moment, she found that the platform was solid beneath her feet, the metal rope smooth in her grasp, and that her upward motion created a slight breeze that felt wonderful against her heated cheeks. Rising effortlessly was a strange sensation, one that she realized filled her with excitement.

"Gredin Vennan, you good?"

Looking up, she saw Nitikikani peering down the shaft at her.

"Yes!" she called up in reassurance. "Much good!" Emboldened, she grasped the rope with her other hand and moved her feet in tiny steps until she had managed to turn around. As the step brought her gradually level with a new room, she was able to hop nimbly off of the little platform and land securely on the floor.

"Good. This my room," Nitikikani said. "You sit. We talk."

Gredin tried not to stare. The room where they now stood was softly lit and welcoming, its walls covered in textured hangings, its floor thickly carpeted. The area toward which Nitikikani urged her held a grouping of four large orbs, like a giant arrangement of the sort of hollowed gourds she had sometimes set out for birds to nest in. One rested directly on the carpet, while the others were mounted upon pedestals of varying heights.

Chairs. She realized that they were intended to act as chairs.

The highest chair had something suspended from the top of it, a slender metal rod that extended for a little way out into the room. Two tall triangles descended from the tip of it, with a length of cloth strung between their bases. If she had seen such a thing at home, in the gardens, she would have assumed it to be an art piece designed to interact with the breeze. Here within the confines of the Hesch ship, its purpose evaded her entirely.

Avoiding that chair, Gredin ducked her head and seated herself in the next-tallest chair. Its circular interior was padded with a generous number of cushions of varying shapes and thicknesses, and the top of the 'gourd' that curved high over her head had been incised so that the room lights created an intricate pattern as they shone through the thin places. It reminded her of the lace cradles Hayla had fashioned for the luminth at the reception, designed to make the light itself an ornament.

And now, according to Khest, those same lace cradles were being used in the Bereft's new enclave…

The very thought of the Bereft jolted her thoughts back to the urgency of the present moment. She saw Nitikikani speak quietly into a panel on the wall, then settle into the tallest chair and swing his injured foot up to rest on the cradle of suspended cloth.

Gredin's conscience twinged. *Not a piece of art. Accommodation for his injury.*

Nitikikani leaned far back, cushion-propped. "So, Gredin Vennan. Why you here Tradepoint all these days? Vennan come, Vennan go. Vennan not stay long." A slow lift of his lengthy bill. "You stay long."

The inquiry was mildly put, not like the day when Nitikikani had threatened to lodge a new demand for Judgment with Wyve because of Gredin's continued presence on Tradepoint. But it was a clear question, all the same. She could offer Nitikikani some half-truth… or she could honestly explain.

Ordering her thoughts, she began.

"Nitikikani at Trisectoriana reception. See many, many Vennan, yes?"

A nod.

"I tell you now, all Vennan at Trisectoriana reception still on Tradepoint."

A sharp cocking of the bald, black head. "All?"

"Yes."

"Is many day. Is many Vennan."

"Yes."

"Why?"

Did she have the words in Tradetalk to make Nitikikani understand? She would have to try. "When Hesch leave Tradepoint, Hesch go home to Hesch world, yes?"

A nod.

"Nitikikani remember reception, remember Vennan man come, Vennan man drop down. Much talk. Reception stop. Yes?"

A slower nod. Then Nitikikani said, "Cirin."

"Yes. Cirin come. Cirin… stop." She had no Tradetalk word for *die*, and certainly no Tradetalk word for *evanesce*. "Wyve tell all other go out. Nitikikani go out."

"Yes."

"Before Cirin stop, Cirin tell all Vennan bad thing. Big thing."

Nitikikani watched her.

"Cirin say… Venna home stop. Venna no more. So all Vennan need stay Tradepoint. No Venna home. All Vennan no can go."

Silence from Nitikikani. Did he understand?

"All Vennan fear. All Vennan worry. No home. Where go? What do? Talk Wyve. Tell need stay Tradepoint more day. Need find new home. Old home stop. No more Venna."

Slowly, Nitikikani said, "Vennan tell Wyve. Now you tell Hesch. You ask Hesch no tell?"

Gredin sighed. "No. Too many day. I speak true to Nitikikani. Nitikikani tell if want. Many, many Vennan on Tradepoint. F'lala see. Soon, other see, too. Time for truth. Venna no more. Vennan here on Tradepoint only Vennan left now. All other Vennan… stop."

Before Nitikikani could respond, one of the cloth panels on the far side of the room shifted, and another Hesch entered, carrying two small trays.

"Gredin Vennan," Nitikikani said, "is Arakikani. Bring eat, bring drink."

Strange food and drink? Common sense told Gredin not to take that risk. But she honestly felt that she and Nitikikani were developing a rapport, and that made her reluctant to refuse his hospitality. Even Burlon had admitted to taking a few risks when establishing a new Trading relationship.

The new, smaller Hesch was glossier than Nitikikani, with gauze clothing of green and white. Was this a female, and Nitikikani was male? Or was this new Hesch simply younger? Gredin was unsure. "Greet. Peace," she said to the newcomer. Nitikikani made no effort to rise and so Gredin stayed seated in her chair, as well.

Arakikani gave the first tray to Nitikikani, then approached Gredin's chair.

As Gredin reached out and accepted the offering, her mouth

watered as she saw what the tray held: a cup of some unfamiliar beverage, steaming visibly, and a small plate which held a trio of tiny unfrosted cakes.

When the aroma of the little cakes reached her, her insides made a noise which she feared must have been audible to both Arakikani and Nitikikani. "Forgive," she said, and felt her cheeks grow hot. "Much thank."

With a graceful inclination of the head, Arakikani left them, vanishing behind the wall hanging.

"Eat," Nitikikani said.

Putting caution aside, Gredin gratefully obeyed, trying to be mannerly despite her hunger. The first cake was simple and pleasing, its golden interior enhanced with black seeds so small that they seemed little more than specks. The beverage in the cup, almost too hot to sip, was thick and sweet, as if honey had been stirred into it. The second cake was crammed with a variety of dried fruits, each giving off its own subtle taste when chewed. The final cake was dense, almost as dense as d'limten bread, but with none of that grain's assertive flavor. Instead, the little cake had a gently wholesome taste, one that Gredin could imagine eating again and again without tiring of it.

When she had eaten all three cakes, and sipped the last drops from the cup, Gredin sighed with satisfaction. She felt warmed to her core and nourished in a way that her tense meals at the enclave never seemed to manage.

"Put tray on floor," Nitikikani advised, suiting his actions to his words.

Gredin bent forward in her chair and did the same, then leaned back into the embrace of the cushions. She didn't feel drowsy, just deeply relaxed, as if some fundamental tension within her had finally found a release. "Good drink," she said. "Good, good food. I thank much."

"You hunger." Nitikikani removed his foot from the cradle and thrust his head forward, seeming to peer at her. "Vennan people hunger?"

Pride and caution advised her to deny it. Instead, again, she answered with honesty. “Vennan people hunger some. Not empty, not full. We make deal Beng grain. Then Beng go, cancel contract, say Wyve no sell Beng grain to Vennan. Hard now. Make some other Trade soon, we hope.”

Nitikikani appeared to ponder her response, then asked, after a lengthy silence, “You say Venna stop. How?”

“Not know. But Venna no more.”

More silence. Then, “Where you go?”

“New home. We look. Soon, we hope find.”

“Hard look. Danger. Tradepoint safe.”

“Need home. No stay Tradepoint long. Now, yes. Need time. Many, many, many Vennan stop when Venna stop. Gone. Tradepoint Vennan much sad. But Tradepoint Vennan strong. We find new home. We not stop.” She took a grip on her emotions; it was time to return to the issue that had brought her here. “Tradepoint Vennan need be good with all. Vennan and Tradepoint be good. Vennan and Shodekekeen be good. Vennan and Mamora be good. Vennan and Rodorno be good. Vennan and F’lala be good. Vennan and Polpethtira be good. Now Vennan and Hesch be good.”

“Vennan be good with Thalken?”

Cautiously, Gredin said, “Gredin te Balamont not know Thalken. Only see one time, at reception. Nitikikani ask Burlon te Laith about Vennan and Thalken, get better answer.” She didn’t mention that the Thalken made her uneasy; she had no solid reason for that feeling, just an unfounded instinct.

“Vennan be good with Beng?” Nitikikani asked next, and the Hesch’s face was too unreadable for Gredin to tell whether the question was seriously put.

Honesty.

“No,” she said. “Vennan no be good with Beng. Beng hurt Gredin te Balamont. Beng try take firestone, try take hlao, try take hlette. Beng cut Gredin te Balamont with knife. Beng kick Gredin te Balamont. Beng cut off Gredin te Balamont hair. Beng cancel Vennan grain contract, run away. Vennan no trust Beng. Vennan no like Beng.

Vennan no good with Beng. Beng leave Tradepoint. Vennan say good, Beng go, hope no come back."

She hadn't meant to be quite so outspoken about it, or to carry on at such length, but everything she'd said was true.

Nevertheless, it had drawn her off the point. Again. Determined to address the other vital issue before Nitikikani decided to bring their visit to a close, she reached around to her nape and unknotted the slender cord from which Dreff's flamestone hung suspended.

Instantly, she had Nitikikani's full attention. She could feel it.

"You say Vennan and Hesch good now, yes?"

A nod.

"Vennan and Hesch Trade again? If Burlon come Hesch maartza, no call Prett Security?"

A nod, but then Nitikikani asked, "Why you care? Hesch no trade grain. What Vennan want trade from Hesch?"

"Many thing. Hesch have good thing to eat. Vennan need. And Hesch have amarantha wine. Vennan need amarantha wine."

"Wine is want, not need."

"No. True before. Untrue now. Before, wine happy, taste good. Now, Vennan need wine for..." She groped for words, wishing she knew more about the Hesch culture. "Vennan man, Vennan woman, come together, stay together always. You understand?"

Nitikikani nodded. "Hesch same."

Maybe so, maybe not. It was at least a place to start. "Vennan man, Vennan woman together. Vennan man come Tradepoint Trisectoriana, four days, Vennan woman stay Venna. Then Venna stop. Venna gone. Vennan woman gone. Vennan man alone."

"Why Vennan man not bring woman Tradepoint? Hesch man, woman, travel same."

Gredin shook her head. "Small trip. Four day. Not travel same. Some come. Some stay home. Safe, we think. Man, woman, together soon, we think." Her fingers closed around the flamestone. "Now, never together again."

A pause. Then Nitikikani asked, "Is you? You come, other stay, now gone?"

She nodded.

"Sorry hear. Much sorry, Gredin Vennan."

She nodded again, this time in thanks and acknowledgment of his sympathy.

"Understand," Nitikikani said. "But why wine?"

She looked for a way into her explanation. "Vennan man, Vennan woman. Two together drink Hesch wine, wine be good thing. Happy thing. Good but not important. Have wine, not have wine, not matter. Wine nice, wine good, but wine not important." She swiped her hand from right to left, as if setting that image aside, and began again. "Vennan man, Vennan woman. Venna stop. Vennan woman stop. Vennan man only. Bad thing. Not happy. Time, Vennan man get bad. More time, Vennan man get more bad. Not walk. Not talk. Just sit. Not good. Amarantha wine make better. Not know why, but amaratha wine make better. Same Vennan woman with no Vennan man. Get bad. Get more, more, more bad. Not drink for happy. Drink to be not bad." Again, she wiped away the story she was trying to relate, to begin a new point. "Vennan enclave, many Vennan man with no woman. Many Vennan woman with no man. Bad. Get more bad. Soon get more, more bad. Need amarantha wine for these. Not for happy. For make not bad. Need Trade with Hesch, get amarantha wine, save many Vennan man, many Vennan woman."

She didn't know what more she could say. There had seemed no point in confusing the issue by speaking of those like Keegan who were Unchosen and could see to their own Balance. It was enough if Nitikikani understood that mated couples had been broken apart by Venna's destruction, and that the surviving member of each such couple was now in danger.

Saying nothing, Nitikikani leaned back, his face lost to view in the shadows within the hollowed bell of the chair. Thinking, perhaps. Or, if her language skills were less effective than she hoped, simply trying to piece together a coherent account from what Gredin had said in Tradetalk. It would be a leap, surely, to realize that a Trade item like amarantha wine might serve more than one purpose. Would Nitikikani believe her or simply assume that the Bereft wanted to drown the sorrow of their loss?

It might not matter. So long as the Hesch were willing to trade or sell the wine to the Vennans, the need could be met… but it was vital for the Hesch to be willing to go *on* meeting that need. She wasn't seeking a one-time Trade. That needed to be clear.

"Nitikikani," she said, "this be new problem for Vennan. Never before. So I talk new contract. Vennan need amarantha wine long-time always, keep Vennan man, Vennan woman safe. Understand?"

"Understand."

"Agree?"

No response.

Gredin sighed. "I, Gredin, not Trader. Not know maartza. Not know contract. Only know need of Vennan man, Vennan woman. You want I have Trader come talk this thing?"

No response.

With a heavy heart, she swept her hand from right to left again, setting the matter aside. Perhaps one promise needed to be kept before another could be contemplated. Taking great care to avoid the tray she had set on the floor, she wriggled forward to the edge of her chair and stood. *Don't think*, she told herself. *Just act.*

She had been clutching the flamestone in her hand long enough for it to absorb her body heat. Now, standing, she walked to within a few paces of Nitikikani's chair and opened her palm.

Exposed to the soft light of the room, the stone seemed to glow with an inner radiance.

"I Gredin, Vennan woman. My Vennan man, Dreff, stop. Gone. He smooth this stone. He wear this stone, long time. He find me, give this stone me, say I wear. Now I, Gredin Vennan, give this stone you, Nitikikani Hesch. Vennan and Hesch good. Gredin and Nitikikani good. Yes?"

With difficulty, Nitikikani began to rise, then sank back into the chair, pointing suddenly at her arm – not the arm that bore the hlette, and the hand that held the flamestone, but at her other arm.

"What?" Gredin asked. "What want ask?"

"Prett *griimoni,*" Nitikikani said. "Vennan be good with Prett?"

She glanced down at the wristband with its pretty jewel. "Yes."

"At Judgment, why Gredin Vennan not talk Prett, say Nitikikani hurt Gredin Vennan arm, ask Prett make Judgment on Hesch?"

It was too complicated to explain. Instead, Gredin settled for saying, "Gredin Vennan do big hurt Nitikikani. Much, much sorry. Not important Hesch do small hurt Gredin Vennan."

Nitikikani's head tilted, and the glittering black eyes seemed to search her face. Then, unfolding stiffly, the Hesch rose and spoke.

"I, Nitikikani, take firestone to be my *ta'ak.* I, Nitikikani, take Gredin Vennan to be good to Hesch. I, Nitikikani, be good to Gredin Vennan, be good to Tradepoint Vennan. Yes?"

The flamestone – which Nitikikani called a firestone – was about to pass out of her possession and become Nitikikani's *ta'ak.* She was exchanging it for peace between the Vennans and the Hesch. That much she understood and believed. Whether that exchange would also procure the ongoing supply of amarantha wine they so badly needed seemed… less clear. But she had a feeling that she had pressed the matter as far as she could, at least for this day. The time had come to fulfill her promise.

"You want hold or you want wear?" she asked.

Nitikikani hesitated.

"You want hold, I give now. You want wear, I help…" She knew no word for 'fasten.' Instead, she said, "I help make stay."

"Wait."

That was not the response she had expected but she nodded and, unable to help herself, closed her fingers again around the flamestone.

Turning toward the cloth panels on the far side of the room, Nitikikani lifted his long bill toward the ceiling and uttered a quick series of piercing trills.

Arakikani appeared almost instantly, head cocked as if in inquiry.

Nitikikani spoke at some length in the Hesch language. Gredin listened with interest, though she could make no sense at all from the sounds.

Arakikani nodded and vanished, returning quickly with another small tray. This one bore nothing to eat or drink. Instead, it held a simple wooden box with a hinged lid.

Arakikani brought the tray within Gredin's reach.

Uncertain, Gredin looked to Nitikikani. "What you want me do?"

"Sit. Take box. Open box. Look. Inside, things I make over long time, since small." Nitikikani lowered a hand to indicate what might be the size of a Hesch child. "Make how I see my ta'ak. You look. You understand."

Gredin sat down again. Gingerly, she placed the box on her lap, gripped the front rim of the lid, and lifted. The lid rose smoothly on well-oiled hinges, revealing the contents of the box: a stack of papers in various sizes and shades, some smooth-edged, some ragged. Only the image on the top sheet was immediately visible.

And it took her breath away.

There, depicted on a sheet of rough, grey paper, was a color drawing that precisely depicted Dreff's flamestone.

She drew the papers out of the box, one by one, making a careful stack. There were twenty of them, some sketched in black and white, most made in color, and the twentieth, which resided at the bottom of the box, was clearly the work of a very young child. Far cruder than the later renditions, it still spoke to her strongly with the vividness of its colors and the precision of its size. This was not just some random flamestone. It was Dreff's stone, undeniably.

Gredin looked up at Nitikikani. "How?" she whispered.

"Ta'ak. Sleep-see. Since long, I sleep-see this ta'ak."

Was he saying that a vision of Dreff's stone had come to him in a night-thought? She didn't understand how that could be possible, but who was she to deny the truth of a night-thought? Had the Power not come to her in her sleep to warn her of Venna's destruction and counsel her about the new role she must play if her fellow survivors were to find their new home?

"You show ta'ak to Arakikani?" Nitikikani requested.

Nodding, Gredin extended her left hand and opened her clenched fingers to display the flamestone resting on her palm.

An odd sound escaped Arakikani: not quite a squawk, but clearly unintentional. Black, taloned fingers rose hurriedly to clasp the long beak shut, and Gredin felt a pang of sympathy; in her youth, she had covered her own mouth with her hands in embarrassment on more than one occasion when some unseemly yelp of excitement escaped her.

With care, to give Arakikani time to recover, Gredin began to tidy the drawings back into the box.

"Wait," said Nitikikani. "One you keep."

"What?"

"Many in box. One you keep. Choose."

A memento of Dreff's stone. Something tangible to remind her of what she no longer had… and why she had done it.

When she thought about it like that, there was no doubt in her mind about which picture she wanted. Sifting down through the stack, she withdrew the bottom sheet, the child's depiction, the excited attempt to recreate that very first night-thought of the *ta'ak*.

Not certain that her choice would be permissible, she held it up for Nitikikani's inspection. "This one I keep? Yes? No?"

"Yes."

She placed the others back in the box, closed the lid, and replaced the box on the tray Arakikani offered. Rising, she turned and placed the early drawing on her chair, then stepped up to where Nitikikani stood.

It was time.

"Bring head down," she directed. "I put *ta'ak* on Nitikikani."

[17]
SPRYGALE

With a pang of regret, Burlon left the swift current of the River and came to rest on his own two feet, swaying slightly as his body adjusted to the change.

Sunshine in his eyes made him squint.

The tang of a sea breeze tickled his nose.

Sprygale!

An upwelling of relief tightened his throat. Although he had never given much credence to Gredin's fear that Sprygale might have met the same fate as Venna and Palomar, it had been impossible to dismiss the worry altogether. But now he stood atop the familiar dune designated for his arrivals and departures, and it was clear at a glance that nothing here was damaged.

On his left, the ocean glittered, stretching to the far horizon. Straight ahead, as well as behind him, the beach dipped and curved, forming the first of the line of coves so essential to the harvesting of geddel crystals. And to his right, on a rise, was the village of Benbatahl, which was built around the *Simati Dobria*, the Mother House, where the ruler and her daughter resided.

The nearest edge of the village was a fair distance away, since the sea was not always the calmest of neighbors. Even from the dune, however, Burlon could see the colorful banners that signaled an event of immense importance: Q'iari, daughter of Majaya, the Ruler of the Southern Seas, was to join her life with that of Jostan, eldest son of the Ruler of the North Reaches.

Out on the sparkling water, fishing boats were visible, but no one was currently on the beach except for a trio of dark-haired little girls busily weaving fronds under the shade of an awning. Burlon unbuttoned his jacket and decided to call out to them, to help revive his ease with the Sprygalian tongue.

Happily, it was a language that did not vary much between the Southern Seas and the North Reaches, except in the vocabulary of their respective interests. But it was different enough from Vennan to make the initial adjustment an awkward one on each new visit, until he fell back into the rhythm of their speech. He had long since committed certain pertinent words and phrases to memory, but casual conversation and local gossip were more of a challenge.

Removing his jacket altogether under the influence of the powerful sun, he waved to the girls and called out, "Fair seas to you, young ones!"

At the sound of his voice, the girls looked up from their work. Instead of simply waving back, all three girls thrust their work aside and came pelting toward him.

Intrigued by their enthusiasm, Burlon walked down the dune so that he could meet them at its base. Perhaps they were eager to share news of the upcoming ceremony.

But as they neared, the shortest one cried out, "You come to save him? You come to save him?"

What was amiss? "I come to bring *timte* gifts for Q'iari. Who needs help?"

"Man! Sick man. You come to save him?"

Burlon hesitated. He was no Healer. Was there illness in the village? That would be a shame, so close to the celebration day. "What man is sick?" he asked. "Fisher man from village?" He hoped it wasn't one of Q'iari's brothers.

"No, no!" All of the girls were speaking now, trying to explain, and their swift, urgent words were overlapping. He caught the word 'traderman,' which was what many of the Sprygalians called him. He heard the word for 'bed' and 'wait,' and 'sick.' But everything else was a jumble of sounds.

Burlon put down his carrysacks and put up both of his hands in entreaty. "All talk at once, confuse traderman." He pointed to the tallest. "You only, please. Slow. Tell me."

Reluctantly, the other two stopped talking. The tallest girl composed herself and said, "Traderman not you sick. Other tradermen care for him, wait many days for you to come. You save traderman now, take him home?"

Traderman not you… Other tradermen…

"Where sick traderman?" Burlon demanded. Reaching down for his carrysacks, he found that his hands were shaking. "Where other tradermen?"

The girls looked at him as if he had lost his senses. "Trade house," they said.

Of course. The 'trade house' was the lodge he and his Tradeteam were always given to use when they came for a shipment of geddel crystals. "I go there now, try to help," he told the girls. "Talk later."

He wanted to Send directly to the trade house, but that might not be safe if others were already there. And his Control wasn't quite what he might want it to be, since he could not stop himself from trying to imagine who those 'others' might be.

Instead, to be safe, Burlon Sent himself and his carrysacks to the outskirts of the village, then hurried on foot between the various lodges until the familiar trade house came into view.

Three people were sitting in its open doorway, no doubt enjoying the way the sea breeze softened the midday heat. Two women and a man. The man and one of the women had dark hair, as all Sprygalians did.

The other woman's hair was the color of beach sand.

Burlon's breath caught in his throat, and his vision blurred. He stumbled closer, swallowing, and was finally able to rasp, "Osla! Osla te Kendar!"

Osla looked up at the sound of her name, then surged to her feet and bolted toward him. “Burlon te Bentain! Oh, by the Power’s light, have you come to bring us home? Why didn’t Demni and Tremena come back for us?” Against all Vennan custom, she flung herself against him, and he dropped his carrysacks and wrapped his arms around her in return, feeling her body shake as sobs escaped her. Then her tears turned to ragged laughter, and she pulled back just far enough to cup his face between her hands and proclaim, “You are a beautiful sight! I am so relieved. You have no idea what we’ve–”

“Osla. Listen.”

He said the words softly, but something in his gaze must have warned her, for she quieted instantly. Her hands slid down to grip his upper arms, and she recoiled when her fingers encountered First Traveler’s hlette beneath his shirtsleeve.

“I want to hear all that has befallen you here,” Burlon assured her, “every bit of it, but I am also the bearer of news you need to hear. If you will be patient with me, I would like to see everyone else who is here with you, and listen to your tale, and then I will tell you everything. I hear that one of your Tradeteam is unwell?”

Her mouth twisted. “In a sense. It is what we told the people here, because it was true enough and far simpler for them to understand. But… Well, come inside, come inside. The others are there, and we will explain.” She clutched his arm again. “You will take us home, yes? You will not leave us here or make us wait any longer?”

“When I leave, I will take you with me,” he promised, selecting his words with care.

It seemed to satisfy her. She let go of him and stepped back, looking embarrassed. “You know the way, of course,” she said, and accompanied him to the entryway, where the two Sprygalians with whom she had been talking were still sitting.

They rose as Burlon approached, and he said, “Fair seas to you. Tell Majaya that Burlon has come with the *timte* quilt. I will speak with her soon.”

“Fair seas. Good to see you come. You will help sick trader?”

That again. Scabs. “Yes,” he said to reassure them, and waved them on their way. The sooner he saw what was going on, the sooner he would know whether or not he could help.

He went inside with Osla, through the spacious public room into the sleeping chamber at the back of the lodge. Shutters had been closed over the windows, making the interior dim even at midday, but he could see a Vennan man sitting cross-legged beside a sleepmat where another Vennan man was stretched full-length. As he and Osla drew closer, he recognized the sitting man as Chappal te Kendar. The other man appeared to be asleep, his face turned away.

Chappal pressed his hand to his chest in an expression of relief and gratitude. “Burlon!” he exclaimed, keeping his voice to a murmur.

But Osla shook her head. “Wake him,” she said, nodding toward the sleeping man. “The four of us have matters of importance to discuss.”

Chappal nodded and reached down to shake the man’s shoulder. “Time to open your eyes, kinsman. We are finally going home!”

The man on the mat jolted awake and stared up at the new face among them. “Burlon te Bentain!” he exclaimed.

Recognition dawned. Dumbfounded, Burlon looked down into the deep-shadowed eyes of Zanther te Kendar, Miri’s Chosen.

[18]

0740 OF 2000 ORBITS REMAINING: 31BLUE

The flamestone gleamed where it hung around Nitikikani's neck, a brilliant flash of colors against the black feathers and black gauze.

Arakikani touched Nitikikani's sleeve and made soft trilling sounds that tickled oddly inside Gredin's ear.

Stepping back to offer the pair a modicum of privacy, Gredin turned away slightly, raising her hand to rub unobtrusively at her ear – then stiffened as she saw the bottom of the wall hanging sway slightly, as if something low to the ground had bumped against it.

Don't be ridiculous. You're just upset about the flamestone…

Then the hanging shifted again, and a waist-high figure scuttled into sight.

Beng! It's a Beng!

That was what her mind warned. But her eyes told her differently. There was no pair of green coveralls, no brown hair, no pale skin. This was a grey bundle of fuzz, with a half-sized beak beneath round, dark eyes.

A tiny, naked Hesch.

At the sight of her, it screeched and froze.

On instinct, Gredin sank to the floor, bringing herself closer to its size.

“Sorry,” Nitikikani said, and Arakikani said something sharply to the little Hesch.

“No, please.” Gredin extended one hand slowly toward the miniature intruder. “Arakikani, Nitikikani, let small Hesch stay. Please?”

Nitikikani let out a huff of air, then sat down, gesturing for Arakikani to do the same.

The little Hesch looked from one of them to the other, and back at Gredin. Then it hurried over to the lowest chair, the one that sat directly on the floor, and clambered inside, retreating to the very back of the curved interior so that only the gleam of its eyes was visible.

Settling herself more comfortably on the floor, Gredin thought for a moment, then drew out her pouch of stones and let them trickle onto the carpet. Stirring through them with one fingertip, she said, “Gredin not know Hesch have sleep-see. Is how Nitikikani first know *ta’ak*, yes?”

“Yes.”

“Hesch say sleep-see. Vennan say night-thought.” Her finger moved through the stones, and she drew comfort from their familiar contours. “Night-thought come to Gredin, say Venna stop, two night before Cirin say same.” A shiver shook her. “Nitikikani sleep-see more happy.”

Nitikikani looked toward Arakikani and spoke in Hesch, perhaps translating Gredin’s words, or explaining about Venna’s loss.

As the two full-sized Hesch spoke with one another, Gredin saw the little Hesch scoot forward to the front rim of its chair, watching her closely as she shifted the stones. Unlike the adults, its head and body were covered in short, fluffy feathers. Were those feathers like a young Vennan’s child-curls, destined to change as the little Hesch grew older? In a Vennan’s case, the curls became waves, and finally gave way to sleek, straight hair after maturity was reached. Judging by the difference in appearance between Nitikikani and this little Hesch, the coverage of grey feathers might be destined to fall out altogether as maturity approached.

Scooping up her stones, Gredin let them sift through her fingers onto the carpet again. A clear, oval stone with feathery black inclusions bounced off of the pile and rolled until it came to a halt a short distance from the little chair.

A feathered arm ventured out, reaching, but the stone was too far away.

Nitikikani made a low noise that might have been a chuckle.

The little Hesch crept closer to the edge of the chair and tried again. When the stone was still beyond its grasp, it leaned out, ever more precariously, fingers stretching... and tumbled out of the chair, onto the soft carpet, where it rolled in an uncoordinated scramble of limbs until it bumped, finally, against Gredin's knee.

"Peace," Gredin said, smiling down at the little face, its beak agape, its eyes enormous orbs of alarm. When that failed to ease the situation, she soothed, "*Chee, chee, chee... Chee, chee, chee...*"

The beak closed.

She extended her hand, and the errant stone rolled back to her and hopped onto her palm.

The fledgling's head tilted, the better to focus on the stone. It shifted one fluff-covered arm, extending its hand until it could tap a single talon against the stone's smooth surface with an audible click. Then, as if frightened by its own success, the little Hesch scooted back on the carpet until it was sitting an arm's length away from Gredin.

For answer, she turned toward it and sent the stone rolling its way.

The little Hesch sat as if frozen, watching.

Gredin called the stone back to her, then sent it rolling forward again.

The little Hesch watched.

Three times, Gredin repeated the pattern. On the fourth iteration, the little Hesch reached down, grasped the stone, and rolled it back to her.

They played that simple game of trust – *roll it to me and I will roll it back to you* – half a dozen times before the stone, on its return journey, rolled on and came to rest against the mound of its fellows.

Gredin sighed. This had been a sweet respite, a chance to slip back into a child's state of mind, where the demands of the world were as simple as watching a stone traverse a carpet, forward and back. But the carpet was on a Hesch ship, and the exchange of trust here involved far more than a down-covered alien child. Her days of light-hearted play were behind her forever. Larger responsibilities called, and time was passing.

Still, there was no need to be unkind. Lifting the empty pouch a few inches into the air, she widened its mouth and caused her stones to hop up into it, one by one, leaving the black and white stone for last. At her prompting, it launched itself high into the air, then landed inside the pouch with a satisfying click.

The little Hesch bounced where it sat.

Gredin tucked the pouch into her pocket and rose slowly to her feet.

The little Hesch did the same.

Gredin crossed her palms and bowed her head.

Awkwardly, the little Hesch did its best to mimic her movements.

Nitikikani and Arakikani had risen, as well. Gredin crossed her palms and bowed to each of them in turn. Arakikani imitated the gestures with smooth grace, then held out a hand to the little Hesch.

Nitikikani said, "I take you down," and gestured for Gredin to proceed him out of the cozy room.

But she circled back hurriedly to her chair, instead, and reclaimed the drawing of Nitikikani's *ta'ak* – Dreff's flamestone. Unwilling to bend or fold it, she grasped it firmly by one corner, then went out the way she had entered, and retraced her steps to the alcove.

"No," Nitikikani said from behind her. "Is for up. Come. We go down."

She followed him ten steps farther, to another alcove. It was also equipped with a moving metal rope and platforms, but these appeared from above and sank into the unseen depths below.

"Simple," Nitikikani said. "See step come. Get on, go down. I go first, help at bottom. Yes?"

"Yes," Gredin said, with more conviction than she felt. Coming up had been exciting. She had even looked forward to repeating the experience. Going down, however, seemed altogether more intimidating. Still, she had little choice.

"Next step come."

She watched with close attention as the step appeared, descending. As soon as it was below waist-height, Nitikikani took a loose hold on the metal rope. Then, as the step reached the level on which they stood, Nitikikani's grip tightened, and the taloned feet and support stick moved nimbly onto the platform.

Nitikikani's bare black head sank from view.

Her turn next.

She was ready. Indeed, she found herself suddenly anxious to return to the Vennan enclave and the privacy of her own room, where she could reflect at length about all that she had seen and heard and done with Nitikikani on the Hesch ship. How long had her venture taken? It would serve her right if she had missed evening meal…

The next step appeared above her, moving smoothly down.

Imitating Nitikikani, she waited, took a loose grip on the metal rope with her free hand, then stepped out onto the platform.

Down.

Belatedly, she remembered that she would need to reverse her stance in order to step off. She began to shift her feet and turn around, impeded somewhat by the paper she carried. When the light of the next opening reached her, she had only turned partway.

"Let go," Nitikikani said, and plucked her from the step with both hands, allowing his stick to clatter to the floor.

"I thank," she said. Establishing her balance, she bent, retrieved the support stick, and handed it to him, all the while protecting the picture that she held. "Sorry. No go down before."

"You come other time, practice," Nitikikani said, and Gredin couldn't tell whether it was a joke or an invitation.

They retraced their steps down the hallway they had traversed earlier, this time with the solid wall on their left and the doorways on their right, until they reached the thick door that led to what Nitikikani called the 'ship between place.' As they prepared to exit through the door on the room's opposite side, Gredin felt her mouth go dry with apprehension. Next, they would enter the long corridor that connected Nitikikani's ship to Tradepoint itself. The thought that there was nothing solid beneath the floor of that corridor frightened her. No ground. No air. Just emptiness…

Nitikikani touched her arm briefly. "No be worry."

Ashamed to have revealed her emotions so openly, Gredin said, "Sorry. First time come Tradepoint."

"First time, you?"

"Yes."

Again, that brief touch on her arm. "Hesch walk ship to Tradepoint this way many time. Nitikikani. Other Hesch. All walk. All safe. No scare."

"Safe," she repeated, and tried to look reassured.

Nitikikani opened the door.

Waved her through.

Came out to join her.

Refastened the door.

Then he gripped her wrist – not painfully, but firmly.

"We walk now," said Nitikikani. "You safe."

The corridor had seemed long on their way to the Hesch ship. Now, returning, it seemed endless. Gredin tried to concentrate on Nitikikani's thin fingers around her wrist, the skin dry and black, the steady grip drawing her on.

She would have sifted through her stones in an effort to calm herself, but she had no hand free to touch them. Nitikikani had captured one, and she held his drawing of the *ta'ak* in the other. She could only count her steps, placing her feet with care, not wanting her feet to strike too heavily on the corridor's floor.

The number in her head mounted and mounted. Had the corridor been this long, on their way in, or was Nitikikani taking her back to Tradepoint by some different route? Had anyone ever encountered a difficulty in these long, connecting corridors that stretched between Tradepoint and the ships? If this one suddenly gave way, could she hold her breath long enough to Send herself and Nitikikani to safety?

"Gredin Vennan."

Nitikikani's voice drew her back from the edge of panic.

"Yes?"

"You look me."

Reluctantly, she raised her gaze to his.

"Nitikikani say this walk safe. Safe bring Arakikani here. Safe bring kekeli here."

Automatically, she said, "Not know word *kekeli*." Such was her gyfte that, even if she were in the act of evanescing, she would likely find the strength to ask after an unfamiliar word.

"Kekeli," Nitikikani repeated, then clarified, "Little. Small. You sit floor kekeli Hesch."

Well then. If Nitikikani proclaimed this corridor to be safe enough for them, it was certainly safe enough for her. She knew little of Tradepoint, but if it was a choice between heeding Tetralanna warnings or trusting Nitikikani's assurances, she knew where she would place her confidence.

At last, the end of the corridor came into view. Mindful of Nitikikani's injury, Gredin was careful not to quicken her pace, but she couldn't prevent the sigh of relief that escaped her when they reached the heavy doorway. Pointing at it, she said, "Door, then between place, then door, then Tradepoint, Hesch enclave, yes?"

"Yes," Nitikikani said, pressing buttons on the panel.

Three beeps and a click.

The door opened, and they went in.

The process was becoming almost familiar to Gredin. She could feel her body begin to relax as they prepared to open the final door and step back into the safety of the Hesch enclave. "I thank," she said to Nitikikani. "Much walk for you on bad foot to bring me here. Sorry. But I thank to see Hesch ship. I thank for words. I thank for peace for Hesch and Vennan, for Nitikikani and Gredin."

"I thank much for ta'ak," Nitikikani said, then hesitated and asked, "You want touch ta'ak before go?"

She understood instantly what he meant. Here in the between place, it was just the two of them. Once they passed through the door, they would be back in the Hesch enclave, in Tradepoint itself, and such a contact between them would draw curious – even censorious – eyes. Here, it was no one's business but their own.

“Please,” she whispered, and reach up with great care to close her fingers around Dreff’s flamestone.

Its familiar contours nestled into her palm, comforting her.

She held it for the space of three unsteady breaths. Then she made her fingers uncurl, releasing the flamestone to rest against Nitikikani’s chest.

“Thank,” she said, and swallowed hard. “Time now I go back Vennan enclave.”

“You, me, we talk soon, Gredin Vennan.”

“We talk soon,” she affirmed, and watched as Nitikikani pressed the final buttons.

Three beeps and a click.

The heavy door opened.

Gredin stepped over the high sill, setting foot back inside Tradepoint – and jumped in alarm as the Prett wristband she wore began to vibrate wildly, buzzing like an outraged hive of Chenna’s bees.

[19]
SPRYGALE

"What has happened?" Burlon demanded, looking from one Kendar Trader to another. "What ails Zanther? Why are you still here?"

Chappal and Osla exchanged glances, and it was Chappal who said, "I'll explain. Sit, if you will."

Burlon settled on the floor of the lodge, setting his carrysacks carefully to the side. "I am listening," he assured Chappal. "Tell me everything."

Chappal sighed. "There should have been no story of any interest to tell. A team of five of us from House Kendar ventured here to see if the *ginglin* had begun their migration. *Ginglin* make very fine eating, and the fishers here on Sprygale are very fine at catching them, but the run only lasts five days or so, and *ginglin* are best eaten fresh. We missed the run, last year, to the House's regret. This year, we were determined to do better. But when we arrived, we learned that the weather had taken a chilly turn, and there had not yet been any sign of the *ginglin* run. We Traders decided to wait it out, but our Travelers had other matters to attend to. The Sprygalians were willing to have us remain, and so we told Demni and Tremena to go back, and then return for us in eight days' time. If the *ginglin* run had not started by then, we would journey home and another set of Traders would come in our place. That was the understanding. We were all agreed. But the eighth day came and went, and Demni and Tremena did not arrive."

By then, Burlon thought, *Venna was gone, and Demni and Tremena had returned to the Source*. But he said nothing, gesturing for Chappal to go on with his account.

"We told ourselves that they would come the next day, full of excuses and apologies for their tardiness. But they didn't. Nor the next, nor any day thereafter. Fifteen days have passed since then, and we have long since run out of tales to tell each other to explain how such a thing could occur. We fear greatly for Demni and Tremena, and we cannot imagine why the House has not dispatched someone else in search of us. Still, as frightened as we were, we knew that you were expected soon. Q'iari and her upcoming Choosing with Jostan have been the talk of the village, and we were told you would soon arrive with the *timte* gifts. And here you are, to our great relief!"

Osla looked at Chappal. "You haven't yet explained about Zanther," she said softly.

Chappal grimaced. "A truth. Your pardon, Burlon. Like you, Osla and I are Unchosen, so the delay posed no great personal difficulty for us. But Zanther has a Chosen, and he has now been separated from her for nearly thirty days. I doubt you are aware, but a prolonged separation from one's Chosen can result in a number of difficulties."

It seemed unkind to let Chappal labor on with an explanation that Burlon did not need. "You are referring to the difficulties faced by Ulm te Kendar, are you not?"

The Kendar Traders stared at him, clearly astonished.

He waved their reaction aside. "I will explain shortly," he said. "But first I would ask how severe Zanther's difficulties have become."

"Not all that bad," Zanther himself answered, although his appearance contradicted his words, "due to the kindnesses of my fellow Traders here. Because we knew the danger, I began to conserve my energies as soon as we realized that something had gone amiss with Demni and Tremena. I have made very little use of my gyftes, and have rested a good deal. Osla and Chappal have been wonderfully thoughtful, attending to my needs. But the past few days have been increasingly difficult. I have trouble falling asleep, and I have little appetite. Still, all will be well, as soon as I am back with Miri. I am certain of it."

"You are *not* certain of it," Osla said, "nor are we. There truly is no time to lose. As soon as Burlon has had a meal and a chance to sleep, and has delivered his goods to Majaya, he will take you home."

"That, I sorrow to say, is not the simple matter it should be," Burlon said.

Osla stiffened. "Oh? And what is more important than Zanther's Balance?"

He held up a cautionary hand. "Hear my news before you judge me, Osla. Matters are not as you believe them to be."

The anger and indignation did not leave her face, but she and Chappal sat silent, giving him the chance to speak, and Zanther watched him anxiously from the bedmat.

"Is there something I could drink?" Burlon asked. "Mine is not a short tale, nor a happy one. I have just come from the River, and I–"

"Our pardon," Chappal said, looking stricken. "Of course. Let me bring you something." He stood up but, before he left, added, "Don't begin without me!"

The three of them who remained sat in uneasy silence until Chappal hurried back in, followed by two young Sprygalian boys. One of them handed a tall cup to Burlon, while the other offered a woven platter that held a bowl of sliced fruits, a generous piece of *sama* bread, and three small fishcakes.

"I thank," he told the boys, accepting what they offered.

Smiling broadly, they ran out of the room.

"Zanther," Burlon said, "your fellow Trader has arranged quite a feast for me. If anything here attracts your eye…"

But Zanther shook his head and looked away.

"Well then, if the three of you will allow me time to take a few bites and sips, I will then turn my attention to the matter at hand."

A swallow of *pimar* juice to slake his thirst, a fishcake, a cool bite of *toto*, which always reminded him of the pink-fleshed melons that grew at the Bentain Holding, and a chewy mouthful of *sama* bread, still warm from the baking ovens. Then one more sip of *pimar* juice.

"There. That should begin to fill the empty chasm within me. My apologies for making you wait." He glanced at them, envying their ignorance, but the time had come to share the tale. He searched for a way to begin. "I should start by telling you that Miri is still on Tradepoint."

Chappal groaned. Osla said, "Then you will have to take Zanther *there*, rather than home. Perhaps you don't properly understand the import of Ulm's tale. Zanther needs to be reunited with his Chosen without delay."

Burlon gave her a level look. "Oh, I fully understand the import of Ulm's tale. And I agree that Miri and Zanther need to be brought together quickly. What *you* three do not yet understand is that *everybody* who came for the Trisectoriana is still on Tradepoint… and that they, and you three, and I are the only survivors of our kind. On the first night of our stay on Tradepoint, word reached us that Venna had been destroyed. It is gone, and everyone who was there when that horrible event occurred has now returned to the Source."

They said nothing, their faces frozen in looks of bewildered alarm.

Slowly, pitying them, Burlon said, "Our world no longer exists. Venna is gone. All who were at home have perished. The only Vennans whose lives were spared are the four of us, some nine hundred of our people who came to Tradepoint for the Trisectoriana, and one other Tradeteam, made up of members from House Avilar, House Kendar and House Calidane. Every other–"

"Who?" Osla demanded. "Which Kendar Trader was it?"

"It was not a Trader. It was a Traveler, Plithik te Kendar. Everyone else we know and love has returned to the Source. And of the thirty-three Houses into which Venna has always been divided, only thirteen of them remain. Indeed, you could almost argue that the number has been reduced to twelve, for Keegan te Fliss, who came with us to Tradepoint in the role of historian, is the only member of House Fliss to have survived."

The pain in Zanther's gaze seemed to plead for Burlon to stop, but there was more of importance that he needed to impart.

"We have lost Cirin te K'lar, as well. He tried to return home and found that both Venna and Palomar are no more. He ventured to Zrach, to rest up for his return to us, but he was attacked there and barely managed the return to Tradepoint before his wounds ended his life."

Despite the midday warmth, Chappal was shivering visibly, and Osla had begun to weep. Zanther lay motionless, his eyes huge as he listened.

Burlon removed his shirt, revealing First Traveler's hlette on his upper arm. "This was left behind when Cirin evanesced. The surviving Travelers assembled, and the hlette has come to me, as you see."

Now they were regarding him as if he were a stranger.

It was hard to know what to explain next, but nothing could be as terrible as learning of Venna's loss and the death of most of their kinsmen, so Burlon spoke on, giving them time to adjust. "Do any of you know Gredin te Balamont?" he asked.

Osla and Zanther shook their heads, but Chappal nodded. "I have heard others mention her – the youngling who wanted to learn Tradetalk."

It was so incongruous a description of her present role that Burlon almost laughed aloud. "Yes, that is Gredin. She joined the delegation to Tradepoint to act as interpreter. But on our first night there, the Power came to her in a night-thought and informed her of Venna's fate. It returned twice more, on the nights that followed, first to entrust her with leadership of those who survived, then again to state that the Travelers must venture out upon the River and find the world that will become our next home, New Venna."

"What nonsense is this? Her hlao is still unfurled!" Chappal protested.

"She is no longer a youngling, as you remember her. She found her Chosen and experienced her dydanin, shortly before our journey to Tradepoint. She is a Speaker. Indeed, she now bears First Speaker's hlette. In front of the entire community, that hlette abandoned

Tetralanna te Balamont, who was serving as the Voice for our delegation, and went to Gredin."

"*That* must have caused a stir," Zanther murmured.

"Oh, the community was already in the midst of a stir, and I was at the center of it. You see, I am no longer Burlon te Bentain."

Osla dashed the tears from her eyes and said crossly, "You most certainly are."

"No. I tell you most sincerely that I am not. While I was dancing at the reception, I found my Chosen. Her name is Chenna te Laith. I aligned with her House, and so I am Burlon te Laith, now and for the rest of my days." He gestured to his hlao. "This is Laith's knot."

"So it is," Chappal confirmed. "But what is this talk of finding your Chosen in another House? A person cannot simply decide to 'align' with some other House if their own House displeases them."

"House Bentain did not displease me. But yes, a Chosen can come from a different House, and a person can align with a new House. I know because I have done both. Indeed, we were advised by Gredin te Balamont not to proceed with our dydanin until one of us had done just that, to make it clear which House would claim the allegiance of any children born to us. And it is fortunate that I did, for Chenna had three glim upon her cheeks when I left her, this morning, to journey here."

Zanther voiced a groan. "You torture our emotions, Burlon. I rejoice with you for your new-found Chosen and your child-to-be, and yet the loss of so many loved ones within House Kendar makes me long to turn my face to the wall and weep."

"You would hardly be alone," Burlon said. "Many tears have been shed by the other survivors, and many sleepless nights have been endured."

He grimaced, feeling a twinge of guilt when he considered how the joy he shared with Chenna had softened the impact for him. That and his reunion with the Rodorno. The losses were still real and inescapable, but he was a Traveler, and Travelers were accustomed to living their lives in segments, now in one place for a time, now in another. Each place was real and engrossing. It somehow made Venna feel as if it were a place to which he might one day return, even though he knew that to be untrue.

He forced his attention back to his tale. “As things stand, House Kendar sent many members to the Trisectoriana – more than any other House except Avilar. When we return, you will find that the Kendar survivors have an enclave all their own – a sort of miniature House, I suppose you could call it. They will welcome the three of you with astonishment and joy, since they believe you to be dead. But you will find matters very different from what you usually encounter on a visit to Tradepoint. The Hesch are currently refusing to communicate or Trade with us. And I negotiated a contract with the Beng–”

“The Beng!” Osla exclaimed.

“Yes. For grain, since the Wilra aren’t in port and we now have nearly a thousand people to feed. On the Beng’s final night in port, however, they cancelled the contract and physically attacked Gredin te Balamont.”

Chappal gaped. “Have they gone mad?”

“It was greed. They came upon her alone in a corridor and thought they could take First Speaker’s hlette and her hlao, as well as a flame-stone pendant she usually wore. Fortunately, I had already advised her to stop wearing the pendant outside of our enclave. And the Beng couldn’t, of course, dislodge the hlette or hlao. Out of spite and frustration, they cut off Gredin’s braids, instead. You will have no difficulty identifying her. She is the only Vennan on Tradepoint whose hair has been reduced to child-curls.”

Osla bristled. “And what has the Director done about it? I have never heard anything so outrageous!”

Burlon sighed. “The Beng had already undocked and departed before their violence became known. It remains to be seen whether they will ever return.”

There was much more to the tale, beginning with the original incidents in the Traders’ Market that resulted in both the Vennans and the Beng being held responsible in a Judgment that would benefit the Hesch. But Burlon hesitated to go into those details. There would be time enough, once they were all safely back on Tradepoint. For now, the Kendar Traders simply needed to know that relations on Tradepoint had shifted in major ways, and that they would be wise to confer with other Traders before they ventured beyond the Vennan enclave.

"The organization of our enclave has proven contentious, as well," he cautioned them. "You would think that Gredin, having been directly addressed by the Power, would receive everyone's support, especially since no Heads of House made the journey to Tradepoint. But no. Each House was asked to find a volunteer to act as a spokesman for their House's concerns, but those volunteers have now taken to calling themselves Heads of House, and they claim that they form a High Council. Some Houses – the more traditional ones – resist Gredin's guidance at every turn. Others – like your own House of Kendar and House Avilar – support her." He shook his head. "It has been a deeply unsettled time for everyone. Unhappiness is common. Tempers are short. There is much uncertainty. Food is sparse, with little variation. Some people have no outlet for their gyftes. All miss the chance to stand under an open sky and feel a breeze touch their face. They miss the sight of the sun, and the feel of its warmth. Many of them are frightened of the other races at Tradepoint, and the Beng's attack on Gredin deepened their fears, even though we assure them that the Beng have departed. People only came prepared for a four-day trip, and now they find themselves stranded, with no home to which they can return."

He drew breath to tell them about the hundreds of survivors who had lost their Chosens, and what an increasing source of difficulty that had become. But if he mentioned it, he would need to explain that, through the Prett, a solution of sorts had been found… And that, he realized, was going to be a particularly thorny topic, one he needed to think about before he spoke. One he would need, perhaps, to broach privately with Zanther.

Burlon held up his hands. "Enough. We can discuss all of this in greater depth later. If I try to tell the three of you everything that has happened since we all left Venna, the afternoon will be gone and darkness will be upon us. Before that happens, I need to go to the Sprygalians and present myself. If you will pardon me…?"

Osla and Chappal quickly gave their consent. Zanther, looking up at him with a troubled air, said nothing.

Burlon put his shirt and jacket back on. "I will return soon," he promised them. Then he picked up his carrysacks, left the lodge, in search of Majaya, Ruler of the Southern Seas.

Once Burlon had emerged into daylight, he made his way steadily uphill. The Mother House was a large, airy, graceful structure that looked down over the village much as a water hen might survey her chicks. As he walked toward it through the broad lanes that linked the various lodges, it struck Burlon that the village seemed unusually busy. Despite the midday heat, people scurried to and fro, many carrying bundles or baskets. It was the sort of activity he would have expected to see on his next visit, when everyone was getting ready for the royal Choosing ceremony, but not now. The normal pace here in Benbatahl was relaxed and cheerful. Today, cheerfulness was still apparent on the faces that he passed, but their pace had perceptibly quickened.

Well, perhaps the preparations were beginning sooner than he had imagined would be necessary. After all, Q'iari was Majaya's only daughter. The ceremony was bound to be elaborate, at least by Sprygalian standards.

The closer he came to the *Simati Dobria*, the more the aromas in the air began to tempt him. His hasty, half-eaten meal in the Trade House had taken the edge off his hunger, but Traveling the River always left him ravenous. If he was fortunate, he and Majaya would sit down to a civilized talk that was accompanied by a substantial meal and a generous cup of…

It was then that Burlon heard a sound that should not be occurring: the grumbling snort of a *morg*. No, not just one *morg*. Several of them. And that could only mean one thing: the group from the North Reaches had already arrived.

Burlon had doubted his eyesight, the first time he saw a *morg*. They were massive, burly animals, covered in a tight-curling pelt as white as the snows in which they lived, and they were substantially taller than a full-grown Vennan, let alone the shorter Sprygalians. But the people of the North Reaches had mastered the art of riding the beasts, using them to cover the long distances between one settlement and another with relative ease, even in bitter weather.

And now, apparently, they had ridden them south.

A trio of *morg* appeared, each with a Northern Sprygalian sitting atop it. The local Sprygalians had apparently become accustomed to this phenomenon, for there were no cries of alarm, but people rapidly vanished through the nearest doorways, leaving the lane to the big beasts.

Burlon stood his ground.

"Traderman!" a mellow voice shouted, and the rider of the leading *morg* waved his arm. Burlon saw that it was Jostan, the royal son who was to be joined with Q'iari. Jostan's curly black hair was straggling over his brow in the heat, and his face glistened. "Have you brought the gift?" he called.

Burlon raised one of the carrysacks to shoulder height, then lowered it again.

"Fine! Fine! The *morgs* are hot. We are taking them down to the sea, to let them swim. Do you wish to come?"

In the past, he would have welcomed such a bizarre adventure. But he was no longer Burlon te Bentain. Now he was Burlon te Laith, with a Chosen, and soon a child, and a community that relied upon him.

"My thanks, but no," he shouted. "I am expected at the *Simati Dobria.* I will find you later and deliver the package safely into your hands. It would not be improved by a dousing of sea water."

Jostan took his refusal in good spirits, and the trio of *morg* rumbled past, leaving a cloud of dust in their wake. As it settled, people emerged from the surrounding lodges to resume their errands. Burlon continued on his way, as well, looking forward to hearing an explanation of why Jostan and his group were already present in Benbatahl.

The answer was not long in coming. By the time he had mounted half of the forty steps that fronted the *Simati Dobria,* a dozen members of the royal household had gathered around him, greeting him and offering to relieve him of the burden of the carrysacks.

Burlon laughed. "No, no. My thanks, but I will not hand these over to anyone but those who ordered them. However, if one of you could run ahead and inform the Ruler that I am here and wish the honor of an audience with her…"

The people around him laughed, in their turn. "Do you suppose your arrival has not already been noted and announced? You are eagerly awaited, Traderman."

"Wonderful. So tell me, when did Jostan and the rest of the party from the North Reaches arrive? I thought they were not expected for another full turn of the moon."

"Just so. Just so. But the Yebda Pass cleared earlier in the season than it has in many a year, and Jostan told his father that they should leave immediately on the journey to Benbatahl, before the weather could turn against them."

When Burlon reached the entry doors, they offered to take his boots, his jacket, even his shirt. He shed the boots, knowing that it would be considered poor manners to wear them inside, and cheerfully surrendered the jacket. He would like to have shed the shirt, as well, but the occasion was an important one, and so he kept it on.

It was a decision he regretted when he was presented in the audience hall. Both Majaya and Q'iari were there to welcome him, dressed in loose, filmy robes that welcomed the slight breeze from the high windows. The mode of dress here reminded him of home – not the pants and shirts and jacket that he wore as a Trader, but the teslans or felks he had always worn when he was back at House Bentain and had no one to please but himself. Sprygalians – at least those who lived in the south, where the weather was reliably balmy – were as comfortable in their bodies as Vennans were, dressing more from a love of color and the fun of ornamentation than from any wish to hide their appearance away beneath layers of cloth.

On Tradepoint, in the public areas, caution and decorum dictated his clothing choices. Even inside the Vennan enclave, it was hard to feel relaxed. But they would eventually find New Venna; the Power had said it would be so. And when they did, Burlon looked forward to the many benefits that would come from being on their own world, free to indulge in their own practices and preferences once again.

Right now, however, he had a Trade to complete – perhaps the most important Trade he had ever managed.

Setting the carrysacks down, he crossed his palms to the two women seated before him and bowed his head. "Ruler of the Southern Seas," he said first, as was proper. Then, shifting the direction of his bowed head slightly, he added, "Q'iari, soon to be Ruler of the Middle Realm. I greet you both and wish you health and happiness on this fine day."

"Welcome, Traderman," Majaya said, her rich voice making the words sound like a fragment of song. "You have brought what I requested?"

"Indeed I have."

"Show us!" Q'iari urged, her voice higher but no less melodious.

Burlon was too canny a Trader to fall into that trap. "Ah, how I wish I could. It pains me to deny anything that you ask of me. But I have been instructed by your mother to say nothing of the object's nature, and not to allow you even the briefest glimpse of it until the time of waiting is ended and she presents it to you, herself."

"Well, at least give me a hint," she entreated.

"Certainly. I can tell you, with absolute assurance, that it is not a *morg*."

She laughed, and it was a lovely, care-free sound. Burlon drank it in like wine, glad to escape the pervasive sadness that plagued the Vennan survivors.

"Do you know," Q'iari said, "I believe that Jostan intends for me to ride one of those creatures when we depart, after the ceremony. Do you suppose I can manage such a feat?"

"I believe you can accomplish anything that you set your mind on doing. And I am confident, as well, that Jostan will do nothing that puts you at any risk of harm. I passed him in the lane, on my way here, and I do not know when I have seen a man more filled with happiness and anticipation. He would do battle with the sea itself to keep you safe."

"Pretty words, Traderman," Majaya said, reaching out to pat her daughter's arm, "but you and I have business matters to discuss." She rose. "You will come with me. And *you,*" she said, pointing a finger at Q'iari, "will not follow us and listen at the doorway or attempt to peek in, or I will give you nothing at the ceremony but a necklace of seaweed. Do you understand?"

"I understand," Q'iari assured her. "Besides, it is much too warm to creep about, today. I give you my word that I will not move from this room until you return and grant me permission."

"Such fine behavior," Majaya marveled, turning to Burlon. "Where do you suppose this docile girl has been hiding, all these years, while I exhausted myself with her mischievous shadow?"

It was not a question that required – or even desired – an answer, so Burlon gave none. He simply nodded a respectful farewell to Q'iari, picked up both carrysacks, and followed Majaya out of the audience hall and along an open breezeway that took them to another cluster of rooms.

At the first of them, she opened the door and gestured for him to enter.

The room was spacious, with a high ceiling, large windows that stood open to the languid breeze, and walls of purest white. In fact, everything in the room was either white or made from the light-hued wood called *bima* that predominated in the southern areas of Sprygale. The only furnishing in the room was a large, thick sleepmat in the center of the floor, covered in a pristine white spread.

Burlon could not have asked for a better place to display the *timte* quilt.

"So now," Majaya said, placing her hands on her hips, "you will show me what you have brought." She was a big woman, tall and majestic, and her stance was a challenge for him to impress her, but he could also read the worry in her eyes – worry that this gift for her only daughter would not be grand enough to do honor to the girl and the occasion.

Burlon had no such worries. "Turn away," he said.

"What?"

He put down the carrysacks and gestured toward the green one. "I wish you to see the quilt at its best. If you turn away briefly, that will allow me to unpack it and spread it upon this bed for your inspection."

"And what is in the blue bag? Will you display that for me, as well?"

"No. It is the gift that the Ruler of the North Reaches and his son have requested for your daughter."

"Oh, I am certain Rangh and Jostan would have no objection to my seeing it."

"Before they have even seen it for themselves?"

"They are my guests. I am eager to see their gift."

He couldn't afford to irritate Majaya, who was very used to having her own way in all matters. Nevertheless, it would not be right or proper to allow her to be the first to view the coat.

Donning a smile, Burlon said, "I understand perfectly. I am certain they are eager, as well. Perhaps you wish to invite them here to this chamber, and the three of you may gaze upon both gifts together."

For a moment, Majaya scowled. Then, with a wry smile, she said, "Oh, very well, Traderman. Simply tell me this, then – are *you* content with the gift they are giving to Q'iari?"

"Entirely," he was able to answer in all honesty, envisioning the elaborate embroidered coat Ingarra had made, and the beautiful scarf Nunellin te Vell had woven to accompany it. "The gift does your daughter full honor. Now, Ruler, if you will turn away…?"

She did so, saying, "Don't be long about it."

"I won't be." Quickly, he unfastened the carrysack, drew out the quilt, settled it onto the bed, and Freshened it to remove the small travel creases. Then he said, "This quilt will remind Q'iari of the southern sun of her childhood home, and keep her warm at night, even when Jostan is away. You may look."

Majaya turned.

The sun from the windows invigorated the bold colors of the quilt, making them seem to glow.

"Allow me to turn it over and show you the reverse," he said, and flipped the quilt, revealing the dark latticework and jewel-like insets of the quilt's reverse side. Then he turned it back again, to display the gleaming sun.

As Majaya gazed at the quilt, tears gathered in her eyes, then coursed down her cheeks. "Traderman," she said at last, pressing a hand to her chest, "you have outdone yourself."

"Then I am content," he said, although his overwhelming emotion was one of immense relief. *He* had been impressed by Ingarra's quilt, but there was always a concern, when dealing with another race, that their reaction might differ. He had dealt with the Sprygalians for long and long, but this was a unique occasion, and Majaya could be opinionated, objecting to matters that he considered to be trifles. Now that her approval had been won, the path ahead seemed far smoother. "So then," he ventured, "you have the twelve chests of geddel crystals we agreed upon?"

"Nearly. Ten are filled, and our fishers will finish harvesting for the eleventh and twelfth chests soon."

"Soon?" Burlon stiffened. "How soon? I need to leave no later than two days from now."

"We will need more time than that. Those from the North Reaches arrived sooner than expected. As a result, the date of Q'iari's joining with Jostan has been advanced, which means that our preparations for it needed to be advanced, which in turn has meant that many of our fishers were diverted to other tasks. The delay is not a long one – a few days only. Relax. Be our guest. You had planned to attend the ceremony. You will simply do so, sooner. The geddel crystals will be ready for your departure on the morning after Q'iari's joining."

"In how many days' time?"

"On the fourth sunrise."

Burlon resisted the urge to bury his face in his hands. "You are aware, are you not, that other Traders from Venna currently inhabit the Trade House, and that one of them is unwell? He needs to be taken to our Healers. The others here do not have a gyfte for Traveling the River. They are relying on me to take him."

"Is he dying?" Majaya asked, her tone cool. "Within the next five days, will he perish?"

Blood and bruises, had the woman no sympathy? "No," Burlon admitted, "but his condition will worsen." Figuring frantically, he said, "All right, I will take him back tomorrow morning. With good fortune, I will be well enough to return on–"

"We prefer that you not leave until after the ceremony."

We prefer. Coming from Majaya, those words were the equivalent of a command. Burlon sighed. "Perhaps I have not explained our situation well," he said. "It is important that I return this man to–"

"Stay. There will be dinners and entertainments in honor of our guests from the North. We require your presence. Now, tuck the quilt back into that bag of yours, to keep it out of Q'iari's inquisitive sight, and you and I will join her for a cool drink and something to eat."

He could defy her. He wasn't a prisoner here. But Majaya was a woman of moods, a ruler accustomed to obedience from everyone around her. And her nerves were no doubt more brittle than usual, having had to advance all of the plans for the ceremony, and contemplating the sooner-than-expected departure of her only daughter.

At nearly any other time, Burlon would have ignored Majaya's preferences and taken Zanther directly to Miri. But there were limits to how soon he would be fit to return, if he did so, and he had promised Chenna that he would take care and keep himself safe.

And there was the matter of the geddel crystals. This was not the time to return to Tradepoint with less than the contracted amount, nor was it a time to risk disrupting Majaya's willingness to Trade with him in the future.

He would make it up to Chenna. And Zanther could manage a few more days, if he continued to take precautions. Two extra days. That was all it would be. The alternative was too dangerous to chance.

"That sounds delightful," he said, and put the quilt away.

A fair time later, with his physical hunger appeased, and Majaya's praise still ringing in his ears, Burlon left the *Simati Dobria* and walked back to the Trade House for a much-needed rest. He had left the precious *timte* quilt in Majaya's care, secure in its concealing carrysack, but the blue carrysack containing the coat was slung over his shoulder. Until he could deliver it directly into the hands of Rangh or Jostan, he would not let it leave his possession.

When he reached the Trade House, Osla and Chappal were nowhere to be seen, and Zanther was asleep. Replete from his meal with Majaya, Burlon stretched out on an unused bedmat and fell into a doze, with one arm draped over the blue carrysack as if it were Chenna drowsing at his side.

He awoke a while later, uncomfortably warm. The breeze had dropped. It was still daylight. And Zanther, he realized, was awake.

"Can I get anything for you?" Burlon asked, sitting up and shifting to face him.

"You can tell me how Miri is faring," Zanther said.

Well, there it was. From the silence around them, it seemed clear that Osla and Chappal were still gone. He might not get another opportunity to talk with Zanther privately. Sobered by the unwanted responsibility that had fallen into his lap, Burlon said, "She was crushed when she thought you must be dead, but she has been kind and brave. I have gotten to know her quite well, and we have become good friends. Would you like to hear how?"

"Indeed," Zanther said. "She is not a Traveler, and not a Trader, and not of your House – that is to say, not of either of your Houses. And so I am at a loss to think how you and Miri could have become acquainted, let alone how you struck up a friendship with her. Tell me everything. I long to hear it all. I was worried about her, even before you brought the news of Venna's loss to us, because I knew what my absence must be doing to her."

"Yes, well, it began when Cirin and I selected her to organize and manage the kitchen Tenders who planned to attend the Trisectoriana celebration. There were so many of them, from so many different Houses, that we feared the kitchens would be in chaos. But your Miri has a sweet but firm manner, and a great deal of tact. The preparations for the reception went smoothly under her direction, and both the diners and the kitchen Tenders were well pleased with the result." He shifted restlessly. "But the reception was the last of our happiness. Midway through that evening, Cirin appeared, and announced the destruction of Venna and Palomar. Then he evanesced, too injured for the Healers to save him. The guests were told to return to their enclaves, and most of the Vennan delegation gathered, House by House, to mourn their losses. But with the reception ending so unexpectedly, the tables were still mounded with food, and it was Gredin who realized that food was soon apt to be scarce. She and Miri and a few of the others packed up everything that was left and stored it, to give us a little buffer of time in which to figure out how to feed everyone in the days to come."

"You say that as if it all happened to someone else," Zanther observed.

"In a way, I suppose it did," Burlon admitted. "I wasn't there. Chenna and I had realized we were Chosens, earlier in the evening, and so our ceremony was held, and the two of us retired to our dydanin. We knew nothing of Cirin's return until the next morning."

It wasn't quite accurate; he had already known about Venna's loss from Gredin, although Chenna had not. But that wasn't a part of the tale that Zanther needed to hear. His attention, quite properly, was all for Miri.

"Because Miri had stayed calm and been so sensible, and knew so much about our kitchen supplies, she was asked to join a small group of us who began meeting daily with Gredin to manage matters and keep people from panicking. That's how I got to know Miri as more than just a kitchen Tender. But lately she and Gredin had begun to react more emotionally to problems, and to suffer small mishaps when they exercised their gyftes. And it was Miri who finally recognized the problem for what it is, because of Ulm."

Zanther groaned. "My poor Miri. She must be so frightened. How soon can we return? I *need* her, Burlon, and she needs me."

"I understand. Truly, I do. But the problem is much bigger than that. Listen to me, Zanther. Listen, and think about what I'm saying. We have hundreds of people on Tradepoint now whose Chosens have returned to the Source. Can you imagine, given time, what the result of that will be, if nothing is done to help them?"

Zanther shook his head. "If? There is no 'if.' There is no way to help them. Miri and I will be spared, because we have each other, but those others…"

"No. Listen. What if I told you that we have found a way – one way – to save them from that fate? Would you advise them to take it?"

"If you had seen Ulm, seen the life she was forced to live, you wouldn't even ask. Of course I would advise them to take it. I would tell them to do anything they could, to escape Ulm's fate. Anything."

I will hold you to those words, Burlon thought grimly.

"Then listen to me," he said. "Miri was told, as we all were, that Venna had been destroyed, and that everyone who was not with us on Tradepoint was dead. She believed that *you* were dead. She didn't know you'd been delayed here on Sprygale. She believed she had lost you and would be without you forever. She believed that Ulm's fate would be her own. When she realized that every Vennan on Tradepoint who had lost their Chosen was doomed to Ulm's fate, she went to Gredin and warned her what to expect. At that point, Miri had no hope."

Zanther rested his forearm across his eyes, his breathing troubled.

"But Gredin consulted the Prett, and the Prett came up with a possible solution. It wasn't one that Gredin wanted to hear, but she was at a point where she had to consider any possibility at all, however unlikely, if there was a chance that it could save hundreds of our survivors from descending into Ulm's state of helplessness. And so, as alarming as she found it, Gredin herself tried the Prett solution. And it worked."

Slowly, Zanther lowered his arm. "It worked?"

"Yes."

"And has Miri undertaken this solution? She is all right?"

Burlon nodded. "Yes. Indeed, she is in far better Balance than you are."

"That is wonderful. Astonishing. I am so relieved!" Zanther smiled up at him. Then his smile faltered. "Why do you look so worried?"

"Because I have not yet told you what the Prett solution entails."

"What does it matter, if it saves them from suffering?"

"For the rest of them, you are right. It doesn't matter. But for

Miri…" Delay was no kindness. Osla and Chappal might return at any time. "The remedy for the loss of hlinga and lack of Balance suffered by those who lose their Chosen can be found in completions, just as they are for a Chosen pair. But once their Chosen has returned to the Source, they find can no longer achieve a completion on their own. And so the Prett's solution was that the Bereft – for that is what we now call people in such a situation – should mate with one another. They have not yet had much time to implement the plan, but already there are many whose hlinga is much improved." He met Zanther's gaze. "Including Miri."

Zanther said nothing for the space of ten breaths, and Burlon waited, unwilling to be the one to break that silence. When Zanther finally spoke, it was only to say, "I thank you for telling me. I think I will sleep again, now."

Burlon felt words rise within him like bubbles. He was genuinely fond of Miri, and he wanted to defend the wisdom of her decision. He wanted to tell Zanther how brave and generous Miri had been, how steadfast in the meetings of the circle of five, how stalwart as she ran the kitchen for the community under conditions of increasing shortage and uncertainty.

But Zanther already knew Miri's worth; he was her Chosen, and must love her as dearly as Burlon himself loved Chenna. Moreover, there would be time enough, in these next few days on Sprygale, for him to regale Zanther and Osla and Chappal with tales of how the community on Tradepoint was coping. And if those tales happened to shine a light on the many good things that Miri had done, well, that was only fair.

Zanther had all of the necessary puzzle pieces. He only needed time to assemble them properly. In other circumstances, Burlon might not have worried, but Zanther's attempts to deal calmly with what Burlon had told him would be seriously compromised by his lack of Balance. For now, Burlon could only trust in the Power and leave Zanther to find what rest he could, in the hope that it would help him to think clearly about so vital a matter, for his sake and Miri's.

[20]

0740 OF 2000 ORBITS REMAINING: 31YELLOW

Frightened by the buzzing *griimoni* encircling her wrist, Gredin looked up at Nitikikani. "It does this why?" she demanded. "Broken?"

His bony shoulders lifted and fell. "Not know. Gredin *griimoni*, not Nitikikani *griimoni*. Prett no give Hesch such *griimoni*."

"But Hesch understand *griimoni*," she protested, trying to remove the wristband. "Vennan not."

Nitikikani's hand touched her arm lightly. "Hurt?"

"No," she had to admit. "Just want stop!"

"Maybe simple. Maybe Director want. Call. Ask." He gestured ahead. "Panel near entry. Come. You call Director."

They moved through the Hesch enclave at the best pace that Nitikikani could manage. Gredin tried to overcome her sense of panic, but the jangling wristband made that difficult. When they finally reached the panel, Nitikikani pressed its buttons and said, "Speak Director. Urgent."

"Who call?" an unfamiliar Prett voice asked, its tone calm and unhurried.

"Nitikikani of Hesch with Gredin te–"

"One moment," the voice interrupted.

A pause.

"Gredin te Balamont?" It was Wyve's voice, and it vibrated and rumbled with intense emotion. Anger? Had she broken some rule by approaching the Hesch and boarding their ship?

"I am here," she said.

"Where?"

"The Hesch enclave. My wristband is–"

The wristband abruptly fell silent, its vibrations ceasing.

"Come to the Clinic. Bring your best healer. Keegan te Fliss is dying."

Heat surged through her, and her body stiffened in repudiation of Wyve's words. "I am coming," she said, and realized she had no time to waste on bio-mist chambers and corridors. Instead, with a quick nod of thanks and farewell to Nitikikani, she closed her eyes, Focused, and Sent.

In the same breath, she was in her sleeping chamber. Gathering her resolve, she hurried out into the room where she and the other four habitually gathered for their morning meeting, and felt a pang of anxiety as her gaze strayed to Keegan's empty room. But she didn't pause. There was nothing to be gained by lingering. Exiting their small suite of rooms, she heard nearby voices raised in confrontation. Then Tetralanna's voice cut through them all, shrill and angry as she proclaimed, "Be quiet, all of you! We are *not* going to risk the delegation's only ranked Healer for the sake of a mere historian!"

Gredin's own temper surged as she entered the reception hall and saw the people gathered there: Tetralanna and Rig te Indirin facing off against Sill and Miri, while First Healer Salderon te Indirin and his Assessor, Cayman, stood to the side, clearly distressed by the debate.

In an instant, all six of them spotted Gredin as she strode toward them, and Tetralanna shrilled, "This is none of your affair. Stay away. You have no business showing up now, when matters have already been decided, trying to push your way in. We have no need–"

Ignoring her, Gredin turned to Salderon. "Are you willing to aid Keegan te Fliss?" she asked him.

"Yes!"

She had nearly reached the group. "What do you need?"

"Just Cayman."

Sill and Miri were speaking urgently now, as well as Tetralanna and Rig, but Gredin had no attention to spare for them. Reaching out, she placed one hand on Cayman, the other hand on Salderon, and Sent with them directly to the Prett Clinic.

[21]

0740 OF 2000 ORBITS REMAINING: 31ORANGE

A crushing sense of guilt glued Wyve's feet to the floor of Room Six.

He had taken up a stance well clear of the activity surrounding Keegan te Fliss's bed. Standing close to the wall near the door, he could easily see the monitors, as well as the actions and reactions of the medical team. They continued to work swiftly and professionally, their well-trained motions betraying nothing of their thoughts.

But Wyve was no fool. He could smell the team's distress and that, along with the wavering and dipping of the measurements on the bio monitors, revealed the truth of the situation.

The Vennan was, indeed, dying.

Nothing the medical personnel had done so far seemed to have helped. Wyve grimaced as he watched Binn insert yet another access port and begin to administer an additional drug. What were the chances that this treatment would prove any more successful than the others she had tried? Should he step forward to warn all of the dariiseri of the evanescence that would occur when Keegan te Fliss died? He had been reluctant to disrupt their efforts when he first arrived. Now, however, with no improvement in Keegan's condition, perhaps it was time.

Unexpected movement in his peripheral vision snagged his attention. Wyve turned his head, and his pulse jumped as he realized that

Gredin had just… arrived, as she had promised only a short while ago. He could only hope that the two individuals with her, a woman and a man, were the Vennan healers he had ordered her to bring.

The three Vennans approached the bio bed, Gredin leading the way. The unknown woman followed her closely, while the male lagged several steps behind. Binn remained in position at the control panel, but the remaining medical team stepped back with a respectful nod of their heads. No doubt, Wyve thought grimly, it was more to allow the Vennans an opportunity to say their goodbyes than from any real belief that the newcomers would find a way to assist the dying Vennan.

As Gredin reached Keegan's side, she spoke sharply in Prettian. "Stop! Do nothing more to his body." She seemed stunned by what she was seeing. "Cayman, can you Assess him with all of these… these *griimoni* attached to him?" she asked in Vennan.

The female stranger looked uncertain. "I will try. But it would be better if they were not present."

Gredin wasted no time. Reverting to Prettian, she ordered Binn, "Remove all of these things from his body."

"He will die without the support they provide!" Binn protested.

"He will die if they remain," Gredin countered, her tone adamant. "Remove them or I will do it myself."

For the first time since Wyve had entered the treatment room, Binn looked to him for direction.

"Do as she requests," Wyve said. "Quickly."

"But, sir, we are supporting his heart and other vital functions."

Wyve pointed to the monitors above the bio bed. "He fails despite your interventions, Binn. At worst, removing everything will only hasten the inevitable." He offered her a gentle smile. "You have done your best. Now let the Vennans have their way with him."

Looking sad and reluctant, Binn nodded, then swiftly began to strip the Vennan of all ports and devices. A trickle of bright red blood marked each removal site, and Binn quickly applied a pressure spray to prevent further bleeding.

By the time she finished, the monitor readings were even more erratic, and Wyve's heart grew even heavier.

"I thank you," Gredin said in Prettian, and stepped back, giving the Vennan woman at her side easy access to the bed.

"Keegan te Fliss," the woman said softly, "I am Cayman te Indirin. Be at peace, for I have come to Assess you." Cayman placed a hand on Keegan's chest, and her blue eyes slowly closed.

A taut silence held for a breath, two, then three.

Cayman's eyes opened wide. "We must hurry," she exclaimed urgently in Vennan. "Keegan's hold on life is weak. They have damaged his vessel within and without, and strange substances poison his body." Cayman removed her hand from his chest. "Salderon, he is within your gyfte. I give you permission to perform this Healing."

Wyve blinked, bewildered. The woman had only touched Keegan for a few moments, and yet she spoke with certainty of his condition. How had she known of the internal damage from the tissue samples? He had said nothing about that harvesting to Gredin when they spoke. Given the dire situation, he had elected to withhold details until there was time for discussion. Cayman had used nothing but her hand to examine Keegan, and yet she seemed to have acquired the pertinent facts. More oddly still, Keegan's monitor parameters had steadied as she did so.

Wyve saw that Gredin did not share his bewilderment. Indeed, her posture eased as the man, Salderon, stepped to the bedside. Cayman remained close to Salderon as he raised both hands. "Keegan te Fliss," he called out in a warm, mellow voice, "I am Salderon te Indirin. Be at peace, for I have come to Heal you."

But the healer didn't stop there. Before Wyve could react, let alone raise an objection, Salderon climbed nimbly onto the bed itself. Stretching himself full-length beside the motionless body, he wrapped his fingers around Keegan's wrist, as if seeking his pulse. "May the Power bless my efforts," Salderon murmured, and closed his eyes.

The display above the bed had become chaotic as it attempted to track and reconcile two sets of inputs. Binn's fingers flitted over the controls, silencing alarms and reconfiguring until, suddenly, two sets of readouts appeared, side by side.

The other dariiseri looked on helplessly.

Wyve kept his gaze trained on Salderon.

Salderon took a deep, shuddering breath, then grew utterly still.

Wyve's heart leapt in alarm. Were they about to lose both men?

"The Healing has begun," Cayman said quietly, a thread of relief in her voice.

Gredin smiled. "Do not worry, Binn. Keegan will be fine, once Salderon completes the Intercession. Healing is his gyfte."

Her words in Prettian were clear, but Wyve wondered how much reassurance Binn drew from them. He, too, had heard the words, and the confidence that underscored them, but he knew that there was no scientific basis for Gredin's conviction.

Gredin left the bedside area to join Wyve, her blue eyes gleaming. "All will be well now. In the days to come, our people will offer many thanks to the Power for restoring Keegan to us," she said in Prettian, her fingers touching the hlette on her arm.

She spoke as if Keegan's return to health were an accomplished fact. "What is happening?" Wyve asked, keeping a cautious eye on the monitor. "It appears to me, and likely to the dariiseri, as well, that Salderon is merely touching Keegan's wrist."

Gredin smiled, and Wyve was struck by how poised she seemed, her alert gaze a sharp contrast to the last time they had been in the Clinic together, after the Beng attack, six sect ago.

"Salderon is performing an Intercession – a Healing – on Keegan, using his gyfte. When he has finished, all of the damage Binn caused will be gone, and Keegan will be as he was before, whole and healthy."

"How long will that take? How is such a thing possible?"

Gredin shrugged. "Not long. But Keegan and Salderon will both need to sleep and rest for several days afterward, to recover. A Healing takes much from both the Healer and the petitioner."

"Petitioner?"

"The one who requires the Healing. Keegan, in this instance. And, since Keegan was close to death, his recovery will take longer, and he will be easily fatigued for a time thereafter."

"But you just said he would be 'whole and healthy' when Salderon completes the… healing," Wyve protested.

Gredin sighed. "Keegan's body, his vessel, *will* be whole, with all damage erased. But vitality and strength are another matter."

Wyve's conscience writhed. "I hope you understand that Binn did not intend to harm him."

"Of course. Keegan is quite fond of Binn and has always spoken highly of her care and dedication. But those *grïimoni* that made his skin bleed… Vennans do not manage well when the integrity of their vessels is compromised. And Cayman's Assessment found that there was also damage deep inside, yes?"

Wyve nodded. "Binn performed the tissue and blood sampling today, rather than finish the food challenges. She thought Keegan needed a respite from the vomiting that the food tests were causing. She was concerned about his weight loss and wanted to prevent a further decline."

"Was she able to salvage the samples?"

"Of course," Wyve assured her, horrified that Gredin might think them so careless. "They are in the lab, safely secured. I promise you that Keegan's ordeal has not been in vain. We will use the blood and tissue to learn much about Vennan praaten and liipraaten."

Gredin's brow pleated. "I do not understand all that you just said, Wyve. What is *praaten* and *liipraaten*?"

Why can't Vennans know at least the rudiments of science?

"Praaten is the detailed study of how a living thing is constructed," Wyve said slowly, taking care to choose words that Gredin might better understand. "It explores what structures hide on the inside of a living thing's body. Liipraaten studies how those structures work at the smallest level, and why they do that work."

"Vennans do not find such things important," Gredin confessed. "Our Healers care for us when we are injured, but injuries are not common for adults. We treat our bodies with respect and take sensible precautions to prevent accidents."

"Be assured, we will use Keegan's samples to develop treatments that can aid Vennans, should a healer not be immediately available. And I suspect we should begin with a more detailed discussion of the Vennan concept of the 'integrity of the vessel.'"

Gredin nodded, her face sober. "The extreme rending of Cirin's vessel caused him to evanesce. His wounds were longer and deeper than Keegan's. But Keegan's vessel had been pierced enough times, and for long enough, that his life also began to fail, just more slowly."

This debacle had, at the very least, made it clear to Wyve how fragile the Vennans were as a race, despite the startling and unexplained abilities they possessed. No wonder the Vennan traders and travelers had resisted the pleas of every Director for three hundred sectora for tissue and blood samples. They journeyed unharmed through space without ships… but a mere cut or puncture caused serious repercussions.

"Burlon should be included in that discussion, once he returns from Sprygale," Gredin said, her gaze still on Keegan's bed. "He understands Prett science words far better than I. Salderon may be of assistance, too, once Cayman judges him to be recovered from the Intercession."

Wyve felt another layer of guilt descend. He had summoned Burlon te Laith to his office and practically ordered him to acquire the next shipment of geddel crystals. Surely, he hadn't sent the trader into harm's way? Burlon had always made it sound as if trading for the geddel crystals was a straightforward task.

Wyve cleared his throat. "Gredin, I am responsible for Burlon's absence."

"Oh?" Her gaze swung to his.

"I called him to my office yesterday. I informed him that the Vokastra were growing increasingly uneasy over the presence of nearly a thousand Vennans on Tradepoint, and that he should do everything he could to appease them."

"They are far from here, are they not? And it is you who is the Director on Tradepoint, not them."

Her naiveté was almost amusing. Almost.

"Gredin, the Vokastra have authority over all Prettian matters. My authority on the station was, and continues to be, granted to me by the Vokastra. If they become displeased, or fearful, or weary of the drain on our resources that housing the survivors from your world represents, they can order all of you evicted from the station. I would either have to obey or be removed from my duties here. And the same is true for Figg."

Gredin was silent.

"I am resolved to do everything I can to prevent that from happening," Wyve said, trying to offer what little comfort he could. "For the remaining sectora that I am Director, I promise you that I will devote my efforts to protecting and defending your people, regardless of what the Vokastra wants." He offered her a small smile. "Figg and Pord and I have developed ways of dealing with those who currently compose the Vokastra. We often are called upon to make suggestions and provide an informed view on issues involving our station. Be assured, the three of us will do all we can on your behalf."

"I thank you," Gredin said, "not only for your friendship, which I treasure, but for your blunt words, Wyve. I begin to understand more of the pressures that rest on your shoulders. And I now understand why Burlon departed for Sprygale against my wishes."

"He did not have your permission to go?" Wyve asked sharply.

"No."

"But…" He didn't know what to say. Another apology seemed foolish.

"No doubt he thought I would again refuse his request to leave Tradepoint." She made a rueful face. "I have not been at my best for some time, dithering over decisions, fearful of making a wrong choice due to my loss of hlinga. But taking an alliance partner at regular intervals has largely restored me to Balance, and I see what needs to be done much more clearly."

"I am glad for you," Wyve said. And for himself, and for Figg. This new, confident Gredin would be much easier to work with, when the need for incisive decisions arose.

"Burlon likely thought to spare us both by taking the decision into his own hands. The last time he asked, I denied his request."

"Really? Why did you disagree with Burlon on this matter?" Wyve asked, curious. "He is an experienced traveler and trader."

"Burlon needed time, like the rest of us, to regain his Balance,"

Gredin replied. "Grief and loss such as we have just experienced are not quickly banished, and can erode one's Balance in odd ways. Besides, we have no way of knowing whether Sprygale still exists, or whether, like Palomar and Venna, it has been destroyed."

In which case they might lose Burlon as they lost Cirin.

Burlon was newly coupled and his mate was pregnant.

And the geddel crystals might no longer exist.

Wyve felt suddenly hollow.

A stir at Keegan's bedside snared his attention. Cayman was murmuring to Salderon, whose eyes were now open.

"The Intercession has been completed," Gredin said, brightening. "Keegan is Healed. I must go, Wyve, but I will return when I can, to hear more about the Vokastra and our relationship with them. And to tell you about the Hesch. You will no doubt be interested to hear of my visit with Nitikikani and his family on their ship. But, for now, a good day to you, Wyve." Gredin bowed briefly with crossed palms, then walked to Keegan's bedside.

Wyve blinked, trying to order his thoughts. Gredin had been not just in the Hesch enclave but aboard the Hesch ship? And Nitikikani had a *family* with him, here at Tradepoint*?*

With only half his attention, he watched Gredin speak to the other Vennans, unable to focus enough on their words to understand them. Abruptly, he became aware of the twinned readout on the monitor over Keegan te Fliss's bio bed. Both sets of parameters were level and steady.

The Intercession is complete, Gredin had said. *Keegan has been healed.*

Cayman and Salderon abruptly vanished.

This time, Wyve's pulse didn't even leap.

Dazed, he watched Gredin bow to Binn, the line of her spine graceful, her riot of pale curls gleaming under the bright bio lights.

Then she and Keegan te Fliss disappeared, as well, leaving Binn and the other dariiseri to stare at Wyve, clearly craving answers he could not possibly provide.

[22]
SPRYGALE

Zanther had not spoken for the past two days. It was as if the ebbing of his hlinga had suddenly overwhelmed him, in spite of his many precautions. He slept only fitfully. At meals, he drank little and ate even less. When Burlon or Osla or Chappal expressed concern, he simply closed his eyes, perhaps to doze, perhaps only to dissuade them from trying to engage him in conversation.

As Burlon had expected, the Kendar Traders responded with dismay when he revealed the two-day delay in their departure date. He did his best to explain the complicated connections between the demands of the Prett Vokastra, the belated completion of the Sprygalian geddel crystal harvest, and the need to stay in the good graces of Majaya, Ruler of the Southern Seas. But Osla and Chappal were understandably desperate to return to the surviving members of their House. And, although Zanther remained mute, Burlon was aware of his reproachful gaze.

On the morning of his first full day on Sprygale, Burlon had returned to the *Simati Dobria* and been granted a second audience with Majaya. During their talk, he negated the tentative arrangements that the Kendar Traders had originally made. The fishers had still seen no sign of the expected *ginglin* run, and Burlon was certain he could barter the Kendar Tradegoods for things that would be of far more benefit to the community. It wouldn't make him popular with Osla and Chappal, but they had not yet experienced the reality of the enclave of survivors, and so did not yet comprehend why the concept of communal goods, rather than House goods, was essential.

On the morning of his second full day on Sprygale, which *should* have been the day of his departure, he was fidgety and out of sorts, unable to escape an awareness that Chenna would be waiting eagerly… then waiting impatiently… then waiting anxiously. The weather was sunny and warm, and the village was abuzz with final preparations for the ceremony that would join Q'iari with Jostan, but Burlon had trouble responding to the smiles around him.

That afternoon, he finally met with Rangh and Jostan to deliver the coat Ingarra had made. Determined to make the best presentation he could, he convinced Osla to accompany him to the guest lodge where Rangh and Jostan were staying. She was taller than Q'iari but just as slender; he was confident the garment would fit her.

"The *timte* coat is in this carrysack," he explained when he and Osla were admitted to the room where the Ruler of the North Reaches and his son sat. "If it is your wish, I will open the sack and simply show you the coat. But a coat, like any garment, is meant to be worn, and so I have asked my fellow Trader to come, in case you would rather see the coat displayed on an individual. What is your preference?"

The men conferred briefly. Then Rangh said, "It would be a pity to waste the presence of your pretty companion. Have her don the coat."

"Very well. Then close your eyes or turn around while she puts it on. I will tell you when we are ready to have you look."

The men complied, although not without a grumble from Rangh.

Burlon unfastened the carrysack and drew out the coat, Freshening it as he did so. Helping Osla to slip her arms into the sleeves, he murmured to her, "This is a warm day, and a very warm coat. I thank you for putting up with this display."

But Osla seemed quite delighted with the garment, buttoning it fully and even allowing Burlon to drape the woven scarf artfully over her hair and around her neck.

"You may look now," Burlon told them, and stepped aside so that Osla and the coat were their sole focus as she turned slowly, showing it off to best advantage.

Burlon stole a glance at the father and son from the North Reaches.

Rangh was nodding. "I doubt Majaya's *timte* gift for the girl will be half so fine," he said, with a look of smug satisfaction that allayed most of Burlon's worries.

Beside him, Jostan seem entranced. "And look, Father. There's a slit at the back that will help the skirt of the coat spread properly when Q'iari rides atop a morg." He offered Burlon a nod. "Cleverly done, that."

Burlon bowed his head in recognition of the compliment, even though the slit at the back of the coat had been entirely Ingarra's notion. Had she somehow foreseen the need for such a feature, even though she had never seen a Sprygalian, let alone a morg? A happy accident? Or a subtle sign of the Power's favor in this endeavor?

No matter. Jostan was pleased. Therefore, Burlon was pleased.

When the two men from the North Reaches fell silent, Burlon said, "I will remove the coat from Osla now, before the heat overcomes her." He set to work on the buttons. "Would you care to examine it more closely, or shall I pack it safely away for you until tomorrow?"

"Best to pack it away," Jostan said. "My father and I have many skills, but needlework is not among them. It is an attractive garment, but are you certain it will be warm enough, come winter?"

"Absolutely," Burlon said. "Ingarra te Balamont fashioned it with a special lining that imparts great warmth without great bulk. In this coat, Q'iari will be both lovely and warm."

Rangh gave his son a wry grin. "Now see what you have done? Your mother will be envious."

Burlon smiled. "I am certain Ingarra could be persuaded to sew a coat for your wife, as well, should that become your desire."

"Yes, well, we'll see. First, my son and I need to recover from the cost of this one, Traderman." With that, he unfastened a large leather pouch from his belt and tossed it to Burlon. "You'll find our agreed price there."

Beside him, Jostan unfastened a smaller pouch from his own belt. "And a bonus, for making so fine a job of it," he said, and tossed it Burlon's way.

Having caught both pouches deftly, Burlon handed them to Osla. "If you will mind these for the moment," he said, "I will pack this coat away so that no harm comes to it, and so that no curious eyes have a chance to behold it before tomorrow night."

When he had done so, he handed the carrysack over to Jostan, reclaimed the pouches from Osla, thanked Rangh for trusting him with such an important commission, and left the guest lodge at a lively clip, grateful to have shed the last of his responsibility for the *timte* gifts.

Osla caught up with him a few steps farther down the lane. "There. You've delivered your goods. Now take Zanther to Tradepoint."

"You know that I can't. I've explained why I can't. Majaya insists that I be there for tomorrow night's ceremony. I can't Travel to Tradepoint with Zanther and make it back in time. The day after tomorrow, at dawn, I'll take all three of you back. Until then, leave me be."

She dropped back a pace.

With a sigh, Burlon turned to face her. "Your pardon, Osla. I do not mean to snap. I know this has been a frightening time for you and the others. But you might also spare a thought for how difficult it is for me. I would like nothing better than to return to Tradepoint and spend tonight in the arms of my Chosen. But I refuse to do that at the expense of the surviving community. The Vokastra is decidedly displeased to find itself sheltering nearly a thousand homeless Vennans. Given half an excuse, they will demand that we leave. The only way to pacify them is for me to deliver the promised geddel crystals – the very crystals that Majaya's fishers have been too busy to finish gathering because of the self-same joining she insists I attend. I am trapped between the Vokastra's demands and Majaya's, and so I stay, although I know to my sorrow that my unexpected delay here is frightening my Chosen. So I ask you to forgive me for venting my frustration on you, but I tell you plainly that I cannot yet do as you would have me do."

"And so," Osla said, "am I to take that as the apology you claimed it to be or as a scolding? I find it difficult to tell."

"Take it as you will. I am going swimming."

"Then stay close to shore. The currents here are unlike those at home."

Burlon eyed her indignantly. "Have you become my Guide?"

"Far worse," she snapped. "I have become one who must count upon your safety if I am ever to see my kinsmen again."

Her words cut through his dark mood. Shaking his head, Burlon said, "I am ashamed, Osla. I *do* ask your pardon. My temper is frayed, but that is no excuse for venting it on you. I will forego the swim. Shall we see how Zanther is faring?"

The next dawn introduced the day of Q'iari's ceremony, the final full day that Burlon and the others would spend on their extended visit to Sprygale. The ceremony would not begin until sunset, and so Burlon supposed that most of the villagers of Benbatahl would spend their day in last-minute tasks: the gathering of flowers and fruits, the ritual cleansing of the *timte* canopy, kitchen preparations, and more. Instead, moments after the sun cleared the horizon, an unexpected cry went up, swiftly spreading throughout the village: "Ginglin! Ginglin in the bay!"

The sound of running feet amplified as more and more villagers ran down to the boats, whooping with excitement.

Burlon cast a glance at Chappal. "Poor Q'iari."

"Why 'poor Q'iari'? This is the day of her joining ceremony."

"Indeed. And that," he said, hooking a thumb at the open window, "is the sound of every able-bodied villager heading away from the *Simati Dobria* at top speed, intent on spending the entire day fishing. Q'iari and her mother will be fortunate if there are half a dozen folk left to help with the final preparations for the celebration. Jostan himself may have caught a ride in one of the boats, and his father, as well." With a groan, he rose from his sleepmat and began to dress.

"Are you going down to the beach to join them?" Chappal asked with an air of alarm.

"No," Burlon assured him. 'I'm heading up to the *Simati Dobria*, to ask Majaya if she needs some help. You might consider doing the same, after morning meal, if you're feeling charitable."

"But... why?"

"Well, if we aren't needed, we'll at least have done the polite thing by offering, since they have housed and fed us for days. But I suspect she'll be grateful and will put us to good use. I've never been here to witness such a run, but the fishers have told me tales of how the other villagers head down to the coves in the hope of harvesting *ginglin* as the fisher boats drive them closer to shore." Fastening his final button, Burlon said, "Come or not. Suit yourself. But I am heading up to the *Simati Dobria.*"

"Without your morning meal?"

Burlon smiled. "I don't think Majaya will let me starve."

When he reached the *Simati Dobria,* Majaya was in a temper and Q'iari was in tears, but it soon turned into quite a merry morning. Burlon found himself wishing for Keegan te Fliss and his tidy lists, but he managed to cajole Majaya into naming the various tasks that were still uncompleted, and together they worked out the order of importance, from most vital to least. Soon thereafter, Chappal showed up, explaining that Osla had stayed behind to look after Zanther's needs. Burlon put him to work, lending strength where it was needed to supplement the more delicate efforts of the serving ladies. Burlon did the same throughout most of the morning, but eventually found himself recruited to sit cross-legged on the floor of a veranda with Majaya and Q'iari, helping them string blossoms for Q'iari's *timte* crown. As an extra kindness, unbidden, he used a touch of the Power to keep the blossoms cool and unwilted, so that they would show to best advantage when Q'iari wore them for her joining.

As Burlon had hoped, they ate and drank while they worked. And, inevitably, they talked, speaking at first of the upcoming ceremony and the unexpected *ginglin* run. Then the conversation moved to the newly delineated Middle Realm, which had long been a disputed area between Majaya's Southern Seas territory and Rangh's North Reaches. After tonight, it would become a peaceful region ruled jointly by Q'iari and Jostan.

In an unexpected turn, Majaya asked, "And all is well on your world, Traderman?"

He could have murmured some vague affirmative, and the conversation would likely have shifted again. But the untruth stuck in his throat. Instead, after a sip of *pimar* juice, Burlon said, "Regrettably, no. But that is a topic for another time. Today is for rejoicing as we celebrate the union of Q'iari and Jostan."

"Sweetly said, but I am curious and concerned," Q'iari objected. "What is the difficulty? Is there sickness among your people? A blight on your crops? Difficulty with a quarrelsome neighbor?"

"No. Nothing like that. The problem is with the world itself. It has… ceased to be."

Q'iari blinked. "I don't understand."

"Neither do we," Burlon admitted. "A large group of us Traveled to Tradepoint for a celebration in honor of one of our Travelers. While we were there, word reached us that our world had been destroyed, causing the loss of all those we left behind… except for the three Traders you so kindly sheltered here, and a group of five who had been away on a Trading mission when the disaster occurred."

"Then where are you living now? Majaya asked, ever the practical one.

"On Tradepoint, for the moment, while we seek a new home world."

"Ah! So that is why–" Majaya began.

"Yes," Burlon affirmed.

Q'iari looked from one of them to the other. "What? That is why *what*?"

Burlon said nothing, and Majaya said only, "Traderman came to me to barter the goods brought by the other traders. Although, now that the ginglin run has started, he may wish to reconsider…"

"No. Our arrangement stands," Burlon told her. "But if the *ginglin* run is bountiful, we might discuss them, as well."

She nodded, saying nothing, and her clever fingers continued to thread blossoms.

When midday came, Majaya dismissed him. "Q'iari and I are going inside to rest," she said. "You should return to the Trade House and do the same. We thank you for your assistance, and we look forward to seeing you at sunset for the ceremony."

Dismissed, Burlon wandered back through the deserted lanes and passed the Trade House by, intent on reaching the beach to see what was happening there. As he walked, he tried to stay alert to the details of the natural world around him: the packed earth of the lane beneath his bare feet, the heat of the midday sun on his head and shoulders, the various scents of sea and plants and food carried by the slight breeze, the sight of seabirds wheeling overhead and the sound of their high-pitched cries. When he returned to Tradepoint, he would ask Sill to Harvest the memory so that it could be shared with the community, and so that Chenna could see where he had been during his extended absence.

When he stepped beyond the last of the lodges and scanned the beach, he was amazed by the variety of actions he saw, and the sheer number of villagers who were there. It seemed as if every resident of Benbatahl was present, taking part in the frenzied harvest. Many were out in the fleet of small craft that rode the waves, driving the *ginglin* inland toward the beach. Others waded in the shallows, scooping up net after net of the glistening silver fish. Some of the nets were then emptied into woven fish cages that could be kept submerged in the cove to be dealt with later. Other nets were dragged laboriously ashore, where people from the village waited with knives and boards and pots, dealing with fish that would no doubt be added to that night's feast. Small children ran excitedly from one individual to another, watching everything with the pale green eyes that marked them as southern Sprygalians. The older children helped wherever they could.

It was a well-coordinated effort, the entire village working in harmony. If he offered his assistance, they would probably accept but it would be out of politeness, not necessity. This work was best left to those accustomed to it. Perhaps Majaya and Q'iari had had the right idea, after all: retire for a short rest, the better to handle the coming evening's ceremonial activities. He would be there for the joining, since that was Majaya's command, but he would not stay late. In the morning, by dawn's first light, he would gather Osla and Chappal and Zanther, as well as the goods he had Traded for, and take them all back to Tradepoint.

Firm in his resolve, he turned away from the excitement of the *ginglin* run and trudged back up the rise until he reached the Trade House.

Osla was there, coaxing Zanther to eat something for his midday meal.

"Have you eaten?" Burlon asked her, joining them.

"Yes."

"Then I will take over here with Zanther. Go down to the beach and watch them deal with the *ginglin* run, if you like. It is quite a sight. Later, we can discuss whether you or Chappal or both would like a chance to take part in tonight's celebration. And then, at dawn, we depart."

That, at last, brought a smile to Osla's face. She handed the tray to Burlon and stood, saying, "I will be back, Zanther. Try to eat." And she left them there together.

Burlon set the tray aside and, leaning over, grasped Zanther beneath the arms and pulled him higher, so that his back was braced by the wall. "You will eat," Burlon told him firmly, "so that you can withstand tomorrow's journey and arrive in a condition that won't frighten Miri." Sitting down, he took the tray onto his own lap and dipped the spoon into a bowl of chowder. "Here. You need not eat for pleasure. You are eating for strength." And he thrust the spoon unceremoniously into Zanther's mouth.

When roughly half of the food had been consumed, Zanther turned his face away. "Enough. I will try again at evening meal."

"Fair enough," Burlon conceded. He was not displeased, since it was more than he had seen Zanther eat at any one meal under Osla and Chappal's gentle care. He set the tray aside. "By this time tomorrow, you will be with Miri," he said into the silence.

Zanther made no reply.

"She is your Chosen."

"I know what she is," Zanther said, not meeting his gaze.

"She–"

"No. You and I have no further need to discuss her. I am going to rest now. I suggest you do the same." And Zanther slid down full-length on his sleepmat and rolled onto his side, turning away from Burlon.

Dispirited, Burlon ate the food remaining on the tray, then collapsed onto his own sleepmat, not expecting to sleep but reasoning that he could, at least, relax before the night's festivities. Thinking about the hard-working cheerfulness he had seen the Sprygalian community demonstrate on the beach at the *ginglin* run, he closed his eyes.

And opened them to long shadows and the sound of a man and a woman chatting in the outer room. Bewildered, he looked around. Moments ago, he and Chenna had been…

No, he realized. He was on Sprygale, and Chenna had been no more than a night-thought. The real Chenna was on Tradepoint, awaiting his return – or perhaps, by now, as convinced of his demise as Miri was of Zanther's.

Tomorrow, all of that would change. He and Chenna would reunite. Zanther and Miri would reunite, as well… or so he hoped. How could it be otherwise? They were Chosens, selected for one another by the Power.

But never, since the creation of the Sixty-Six, had a situation existed where a member of a Chosen pair mated with someone else.

Had he been wrong to tell Zanther of it? Miri seemed so guileless that he could not imagine her attempting to hide the truth from Zanther. And yet that should, perhaps, have been her own decision to make. Burlon longed to know what was going on in Zanther's mind, but the man seemed determined not to discuss the matter any further with him.

Rubbing the sleep from his eyes, Burlon realized he had slept the afternoon away, and that the conversation he could hear was Osla speaking to Chappal about the approaching ceremony, and whether Burlon and Zanther ought to be wakened.

Not entirely refreshed, Burlon stumbled out to join them. "I am up. But why wake Zanther?"

Osla made a wry face. "Q'iari has decided she wants all four of us to attend the ceremony, and so Majaya is sending some sort of carrychair for Zanther. They are adamant that he be there. And we are all to go barefoot."

"Then we will have to humor them," Burlon said. "It is the final night. We leave at dawn. We have only this evening's festivity to get through, and then I will take us all to Tradepoint."

"Most of the Sprygalians will be up before dawn, as well," Chappal said. When Burlon looked askance at him, he clarified, "The second day of the *ginglin* run."

"Indeed." A glance out of the window showed him that the sky was beginning to blush, and he could hear the first faint sound of drums. The ceremony would soon begin. "Well, if the two of you can help Zanther, I will ready myself for tonight."

They had barely completed their preparations when a pair of Sprygalian men appeared at the entrance to the lodge, supporting a chair mounted between two poles. With less fuss than Burlon had feared, Zanther was placed in the chair, and they all headed down to the beach for the joining ceremony.

Torches lit the deserted lanes, and the sound of the drums grew louder as they left the village behind and made the final descent to the beach.

Burlon had expected to find the villagers of Benbatahl gathered on the sand. Instead, he saw that they were all standing ankle-deep in the surf, some with torches in hand, some with drums, while children carried fronds and sprays of flowers. All stood with their backs to the water, their faces turned toward the village.

The two Sprygalians bearing Zanther's chair took it straight down to the water's edge, and Burlon and the others followed, taking their place among the villagers.

The water felt cool and welcoming as it ebbed and flowed around Burlon's ankles, and the wet sand shifted slightly beneath his feet with each new wave. The torches crackled and smoked, giving off a pungent herbal scent as they burned, and he could feel the heat of the nearest one on the right side of his face. Some of the drums were small, with a thin, changeable pitch that sounded almost like people conversing. Others were much larger, supported by a rope of braided vine that passed diagonally over the shoulder and around the body of each drummer. They produced a full, rich tone that Burlon could feel in his bones.

Then the flutes began, high and sweet, blending and separating like birdsong, and the people around him murmured, looking to the left and right.

He heard a deep, guttural chant, somewhere off to the left. Gazing over the heads of the shorter Sprygalians, Burlon saw a dozen men from the North Reaches striding down the beach in tight formation, with Rangh in the lead. They wore rough capes of fur, and Burlon's first thought was that they must be miserably hot. But this ceremony wasn't about comfort. It was a display of might and worth and tradition.

The sound of female voices singing drifted on the evening breeze. Turning to his right, Burlon spotted the women of the royal household of the Southern Seas walking at the edge of the water line. No, not walking. Dancing. Their light steps traced a graceful pattern, with Majaya at the head of the cluster.

The men of the North Reaches were closer now. They did not dance, but their walk took on the cadence of a march, punctuated at intervals by a stomping step accompanied by a wordless cry.

The women's song shifted, adapting itself to the rhythm of the men's footfalls, merging into a unified performance of chant and song, supported by the drums and flutes.

As the two groups met, Rangh and Majaya faced off against one another in ritual confrontation, inching forward until they were practically touching, neither willing to retreat. The drums grew louder and more insistent, and the warriors from the North Reaches added sharp claps to the rhythmic stomping of their feet.

A sudden trilling cry arose from far back in the group of women.

Everything else – the chanting men, the singing women, the drums, the flutes – fell silent. Only the ocean still dared to whisper as it crept up and back, up and back.

A single female voice began to sing, and the group of women from the royal household shifted and split, some moving to their right, some to their left, clearing a path down the center. Over their heads, Burlon could see something tall and brightly colored swaying as it moved forward through the ranks of women. Fronds? Feathers?

Q'iari emerged from the women's midst, stepping forward to place her hands on Majaya's shoulders from behind. The girl was an impressive sight, wearing a towering headdress made up of feathers, fronds, and the flower crowns that Burlon had spent much of his morning helping to make. One of Q'iari's arms was bare, while the other was almost totally covered from wrist to shoulder by a series of bracelets and cuffs, some narrow, some broad, some made from gleaming metal, others of beadwork, or of clay that had been painted with bright colors in brilliant designs. Necklaces of fresh flowers hung down to cover her breasts, swaying as she walked. A panel of painted cloth was wrapped around her lower body, knotted high at her left hip, ending just above her knees. Her feet were bare, and each slender ankle was adorned with a ringlet of flowers.

As she continued to sing, the men parted, left and right, until finally Jostan came into view, swathed in furs. He took up a position behind his father, resting his huge hands on Rangh's shoulders.

A little pantomime ensued, with Q'iari and Jostan taking turns leaning to peer around their parent. Finally, both leaned at once. Their gazes locked. Q'iari's song took on a new urgency, and Jostan voiced the chant of the men of the North Reaches.

Still singing, Q'iari turned Majaya to face her, pressed her check to her mother's cheek, then gently guided Majaya into the waiting arms of the other women before turning back, alone, to face Jostan and Rangh.

Jostan turned Rangh around, enveloped his father in a crushing hug, then thrust him into the crowd of men from the North Reaches. When they had absorbed Rangh into their ranks, Jostan turned to face Q'iari. Taking two strides, he held out both of his hands, palms upward.

Q'iari took three small dancing steps forward and placed her palms upon Jostan's.

Burlon jumped as the villagers around him began to chant. Concentrating, he made out the words: *We stand between you and the ocean, ready to protect you both*, they said, repeating the phrase three times.

Then the men of the North Reaches chanted: *We are of the land, and the land will welcome you.*

As soon as they fell silent, Q'iari and Jostan turned and made their way up the beach to the *timte* canopy. Everyone remained where they were, although Rangh and Majaya moved to stand at the front of their respective groups.

Starting at the very edge of the *timte* canopy, Q'iari and Jostan began to walk a pattern that had been drawn in the sand beneath it. By the time they reached the pattern's end, they were at the very center of the space defined by the canopy.

Q'iari extended her right hand. "Come and join us, Rangh of the North Reaches." And Jostan extended his left hand and called, "Come and join us, Majaya of the Southern Seas."

The two rulers walked together to the canopy to join the couple. Behind them, each man of the North Reaches accepted the hand of a woman of the royal party of the Southern Seas to walk, two by two, and take their place in the circle that was forming.

When everyone from those two groups had taken their places, the villagers standing around Burlon let out a happy cry and left the surf to follow them. The two villagers who had brought Zanther's chair down for the ceremony picked it up again and carried him onto the beach, as well.

As soon as everyone had gathered under and around the canopy, Q'iari and Jostan moved to the very center of the pattern again. Jostan lifted Q'iari high into the air and turned in a slow circle, then lowered her gently and proclaimed, "I belong now to Q'iari, and beseech her to join me in ruling the Middle Realm."

"And I belong now to Jostan," she caroled, "and agree to rule with him over the Middle Realm, where we will live in harmony with both the North Reaches and the Southern Seas."

Trilling cries went up from the gathering – signs of enthusiastic approval, Burlon surmised.

When the uproar finally faded, Q'iari raised her voice again. "I am a young woman not known for her patience, as those who live here know well. For days, I have heard rumors of wondrous timte gifts brought from afar. My curiosity is aflame. Would this not be a fine time for them to be presented?"

Majaya placed her hands on her hips. "No, daughter, it would not! They are to be viewed back at the grand hall, not down here where they would soon be covered in sand."

"Well then," Q'iari said, with a dramatic sigh, "let us walk through the village and mount the steps to the Simati Dobria, where a fine feast awaits us all on this most joyous of nights. And then perhaps, at last, my *timte* gifts can be revealed."

Burlon swallowed a groan. If the gifts had been displayed here, he and the Kendar Traders could have excused themselves afterward and sought their beds. As matters now stood, Majaya would likely expect him to linger until the presentation.

Q'iari's impatience had just become his best hope for an early night. And, he reasoned, he needed a meal almost as much as he needed sleep. Tomorrow morning, he would be Traveling back to Tradepoint with a fair load to juggle: the three Kendar Traders, the geddel crystals, the results from his renegotiation of the Kendar Trading goods, and the cargo from his own last-minute arrangement with Majaya. The bulk would be considerable, and managing it all safely was paramount. He did not intend to meet Cirin's fate, especially now, when he had every reason to live: Chenna, their coming child, the search for New Venna…

Tomorrow morning would be a time to take the greatest of care.

Despite entering the Simati Dobria in a dour mood, Burlon soon found himself enjoying the celebration. He reminded himself again not to take these flowers and festivities for granted; tomorrow, he would be back in the enclave, where life was far less gracious. Sitting now at a table in the great hall, where heaping platters of food were being passed and every face was smiling, he longed for Chenna to be able to enjoy it at his side.

A strange, loud, resonant note pierced the jumble of laughing voices, then repeated itself in the silence that followed.

Looking around, Burlon saw Majaya standing at the head of the room, lowering a large seashell from her lips. "The time has come," she announced, "for the *timte* gifts to be revealed. Q'iari, if you will come here to me…?"

When she did, Burlon had to smile; the girl was aglow with happiness and excitement.

"Bring the bag," Majaya commanded.

Two of her helpers brought the green carrysack forward, while six more followed behind them.

When Burlon realized that Majaya intended for the women to unpack the quilt, and that they might then display it on the floor in the center of the hall, he quickly Cleansed the pale *bima* planks, banishing the traces of sand and dirt that the guests had brought in on their feet. Then he sat back and folded his hands, reminding himself sharply that the quilt and coat were no longer his business. He had handed them over to Majaya and Rangh, who would give them now to Q'iari, and all three of them could treat the items however they wished, without any interference from him.

Actually, the presentation of the quilt went quite well. He suspected that the women must have practiced, earlier in the day, for their movements were smooth and coordinated as they drew the quilt from its carrysack, grasped its edges at careful intervals, and then backed away from each other in smooth rhythm, allowing the quilt to unfold between them.

The people in the room made sounds of admiration, and Q'iari clasped her hands, exclaiming aloud in delight.

Then the women stepped together again and, in a complicated little twist of moves, managed to invert the quilt so that they revealed its reverse side when they backed away from each other for a second time.

The observers, clearly startled by the transformation, were even louder in their praise, and a number of them called out for the women to reverse the quilt again, which they did, to everyone's audible pleasure.

Majaya spoke up, at that point, and the quilt was folded and returned to its carrysack while the room's admiration of it was still at full flood. At no point had the quilt touched the floor, and now it was tidied away, out of sight, leaving people to compare their impressions of it without the opportunity to grow tired of the sight or attempt to find fault with it.

A canny woman, Majaya.

Now it was up to the men of the North Reaches to provide a comparable spectacle.

As soon as the women with the green carrysack left the floor, taking the quilt to safety, Jostan and his father walked to the center of the room. Rangh carried the blue carrysack. Jostan had shed his furs. Tall and strong, wearing a white shirt and white pants, he strode up the hall to where Majaya and Q'iari stood, then extended his hand in invitation to his new mate.

Never one to balk at being observed, Q'iari came to him with slow, deliberate steps.

He bent and murmured something in her ear.

She drew back, her eyes wide.

He bent and murmured again.

This time, she smiled. Slowly, with great ceremony, she removed the elaborate headdress of flowers and feathers, and handed it to Majaya. Then, one by one, she slid the bracelets from her arm and piled them at her mother's feet.

Kneeling before her, Jostan slid his palm down the pretty curve of her left leg and removed the flower circlet from her left ankle, then did the same on the right.

"Come and receive your gift," he said to her as he rose.

Hand in hand, they walked to where Rangh stood with the blue carrysack, which he had now unfastened.

"Look back at your mother," Jostan directed.

As Q'iari turned around to do so, he pulled the coat from the sack and deftly slid her left arm partway into the first sleeve, then captured her other hand in a gentle clasp and guided it into the second sleeve. In one smooth motion, he drew the coat up and settled it on her shoulders, then stepped around in front of her and began to button it.

He took his time about it, letting his hands find the shape of her through the embroidered fabric, smoothing the coat over her breasts and encircling her slender waist with his hands for a moment before kneeling again before her to fasten the lowest buttons. Finally, he draped Nunellin's scarf around her neck and twisted it into a hood with the ease of a man accustomed to bitter weather.

Q'iari tucked her chin, the better to see the intricate decorations on the front and sleeves of the coat. But Jostan rose and tilted her face up to receive a kiss from him before saying, "It is lovely on the back, as well as on the front. Turn slowly and let all admire you. Then we will remove it so that you can see all its wonders for yourself, before you grow too warm. This is a coat for your future as the Ruler of the Middle Realm, where winter pays a visit every year. It is not suited for long wear here in the Realm of the Southern Seas."

Rangh had already retreated to the edge of the crowd. Now Jostan did the same, motioning for Q'iari to display herself for everyone's pleasure. "Turn, beloved. Let those who have been your people admire your beauty before we depart tomorrow to make the Middle Realm our own."

She obliged him with a series of slow, graceful twirls, and again the people in the room made sounds of appreciation that left Burlon quite certain they were admiring both their Ruler's daughter and the exquisitely embellished coat that enveloped her.

Like Majaya, Jostan knew when to bring the display to a close. He began by joining Q'iari for three slow revolutions, as if they were dancing. Then he drew her to a halt and divested her of the coat as sensuously as he had helped her into it, before gesturing for his father to bring the blue carrysack out to them again.

After that, the evening settled down to a genial mix of food, drink, and talk. Burlon took advantage of the milling crowd to approach Majaya and say, "Our visit ends at dawn. We thank you for the extraordinary hospitality that you and your people extended to our stranded Traders. Q'iari is a vision tonight, and we wish her every happiness in her new life with Jostan."

For the first time in their acquaintance, Majaya looked old. "I have raised her, and now I have spent her like coin to purchase peace with our northern neighbors."

"That may be so, but Jostan seems to esteem her honestly, and she is a strong-minded young woman who knows her own worth. Besides, she will not be living so very far from here. You will still see her often. And your gift of the *timte* quilt will be there upon her bed to remind her of your love, every night." He smiled. "I suppose your next task is to finish training your sons, so that they may help you rule the Southern Seas when they have gained enough years."

She nodded, looking less worn. "Life is good, Traderman." She glanced around and said, softly enough that the words reached no other ears but Burlon's, "You have done us many kindnesses, and we are grateful. The geddel crystal harvest is complete. When you rise to depart in the morning, you will find everything you have asked for waiting for you at the top of the dune. Travel well and be safe. We look forward to your next return."

"It will be as it has long been," Burlon assured her.

"And you wish this new addition to the trade to carry forward?"

"Yes. Until I notify you otherwise, I would take it as a kindness, as would my people."

"Then that is how it will be. But I suggest, now, that you take your group back to the Trade House. One of them seems to have fallen asleep in his chair."

"That would be the one whose health has been poor," Burlon said. "He means no disrespect. And do not alarm yourself. It is not an illness. Once we return to our people, he will soon mend." At least, Burlon hoped that would be true. And it *would* be, unless Zanther's condition caused him to make a disastrous decision about his situation with Miri. "But you are right. I will take them all back to the Trade House now."

"Do you need assistance? His chair can be carried again."

"Thank you, but there is no need. We will assist him ourselves.

And I will look forward to the next time I see Sprygale's skies. Fair seas to you, Majaya."

"And to you, Traderman."

With a proper leave-taking accomplished, he was free to retrieve the others and call an end to this long day. He made his way back to where the three members of House Kendar sat and said, to Osla and Chappal, "Let us leave these revelers. Chappal, if you will help me support Zanther between us until we are outside and away from the lights, I will gladly Send with him back to his bed."

"No, I will Send with him," Chappal said, his tone firm. "You have a Chosen now, and your hlinga has had several days in which to ebb. Osla and I will feel more confident if you sleep, and eat again when you rise, since we must trust you to return us all to Tradepoint."

"Very well, although I am quite fine," Burlon said, chagrined to realize that old habits had entrapped him. Chappal was right. It was only sensible to be cautious. "Let's deal with getting Zanther back to the Trade House. Then we can settle into our beds, knowing that our departure is but a single sleep away."

[23]

0547 OF 2000 ORBITS REMAINING: 24GREEN

Keegan didn't want to open his eyes… which was fortunate, because his lids were far too heavy.

Suspended in comforting darkness, he floated, boneless and half-aware. The softness of the bed beneath him, combined with the warm weight of the bedclothes covering his body, tempted him to return to the deep well of sleep from which he had just emerged.

The room was so quiet that Keegan could hear nothing but his own, slow breathing – until a muffled, chinking patter caught his ear, then abruptly stopped.

Something brushed the covers near his hip. Or was it someone?

The gentle noise ceased, as did the movement, and silence returned. His thoughts began to drift…

Plink.

Plink.

Clatter.

Plink.

The metallic noise, oddly rhythmic and overly loud in the quiet room, roused him.

"Desh," someone hissed, and the air around him stirred.

'Desh' was a word he had accidentally taught Binn on a day when he couldn't seem to stop vomiting, forcing her to bring him the capture pouch again and again.

Was it Binn, now, moving about the room?

Was she about to begin another procedure with the clinic *griimoni*? One that would bite even deeper into his vessel in its cold, remorseless quest for more samples?

Afraid that Binn might even now be positioning a strange new machine over him, he forced his lids apart, readying himself to tell her to stop–

"My apologies for waking you, Keegan. The stones suddenly developed a mind of their own and flew everywhere about the room."

Not Binn. Gredin smiled down at him.

And not the clinic. He was in his own room in the enclave.

Relief swept through his body. He wet his lips, which had gone even drier at the thought of more *griimoni* being unleashed upon his body.

"Are you thirsty?" Gredin asked. "I have chilled *tharaman* tea here. As I recall, you found it quite delicious."

Keegan nodded and tried to raise himself on the bedmat.

"Don't exhaust yourself," Gredin ordered, looming over him, her slender height accentuated by the disparity in their positions. "I will help you sit."

After levering him up against a mound of pillows, Gredin offered him the tea, then folded herself down to sit on a rug that was unfamiliar to him, next to his bedmat. Keegan eyed her for a moment, then drank deeply, slaking his thirst on the cool, sweet tea. He felt as if he could drink cup after cup of it, relishing the taste and the feel of the liquid on his parched tongue.

He swallowed in great gulps, ignoring Gredin's admonishment to proceed more slowly. Finally, he handed the drained cup back to her. "My thanks," he said, panting. "My thirst got the better of me."

Gredin gave him a considering look and set the cup aside. "You look more alert, this awakening. Would you like more to drink? Or something to eat? Some solid food, perhaps, instead of broth?"

Keegan felt too tired to lift a spoon but his stomach growled eagerly at the suggestion of food. "I will try. My insides favor the idea, but my vessel is unsure it wants to make the effort."

"I will gladly feed you if you cannot manage on your own. Cayman says it is important that you eat and drink as much as you can, each time you are awake."

"I will try," Keegan said again. "But don't bring much, Gredin, please. Miri's porridge is filling but bland. I wouldn't want to waste any, if my appetite is satisfied before the bowl is finished." He made a face. "Porridge doesn't sound at all appetizing, and yet I am far too empty. Your pardon. I do not mean to be so disagreeable."

Gredin smiled. "You are fortunate, then, for I have something which I think may please you, as well as a full pitcher of *tharaman* tea. Miri prepared both herself, just for you."

Keegan watched Gredin as she Fetched first the tray, then the pitcher, placing both objects on the colorful rug. The pitcher was a deep, rich rose, smoothly polished, and it gleamed in the light of the luminth placed here and there about his room.

Gredin picked up the pitcher and refilled his cup, the stream of tea making a musical sound as it flowed. "Miri likes using this pitcher for the *tharaman* tea because it and the undiluted *tharaman* liquid are nearly identical in color."

"That sounds very much like Miri. Such touches bring her pleasure."

"I'll set the cup aside until you want it. For now, I suspect you'll find the food as much as you can deal with," Gredin said, Fetching the tray into place on his quilt-covered lap. And then she smiled as he gaped at what it bore.

He had been braced for porridge and perhaps a slice of bread with a thin smear of jam, given what he knew of the state of their food stores. Instead, there were pravelin, dotted with glistening drops of infused oil; a small slice of grilled ruparo on a bed of sautéed greens; a plate of pastries, including several tiny rostti and a jam tart; and, finally, a golden-brown braided yeast roll.

Keegan looked at Gredin, bewildered. "Where did all this come from?"

"The cold units. I ordered some of the remaining reception food to be taken from storage for both you and Salderon. After an Intercession, the appetites of both petitioner and Healer are apt to be finicky, according to Cayman. Miri and I hoped these offerings might tempt you both."

"I hardly know where to begin," Keegan said, and felt tears of emotion well up. "It is too generous an offering for one such as me."

"Don't say such a thing," Gredin admonished indignantly. "You are far more important to this community than you seem to realize. And you are a good friend to many, including myself. Indeed, I had to insist on having this turn to sit with you. A number of different folks have been at your bedside, keeping watch to bring you comfort when you awoke. You may be the last of your House, but there are many who care deeply about your welfare. Ingarra and Beda, Hayla, Khest, Ellis, Chenna, Nunellin, Sill, and Miri have all sat with you for a time while you slept. Between us, we made certain that you were never alone."

His throat tightened. "I don't remember them being here."

"Cayman warned us that you would likely have little memory of your first few awakenings. But we each managed to get at least a few sips of liquid into you before you slept again." Gredin grinned. "Cayman said it should be nearly time for your first true awakening, so I claimed the honor of being here. And my stones kept me company while I waited."

"Is that the noise I heard?"

"Yes. It brings me comfort to hold them and feel their shapes in my hand before I cast them. Usually, they are content to make pretty patterns on whatever surface I use. But sometimes, when I cast them from my hand, I find my thoughts straying to some unexpected topic, as if the stones are telling *me* what they represent while they are still in motion."

Keegan could no longer resist the aroma rising from the food tray. He picked up the roll and took a bite of the warm, yeasty bread. It had been flavored with ranomen, a mild spice redolent of the world they had lost.

Chewing slowly, he savored the blissful mouthful. Finally, swallowing, he asked, "And what was it, this time?"

"This time?"

The taste of the bread had roused his appetite, and he picked up a pravelin next. Before placing it in his mouth, however, he clarified his question. "Did the stones tell you something, or were they just making a 'pretty pattern' this time?"

Gredin laughed. "Well, it was definitely not a pretty pattern. I didn't cast them any differently than I usually do, but instead of landing on your bedmat, they flew all over the room. Not one of them stayed on the quilt. Instead, they went in every direction! It took me a while to gather them up. One had even landed behind your storage chest."

Keegan ate a second pravelin, then luxuriated in a bite of the ruparo, reveling in the delicate yet rich taste of the ocean fish. "It sounds a bit like that time at our group meeting when one of the stones developed a mind of its own. I had to go all the way to the door to find it and bring it back to you, remember?"

Gredin nodded, looking thoughtful.

"That was when you told Sill and Miri and me that Burlon had gone to Sprygale. You said the stone had told you."

"And today I was thinking about when to begin the search for New Venna," Gredin said slowly. "With Burlon overdue, I was wondering whether to delay the quest for our new home yet again."

"It sounds as if you received your answer," Keegan said. He took another bite of the ruparo, this time with a forkful of greens. Then he looked at her in consternation, as her words belatedly penetrated. "Burlon is overdue? How seriously? How long have I slept?"

"You have been asleep or drifting for the past four days."

He almost laughed aloud at her jest, then realized that she was serious.

"We expected Burlon's return two days ago." Gredin sighed heavily. "We are increasingly worried, particularly Chenna. Hayla is nearly as bad – although, to her credit, she wears a calm face when she and Chenna are together. Even Khest te Bentain, who remains his good friend despite Burlon's change of House, is troubled. Khest is normally the steadiest of individuals, but now he is so worried that he finds it hard to Focus when he exercises his gyfte. He has been attending you regularly, since the rest of us sitting vigil here have no gyfte of Touch, while several of Salderon's protectorate do."

Keegan found that he had lost his appetite. "What do you think has happened, Gredin? Burlon knows the River's path to Sprygale well and has Traveled it for long and long."

"As Cirin had, to Venna and Palomar."

The comparison was appalling. "But the situations aren't the same. Sprygale is not a hostile world, like Zrach."

"True… if it still exists. I have talked with the Travelers, and they assure me there are other worlds on the River's path past Sprygale where he could shelter, but…"

"But…?"

"Burlon is not Cirin, for all his self-confidence."

"Burlon is not a foolish man," Keegan protested. "And he is First Traveler."

"He is First Traveler of those few we have left to us," Gredin said grimly, and threw up her hands. "If we have lost Burlon and First Traveler's hlette, it will be my fault, not his."

Keegan let his heavy head drop back against the pillows. "That makes no sense. Burlon left without your permission."

She looked at him soberly. "I have done much thinking while sitting here, casting my stones. I have been guilty of judging everyone else's Balance by how disrupted my own has been. The majority of the community is farther along the road of recovery than the Bereft. I am improving steadily now, but only because I have found a persistent alliance partner who has my well-being uppermost in his mind. With my hlinga nearly restored, I can see that my insistence that no Traveler leave Tradepoint was mostly a panicked desire to keep everyone safe and to do absolutely nothing that might further upset our precarious existence here."

"You were being cautious."

"I was denying the Travelers the use of their gyfte, and that realization shocks me." Gredin offered him a thin, humorless smile. "I do not enjoy remembering the Gredin who existed prior to having my Balance restored. It is past time for me to reconsider the issue, even given Burlon's continued absence."

Exhaustion and sleep pulled at him but Keegan fought them off. "If I hadn't foolishly allowed Binn to take her samples, I would have been available to offer you support and encouragement. Your pardon, Gredin, for making the past few days even more difficult."

"*Chee*, *chee*, *chee*," Gredin soothed. "Truthfully, much that is positive has happened while you slept."

Hope fluttered. "Tetralanna and her group have changed their minds?"

Gredin's shoulders slumped. "No. They continue to refuse to take alliance partners, despite the improvements of the Bereft in their own Houses who have done so. I know they fear change and feel honor-bound to preserve our traditional customs, but they are harming themselves, and the damage may soon be irrevocable. I need to find a solution to their stubbornness."

"I will think on it, as well," Keegan murmured, allowing his lids to close.

"You need to sleep," Gredin said firmly. "My news will wait for another time."

Keegan forced his eyes open. "No, please, I want to hear. What good things have occurred while I was senseless?"

"I went aboard the Hesch ship with Nitikikani."

"What?!"

"I went onto his ship, and I met his mate and their child. I explained that Venna's destruction was why our community is still on Tradepoint. And I gave him my flamestone pendent as a sign of my – our – good intentions for the future."

Shock and curiosity now had him wide awake. "But your flamestone necklace was given to you by your Chosen. You treasure it!"

"Yes… but Nitikikani told me that it was his *ta'ak*, a thing of spiritual significance. He has seen the flamestone in his night-thoughts since he was a young boy. Oh, Keegan, I wish you could have been there with me! Nitikikani had a box that contained drawing after drawing that he had made of it, over the years. He even gave one to me before I left his ship, as a kind of… comfort for my loss. It is the first drawing he ever made of it, done when he was very young. I will Fetch it for you to see!"

A delicately framed, rectangular object appeared in Gredin's hands. The frame itself was made of glinn wood, and was carved with a motif that echoed Gredin's First Speaker's hlette.

"Isn't it beautiful?" she asked, turning the frame so that he could more easily view the picture itself.

Beautiful, indeed. And strange. And oddly compelling.

The young Nitikikani – now *there* was a strange thought, as Keegan tried to envision the menacing bird man as a youngling – had accurately drawn the shape of the flamestone, although he had depicted it several times larger than it actually was, and a bit bolder in hue than Keegan remembered. Bright, saturated colors mingled, causing the glowing portrait to look newly painted, as if the pigment were still wet.

And then he realized something that his tired mind had failed, at first, to notice: the rendering was done on *paper.*

"It is wonderful. Mesmerizing," Keegan praised absently.

Gredin beamed. "I keep it on the shelf with the Polpethtiran baskets and the *amarantha* wine. When I look at it, Dreff's gift doesn't seem as… gone."

But Keegan's gaze remained riveted on the pale grey paper stretched tautly within the frame. His thoughts churned. Nitikikani of the Hesch had used paper… which meant that the Hesch had both the concept of paper as a medium and a source for it.

"Gredin," Keegan asked hoarsely, "do you think it possible that the Hesch could supply us with paper? That sheet handled the paint well, without any running or blurring. Perhaps it could do the same for my inks! And if, even as a child, Nitikikani was permitted to use paper, maybe it is not a rare thing for the Hesch, and would not be overly costly!"

Gredin looked chagrined. "I was so intent on the portrayal of the flamestone, I failed to see the background for what it was. Your pardon, Keegan. When I next see Nitikikani, I will make inquires on your behalf. Or, if you prefer, I can wait until you are fully recovered and can accompany me to the Hesch *maartza*."

Keegan was rescued from attempting a coherent reply by the sudden arrival of Ingarra te Balamont. Gredin's former Guide had her sewing bag in one hand, but now, instead of her usual smile, she wore an excited look, and her eyes were bright.

"Gredin, hurry to the reception hall! Burlon has returned!"

Keegan watched Gredin scramble to her feet, a huge smile of relief and joy lighting her face. Indeed, she nearly knocked over the cup in her excitement. "Burlon? You're certain? Oh, praise the Power! Can you stay with Keegan? He has eaten a little, but he'll likely need another drink before he sleeps again."

"Go, go," Ingarra said, shooing Gredin toward the door. "We can manage here just fine without you."

Gredin appeared quite used to the loving grumble. She gave Ingarra a swift hug and hurried out of the room, still beaming.

"Now," Ingarra said, surveying the tray, "why not eat one of those rostti before you fall asleep again? I don't want Cayman chewing my bones about how poorly we've tended you. Yes," she nodded firmly, her eyes kind, "a rostti and a drink of *tharaman* tea should do you quite nicely. Then a good nap. Unless you want to relieve yourself first?"

Ingarra must have been a wonderful Guide, Keegan reflected, amused. "No need," he said, selecting a rostti as she had bidden. "Perhaps later, when I wake again." He dutifully popped the pastry into his mouth and chewed, savoring the rich, sweet taste.

Another reminder of things that will never be again...

The thought brought tears perilously close.

Perhaps sensing his sadness, Ingarra opened her sewing bag and withdrew an impossibly small teslan made of white linen. "I am making this for Chenna's baby." She leaned forward, holding it up for his perusal. "What do you think? Will she like it?"

Keegan swallowed the last of the rostti, tasting the salt of his unshed tears along with the food's sweetness. He peered at the tiny figures Ingarra had embroidered around the neckline and sleeves. The same figures partially adorned the hem, as well. He took a closer look. "I'm not sure I recognize…"

But then he did. *Bees. Tiny golden bees with widespread wings.*

"Little bees," he said hoarsely. "To honor Chenna's gyfte."

"Just so," Ingarra said, looking well-pleased. "A sweet symbol for a sweet young woman." She carefully placed the garment on her lap. "Now, let's have you take a small sip or two and get settled. Then I will tell you about something else I plan to make for Chenna and Burlon's coming child."

In what seemed like moments, Keegan found himself flat again on the soft bedmat, a single pillow beneath his head. He felt replete, comfortable, and impossibly drowsy. His eyes kept closing, despite his best attempts to keep them open. "Tell me about the other gift," he entreated.

"Well, it really started with Nunellin te Vell. Beda and I helped her move her loom when Vell's new enclave was finished. You should see how much rista wool she had brought along to Tradepoint for the demonstrations! Who would have thought that someone besides me felt compelled to bring half the contents of their chambers along on the journey?" Ingarra asked, and chuckled.

Eyes now closed, Keegan felt his own lips twitch in amusement.

"I felt safe in teasing Nunellin a bit about it, since we'd gotten to know each other quite well while we worked on the Sprygalian *timte* gifts. At any rate, the sight of all that rista wool made me wonder…"

They were the last words Keegan heard before sleep reclaimed him.

[24]

0546 OF 2000 ORBITS REMAINING: 25ORANGE

There was little sense of the passage of time on the River. No sense of heat or cold. With First Traveler's hlette encircling his arm, Burlon didn't even feel strained as he Traveled along the golden ribbon that was the very essence of the Power. He was a bird in air. A fish in water. Safe. Secure. Content.

More than just content. Happy. Fulfilled.

Ahead, a familiar looping coil of the path alerted him that he was nearly at his destination. Instinctively, he firmed his hold on his cargo, people and goods alike. At the proper moment, he exited smoothly from the River, experiencing a faint sense of regret as he did so. And then, abruptly, there was something solid beneath the soles of his feet, and time began again. He drew a breath, and his nose filled with bio-mist.

Tradepoint.

It was as if recent memory lagged behind, racing to catch up with him. He knew that he was Burlon. He knew that bio-mist meant Tradepoint. Both of those facts had long been true. But he was startled when he opened his eyes and saw, through the mist, through the curve of the dome, a sea of people seated at long tables, staring at him. No sound reached him, but he could see lips moving, fingers pointing, folk starting to surge to their feet…

=Burlon!= Crisp and unmistakable, Gredin's mind touch reached him. =Are you well? Who is with you?=

Who is…? Ah. Memory flooded back. =I am unharmed,= he assured her. =I bring three Kendar Traders who were stranded on Sprygale – Osla, Chappal, and Miri's Chosen, Zanther.=

=Zanther?= He felt the thrill of her joy at the news, and sensed it in her reply. =I will tell the community. I will tell Miri!=

The heads of the people in the room suddenly swung to look back and to their left in a single united movement. Peering in that direction, Burlon spotted Gredin's curls, just visible at the back of the room, where the little corridor connected her suite with the reception hall. And then her voice rang out, reaching him even through the dome.

"Hear me! Rejoice! Burlon te Laith is safely returned, and he has recovered three more of us who were believed to have returned to the Source! He found them stranded on Sprygale, and they are all from House Kendar. Traders. Their names are Osla, Chappal, and Zanther."

The mist was thinning. Straining his eyes, he looked toward the kitchens, and was rewarded by the sight of Miri appearing in the doorway, her face transfigured by the news. Then a group of people surged to their feet, and he lost sight of her.

But he was relieved to see that it was only a group, not a mob of frenzied people such as those who had alarmed him on the morning he first emerged from his dydanin. The community, silenced by the dome, gave off an impression of excitement and high spirits. He saw smiles as well as tears. No one jostled or pushed to approach the arrival dais, although he was sure that House Kendar's survivors, who were numerous, must be anxious to reach the Traders he had rescued.

He offered Osla, Chappal, and Zanther a smile. "Prepare yourselves. You are about to be welcomed not only by your House but by the entire community," he informed them.

As soon as the dome began to ascend, waves of sound reached him, voices raised in wonder and thanksgiving. And one voice stood out from all the others.

“Zanther! Zanther te Kendar!”

Looking toward the voice, Burlon was gratified to see that even Tetralanna te Balamont had been caught up in the happiness of the occasion. She was holding Miri by the wrist, forging a path for her through the crowd, brooking no delay.

For himself, Burlon lacked even that much patience. Stepping clear of the dome, he closed his eyes and reached out. =Chenna?=

=Burlon!=

At the first touch of her mind against his, he Focused and Fetched her to his side. He supposed it was a reckless thing to do, having just completed a journey on the River, but he could endure their separation no longer. He clasped her to him, then stood back long enough to look at her beloved face. “Eleven glim,” he announced with delight, and bent to kiss her.

When he emerged from that kiss, he saw that Osla and Chappal were supporting Zanther as he made his way gingerly down the steps of the dais. Just as they managed to ease him onto a bench, Tetralanna and Miri reached the front of the crowd. Miri had gone pale, and Tetralanna’s cheeks were flushed a deep red.

With a glare and a toss of her head, Tetralanna met Burlon’s gaze, and he realized how drastically he had misread her intent. She was not hurrying to enable a reunion. She was intent on a moment of reckoning.

“This woman!” Tetralanna declaimed, her voice issuing forth with shocking force and clarity. “This woman, Miri, has betrayed the trust of her Chosen, Zanther to Kendar. He returns to us today, spared by the Power itself. And what does he find? That his Chosen has taken another man into her bed while he was away. I counseled against it. I did all that I could to make people understand that we are meant to share our bodies with our Chosen, and with no one else. The Power gave us a clear sign when it restored the Avilar Tradeteam to our delegation. But Miri, like so many others, could not be bothered to trust or wait. And now her day of account is upon her, for here is her Chosen, a good and faithful man. And what does he find? A tainted and unworthy woman, unfit to–”

"Stop!" Gredin burst through the front ranks of the people who stood transfixed by Tetralanna's words. Snatching up the older woman's hands, she thundered, "Hear me, Tetralanna te Balamont, and attend. You will not pervert what is left of your gyfte by using it to berate a member of this community who has done no wrong. You are Silenced – not just for this day, but until such time as I have seen enough improvement in your Balance to believe you can make responsible choices about how you wield gyfte of Speech, which should be precious to us both."

Tetralanna's mouth worked angrily, trying to shape sounds, but no words came out.

"I would speak."

The words were faint, and at first Burlon was uncertain who had spoken them. Then he realized that it was Zanther, who reached out an unsteady hand to touch Gredin's arm in a bid for attention.

"I am listening," she assured him.

"No, please, I would like to speak to everyone. Can you… Can you make that possible?"

Burlon felt a wave of dread, unsure what Zanther would say.

But Gredin, although she looked puzzled by the request, said, "Of course." Releasing Tetralanna, she grasped Zanther's hands.

"Miri is my Chosen."

The words penetrated the room, prompting everyone to fall silent again.

"We are of House Kendar," Zanther continued. "Ulm was our kinswoman, and so Miri and I both grew up knowing what happens to one who is separated from their Chosen for too long, or who loses them altogether. It terrified us then, as it does now. I am grateful to the Prett for finding a way for us to escape that fate. And I am proud of my Miri for being strong enough and brave enough to claim life over decline. Because of her courage, she is now in Balance and can help me to recover. I have loved her since the first day our paths crossed, but I have never adored her more than I do today."

Gredin released his hands.

As if freed from invisible bindings, Miri took the final steps and was enveloped in Zanther's arms. As she wept into his shoulder, Zanther kissed her hair, then looked up to Gredin. "My thanks to you," he said, his voice reduced again to a hoarse whisper.

Hayla approached. "Gredin? Does it not seem to you that these two deserve a sort of dydanin of their own, the better to return Zanther speedily to Balance? We could give them the chamber that Burlon and Chenna used, if you approve. It is nearby, and I can have it Freshened and ready very shortly."

"An excellent idea," Gredin said.

"And *you*!"

Burlon backed up a step as Hayla rounded on him.

"Shame on you for frightening poor Chenna like that. When you say you will return in two days, you should return in two days! How can she learn to trust you if your promises mean nothing?"

Explanations would have to wait. "I will work hard to make it up to her," Burlon said instead. "And to you."

"Me? This has nothing to do with me," Hayla said indignantly.

But it did, and he knew it. Cirin had been late in returning… and Cirin had died. That knowledge must have haunted Hayla for the past two days, whether she would admit it or not. He wondered how she and Chenna would manage to cope, once he began the search for New Venna.

Miri stirred from her haven at Zanther's side. "I will only agree to a dydanin of the sort that Burlon and Chenna had," she insisted. "I'm still needed in the kitchens, and at the food stall, and at our morning meetings. Those duties will leave ample time for us to be together."

Glancing around the room, Burlon realized how quickly his eyes had come to expect to see living things. Plants. Trees. The ocean. The sky. He hungered for the soothing sight of green, and wondered how much sharper the pangs of that hunger must be for a Grower like Beda, or for his own dear Chenna, who had tended the beehives at the Laith Holdings...

"It isn't fair!" a woman's voice complained.

He turned to find Gredin confronted by a dozen or more angry people who had gathered protectively around Tetralanna.

"To take her voice away–"

"To Silence her–"

"Not to let her Speak her mind, just because you don't like her!"

"Just because you disagree!"

"Thank you," Gredin said to them in all apparent sincerity. "In the joy of this reunion, I had almost forgotten that there is more I need to say."

"No! Not until you lift the Silencing from Tetralanna."

But Gredin shook her head. "That isn't going to happen. Not today. Not tomorrow. Not until we have resolved her problem."

"*You* are her problem!"

"No. I am not. But I know what is." With that, Gredin turned her back on them and mounted the dais steps. "Listen to me, everyone," she said – not loudly, but with the inescapable clarity that her gyfte bestowed. "There are several important matters I must share with you."

It was the Voice. No one, not even Tetralanna's friends, could ignore it.

A silence fell over the community.

"Gyftes are meant to be used constructively, to strengthen the community. Because Tetralanna te Balamont used her gyfte of Speech to interfere between two Chosens, I have temporarily Silenced her. But I know that she would never have spoken such hurtful words if she had been in Balance. Most especially, she would never have sharpened the impact of those words with her gyfte. But this is the sort of harm that can occur when someone's hlinga has faded, robbing them of Balance, and such behavior cannot be allowed to continue."

Burlon tried to anticipate where Gredin's words were headed, but found that he could not predict her turn of mind. He could only wait, and trust, and listen.

"Now that my own Balance has been restored," Gredin continued, "I see how unwise I was to stay silent while improper behavior occurred in the community – not just from Tetralanna but from the many individuals who accepted what should have been a selfless role to aid their House and instead turned it into a platform to increase their own authority and influence. As a result, I release the current House volunteers – who were unwise enough to call themselves Heads of House – from their duties. I thank them for their willingness to serve, and I apologize to those who carried out their duties conscientiously, but we will handle matters differently now."

"I suppose you're going to decide everything yourself," Palla te Laith called out.

Burlon expected to see a flash of anger from Gredin at the interruption. Instead, she smiled. "No. We will find the individual in each House with the greatest gyfte of Service, and ask them to represent their House and inform us of its needs."

Burlon almost chuckled aloud. It was an inspired solution. Gyfte of Service was a universal gyfte possessed by every Vennan, to one degree or another. Those whose gyfte of Service was large were, by the gyfte's very nature, kind and thoughtful people, the sort who instinctively nurtured others. They tended to be liked and respected by all who knew them. In troubled times like these, they would be patient, lending a sympathetic ear to all within their House.

"And how are we to identify these folks?" Palla demanded, but even he sounded less belligerent than before.

Gredin hesitated, and Burlon's spirits plummeted. Even the best plan would founder if there was no way to implement it. Hadn't Gredin learned that by now?

But Yohn te Avilar stepped out of the crowd and said, "House Avilar has a kinsman here whose gyfte it is to Sort. We have long called upon him to identify the gyftes of our newborns, and to sort ranked gyftes from minor ones. If asked, he can perform that same service upon our community members."

"You expect him to sort nearly a thousand people?" Palla scoffed.

"No," Yohn said calmly. "Each House is likely aware of those individuals within it who have been notably patient and kind and helpful, these past difficult days. Some folk may even have been told by their Guides, as children, that they possessed a fine gyfte of Service. Let those people's names be put forward – perhaps ten from each House – and we can ask my kinsman, Dard te Avilar, to sort and rank them. Indeed, it might be wise for the top three or four to be identified, since those with a generous gyfte of Service are apt to work more tirelessly than they should. At need, we can rotate the task among them at intervals, to spare them from neglecting their other gyftes."

"Excellent," Gredin said. "Dard te Avilar, if you would step forward…?"

A tall man with a shy manner separated himself from the crowd and came toward Gredin.

"Do you agree with your kinsman Yohn that this sorting and ranking of gyfte of Service would be within your ability?" she asked him.

"Yes. I believe it to be possible. I am certainly willing to try. I have little of consequence to occupy my days, at present." He smiled. "I was heartened to hear that a child will be born to Chenna and Burlon te Laith. It will be exciting to see what gyftes their child bears. In the meantime, however, I will most happily sort these other folk."

"Our thanks to you, Dard te Avilar. I will contact you tomorrow." She looked out over the room. "Houses, please, converse amongst yourselves tonight and see which individuals seem likeliest. If you have more than ten to recommend, feel free to do so. We will take our time and have Dard continue his sorting until we are confident that the right individuals are found."

People stirred, as if already eager to discuss candidates amongst themselves.

But Gredin said, "However, that is not the only difficulty that demands a change."

The crowd subsided.

"Nine days ago, I stood before you all and spoke of the threat faced by those of us who have lost our Chosens. I called us the Bereft, and I described for you the depths to which we would gradually sink if we didn't join with an alliance partner to prevent our hlinga from draining away, taking with it our Balance, and thus our ability to deal rationally with our difficulties. Since that time, nearly all of the Bereft have taken steps to save themselves, as I have, and our community is much the better for it. But some Bereft still refuse to take advantage of the opportunity provided for them, or have been intimidated out of it by a few out-of-Balance individuals. Because of that, we are suffering incidents like the one you saw here today, where Tetralanna unfairly used her gyfte to publicly attack a member of this community. I can only be grateful that Zanther and Miri te Kendar come from a House that understands the cost of being Bereft all too well."

Burlon hugged Chenna closer, unsure what more Gredin thought she could do about the problem. Already, the Bereft who clustered around Tetralanna were whispering to one another, while Tetralanna, unable to Speak, appeared close to attacking Gredin bodily.

"Our community cannot mend and move forward, so long as we harbor Bereft whose hlinga is so depleted and who refuse to take the necessary steps to improve their own condition. And, as each new day passes, they will grow more erratic and less capable, becoming an increasing danger to themselves and others. Therefore, before the opportunity to save them fades away completely, I will do for them what they will not or cannot do for themselves."

She shifted, and her voice took on a new resonance as she tapped more deeply into her gyfte. "Hear me, all Bereft who have not yet taken an alliance partner. You are hereby Compelled to present yourself at the Bereft enclave, where you will mate with a fellow Bereft before the end of the day, tomorrow. And you are hereby Compelled to do so at least once each day thereafter, until such time as you are Assessed and proclaimed to be back in Balance, with your hlinga restored. At that time, when your mind is clear, you may each come to me and we will have a calm, rational discussion about your situation, and whether the Compulsion should be lifted from you."

A wordless moan of protest sliced the air: Tetralanna.

Gredin gave no sign that she had heard. "When we are injured, we must seek a Healer. When we are *Bereft*, we must seek an alliance partner. Both are essential to our health. You are thus Compelled."

It seemed to Burlon that the air in the room suddenly rippled, or perhaps it was a collective shiver running through those who stood listening.

"You can't do this to us!" a man shouted, and Burlon recognized Doboro te K'lar, the man from whom he had removed First Traveler's hlette on the day it became his own. It saddened Burlon to learn that Doboro was one of the Bereft. Like Tetralanna, he had lost much in Venna's destruction: his Chosen, the hlette, and soon his gyfte, if Gredin's gyfte failed to Compel him.

"The choice should be ours!" a woman wailed. "Can't you see how wrong it is of you to force someone to go and… and…"

"And mate with a fellow Bereft," Gredin said, "in order to restore your Balance and save your gyftes. It is my responsibility to see to your recovery until you can see to it yourself, for your sake and the sake of the community. That is why I Compel you to do this, and to continue doing it until your hlinga is restored."

"And then you will let us stop?"

"It is my belief that, once you are returned to Balance and thinking clearly, you will not wish to stop, since stopping means parting yourself forever from the Power and your gyftes."

"But–"

"Protests will gain you nothing. You will do this. And I suggest that those of you who are unhappy about this Compulsion converse with members of House Kendar who knew Ulm and who helped to care for her in her infirmity, so that you fully realize what a burden and a misery her life became to her." She looked away from the woman. "In the meantime, the rest of the community has largely regained its Balance, and it is therefore time for us to take steps to fulfill the Power's final direction to us – to begin our search for New Venna."

New Venna.

The words crackled in the air. Burlon felt excitement pulse through his body, staving off the exhaustion that had stalked him since the moment of their arrival from Sprygale. Gredin was finally going to relent and release the Travelers!

"Over the past two days, I have met with many of our most experienced Travelers. I have discussed the search for our new home with them, and we have debated how that search might best and most safely be undertaken."

Burlon stared at her. She had met with the Travelers? In his absence?

"Until recently, we have had just two classes of Travelers – those with a Chosen and those who were Unchosen. Now, of the fifty-one Travelers among our survivors, we have three classes – twelve who still have their Chosen with them, thirty-five who are Unchosen, and four who are among the Bereft."

The smallness of the numbers made Burlon wince. So many men and women returned to the Source, so many Travelers no longer available for the search…

"Our four Travelers who are Bereft cannot, of course, attempt to Travel the River in their current state. They are far from Balance, their hlinga depleted. But if they avail themselves of alliance partners, their Balance will quickly improve. Once their hlinga is restored, they can join the ranks of our active Travelers conducting two-person trade missions to known worlds. There are twelve of them, which would give us sixteen in all – eight pairs who could make journeys to and from such known trading worlds as Sprygale and Odoro."

Why, Burlon wondered, was she discussing trips to Odoro and Sprygale? New Venna was the goal. Finding it was the most important task for all of the Travelers to undertake. That much was obvious. Yes, they'd still have to see to the geddel crystal deliveries, but…

"In the meantime, we have thirty-five Unchosen Travelers – seventeen pairs of Travelers, with one left over – who can conduct the search for New Venna. As Unchosens, they are still able to maintain their own Balance, and so it is safe for them to undertake the uncertainties involved in these explorations into areas unknown to us…"

Her voice went on, patiently explaining, but it was only noise to Burlon, unable to compete with the refrain echoing so loudly in his head: *I have a Chosen. Only Unchosens will search for New Venna. I have a Chosen. Only Unchosens will search for New Venna. I have a Chosen…*

Chenna's arm slipped around his waist. "Are you unwell?" she whispered. "Should you sit down?"

"I am First Traveler," he said, without meaning to say it aloud.

What was wrong with him? He never felt this drained after Traveling the River. To do so was his gyfte. His delight. He had made the trip to and from Sprygale countless times. But now, instead of simply feeling ravenous, his insides were uneasy, and the reception hall seemed suddenly far too warm.

But he stiffened his knees and made some sort of reassuring noise when Chenna asked again if he was unwell. Gredin would finish Speaking soon, wouldn't she? He needed to tell her about the unexpected goods he had brought from Sprygale. He needed to store the geddel crystals safely in the Vennan warehouse, so that he could divide them before making his delivery to Wyve. He needed to…

He needed, urgently, to sit down.

He did so on the dais steps, drawing Chenna down with him. The Tradegoods needed to be dealt with before he went anywhere. He would discuss them with Miri…

No. Miri would be with Zanther.

Burlon's mouth was dry.

The community, who had been listening attentively to Gredin's words, began to stir and talk, then to disperse. Had she finished her address, or had her gyfte faltered, causing her to lose her hold on them?

With an effort, he blinked his vision clear, and saw that Tetralanna's friends were escorting her from the room, casting dark looks over their shoulders in Gredin's general direction. A crowd of people, most likely from House Kendar, had gathered around Osla and Chappal. Other individuals were leaving the reception hall, but several large groups remained. And Gredin…

Gredin was hurrying toward him, her expression one of exasperated concern.

He recalled, belatedly, that he had journeyed to Sprygale without her knowledge or permission. He recalled, as well, that he was two days late in his return. And he recalled how very much he did not enjoy it when Gredin felt called upon to chastise him, especially in public.

"Take me to our bed, my love," he murmured to Chenna.

But he was too late. Gredin was already upon them, kneeling on the step below so that she could peer up into his face as she said, "Burlon te Laith, you have been a fool."

Burlon sighed. "And a good day to you, First Speaker."

"Were you *trying* to return to the Source?" she demanded, then reached out a hand to Chenna in apology. "I am sorry, Chenna. I know that he would never willingly risk the life he has with you. But what he did was very, very foolish."

"I am not a fool," Burlon protested.

"That isn't what your fellow Travelers tell me. Did you stop to consider the change in your condition before you left? You had only ever Traveled to Sprygale as an Unchosen, quite capable of restoring your own Balance before your return. This time, your state of Balance when you left Tradepoint had to sustain you through the journey there *and* the journey back, not to mention the added burden of tradegoods and three unexpected Traders. What if you had lacked the strength? You would all have lost your lives upon the River, and what would Chenna have done then?"

Gredin was the second woman to scold him today on the pretext of Chenna's peace of mind, when it was also their own that had been troubled by his absence. But there was little point in saying so. He was touched, as well as annoyed, to think that Gredin had been worried about him. There might even be a bit of truth in what she was saying. Perhaps he hadn't paid sufficient attention to the changes his Choosing had wrought within him. He *felt* the same. But, in truth, he wasn't the same…

For now, though, he needed to share the good news of his cargo, before he fell asleep where he sat.

"Chastise me all you like," he said, "but could you do it tomorrow, when I am properly alert? Right now, you need to inform the kitchen Tenders that the large wooden crates at the bottom of the stack contain a fresh catch of *ginglin*. The kitchen Tenders from House Kendar have dealt with *ginglin* before and will know the best ways to prepare them. The crates on top are filled with fruits and vegetables, whatever was ripe on Sprygale. The plain baskets contain fresh-baked *sama* bread. The fancy baskets are left-over treats from Q'iari's Choosing ceremony. The red baskets contain flowers and ferns that can be used to decorate the tables – except for the red basket with the white handle. That one is mine." He Fetched it to himself, then went on. "The wooden trunks are filled with geddel crystals, and should be transferred to the warehouse immediately. Ellis can do that, if you track her down. Oh, and here…" His fingers were unusually clumsy, but he managed to extract the pouches given to him by Rangh and Jostan from his pockets, where they had been weighing down his pants to a dangerous degree. "Coins from the North Reaches. Have Ellis put them in the warehouse, as well. I'll deal with them tomorrow. I'll deal with everything… tomorrow. Except the fish. And the flowers. Those shouldn't wait, although I've done my best to keep them both cool."

Gredin reached down and startled him by touching her fingertips to his cheek for a moment. "You seem to have proven yourself quite a master Trader on this trip. I am grateful. But try not to frighten everyone again, please?"

He nodded, and she withdrew her hand.

On a more casual note, she said, "I gather that the *timte* gifts were well received."

"The quilt and coat were both perfection. Ingarra deserves much of the credit for the bounty you see stacked here."

"Burlon!" Ellis te Vell joined them. "I am so glad to see you back, and more pleased than I can tell you to see the Kendar Traders safely returned to us. I had not thought it possible!"

"There is a bittersweet tale to tell about that, but I will save it for tomorrow."

Ellis looked to Gredin. "What do you require, First Speaker?"

Confused, Burlon looked to Gredin. "Did you summon Ellis?"

"Of course. You said I should."

"Well, yes, but I didn't see you… I mean to say, you and I were still talking, and…"

There was a touch of mischief in Gredin's smile. "Not everyone needs to stop everything that they are doing and close their eyes in order to reach another's private mind."

"I do," he admitted bluntly. Although he was finding it much easier, now that he had acquired First Traveler's hlette.

"I know you do. And it is no shame. Your gyftes are many and fine. No one possesses them all. But I am a Speaker, and such contacts come easily to me. As soon as you said that Ellis's presence would be helpful, I reached out to her. Tell her what it is that you require."

And so he repeated his instructions about the items on the arrival dais, confident that Ellis would manage it all. She was a skilled Trader, and long used to dealing with the warehouse.

"Goods to the warehouse, after I take the food to the kitchens and explain to the Tenders what we're providing," Ellis summarized with a smile when he was done. "It sounds as though tonight's evening meal will be the best we've had in quite some time!" She mounted to the top step, surveyed the stacked goods, then came down and walked off toward the kitchens, whistling.

"Is there more business that you must attend to?" Chenna asked him on an anxious note, then looked to Gredin. "He needs to rest, First Speaker."

"I agree. And there is no need to call me 'First Speaker.' You and I share the burden of dealing with this stubborn man, and so, to you, I am simply Gredin." She extended her foot and nudged the red basket with the white handle which sat next to Burlon. "I agree that you should take him to your nest, Chenna. Before you depart, though, my curiosity would like to know what this basket holds. Burlon?"

A chuckle rose from his weary depths. "A gift… but it is not for you. It is for Chenna."

Gredin smiled. "It seems you have brought an abundance of gifts for the community, and I will enjoy my share of them. It is only right that you also bring a particular gift for your Chosen, who has been through a difficult few days because of you. May I see it, or is it a private thing?"

"It is a very public thing," Burlon told her, and opened the basket. Reaching beneath the layer of damp fronds that covered the basket's contents, he drew out his gift. "Chenna, my Chosen, this is a *timte* crown made of flowers from Sprygale. Yesterday, during the Choosing ceremony, it was worn by Q'iari, who is now their Ruler of the Middle Realm. Will you accept it from me and wear it, as the first token of my apology?"

Her kiss assured him that she would.

When he had settled the blossoms over her braids, it pleased him deeply to see what a lovely picture it made: Chenna, with her flowers, and her glim, and her smile.

"Go to your nest, the pair of you," Gredin said. "If you do not attend tonight's fine evening meal, I will have it Sent to you there."

A glance at the arrival dais showed Burlon that Ellis had already Fetched the crates of fruits and vegetables, and the baskets of *sama* bread and the baked treats. As he watched, the first crate of *ginglin* vanished, as well. He could imagine the excitement of the kitchen Tenders as each new container of fresh ingredients appeared in their midst. Over the course of the day, they would work their wonders, and evening meal would be memorable indeed.

It was only enough for one meal – or perhaps two, if the kitchen Tenders were inventive. But it was a promise of better days to come, when abundance would again be something they could count upon.

For now, it satisfied him to know that Ellis had matters in hand. He was free to set down his responsibilities and take shelter in the arms of his Chosen. Almost, *almost*, he could ignore the sting of outrage and disappointment he felt over not being one of the Travelers appointed to seek New Venna.

No one was Traveling anywhere, tonight.

And he was with Chenna.

With an effort, he clambered to his feet. "Chenna and I will take our leave," he said to Gredin. "And I will see you at tomorrow morning's circle of five, where we can discuss the many ways in which you have once again turned the community upside down and inside out."

She smiled. "And here I thought that was your special gyfte! Go, both of you, before anyone else can delay you. Ellis and I will do our best to prevent Tradepoint from falling from the sky before Burlon te Laith is once again available to steady it."

Several witty retorts occurred to him, but he let Gredin have the final word, content to make his way slowly out of the reception hall with Chenna at his side.

[25]

0511 OF 2000 ORBITS REMAINING: 10GREEN

Gredin gazed at the four figures, each small enough to sit on the palm of her hand.

A clay man with a tuft of white fuzz sticking up from his head.

A stocky, many-legged, long-muzzled creature fashioned from blue cloth.

A large-eyed, large-eared animal curled into a ball, cast in silver metal.

A black bird, thin and angular, carved from gleaming stone.

"What are these?" she asked.

She was in Wyve's office for the second time that day. She had started her morning there, as usual, and then had returned to the Vennan enclave, intending to meet with her inner circle over breakfast, relieved beyond expression to have Burlon safely back with them. And Burlon, after an afternoon and night spent in his nest with Chenna, had the look of a man who had been well loved and was ready to take on whatever challenges the day might offer.

But the group had barely begun to assemble when Gredin's wristband pulsed politely, summoning her back to Wyve's office. A few moments later, Ingarra came in to say that a voice had spoken from the reception hall wall, calling out both Gredin's name and Burlon's.

Gredin and Burlon left the enclave together, only to find a transport pod waiting for them in the public corridor just beyond the Vennan antechamber. It delivered them straight to the Director's office, while Gredin grew more and more uneasy. What could have happened in the short time since her early meeting with Wyve and Figg that required such prompt attention? They had hurried inside to find out… and there, lined up on the edge of Wyve's desk, were the four little figures.

"Sit," Wyve invited.

Gredin settled herself on a bench and waited while Burlon did the same.

Wyve gestured at the line of objects. "These were left for you, just now."

The materials and workmanship were utterly different from one figure to the next. "What are they?" Gredin asked again.

"Tokens," Burlon said.

"Gifts," said Wyve.

Increasingly confused, Gredin asked, "Who brought them? Are we supposed to display them?"

Burlon snorted. "No. That would be pointless. If I may, Wyve…?"

Wyve gestured for him to proceed.

"Sometimes, a foreign tradeteam will offer a gift, out of friendship." He smiled a crooked smile. "Sometimes, it's done as a graceful way to offload left-over goods before a ship heads home. Other times, the gesture is more sincere. And when such a thing is done, the size of the gift can vary. If it is something small, they may just leave it at the maartza of the race they wish to please. But if the gift is unwieldy or heavy, these tokens are given instead. They're entrusted to the Director, while the actual goods are stored in an unassigned warehouse."

Gredin looked at the little statues again. "So someone is giving us a gift. A *large* gift. Or, rather, four such gifts."

Wyve nodded.

Gredin pointed at the first figure. "Is that supposed to be a F'lala?"

"Indeed."

"So the second one must be a Shodekekeen."

"The third is a Rodorno," Burlon stated.

"And the fourth one is clearly a Hesch!" she said, delighted.

Burlon turned to stare at her. "Yes, it is a Hesch, although I can't imagine why it's there, or why you sound so pleased about it. Wyve, I hope you've inspected whatever they gave, to be certain it will neither poison us nor explode."

Wyve looked back and forth between them. "Have you two not talked since Burlon's return?"

Amused, Gredin said, "No. He has been entangled in his Chosen's embrace, with no time to spare for the rest of us."

"Well then, perhaps you should enlighten him as to what he has missed."

"Yes," Burlon said, glowering at her. "What have I missed?"

"Nothing of great import," she said, adopting an airy tone. "Just that I ventured to the Hesch enclave, presented Nitikikani with my necklace, and boarded his ship, where I explained our situation to him and spent a little time playing with his fledgling."

Burlon drew back, eyeing her. "You ventured to the Hesch enclave? Alone? Uninvited?"

"Yes."

"Did you at least tell someone where you were going?"

"No."

"And, instead of summoning Security, Nitikikani actually let you in?"

She nodded, rather enjoying Burlon's consternation, now that the risk had been safely surmounted.

"And you gave him your flamestone?" he demanded. "*Gave* it to him?"

That part of the tale was harder to smile about. But she nodded and said, "He had greater need of it than I did."

Burlon's expression was pained. "Greater need? I'm certain he wanted you to think so. Well, gone is gone. But you went aboard the Hesch ship?!"

She shrugged. "You boarded the Rodorno ship."

"The Rodorno are my friends. My personal friends. I know Artett Abna-gul and have every faith in her good intentions. That hardly describes your situation with Nitikikani."

"How was our relationship ever going to improve if I didn't talk to him?"

"Talk to him. *Talk* to him? Talking with him might have entailed exchanging pleasantries at the Traders' Market. Instead, if I heard you correctly – and I truly hope that I didn't – you 'explained our situation to him.' Does that mean what I fear it means?"

"He knows that Venna has been destroyed," she said, and braced herself for a further outburst of temper.

But Burlon simply sighed. "Well, it isn't as if we could hide the fact indefinitely. But I wouldn't have selected the Hesch as the first people I confided in."

"It was past time to be honest. And Nitikikani had a right to know why Wyve was tolerating my continued presence here, in violation of the Judgment." She might as well tell Burlon the rest, she supposed, while she had Wyve present to act as a buffer. "I told Nitikikani that he could tell others, as he saw fit. I had no real way to prevent him, and so it seemed better to give him permission than to try to exact some sort of promise from him."

Burlon shrugged. "Well, if you were going to tell him at all, it was your only realistic choice."

Gredin felt a wave of relief and pleasure upon hearing Burlon's words. For once, he agreed with her and even seemed, reluctantly, to approve of the course she'd taken. When they'd first arrived on Tradepoint, she had been a useful tool for him – a translator. By the next morning, after the Power's pronouncement to her of Venna's loss, he had reconsidered, adjudging her to be a homesick child, or a fool, or both. In the days that followed, he had agreed with Cirin and Tetralanna that she should be returned to Venna – but, by then, Venna no longer existed. And so she had hidden herself away to avoid being cast into the void, and Burlon's opinion of her had sunk even further.

Cirin's return and tragic death had changed all of that, vindicating her. Together, she and Burlon had tried to impose some necessary structure on the situation, each in their own way. But her ebbing hlinga had made her erratic and undependable, causing her to clash with Burlon again and again. By the time she learned what was happening to all of those who had lost their Chosen, still more damage had been done to Burlon's opinion of her. And then he had gone off to Sprygale, just as her matings with Khest began to steady and strengthen her.

Might this finally be a chance for them to deal with one another respectfully, without friction, coordinating their efforts on behalf of the community?

She became aware that he was looking at her oddly. "What?" she asked.

"Was there really a fledgling aboard the Hesch ship? Are you sure it wasn't just a young Hesch trader? I mean, young compared to Nitikikani?"

She smiled. "No, it was a true fledgling. Only this high," she said, holding out her hand, "and covered in grey fluff."

Burlon shook his head. "Well, that is a wonderment. I had no idea the Hesch brought their families along when they came to Tradepoint. Seems more than a bit reckless!"

"Oh? Your child is going to be born here," she reminded him, and saw him go pale.

A little silence fell. Wyve took advantage of it to ask, "How is Keegan te Fliss faring?"

"He recovers well," Gredin said. "I will tell him that you inquired."

"What do you mean?" Burlon asked. "Did something happen to Keegan?"

Gredin berated herself for not remembering how much Burlon had missed in the four days of his absence. "Things went awry at the clinic," she said, "but now Keegan is–"

"We almost killed him," Wyve cried, looking stricken. "I thought we *had* killed him."

"*Chee, chee, chee...*" Gredin soothed. "He is fine. The matter is past. Salderon–"

Burlon stiffened. "Keegan required an Intercession from

Salderon?" He fixed his stare on Wyve. "What did your people *do* to him?"

Gredin spoke before Wyve could answer. "The Prett foods were all making him sick. Binn was concerned to see that he was getting thinner. She thought to spare him, for a day, by doing something different. She meant it as a kindness, really. Binn had no idea that Keegan would react so badly."

His gaze swung back to Wyve. "She took those samples your people have been after," he accused. "Despite our repeated refusals. She did, didn't she?"

"Yes," Wyve said, his voice a low rumble. "Your people have no proper science. We thought you were just wary of something you didn't understand. But *we* were the ones who didn't understand. We were certain it would be only a minor inconvenience, performed in service to a much greater potential good. But then things went wrong… and the more Binn tried to help him, the worse matters grew, until at last I was certain his bodily systems would fail and he would evanesce before our eyes, as Cirin did."

"But he didn't," Gredin reminded him. "Salderon arrived in time. And Keegan and Salderon will both be back to their usual activities, after a few more days of rest. They are already much improved." She rose and walked behind the desk to place her hand on Wyve's massive shoulder. "Neither you nor Binn meant any harm. And now you both know better than to attempt such a thing again. Vennans are not Prett. And you will listen more carefully, the next time we decline something that you request. Meanwhile, Keegan bears you no ill will, and wishes Binn to know that he looks forward to resuming his work with her soon."

"No!"

The word burst simultaneously from Wyve and Burlon.

"Yes," Gredin said calmly, returning to her seat. "The food testing will not take much longer, and Keegan is determined to see it through to completion. It is his offering to the community. You must allow him that, for his pride's sake. It weighs upon him, knowing that he is the last of his House. If he cannot feel involved with the wider community, then he will be truly alone. And Binn, I suspect, will be doubly vigilant, after the scare we all endured." Determined to lighten the conversation, she said, "Ah, Wyve, I wish you could have seen the beautiful flowers Burlon brought to his Chosen when he returned from Sprygale... although I suspect you are far more interested in the other goods he brought back with him."

Wyve's eyes brightened. "You were successful, then?" he asked Burlon. "You obtained the geddel crystals?"

"They are already sitting safely in our warehouse," Burlon assured him, "awaiting the date of their delivery to the Vokastra."

"Excellent. I am more relieved to hear it than you can easily imagine."

Burlon looked nettled. "Do we make such unpleasant neighbors?" he asked. "Do we stink, like the Mamora, or attack others in the public corridors, like the Beng? The Vokastra are not here. They do not see us. Why does our presence on Tradepoint offend them so?"

"It does not offend them," Wyve assured him. "But they worry about the possible precedent that it sets. We have always adhered strictly to the orbital limit and have reinforced it with monetary penalties. They fear, if we make an exception for the Vennans, that other races will argue for exceptions to be made for them."

"Fine," Burlon growled. "When their worlds are destroyed, they can request leniency from the Vokastra. I do not foresee it happening."

"No, of course not. But the other races come and go from here in ships, and those ships sometimes malfunction. They might request a free extension while they finished their necessary repairs. Or they might wish to linger, in the hope that a preferred trading partner will arrive in port in a few more sects, thereby saving them the cost of offloading the requested goods to us and paying our fee when we broker the trade. So long as we can say 'That is the rule,' and have it apply equally to everyone, there are no grounds for anyone to stand upon to argue. But if we waive those rules for you and your people, the Vokastra fear it will undermine our authority."

"The station is yours. You can make whatever rules you wish. You have Security to back those rules. You manage the master accounts. It seems to me that your Vokastra worries over nothing. What is their *real* concern?"

Gredin wanted to tell Burlon to quit pushing at Wyve, who was their friend. But she was finally coming to understand – no, to accept, deep within herself – that, although Wyve and the Vokastra were both Prett, they were not identical in strength and influence. And so she gave Burlon a moment more to pursue his questions, as much as she wished she could spare Wyve the hint of animosity in Burlon's voice.

Wyve sighed. "Their real concern? Ah, Burlon. That is where the Vokastra and I differ most. My concern is that there are too few of you. Their concern is that there are too many."

"But you have ample room here, do you not? Are you short of warehouses? Short of enclaves?"

"No."

"Then why do our numbers matter so much to the Vokastra?"

Wyve hesitated, and Gredin thought he might not answer. But then he shook his head and said, "You are many and we are relatively few. In the minds of the Vokastra, that poses a threat. They worry that, deprived of your own world, you will decide to stay here indefinitely, and that you will attempt to overrun us and do so by force if we object. It is a child's fear of the dark – groundless but potent. I have tried to explain to them that Vennans do not like living on Tradepoint, and that you lack the first concepts of how to operate Tradepoint's equipment and griimoni. But those are logical answers, while their fears are illogical, and so my explanations do little to ease their concern. That is why I strive to maintain the present equilibrium between politics and your people's needs. It is why I urged you to make the journey to Sprygale. A late delivery of geddel crystals could shift the balance of opinion within the Vokastra sharply against your continued presence here. For now, I have explained to them that you and your people need a reliable place to stay, in order for you to maintain your trading schedules. But if we provide you with that reliable place, and you *still* failed to deliver the geddel crystals, then they would lose their motivation for putting faith in my explanations." He spread his hands, splaying his thick fingers. "You understand, then, why I am so very pleased to hear that the geddel crystals have arrived safely and are in your warehouse, awaiting distribution."

Gredin smiled. "Indeed. And perhaps my news will please you further."

"Your news?"

"Later today, groups of our Travelers will launch themselves upon the River to begin the search for New Venna."

Wyve's gaze flicked from her to Burlon. "But you have just returned from Sprygale!"

"Oh, I will not personally be part of the search," Burlon said, and managed to produce such a calm tone of voice that Gredin smiled at him in gratitude. "With both the Traders and the Travelers to oversee, as well as our maartza and the geddel crystal consignments, and now my Chosen and our coming child to consider, it hardly seemed the best time for me to undertake an open-ended journey of exploration."

"Selfishly, I must say I am relieved to hear it," Wyve admitted.

Gredin felt much the same. She had been braced for a mighty battle with Burlon over the matter of New Venna. If he was truly seeing the sense of her plan on his own, it would make the coming days much simpler. And yet she couldn't help wondering if perhaps he sounded just a little *too* agreeable. Burlon was strong-minded and prideful. She would have to wait and see whether his sensible resolve held firm.

Still, it might, if she could keep him busy enough. The closer time came to the birth, the less inclined he would be to leave Chenna.

Thoughts of the coming birth caused her thoughts to stray back to the Hesch fledgling. Reaching out, Gredin picked up the bird statuette. It was lighter than she expected, and more detailed. From a distance, the fine points of the carving were swallowed up in the ebony darkness of the stone. In hand, however, she could tilt it to catch the light, and see the tiny incisions made to indicate everything from the individual talons on its feet to the leathery skin of its bare head. Even the length and breadth of the miniaturized beak were precise; she could almost imagine it clacking to protest the temerity of her inspection.

"If you take that one and the Shodekekeen," Burlon said, "I'll take the F'lala and the Rodorno."

Gredin looked at him in surprise. "I thought you said we had to give the tokens to Wyve."

Burlon's smile was faintly patronizing. "Not until we've claimed the goods and transferred them to our own warehouse. Once that's done, we return the tokens to Wyve, and he gives them back to the original donor, to be used another time."

"What a shame." She turned the little bird in her hand. "I would have liked to keep this."

Burlon looked scandalized. "The only way to keep a token is to turn down the gift, and doing so would be interpreted as both an insult and a threat."

"An insult? A threat?"

"The implied message would be that you found their gift either unacceptable or inadequate, and that you were holding onto the token until they made up for the slight."

"Oh. Well then, clearly, I can't keep it. We've just come to good terms again with the Hesch. I certainly don't want to disrupt that!"

"Good," Burlon said on a fervent note, and handed her the Shodekekeen token. "Is there anything we should know about these before we go?" he asked Wyve.

Wyve considered the question, looking amused. "You might care to leave the Hesch for last," he said. "And all four are quite bulky. If you wish to leave them where they are, for the time being, I have no immediate need of those warehouses."

Burlon's brow furrowed. "Thank you, but there's no point in our incurring the use-cost of four more warehouses when I've got Traders sitting idle at the enclave who can come and shift things into our own space."

Gredin thought Wyve looked a little put out as he said, "I meant that there would *be* no short-term use-cost for those warehouses."

Burlon sighed. "Wyve, you can't. We're already sliding toward debt, and now our situation is public knowledge throughout the station. If you start ignoring legitimate use-costs that we've incurred, someone will spot it. Let's not give the Vokastra anything irregular to point at. I appreciate your intention. I truly do. But you need to keep a scrupulous accounting of everything we owe, including the new enclave spaces and the charges for Keegan's testings at the clinic."

Wyve stiffened. "We are certainly not going to charge you for the session that nearly cost him his life!"

"All right," Burlon conceded, "but we will need to come to an honest settlement for the rest of it, eventually. For now, the kindest thing you can do for us is to keep yourself out of trouble." He picked up the Rodorno and F'lala statuettes. "Well, Gredin, let's go and see what all of this is about, shall we?"

"Yes." She smiled at Wyve. "I will see you tomorrow morning, if not before. Our thanks to you," she said, and followed Burlon from the Director's office and out into the public corridor.

Burlon took the lead, but Gredin quickened her pace so that she could walk beside him. "What are you doing?" she asked, as he turned the little F'lala upside down and peered at it.

"Checking for the warehouse designation," he said. He did the same with the Rodorno figure, and gave a grunt of what sounded like satisfaction.

"What?" Gredin asked again.

"The two warehouses are adjacent." He stopped in the middle of the corridor. "Turn your Shodekekeen over."

She did as he asked. The cloth creature was mounted on a solid black base, and embedded in that base was… something. A small square with short colored lines embedded in it, going this way and that.

"Good. It's with the others. And your Hesch?"

She turned the Hesch statuette over for his inspection and saw the same sort of little square embedded in its base.

Burlon let out a harsh chuckle. "Typical Hesch. A separate corridor. They always have to be different."

"Don't speak ill of them," Gredin objected. "Under the circumstances, Nitikikani has been astonishingly patient with me."

That drew a wry smile from Burlon, but he said nothing else critical as they set out walking again.

"Why do you suppose they're all giving us gifts?" she asked him.

Burlon shrugged. "Probably because you told the Hesch that our world is gone… and," he added, with an air of reluctance, "because I did the same with the Rodorno."

She halted abruptly. "You did? You told them? And you didn't *tell* me that you'd told them? I've been so worried about how you would react to what I revealed to Nitikikani – and you'd already done the same thing, yourself!"

"It's difficult for anyone to keep their troubles to themselves when the Rodorno are around. So I suspect that either the Hesch or the Rodorno told the Shodekekeen and the F'lala, and the result is that they have each left us a sympathy gift. Embarrassing, but I suppose we would have done much the same, had such a tragedy befallen one of them. Well, maybe not the Hesch, as things used to be. But you seem to have had a positive effect on *that* relationship. Or maybe they just like your hair better this way," he said on a teasing note. Then his smile fell away. "Gredin, I am so sorry about the Beng attack."

"As am I," she said, "but nothing about it was your fault."

"I was with the Rodorno. You couldn't reach me."

She shrugged. "I could have taken someone else along when I went to consult with Figg. And could you honestly have predicted that the Beng would do such a thing to me?"

"Well, no, not *what* they would do. But I should have realized they might do something. They were resentful, and their departure date was upon them, and I'm sure they dreaded having to present themselves at home and reveal the details of the Judgment. I knew they were unreliable. I knew they were greedy. I knew they were desperate. That all added up to a warning. At least, it should have, if I had been paying proper attention."

"Truly? Had they ever physically attacked anyone before?"

"Well, no, but…"

"Has *any* race ever physically attacked another, here on Tradepoint?"

"No."

"Then I hardly think you need to blame yourself. I wasn't paying proper attention. My mind was on what Figg had said. I walked right into the middle of them. To that extent, it is very much my own fault.

But, mostly, it's the fault of the Beng. And now they are gone, at least for the time being, so let us not distress ourselves unduly about it, or spend any more time thinking about them than we can possibly help."

"But this is Tradepoint!"

That much was obvious. She didn't understand why he felt he needed to say so. "Of course it is Tradepoint. What difference does that make?"

"This is my place. I'm a Trader and a Traveler. Cirin and I organized the trip for the Trisectoriana. I helped to bring everyone here." He gestured, as if frustrated in his attempt to find the words he needed. "I assured everyone they would be safe here. I told them that because I *believed* it. And then the scab-ridden, blistered, broken-boned Beng made a liar of me! I hate knowing that they laid their hands on you, and hurt you, and cut you with their knives, and–"

"Only one," she interrupted.

"What?" He blinked as if waking from a dark night-thought. "What did you say?"

She smiled. "I said there was only one knife. And Beda Healed me. There isn't a mark from that night to be found upon me. If it weren't for my hair, no one would even know it had happened." Giving his arm a pat, Gredin said, "The community will think it very odd if you started accompanying me everywhere. Let the matter go, Burlon."

"I can't just–"

"You can. And you should. I give you permission to walk constantly at my elbow when the Beng return, if that is what it takes to calm your fears. For now, however, you and I are here, and they are not, so there is no cause to fret yourself about it. We have far more important tasks to accomplish. I am eager to see what these tokens represent!"

They walked a while longer and rounded a corner before Burlon finally stopped in front of a warehouse door.

Gredin pointed. "That is our symbol – a purple circle crossed by wavy green lines. But why is there another symbol beside it?"

"That three-sided red shape is for the F'lala, to show that this warehouse holds their gift for us." He rotated the small statue and pressed the bottom of it to the panel.

A click. The door retracted.

Gredin slipped inside and stared. The room was lined with ankle-high platforms, and each platform held sacks that were piled higher than her head, some brown, some yellow. One of the yellow sacks had slithered down, escaping its pile, and landed on the floor.

"What is in all these sacks?" she asked, bewildered.

In a solemn tone that shook with emotion, Burlon said, "Grain. Beng grain, from the look of the sacks."

"Won't Wyve and the F'lala get into trouble?" she asked. "Didn't the Beng leave word that we weren't allowed to have any of their grain?"

Burlon was smiling, though his eyes looked suspiciously bright. "Wyve was forbidden to *sell* Beng grain to us. But if the F'lala purchased this grain legitimately through Wyve, there is no rule on Tradepoint to prevent them from simply giving it away." He shook his head slowly. "Such a kindness. And I'm hopeful that the two different colors of sacks mean that they contain two different kinds of grain. Miri will be so pleased!" He looked down at his hands and lifted the Rodorno statuette. "Shall we see what my friends the Rodorno have left for us?"

"Yes!" Gredin replied eagerly.

Burlon carefully closed the F'lala warehouse and walked to the next door. "Rodorno," he said, pointing to a blue oval within a purple oval. Then he pressed the base of the token to the panel.

The door clicked and opened.

Gredin followed Burlon in, as the lights came on.

"More sacks," Burlon said, "this time green and blue." He surveyed the mountainous piles. "Do you realize how many meals we're looking at? How much variety? How much peace of mind? Even this much grain won't last forever, of course. Nothing does. But it is a huge improvement on what we had."

Gredin brandished the Shodekekeen token. "With other things to come," she reminded him.

"A truth." Again, Burlon took care to seal the door. Then he led her past three doors and crossed to the other side of the corridor. "Here. This is the Shodekekeen symbol." It was a blue square, with three purple corners.

Gredin held the statuette out to him.

But Burlon didn't take it. "Would you like to open this one yourself?" he invited.

Pleased, Gredin did as she had seen Burlon do: she turned the statuette onto its side and pressed the bottom of its base to the panel.

Click.

The door opened, and they walked inside.

Again, they found themselves gazing at piles and piles of sacks. This time, all of the sacks were purple.

"Five colors," Burlon said. "If my notion that each color of sack holds a different type of grain, then that would mean…" He looked as openly excited as a young boy. "Gredin, the Beng only have five kinds of grain – stezzin, beek, faralat, doro, and piprill. If each color is a different kind, then that means that at least *some* of what we've been given must be piprill, the grain they wouldn't sell to me. Of course, some will be doro, as well, which I had originally decided not to purchase… but only because I thought it would be too similar to the Wilra's d'limten grain. Now that we have other types to use, and our supply of d'limten is running low from constant use, I'd be a fool to object to the doro." He spread his arms, gesturing at the mounds of purple sacks. "This is so much more than I could have hoped for! And there sat Wyve, not giving the secret away. But he must be tremendously relieved for us, as well."

"Between Zanther's return and this bounty, you're right – Miri will hardly be able to contain herself!" Gredin held up the little black bird. "And there's still one more warehouse."

"Yes," Burlon said. "And it's a bit of a hike from here." For the third time, he made a careful ceremony of securing the door. Then he pointed and said, "The Hesch warehouse is that way, several intersections along."

When they reached it, Gredin saw that the symbol on the panel was simply a black curved line – a feather? And next to it was the Vennan symbol.

"Burlon… does our symbol mean something?"

"I told you – it means us."

"Well, yes, I know that much. But the Hesch symbol looks a bit like a feather, and so I wondered whether our symbol was supposed to look a bit like something, too."

"Oh. That. Yes. The wavy green lines are hills, and the purple circle is the sea. At least, that's what my Mentor told me, in one of my first lessons with her."

"Does *everyone's* symbol look a bit like something?"

Burlon shook his head, chuckling. "I have no notion. And you have too many questions. Don't you want to see whether the Hesch have given us more grain?"

Chagrined, she turned the bird statuette in her hand and pressed its base to the panel.

Click.

Open.

Lights.

She stepped over the threshold…

Tears welled up in her eyes, and she began to laugh and cry, pointing a shaky finger at the shelves. "Oh, Burlon! Look at what Nitikikani has done."

Shelf after shelf held row after row of squat, grey jugs, all facing the doorway, all with their bulging eyes aimed at her, all with their stopper-tongues sticking out.

It was the most beautiful sight she had ever seen.

"We'll need cups," she said. "Lots of cups. And small pitchers or bottles."

That drew a skeptical look from Burlon. "Are we going to sit right here and drink ourselves insensible?"

She pushed playfully at his arm. "Silly man. We'll needs two cups and a small container for each nest in the Bereft enclave. Just *look* at all of this amarantha wine! It could well make the crucial difference for Tetralanna and the others who have been so resistant. And the others, who have already managed to begin, may not need three full cups, but I'm sure a few sips when they first arrive would ease their way and help them set their concerns aside."

Burlon was staring at her again. "You told Nitikikani about the Bereft and their alliance partners? Slivers, Gredin, is there anything about our difficulties that you *didn't* tell him?"

"Likely not – and how can I be sorry, when it has reaped us such a kind-hearted harvest? But be warned, Burlon. If this bounty brings the improvements that I hope it will, we'll need to budget for an on-going supply of amarantha wine. I suspect the demand will ease, over time, as people find partners who suit them, and see the benefit an alliance partner brings them. For now, however, I will encourage its use as an investment in our health and wellbeing."

Burlon managed a wan smile. "I would not have imagined that part of my emergency spending plan for the community would involve massive purchases of wine… but I understand the point you make." He nodded toward the crowded shelves. "At least this gift will put us well ahead of the demand, for now."

Gredin walked deeper into the warehouse, trailing her fingertips with grateful affection over the brows of the carved stone jugs. Then she reached the end of the row and looked beyond. "Burlon?" she said uncertainly, her voice a little pinched in her throat.

"What?" Perhaps alerted by her tone, he hurried to her, then looked past her. "Oh my."

"Oh my, indeed." Gredin took a step forward, then another as her gaze roamed over the back line of shelves. "Can the Hesch really afford to give all of this away?"

All of this was a variety of jars and containers, some of which she recognized, some of which she did not.

"They've done it, whether they can afford to do it or not," Burlon said. "There is no polite way to refuse a gift. And Miri and the other kitchen Tenders would no doubt do violence to me if I tried." Burlon moved past her, hunkering down to examine the lowest shelves. "Baskets of kardin nuts, still in the shell. Containers of chupala nuts, husked and quartered." He straightened to inspect the next shelf. "I think these are all crushed lumik. And my guess is that those matching jars are kardin paste. You can spread it on crackers and breads, or dip uncooked vegetables into it. In fact, there are several different dips and spreads here." He moved up a shelf. "Preserved fruits. Jams. Jellies. And above that is a whole shelf of things I can't even identify. I suppose we should turn those over to Binn and Keegan for testing. But the rest of these are known to me and should be fine." He cast a wary look at her. "What did you do to win this kind of favor from Nitikikani?"

She sighed. "I gave him the *ta'ak* he has been seeking for most of his life."

"The what?"

"The *ta'ak*. In this case, Dreff's flamestone pendant."

"I don't understand."

"I gather it's a bit like seeking your Chosen, if your Chosen were a thing rather than a person. Nitikikani has had night-thoughts about Dreff's flamestone since early childhood. He has sought it, everywhere he's ever gone. He has drawn pictures of it, done paintings of it, crafted models of it. And then he saw it, hanging around my neck, when I first arrived on Tradepoint." She gestured at the laden warehouse shelves. "I believe the Power intended for us to meet."

"You and a Hesch?"

"Yes."

Burlon considered it. "Well, I suppose stranger things *could* have befallen us. If you had to befriend someone unlikely, at least it wasn't a Beng!" He gestured back toward the door. "Are you ready to return to the enclave? This afternoon, Ellis and I will organize the transfer of these goods. We'll have the kitchen Tenders make room for several sacks of each type of Beng grain, and for the known items from these shelves. The rest of the Beng grain can go to our warehouse. Samples of the unfamiliar Hesch foods can be delivered to Binn's attention at the clinic, and the rest can go to the kitchens." He hesitated. "Except the wine, of course. Where do you want the amarantha wine?"

"For now, most of it can go to the warehouse, but we'll need to see about gathering enough cups and pitchers, so that each nest in the Bereft enclave has a small supply of wine on hand."

"I'll talk to Miri and Hayla. If we don't have enough, I can ask Wyve."

Gredin felt a sweet rush of relief. "We may actually weather this crisis," she said. "I feared, for a time, that it would drag us under."

If Dreff had been here, if he had seen how people were suffering, and the larger fate that was stalking us, he would have been the first to understand why I had to let the pendant go, she assured herself. From time to time, unthinking, she still reached up to clasp the absent flame-stone in her hand. But that habit would pass. She was standing in this warehouse, surrounded by an outpouring of benevolence from Nitikikani, because she had united him with his *ta'ak*. The satisfaction of that reality far surpassed any benefit she could have experienced by keeping the necklace for herself.

In order to lead the survivors and keep them safe, sacrifices would sometimes be necessary. She had been called upon to surrender her pendant. Burlon had been called upon to surrender his ambition to be the Vennan who found their new home. And the Bereft, all of them, were each being called upon to surrender their right to hide away in solitude and mourn their Chosen's return to the Source; instead, they were called upon to face life and to serve their bodies' needs in order to retain their Balance and uphold their responsibility to the community.

"We should get back to the enclave," Burlon said. "I want time for a quiet word with the Travelers before they set out."

She nodded her agreement and walked with him to the door. "You know," she said as he secured it, "any one of the Travelers might be the one to find New Venna. The search could take long and long… or it could happen quickly. Imagine, if someone returns in three days' time to say they have found it on their very first attempt!"

"Imagine, also, that it takes until their tenth attempt," Burlon cautioned. "Or their hundredth. Or their thousandth. It will take as long as it takes."

"Yes, it will take as long as it takes," she conceded. "But, in time, it will happen. The Power would not direct our Travelers to embark upon the River to no purpose."

Later, when the entire community had gathered to watch the departure of the Travelers, Gredin recalled those words again: *The Power would not direct our Travelers to embark upon the River to no purpose.* Thirty-five of their survivors were leaving the safety of Tradepoint and embarking upon the River. The thirty-five men and women were all Unchosen, divided into seventeen pairs and a single Traveler – Yohn te Avilar.

This was the beginning of a new period in the enclave. On any day, at any time, the dome might descend over the arrival dais as a team of Travelers returned from their exploration with news of where they had been and whether the journey had proven fruitful. Hopes would rise and fall. New journeys would be undertaken.

But this was the beginning. As Gredin watched, the dome descended over the departure dais, and bio-mist began to swirl. A few folk in the crowd wept but the Travelers stood tall, their expressions eager as, two by two, they began to vanish. By the time the bio-mist cleared, the dais was empty.

"A fine departure," a familiar voice said. "I am grateful to have witnessed it."

Turning, she found Keegan standing in the archway, leaning against it for support.

"You should be in your bed!"

"No, I am much better, and I am weary of gazing at that ceiling." He gestured at the nearest table. "Sit here on a bench with me and tell me what I have missed."

Gredin hesitated, then nodded and joined him. "You will need your *crabe*. Have you recovered enough to Fetch it?"

For answer, it appeared on the table in front of him.

Reassured, she said, "Very well. I will recite for you the names of those whose substantial gyfte of Service has caused them to be selected by Dard te Avilar to serve as their Houses' new volunteers. But first…" She reached into her pocket and grasped the Hesch statuette, which rested atop her pouch of stones. Drawing it out, she set the stone carving on the tabletop beside Keegan's *crabe.*

"What is it?" he asked, clearly intrigued.

"A token from the Hesch," Gredin explained. "I'll need to return this little fellow to Burlon as soon as the Traders finish transferring items to our warehouse, but I thought you might like to hear his tale before I do…"

GET 3 BOOKS FREE!

As a thank you for reading *The Bereft,* book three in *The Tradepoint Saga.*

We hope you enjoyed it as much as we enjoyed bringing it to you. We just wanted to take a moment to encourage you to review the book on Amazon and Goodreads. Every review helps further the author's reach and, ultimately, helps them continue writing fantastic books for us all to enjoy.

If you liked this book, check out the rest of our catalogue at www.aethonbooks.com. To sign up to receive a FREE collection from some of our best authors as well as updates regarding all new releases, visit www.subscribepage.com/AethonReadersGroup.

JOIN THE STREET TEAM! Get advanced copies of all our books, plus other free stuff and help us put out hit after hit.

SEARCH ON FACEBOOK:
AETHON STREET TEAM

APPENDIX

VENNAN HOUSE NAMES

Vennan Houses are extended families. A Vennan has a personal name and a House name, linked by 'te' (basically 'of'). Thus, **Gredin te Balamont** means **Gredin of the House of Balamont**. The thirteen surviving Vennan Houses are:

House Avilar
House Balamont
House Bentain
House Calidane
House Darius
House Fliss
House Indirin
House Kendar
House K'lar
House Laith
House Shelahn
House Torr
House Vell

RACES PRESENT ON TRADEPOINT IN *THE BEREFT*

The tradeteams of twenty-three different races do business on Tradepoint, but only a few of them are there during the events of *THE BEREFT*, as follows:

F'lala: Mild-mannered and stocky, with cloud-like white hair
Hesch: Tall and bird-like, unnervingly interested in Gredin
Nairn: Red haired and bearded, boisterous and fair-minded
Polpethtira: Purple-skinned female tradeteams, tech specialists
Prett: Tall, burly race that owns and operates Tradepoint
Rodorno: Emotional empaths, solid allies of the Vennans
Vennans: Delegation of 937 craftspeople stranded on Tradepoint
Yaylay: Man-and-bird pairs of traders, mutually telepathic

TELLING TIME ON TRADEPOINT

Tradepoint is owned and operated by the Prett. Time designations used on the station are based on Tradepoint's orbits around the planet of Prettig. The Prett personally keep very accurate time, down to fractions of a second, but Tradepoint uses simplified time units for the convenience of the many different races who do business there.

- Each day/night cycle is divided into fifty hours (one per orbit).
- Each day's hours are numbered 1 through 50.
- Each hour is divided into 5 segments, in a progression of colors: purple, blue, green, yellow, and orange.
- Example: A meeting could be scheduled for 23blue (the second segment of the twenty-third hour).

PRETTIAN TERMS FOR LARGER UNITS OF TIME

- Sect: One day (50 hours)
- Sector: One month (40 days)
- Sectora: One year (400 days)
- Sectoria: One century (100 years)

FURTHER INFORMATION ON WEBSITE

Go to: https://jjblacklocke.com/

- Pronunciation Guide to alien words and names
- Art, articles, and reviews for the books of *The Tradepoint Saga*
- FREE e-book novelette, VENNA BEFORE THE END OF THE WORLD

ALSO IN THE SERIES

REFUGE

AFTERSHOCK

THE BEREFT

ACKNOWLEDGMENTS

The Tradepoint Saga (REFUGE, AFTERSHOCK, and THE BEREFT) would not have been possible without the comments, counsel, and real-world assistance of the following individuals:

• Brett Hiorns, beta reader, whose feedback at various stages of this project was invaluable.

• Tory Hunter, whose detailed manuscript critiques and energetic championing of this series kept The Tradepoint Saga on the right track.

• Anne Tibbets, literary agent and author, who took The Tradepoint Saga under her wing and found it a home.

• Vince and Erich at BoileauCommunications.com for their fabulous job on our website.

• Special thanks to our team at Aethon Books:

o Rhett Bruno and Steve Beaulieu at the helm

o Paul Simpson, editor

o Kate Reading, audiobook narrator

o Tom Edwards, cover artist

• And thank you to the many readers who took a chance on a new author and series, and were generous enough to:

o Leave reviews and rankings on Amazon and Goodreads.

o Follow JJ Blacklocke on Instagram and Twitter

o Like and Follow the JJ Blacklocke Facebook page, and join Gredin's Gang.

ABOUT THE AUTHOR

Born in the South and raised in the Midwest, JJ Blacklocke wears many hats, with skills as diverse as public speaking, catering, teaching, and business administration. *The Tradepoint Saga,* which began with REFUGE and TRADEPOINT, and continues here in THE BEREFT, is the result of a private fascination with Vennans and the adventures forced upon them by a twist of fate.

For more about the Vennans and Tradepoint, visit https://jjblacklocke.com/

www.ingramcontent.com/pod-product-compliance
Lightning Source LLC
Chambersburg PA
CBHW030625310726
48979CB00003B/878
* 9 7 8 1 9 4 9 8 9 0 7 5 4 *